"Laura Furman reinforces her characters with engaging detail. . . . This novel is her most ambitious work to date . . . a series of richly composed still lifes."

The New York Times Book Review

"Laura Furman's novel, TUXEDO PARK, is a story told on an epic scale, and as such, gives us a sense not only of time passing, but of the powerful way time shapes and transforms the lives it touches. . . . Her uncanny ability to recreate the warp and woof of childhood, with its idiosyncrasies of thought, feeling, and gesture, is a joy to read."

The Columbus Dispatch

"This book is full of small, wonderful moments, which increase as the story moves towards its expansive end. . . . we are drawn into the novel, its questions, its moral concerns. And if, in the end, the story seems to be more about power than love . . . or even more about self-knowledge, that only makes it a richer blend."

San Francisco Examiner-Chronicle

"Furman's deft and engrossing novel is full of subtle and sad observations on social class, love, and the darker places of the psyche. Her characters are exasperating yet credible, her prose supple, clear, and always engaging."

Worcester Telegram

The critics love

Laura Furman's

TUXEDO PARK

"Families. They have the power to destroy or heal. But they can never be ignored. This is the theme of Laura Furman's powerful novel about the mismatch of Willard Weaver and Sadie Ash . . . a compelling story."

Los Angeles Herald Examiner

"Splendid . . . This novel—full of subtle observations about love, money, and the unpredictability of human nature—is Furman's best book."

People

"Laura Furman's new novel . . . finely crafted, each character lovingly, carefully wrought, each scene meticulously colored, and every detail palpable . . . This is a book that first catches your eye and then grabs your heart. It hangs on and won't let go."

Anne Tyler,
USA Today

"Engrossing . . . Furman's deft hand with character delineation invests her narrative with credibility . . . a compelling story."

Publishers Weekly

(more)

"Most of the people in TUXEDO PARK . . . are brilliantly drawn. Furman is excellent at understated satire, and with remarkable economy she sketches the geographic and social contours of Tuxedo Park."

Dallas Times Herald

"Laura Furman is one of those very talented writers who create characters so disturbingly real that it's difficult to remember they are only fictional. Such a character is Sadie Ash, the self-deluding, exasperating, and completely believable protagonist of TUXEDO PARK."

The Arizona Daily Star

"Beginning with the now classic theme of the effects of a disintegrating marriage upon parents and children, Furman has carefully separated the elements from their usual context and reassembled them against a highly colored background. The result is a collage in which familiar pieces fall into surprising configurations."

Los Angeles Times

"A luminous novel, restrained in emotion and rich in detail . . . The mood of the book is one of dislocation and timelessness. . . . This is a sad story in its sense of lost chances and barriers to happiness. But there is also hope, and the fulfillment of old wounds finally healed."

Bestsellers

TUXEDO PARK

Laura Furman

FAWCETT CREST • NEW YORK

A Fawcett Crest Book
Published by Ballantine Books
Copyright © 1986 by Laura Furman

Library of Congress Catalog Card Number: 86-5928

ISBN 0-449-21406-0

This edition published by arrangement with Summit Books, a divi-
sion of Simon & Schuster, Inc.

Manufactured in the United States of America

First Ballantine Books Edition: November 1987

For Joel

PART
ONE

PART
ONE

One

FROM STREET LEVEL, HIGH ABOVE THE SKATING RINK, his arms braced against the brass railing, he watched as the girl glided beneath the golden statue of Prometheus. In her favor, she had a low center of gravity and a good sense of balance, but her technique was rough; her lips moved as if she were cheering herself on. This almost spring day might be her last chance to practice, he thought. As for him, his feet were wet, and he might be catching a cold. His overcoat felt heavy, wet from hours of exposure to the humid, late winter air, and his fedora was damp to the touch. He breathed in deeply, as if drinking, and settled against the railing.

She pushed off with her back foot, crouching a little low for figure skating. There was a moment of hesitation between step and glide when it seemed as if she might decide to stop altogether. But in that pause she gathered strength and leaned into the air as if into a long-awaited embrace.

In the inner circle where the experts skated, a little boy spun like a pompommed dervish, and a white-haired man, tartan scarf around his neck, rose up and down without a tremor, holding his arms crossed over his chest. She glanced at them, stopped a humble distance away, and practiced her fancy step, turning this way on

3

her right skate, that on her left, tracing half circles on the ice.

Her face was long and thin, and her eyes too close together by the smallest amount. Her long nose and generous mouth, the crowded eyes, made her expression melancholy, not her true face or her true nature, he thought.

She was leaving the center now. She was brave ever to go there—her step wasn't much compared with the jumps and twirls of the regulars. She had come to the skating rink at Rockefeller Center that afternoon with a decisiveness he imagined she brought to everything. She did what she wanted, he thought, whatever was next, like a honey bee, while he had little taste for daily life.

Now she was circling the rink, bent over like a racer. Working her arms, she pressed against the wind. Ice flew from her blades. The notched tips of her figure skates caught the surface. She stumbled and pushed off again, then left the ground with all the force she'd been working for. She traveled a few feet on momentum, treaded ice for a split second, and fell.

Willard ran down the steps two at a time, pushing past the afternoon strollers and office workers, pressing entrance money into an attendant's hand. By the time he was near, her eyes were open.

"Let me help you," he said. He was at the edge of the ice, holding out his hand to her. "Are you all right?"

She looked up at him and tried to move closer. When she saw his face under the brim of the fedora, she said, "Why, it's you."

She took his hand, and he pulled her to her feet. She brushed off her legs and hips with her free hand, picked at the shards of ice stuck to her blue wool skirt.

"Do you remember me—Sadie Ash?"

"Of course I remember you. I happened to be passing by," he said. "I saw you and stopped to watch. The skating looked so . . ."

"Festive?" she suggested.

"That's it. It looked festive." He smiled, a warm expression that was as deceptive as her melancholy look.

"I like skating," she said, "but I'm no good at it."

"You looked swell."

"No. I always wanted to do something—skate or dance—but I'm clumsy. My brother says I have the two most graceful left feet he's ever seen."

She stepped off the ice, awkwardly, as if to prove her point. He let go of her hand, but said, "Let me take you to Rumpelmayer's for something hot."

"I don't know," she said. "I told my brother I'd come home before it gets dark."

"I'll see you home in a cab then. After your fall—"

"I fall all the time," she said.

"Or," he said, "if you're not tired of being outdoors, we might walk. Through the park. Unless you're in a terrible hurry or you're injured."

"Oh, I'm not wounded much," she said. His skin was ruddy from the cold, she noticed, like porcelain lightly glazed. "And I'm not really in such a big hurry."

THE LAST SNOW OF WINTER WAS NEARLY MELTED, though it clung to the boulders in shadowed patches. Tall, curved street lamps competed with the dark blue twilight as Sadie and Willard approached Bethesda Fountain. The view over the little lake was orderly and promising in the evening light.

"I pretend this part of the park is Paris," she said. "You used to live in Paris, didn't you?"

"For a few years. When I finished school—or school was finished with me—I moved to Paris to become a painter. And I painted there until I discovered how terrible I was." She made a sound of protest, and he said, "Not even terrible, I was far worse, I was competent."

"And then you came home."

"No. I stayed in Paris for several more years, five or six. I looked seriously at good paintings. By real painters. And I became a connoisseur, a lazy connoisseur. And since I'm not very brave, I didn't stay to greet the Germans. I came home to help with the war effort, but I haven't been terribly good at that either."

"Do you miss it? Being in Europe?"

"It's the only place I've ever been happy, or almost happy. But I don't miss a place when I'm not there. Why should I?"

"I don't know," she said. "I never thought of missing as being voluntary. You do or you don't."

"And what do you miss?"

"All kinds of things. Times past. People," she said. "Doesn't your family live here? Didn't you miss them when you were away?"

"My father lives in New York," he said. "I didn't miss him."

"But how could you not? Your father."

Sadie quickened her pace until Willard caught up with her and took her arm, slowing her once more.

"What is it?" he asked.

"I live alone with my brother," she said. "I've gotten used to saying whatever comes to mind. Forgive me."

"Don't be silly," he said. "You couldn't offend me."

It had been the same the year before when Willard singled her out from the other students in Professor Albert Stuart Denton's course in European painting, and asked her to dinner and a concert at Carnegie Hall. Another girl in class told Sadie that Willard was a friend of the professor's. He wasn't only handsome and older, almost thirty, he was rich and had lots of women after him. He could have anyone he wanted.

At dinner he was silent except when he answered her questions, the same ones she'd just asked him. She didn't remember his answers because she hadn't listened to what he said, too absorbed in his voice. He'd taken her home after the concert and in the lobby, under the eyes of the night doorman, shook her hand, thanked her for a pleasant evening, and left.

They hadn't spoken again, except to say hello, though she'd watched him during class. His face was neither masculine nor feminine, and he resembled a creature from the paintings they were studying, a Pre-Raphaelite angel or saint. He was medium height, with almost blond hair and muddy hazel eyes. Sadie wondered what it would be like to be beautiful. The term ended and she left Barnard. When she thought of Willard in the intervening year, it was with a feeling of embarrassment, as if she'd failed a simple test.

"It's rude to ask personal questions," she said.

"Not necessarily. I'm flattered that you care to know a thing about me."

They walked companionably, his hand still on her arm.

"Now it's my turn," he said. "I looked for you on campus and never found you. Have you become a biologist or a mathematician?"

Sadie smiled and a dimple showed in her left cheek.

"I transferred to Hunter. I didn't like seeing my brother work so hard to pay for my tuition."

"Shall I carry your skates?" he asked. "They must be getting awfully heavy."

"A little." She had refused the offer when they left the rink, reassured by the weight of the skates; now she handed them to him and he put them over his shoulder so that they dangled from their long laces and knocked against his coat as he walked.

"What does your brother do?" he asked.

"He's a lawyer. Train & Ash is his firm. Some name, isn't it? They have their offices on Forty-second Street. You can see the library from their windows."

They walked slowly through the hushed park, and as they neared the wall along Central Park West, they began to hear traffic and see people hurrying past. At Sixty-fifth Street they left the park and walked over to Broadway, lingering at the bright shop windows, slowing their pace as they neared Sadie's building on West End Avenue, a square gray building that occupied half the block. A bright blue canopy stretched across the sidewalk, held in place by brass poles that the elderly doorman polished in the afternoons.

"Tell me something," she said.

"Anything," he said.

He held on to her skates, feeling the cold wet blades through his leather gloves.

"Why didn't you call me again last year? I mean, I can imagine a million reasons, but . . ."

"I intended to call," he said, "but one thing led to another . . ."

He hadn't thought much of it at the time. He had taken up or been taken up by the daughter of a friend of his father's. She had a place at the end of Long Island and Willard fell into the habit of going out there with her. When the affair ended, he looked around for Sadie, but she was gone.

"You just didn't know where I was," she said.

"Something like that," he said, glad that she supplied his excuse. "I didn't disappoint you deliberately, Sadie. Will you forgive me if I promise never to do it again?"

"Never's a long time," she said. "Cross your heart?"

She smiled but her heart pounded, and she looked at him wide-eyed, as if an important matter would be settled by his reply.

Willard's smile revealed a row of white teeth, its perfection broken by one cuspid slightly out of line.

"Cross my heart," Willard said. "Hope to die."

Two

IN THE SPRING NIGHTS THAT FOLLOWED THEIR MEETING, Sadie was restless in the room where she'd slept all her life. Everything was different now, even the apartment where she'd lived forever, the heavy, carved, mahogany dining-room set, the big couch with its brocade upholstery thin at the arms, the worn Turkish carpet in the living room. Dusting her mother's china vases and figurines every Thursday, as her mother had, Sadie was impatient for the next part of her life to begin.

When she was twelve, her parents had gone to Florida, leaving Sadie with her brother Reuben. It was her parents' first trip together since they were married and went to the Poconos. A second honeymoon, her father said, packing seersucker and cotton in the middle of winter, and we can't take a stringbean like you on our honeymoon.

She didn't want them to go. Her brother was eight years older than she, a law student at Columbia, living in a hotel near campus, in a room Sadie never saw, and he was happy there, his first home away from home. She didn't want him to stay with her while her parents were in Florida, and she sulked until her parents left. When the elevator door shut, Sadie wanted to run after them and say one more thing, Have a good time or Don't leave

9

me. They took a drive one evening in Daytona Beach at sunset. A truckdriver, blinded by the sun, ran into their car, killing them both instantly. At the moment when she answered the telephone and heard the news, Sadie felt that the world stopped. She wondered later if anything would have been different if only she hadn't been there to answer the phone, if she could have postponed death. And time didn't resume until she met Willard skating.

Reuben moved all his things from his hotel room, and he stayed on with Sadie for good. They changed nothing in the apartment. Why should they change a thing? The apartment was theirs and it was not theirs. They lived in limbo, waiting for Sadie to grow up, for Reuben to get established as a lawyer and to marry. Meanwhile what difference did furniture make?

Sadie did her best, fluffing the velvet pillows. In time she consigned her dolls to a hall closet to make room on her shelves for books. She obeyed all the rules Reuben set out for her—wasn't she lucky not to lose her home and to have such a brother?

Reuben was square and solid, like his mother—dark-haired, brown-eyed, heavy-jawed. He tended to be a little overweight and in his lawyer's suits looked older than he was. The only sign of vanity in Reuben, or even of attention to his appearance, was his struggle to make his thick, curly hair lie flat. In most of the snapshots of Sadie as a child, Reuben stood behind her, looking down at her. When she looked at the photographs, she remembered his hand on her neck.

He finished law school two years after the rest of his class because he ran his father's business, a ladies' garment factory, until it could be sold. Sadie's share of Ash Manufacturing he put in trust, "for your rainy days." The small income from the trust was there for Sadie's future. His principal he used to start a law firm with his old school friend Bernard Train. Neither Bernard nor Reuben was drafted—flat feet, bad eyesight, allergies—so not even the war touched their lives.

Nothing had changed, Sadie thought, staring at the engraving on her wall of a little girl skipping rope. Not until now.

It was ten in the morning, she had finished her last exam the day before, and Willard had promised to spend the whole day with her. In the past week, she'd been studying for exams, and couldn't attend a lecture he'd invited her to on Cézanne by a man Willard knew in Paris—an apostle of abstraction, Willard said. She might as well have gone, for she wasted the evening, unable to concentrate on her textbook, thinking of Willard. She opened the bedroom window, feeling the shock of sweet air, and Sadie returned to bed.

How could she have met him and been able to live when he didn't call her again? If it happened now, she thought, there wouldn't be anything to do but die. She put her hand on her chest, counting her heartbeats. How could she have lived without Willard when now the world was made of him?

The year before, months after their date, Sadie had seen outside their classroom a leggy blonde who did not belong among the students and rumpled faculty members rushing past her. She was dressed beautifully in a tailored suit, a fox scarf curling around her shoulders. Sadie guessed that she was waiting for Willard. He emerged from the classroom, greeted the woman, who looked annoyed and then relieved to see him. He took her arm and steered her down the hall. Next to her Willard looked more ethereal than ever.

But that was last year, Sadie thought. This is this year. Now it's me.

She hummed in the tub, "They Can't Take That Away From Me," admiring her skinny legs and her round little breasts. She dried herself, rubbing until her skin was red, dusted with baby powder, and brushed her teeth.

Sadie chose a white linen blouse with a soft collar and

a full cotton skirt. She took rouge, lipstick, and powder
into her parents' bedroom, where even now her mother's
smell lingered, a grown-up woman's smell that disappeared if Sadie tried to find its source or to identify it as
jasmine or rose. Also present, just as elusive, was her
parents' marriage, there in the twin beds pushed together, in the matching bedside tables and lamps, the
plumped goosedown pillows.

She looked at her reflection and tried to see what Willard saw in her. She lifted her reddish brown hair, like
her father's before it began to gray, pulling it back se-
verely from her face, and dropping it again so that it fell
in its ordinary way.

Before Willard had appeared at the skating rink, she
knew nothing of the world or how to live in it. Willard
knew everything and he had access to everything that
mattered: to art, not the boring kind one looked at alone
while killing time in a museum or dutifully taking notes
in class, but art that radiated passion and intelligence,
courage and skill. He knew food and wine. Her family
was in the business but she'd never seen anyone wear
clothing as beautifully as Willard did. Everything he wore
looked custom-made, his baggy trousers and large shirts
falling in effortless pleats. His dinner jacket looked casual, as though he'd invented it.

He could name everything they saw: skyscrapers in
midtown, townhouses in the Village, who built them, of
what material and what style; the furniture they saw
in the Metropolitan and shops along Madison, if it was
overvalued, rare, or fake; binding on fancy books; tech-
niques of engraving, calligraphy, and drawing. He knew
the names of the trees in the park and cloud formations
in the sky. They went to the Brooklyn Museum and wandered over to the Botanic Gardens, where neither could
name the plants beyond tulips and roses. He didn't admire formal gardens, he told her, too demanding, too
fussy.

To be fair, she thought, frowning into the mirror, she
knew other people who could name things. Reuben and

Bernard Train knew about things Willard took no interest in, but they bored her when they talked about politics and the law, their clients' crimes and connivances.

Willard had told her that he loved her brightness, but she didn't feel smart around him. All spring, she'd felt lucky for the first time, but not smart. Never mind, she told herself. She caught her expression reflected in the mirror, the smile of a person with a pleasant secret. Willard saw her as no one ever had, and he wanted her, not someone else. Things were finally changing. Don't question it, she cautioned herself, good things come to good people.

ON THE CROSSTOWN BUS GOING EAST, SADIE TOOK A window seat and watched the women on Broadway pulling their wire shopping carts, the housewives standing outside the butcher and the bakery in twos and threes, talking, their faces turned up to the sun. Her mother had once been one of those housewives, going each morning from shop to shop for the evening's meal, and Sadie used to watch for her from the bus. Seeing her mother when she didn't know that Sadie was watching was marvelous and unnerving.

The only other passengers on the bus were a bristle-haired sailor and his girl, who wore a yellow-flowered dress. They sat twined around each other near Sadie. Sadie watched them for a moment, then turned away, embarrassed as she always was when she saw lovers embrace. Then she turned to look at them again and her eyes met the other girl's. Sadie saw herself in the girl, Willard in the sailor. They were the same, and their sameness had nothing to do with the present—the crosstown bus, wartime, the sailor's white uniform—but with something that had always been, like the housewives standing and talking in the morning sun.

A few days before, she and Willard had driven to Coney Island and walked on the boardwalk, holding hands and eating pink cotton candy. They had looked over the crowd on the beach, at the patterns of flesh colors, a bright umbrella or beach towel, a uniform here and there. Willard said that it was like a Seurat and that each dot of color, each person, was important for what it added to the whole composition. Sadie had tried to see as he saw, but what moved her was the people. That day she, who never liked crowds, felt a part of the mob that moved along the boardwalk, swimming, playing games three for a dime, eating cotton candy and hot dogs, drinking lemonade and beer. She was part of all the other couples who were embracing, half-kidding and self-conscious, in swooning, hungry gestures.

SHE LEFT THE BUS AND WALKED. CROSSING LEXINGton, Sadie heard a distant roar. Bells and sirens were ringing and, all around her, people were running as if the city were on fire. A soldier threw his hat in the air and rushed on, not bothering to wait for it to fall. She stopped, wondering if she should retrieve it for him.

She asked some boys who were rushing past, "What is it? What is it?" but none answered. Around her, people embraced and wept. She stopped at the flower shop at Eightieth and Third, Willard's corner. The old man who owned the place stood in front, his buckets of lilacs and irises leaking on the sidewalk.

"What is it?" Sadie asked. "What is it, mister?"

"It is finished," he said. He had a slight accent, untraceable, like her father's. "Finished."

"Finished?"

"In Europe. The Nazis have surrendered. Germany. Italy. France. All finished."

Her first thought was that her luck had run out. Now Willard would go back to Europe where he had been happy.

She stood in the doorway of Willard's brownstone, hesitating, waiting to feel as wild as the people on the street. The war had been going on so long, like a knot that wouldn't come untied. She had been waiting for it to come to her, and to find her place in a camp—why not her, after all? She had gone on with her life, but she'd been waiting. Now she couldn't believe that the waiting was over and that she was free. Reuben would talk about how it had ended and what would happen next. And Willard would return to Europe, of course. He was in New York only because of the Occupation. The war was an inconvenience to him, not what it was to people like her. She had two quite opposite feelings about Willard: that he was in her life forever and that he would leave. She couldn't imagine him in New York forever, like Reuben, like herself.

Sadie opened the door and began the climb to the third floor up the carpeted stairs. She should have bought flowers from the man in the shop, she thought. She inhaled the lavender that Willard's landlady used in the hallway and let out her breath with an explosive sound, like a child imitating a bomb.

THE APARTMENT WAS FURNISHED SPARSELY WITH pieces from Willard's father, who had invited him to take whatever he liked from the house on Seventy-ninth Street. Willard had chosen as little as possible and then had come away with less when his father decided that, after all, he did not wish to part with this chair or that rug.

A bright Kazak covered the living room floor, and indigo velvet draperies were tied back from white inner curtains that filtered the spring sunlight. A cherry library table was set at an angle to a wine-red sofa. On a miniature brass easel on the table was a reproduction of *The Little White Girl*. Sadie reminded him of Whistler's pale girl standing in white lace before white draperies. (At her feet lay flowers she'd dropped, but she was an obedient girl and didn't break her pose to retrieve them.) The work table was neat; he kept his notes on Whistler hidden away in a portfolio made for him in Venice.

His bedroom was decorated by his Whistler oil of a

Venetian canal at sunset. By a stroke of good fortune, Willard had found the small painting in a junk shop on Third Avenue. He hadn't known for a certainty that it was a Whistler, but he had felt an excitement that was nearly the same as sudden fear or violent sexual attraction. Once in Paris he'd come upon an ancient Chinese jar that he bought for next to nothing and he'd felt the same sensation. It was not only the commercial aspect that brought about his passion—not mere acquisitiveness —it was the sudden apprehension of beauty, whether it might be his own possession or a museum's.

The wide bed was covered by a lofty white eiderdown, reminiscent of his school days in Switzerland. The glow from the Venetian sun gave warmth to the bare room.

HE OPENED THE APARTMENT DOOR AT HER KNOCK.

"Sadie," he said. "I've been waiting."

"You've heard," she said.

"Of course."

The living-room windows were open, and the sheer white curtains moved restlessly in the breeze. She could hear, though faintly, the sound she'd heard on the street, as if the whole city were shouting at once.

"It's something, isn't it? Now that it's happened."

On the small table before the couch was a tray with an ice bucket, a bottle of champagne, and two fluted glasses.

"At noon?" she asked. "How wonderful! I've never drunk champagne at noon. Hardly at all."

"The war in Europe ends only once," he said. "And it's time you learned about champagne."

She sat on the couch and watched him open the champagne and pour a glass for each of them. When she ducked her head to smell the cold wine, bubbles hit her with force, almost hurting her, and she laughed, startled.

Willard was smiling at her, holding up his glass. He wore a pale yellow shirt and gray trousers. The sleeves of the shirt were rolled up to his elbows. She loved to see the tightness of skin to bones in Willard.

"Shall we toast the end of the war?" he asked. "Or us?"

"The war," she said. "Isn't it more important than anything?"

Willard shrugged and said, "To the end." Before he left Paris, the city was crowded with refugees—Italians, Poles, Czechs, Belgians—looking for safety, and Sadie looked a little like the refugee girls. He wondered how many of them had lived to see this day. He had wanted to do something and had saved no one but himself. Willard drank the champagne, then poured more into their glasses and said, "To us."

"The beginning," she said.

She walked around the room, holding her glass, feeling daring—champagne at noon in Willard's apartment.

"Why are you smiling?" he asked. She was so pleasing to him today. She smelled sweetly of soap and looked so girlish in her little blouse.

"I was thinking how sophisticated I am," she said, setting down her glass and going over to Willard, who stood at the window. As she approached, the soft light gathered around him. She was standing so close to him that she could smell the champagne on his breath, the freshness of his shirt.

Willard looked down at her and, with a sigh, took her in his arms, first enfolding her, then kissing her, and he was surprised by the strength of her hold.

THEY CARRIED THEIR GLASSES INTO THE BEDROOM, AND undressed as if they were old, accustomed lovers. Naked, he pulled back the sheet and the eiderdown, then got into bed and waited for her. She looked so shy as she took off her slip that when she came into bed, he almost asked if she was sure she wanted to do this. He was very careful as they made love and very tender, asking her if she was all right, was this nice and did she like it, not nervously but reassuringly, he hoped.

She thought: Why am I doing this? Why now and why this man?

But then she forgot her questions and felt the new pleasures of being caressed and held. At last the questions and the pleasure came together, and Sadie felt brave and wonderful.

Later, as they lay side by side, hands touching, it came to her that she had made the first decision of her life.

"HAVE YOU EVER SKATED BACKWARD?" SHE ASKED. "That's how it felt, Willard. Like nothing and then everything."

"I'm not much of a skater," he said.

"Well, life is certainly strange."

"Is it?" he asked. He ran his hand along her side, thinking dreamily of the blood on the sheet, crimson on white.

"Everything is fate," she said. "If fate has it in for you, or if it's careless and it allows small things to go wrong, then big, powerful, important things might never happen."

"Things such as . . .?"

Sadie turned toward him and rested her head on his arm. "If I hadn't been skating—and I almost didn't go because it was late and I didn't really feel like it. If you hadn't happened to be there. If I hadn't fallen, you never would have noticed me there, and then—"

Then her fate would not be sealed, but she didn't want to say it aloud.

"So you've proved your case," he said. "If it's all fate, then what should we do? Lie back and wait for the next thing?"

"Yes," she said seriously. "To be able to accept your fate, whatever it is, to see it when it comes, to recognize what's important and fated. That's what you can do. All you can do is accept it."

He thought of telling her that he had been there deliberately, watching her; and if he had, things might have gone differently. Instead, he took her in his arms and said, "How young you are, Sadie. How sweet." He considered making love to her again, then asked, "Would it be fate if we were both hungry for lunch? At a nice little restaurant I know? Or would it be coincidence?"

Sadie said, "Habit," and then she added, allowing herself the luxury of hugging him tightly, a familial gesture that she guessed made him uncomfortable, "Oh, Willard, why not be happy? I know all the reasons why not but now it seems so simple to me. Why shouldn't we be happy? Everything that makes sense just doesn't."

Holding her, Willard felt if not happy then content with the turn the day had taken.

Three

IF SADIE HAD HAD A MOTHER OR A SISTER, SHE MIGHT have asked questions about Willard and love. But she had no female resources, and even if she had Sadie would not have believed that anyone else in the world had felt as she did or had done what she and Willard did together. She had an unusual and dangerous privacy with Willard, the first secret of her life from her brother.

She took in the sound of his voice and began to be an expert on when Willard was really cheerful and when he was claiming to be; what he meant when he said he was cross, and why he wouldn't say he was angry. The only life that mattered took place when they were together, and all other occasions were to be gotten through. Her sensations were precious to her, all the more so because they were not voiced even to Willard. They became more than themselves as now Willard was more than himself.

Still, she felt sometimes just before they made love that she should resist him. He pulled her away from herself, made her into another person who might be unable to rise from his bed, to see or speak without him. Once they began to make love, once she even saw that he wanted her, she felt a slipping away that she came to associate with passion. When she returned to herself, Sadie had trouble remembering what she had feared.

When he was distant or indifferent Sadie felt sure that they would never make love again. She sat through movies and meals, followed him around art galleries and museums, through the park, thinking that if he didn't touch her soon, she would go mad or die. When they were apart Sadie worried that he would find someone else, that she would wait in vain for him to remember her.

Her uneasiness was either there or not. If it was present its absence was unimaginable; if absent, it was a silly memory. Lying on his wide bed in the spring afternoons and warm early summer nights with the window wide open, Sadie felt as though she were on a tray, flying over the city, ready to be served to the world. She drew a new line in her life between past and present, before Willard and after.

Soon after they began their affair, Willard bought a white silk kimono for her. She kept it in his closet and when she saw it hanging there, she felt sure that he would make everything right between them. He called her his Whistler girl when she wore it and liked her to be naked underneath the silk. He arranged her hair so that it fell around her head in loose curls. Sadie felt like another person when she wore the white kimono.

Four

FOR BREAKFAST REUBEN LIKED COLD BOILED POTATOES with sour cream. Reuben ate in his shirt sleeves, flinging his tie over one shoulder to keep it away from the food. He read the morning paper as he ate, making a click of annoyance at what he found there, though never one of surprise.

Even when she had been out until dawn with Willard, Sadie struggled to sit in the breakfast alcove with Reuben, a habit left over from her school days when he prepared her breakfast and saw that she was up and dressed before he left for work.

She'd told him about Willard right away, mentioning that she'd met someone from her art history class at skating. "That's nice," Reuben said. She left notes for him: "Gone to dinner," "Gone to the theater," and she told him that she was with a very nice man, Willard Weaver, the one from art history class.

Reuben didn't have to ask anything about Willard. Sadie supplied the plots of plays they'd seen or recounted what she'd eaten for dinner with Willard. Sadie told him about Willard's education, his time in Paris, his wonderful eye for art. When Sadie fell asleep at the breakfast table, Reuben woke her and led her back to her bed, saying that he appreciated her company but if she needed her sleep, she should get it.

A few weeks after school ended, Sadie and Reuben sat at the breakfast table. His sleeves were rolled back, revealing black-haired, muscular arms. The Ashes were shaped like boxes with big arms and legs, Reuben always said. She stared at her brother, feeling nostalgic for the moment that was taking place: the smell of her coffee and his pot of tea; the blue-and-white flowered bowl of potatoes and sour cream; her toast, buttered, covered with peach preserves, neglected.

Now that she was in love, Sadie tried to invent a woman worthy of Reuben, someone who would appreciate his good qualities. He had always been the same, she thought. He dressed the same when he was a student in college, then in law school, and now when he was a partner in his own firm. In the fall and winter he wore a brown suit, gray shirt, and a dark knit tie. For special occasions Reuben had a white shirt and a striped silk tie. For a few weeks in summer he changed to a seersucker suit, which he wore with short-sleeved white shirts and a red tie. "The one thing I learned about the rag trade," he said, "is that clothes don't matter."

The few nights that Sadie and Reuben were both home they ate supper in silence then retired to the living room and read—he *The New Masses,* she the latest Mr. and Mrs. North. They strolled over to Broadway around ten and ate ice-cream cones on their way back home as they always had, but Sadie felt sad, as though she was pretending to be herself.

Reuben was still there in her dreams as he always had been, a figure standing between her and trouble: fire, a dark body of water, a door open to an unlit room.

"I worry about you, you know," Reuben said. He licked his lips of a last smear of sour cream, then patted his mouth with his napkin.

She was looking at her toast, breathing in the smell of the coffee, and thinking of Willard.

"Why would you worry about me? I'm all right."

"I worry," he said.

He would start telling her now that she had to plan her summer. She always had a summer job at Reuben's office, a monotony broken only by single weeks at the mountain cabins or beach houses of half-hospitable relatives. The job kept her under Reuben's nose, and she spent the summers filing, typing envelopes, proofreading interminable briefs, and waiting for school to start.

"Well, don't," she said. "I did fine in school. My health is good. I have—" She had been about to say that she had Willard but it occurred to her that this might be why Reuben was worrying. "I have a good time. And I'll come to the office tomorrow. I promise."

He waved his hand as if he were batting away flies.

"Believe me, I'm not talking about your good times," he said. "I'm talking about your life."

"Maybe we could talk tonight? Or tomorrow?"

"Listen to me, Sadie," he said. "We're born for a reason and it isn't to eat in restaurants."

"Don't start," she said. "I'm too old for you to order me around this way. I'll be twenty in October. It's too late."

"Please," he said. "I'm not ordering you around. Do me the courtesy of listening. It's not just this boyfriend of yours—"

"You'll meet him soon," she said. "I'll bring him to dinner next week."

"I don't mean him," he said. "Not at all. If he enters, he's just a *symbol* of what I mean."

"Oh, Reuben," she said. "Don't start. You know you've never wanted me to do any political work. I'm your little butterfly, remember?"

"I haven't called you that in years. You're grown up now."

"But really. Whenever I try to do anything—a demonstration or helping a committee or something, you give me that look. So I stop."

"As I recall, you think political work is boring. And you act out of guilt—should that make me happy? If you wanted to devote yourself to a cause, a look from me wouldn't stop you."

"Okay, okay. It's all my fault. I'm a butterfly."

"For whom will you live your life? I'm not talking about charity or politics or committees. I'm talking about something deeper. We, each of us, have a choice to make."

"What kind of choice?"

He shook his head, unwilling to be diverted.

"Unless you have your ideas intact, unless you know what you want and you stick to it, your choices are made before you know it. Before you know what you're doing, life sweeps you along."

"I don't know what you're talking about," Sadie said. Once she would have enjoyed hearing Reuben speaking seriously of her future. Too late now, she thought, I'm halfway out of the nest.

"You can live for yourself or you can live for something bigger than you. Belief in an idea. All right—a political movement. The times we live in, the great social movements—I'm telling you, Sadie, for a woman life is a wave coming at her. You stand there with your mouth open, and it hits you. Before you know it, you have a husband, kids you have to raise and give everything to. No more chance to do anything bigger. You've forfeited your chance.

"Ask yourself, Sadie, with each decision you make, For whom shall I live my life?"

Reuben gathered his bowl and spoon, and carried them into the kitchen. She knew he was right about the wave —she'd seen it hit girls at school. They fell in love and that was the end of them. If she saw them on the street, they looked different, softer and bewildered. She had felt sorry for them. Now she was one of them. As for belief in something bigger, at night sometimes, floating toward sleep, Sadie wondered if God knew where she was. He was there when her parents were killed, there at the camps. What did God care about her?

Reuben returned to the breakfast alcove, put on his jacket, cleared his throat.

"I appreciate it that you're concerned for me," she said. "Thanks for talking to me."

He adjusted his round, horn-rimmed glasses on his nose.

"What else is more important? I'll tell them at the office that you'll be in next week. Monday?"

She almost said, Tell me now, tell me what I should do. Instead she nodded, trapped into another summer at the firm, and told him, "Fine. I'll be there on Monday."

LATER, WALKING ACROSS THE PARK TO WILLARD'S, SHE felt the full beauty of the summer day. Watching the old men on the benches and the mothers with their strollers, Sadie wondered if everyone in the world knew about love. She tried to imagine her heavy, faithful brother in love but it would not be the same. Reuben would never know a fraction of what she now knew. And, feeling superior and guilty, she hurried on to Willard.

SADIE'S DESK WAS IN A CORNER OF THE OFFICE NEXT TO the windows that overlooked the Forty-second Street library. By turning in her padded swivel chair, she could see out to the street and Bryant Park, or, in the other direction, Arlie's switchboard, Elsa's desk, and the doors to Reuben's and Bernard Train's offices. Elsa, pink and white, overweight, living with her mother and a brother who drank, sat outside Reuben's office like a palace guard.

Arlie, dark and wiry, clattered on high heels like a Rockette, and answered the phone too loudly. Elsa raised her eyebrows and looked at Sadie, begging for agreement. Arlie, divorced, was raising her two daughters alone. She telephoned the girls several times a day, urging them to study, to wash the dishes, to stop moping: "Go play in the street," she told them. The girls went often to Alexander's and bought the wrong clothes, which Arlie described to the button to Sadie. She let them wear what they wanted. "Everyone's got the right to make their own mistakes."

Arlie and Sadie picked up where they had left off the summer before and went to lunch together nearly every day at Lennie's, a luncheonette on Sixth Avenue, around the corner from the office. She had intended to see Arlie often, but she got to the office only once during the school year. Lennie's window was filled with geraniums that grew on stringy stems up, down, and across the glass, growing strong from the soup and hamburger fumes and the steam off the coffee urns.

"Train and your brother," Arlie said. "They're getting to be two old bachelors, you know?"

"Well, they are," Sadie said. She was trying to remember if the menu had been altered in the year since she had eaten there.

"They don't have to be," Arlie said.

"Reuben could marry Elsa," Sadie said.

"I'm serious, kid. He's getting worse. Wrinkled shirts."

"I guess I should take better care of Reuben."

"It isn't your place," Arlie said. "Reuben just doesn't care. And Train is just as bad, only the opposite. He's so fussy, you know? As if anyone was looking at his clothes." She smoothed down her checked cotton sheath. Arlie's hair was thin and dyed red. She wore it piled on top of her head. Sadie didn't know how she managed to care so much about her daughters and her bosses, even about Elsa. Never me, she thought.

One day at the office was much like the next. Sometimes Sadie thought she was asleep with her eyes open. Mornings were good if she got a call from Willard, a few words to reassure Sadie that she led a life that Arlie and Elsa, her brother and his partner wouldn't understand. She waited for the lunch break so she could be outside, even if only to walk to the luncheonette and back. She waited for five o'clock so she could rush home and dress

for a date with him or run across the street to meet him
by the library lions. Sometimes when she first ran up to
the lions, he wasn't there, but when she looked again, he
appeared, and she was struck all over again by how beautiful Willard was. If Willard didn't call, she was in for
looks from Arlie and sympathy from Elsa. Sadie wished
so hard for the end of each day that the hours between
three and five seemed solid to her, iron gates too heavy
to push open.

She typed endless envelopes that summer, alphabet-
ized address lists for organizations that were clients of
Train & Ash. When Willard called late or when it seemed
that he wouldn't call at all, the letters swam before her
eyes, and Sadie felt a painful yearning, like hunger and
nausea combined.

The summer Sadie was sixteen, Elsa offered to teach
Sadie how to sew. She came to the apartment on Tuesday
evenings with containers of food, and after supper, she
set up Sadie's mother's old Singer in the kitchen alcove
and explained the tedious construction of buttonholes
and linings. Reuben sat nearby on the couch, reading. At
the end of the lesson, they walked to Broadway, where
Reuben waved down a cab for Elsa and pressed money
for the fare into her hand. Sadie hated the look in Elsa's
eyes when Reuben touched her hand to give her the cab
fare. Why couldn't she see it was hopeless, Sadie wondered, and thought, Never me.

One lunch at Lennie's, Arlie told Sadie about her husband. They had been crazy about each other. He kept
losing jobs but so did a lot of other people. He drank too
much but not so much that she would call him a drunk.
He stepped out on her but maybe she was losing her
looks. "Excuses," Arlie said. "That's what you do for
the people you love." But he began to hit her, a slap at
first and then he broke a few ribs and seemed willing to
go on from there. She held on until he hit the older child.
"Everyone's got their line," she told Sadie, taking in her
last spoonful of soup. "The line they draw. You just
don't know what it is until you come to it."

"I never knew . . ." Sadie said.

"Don't feel bad about it," Arlie said. "Something happens to everyone. And I have the girls, right?"

"I guess," Sadie said.

In July, the city slowed and the evening air filled with sunlight and grit. Walking home was like swimming and the men who walked with their jackets slung over one shoulder, the women who loosened a button of their blouses were fish. Sadie stopped at a delicatessen or the cheese store, dreading the moment of entering the hot apartment. Later, soaking in the bathtub, looking at winter dresses in an old issue of *Vogue*, Sadie felt beyond everything.

How could it be, she wondered, how did it happen that one minute you were free and young, the next minute burdened with a crabby old mother and a drunk for a brother, or two daughters who dropped water bombs on passers-by and spent too much money on lipstick? Guilty, repelled, Sadie daydreamed of escaping from them all, and of being with people like Willard, safe and independent, not pinned down by obligations and cares.

Five

IT WAS TOO EARLY TO DRINK AND HE HAD SMOKED TOO many cigarettes to want another. Willard lay on the couch, his hand over his eyes. The clock ticked in the kitchen. He took his hand from his eyes and looked at his wristwatch, four o'clock, and returned to his state of near-sleep.

WHEN WILLARD WAS SIXTEEN, HE CAUGHT A COLD AND was stuck in bed, suffering equally from the cold and from the knowledge that Reed was furious with him for bringing germs into the house. He refused to see Willard, saying that the young always bore more virulent versions of a disease.

As soon as he was almost well, Willard dressed and left the house. When the damp late January air hit his face, he knew he had left his bed too soon. He trudged west toward the park, to take refuge in the Metropolitan.

Other boys had horrible fathers. It didn't take Willard long to figure that out. Some boys he knew at school had no fathers at all or too many. Some had banks or law firms as guardians. Some—the worst off, Willard judged —spent holidays with the headmaster, for they had no-where to go at all. If Reed Weaver was subdued in his paternal welcome, at least it existed. Willard would have invited one of the boys home with him, but he couldn't bear the idea that tales of Reed's eccentricities might be taken back to school. Early he appreciated the convenience of keeping his worlds separate.

Reed had been athletic as a younger man—a champion court-tennis player at Tuxedo, a decent diver at Harvard, not a bad shortstop, a fast miler—now he rarely left his house. Willard's mother had died of blood poisoning when Willard was very young, and Reed clung to his loss —the same thing might happen to him. Willard remembered his mother as tall and slim, blond in a way he would never be. He could recall her presence, could feel her carry him from room to room in Tuxedo, lay him back in his carriage. He left his memories of her hazy, as if he risked losing her altogether if he dwelled on them.

From the time Willard was eight and returned from school abroad, Reed commented on all the invitations the boy must have to answer for parties and outings in New York. When Willard denied that he had anywhere to go or anything to do, Reed commended him on his modesty and warned him that the easiest way to lose his popularity would be to take it for granted.

Willard took the hint. Each day, he informed Reed or Prince, his father's manservant, that he was going to visit a friend. He made the announcement in the foyer, as he was putting on his velvet-collared overcoat and his small-peaked cap with the button on top. Prince surveyed him critically, then stepped back and reached for the doorknob.

The first few times Willard achieved his freedom, he went no farther from home than the Metropolitan Museum of Art, where he stared at Rembrandt's *Old Woman Paring Her Nails* and minor Dutch domestic scenes. He had read of kidnappings of rich little boys and wondered why his father didn't extend his web of caution to include him. He wandered down Fifth Avenue along the park wall, toward the Frick, envying younger children with nannies or mothers and older ones who had each other.

Choosing at random, he began to follow people around Manhattan. If he followed, it didn't matter that he wasn't noticed or that they didn't care about him.

As he grew older he played the game less frequently, for he invented other ways to entertain himself or else avoided coming home entirely. He made a few friends, went to the theater, and visited family friends in Tuxedo Park.

On a bench across from the museum he saw a man and a woman, gloved hands clutching, talking animatedly. Even Willard, whose experience of emotional scenes was limited, sensed their desperation. They embraced, then broke apart. The woman stood and twitched her shoulders like a bird shaking off water. She walked slowly past the man, down Fifth Avenue.

She wore a brown wool coat and a maroon beret that was easy to spot, even when she got far ahead of Willard. When she paused at a shoe store, he saw that she had a sweet face, though now it was distorted by worry. She walked to Madison Avenue and went first into a dress shop, then a bakery.

It began to drizzle, half snow, half rain. Willard shifted his weight from foot to foot, waiting across the street from the bakery.

She appeared again, holding a large cakebox carefully, not allowing it to tip, and walked across the street directly to Willard. Up close, the beret looked the worse for the wear, but the woman was prettier than he'd thought.

"He sent you, didn't he?" she asked. "I know that he did. You didn't see a thing, though, did you, you little sneak. An afternoon of shopping, right?"

"I think . . ." Willard's voice cracked.

"Why, you're just a kid," she said. "He *sent* you. Admit it to me."

She spoke quickly and trembled with anger. Willard took a step away and said, "No. He—"

"He sent you, all right," she said, moving closer. She clutched the cakebox by the strings, tilting it, and with her other hand grabbed Willard's velvet lapel. "A runny-nosed kid." She raised her gloved hand and slapped Willard hard across the face. Tears came to his eyes and he wanted to return the blow.

"Go away," she said, stepping back. "Let me alone. There's nothing left to see."

He thought about her all the rest of his vacation. Willard tried to imagine what would drive a woman to slap a stranger and he tried to guess who she thought had sent him. He had never known anyone before who cared enough to slap him and he enjoyed thinking about the woman. Indeed, when he invented an explanation for her action, he argued with himself until he destroyed his logic. What mattered was that he had been included in a tight circle of feeling and action. He returned to the corner where he had first seen her and the man, but he never found them again.

Willard accepted his nomadic, homeless childhood in time, and didn't speculate on whether it had formed or suited his character. He shared with Reed his ability to turn from people and strike them from memory. It didn't bother him that this reaction grew more involuntary the older he got. He noticed it less.

In later years, in London or Paris, but especially in Venice, Willard turned to see if anyone was following him, but no one did. He had love affairs, enough of them to see the end in the beginning. He always remembered the couple on the bench and the twitch of the woman's shoulders as a standard for feeling. He would have liked to have a friend with whom he was free to discuss his affairs, but the school friendships he kept up didn't include such conversations.

One day at the dull end of winter he saw Sadie at the window of a jewelry store. She was tapping on the glass as though she were keeping time to music. How could he tell her that he'd followed her, watched her on the subway as she read ads or her school books, or hesitated at a crowded street corner? When she fell skating, he acted.

From then on, he willed himself to behave as if something unforeshadowed and unpredictable might happen to him.

Reed Weaver's house on East Seventy-ninth Street had been built as a wedding present for his parents by his maternal grandfather. The house was plain, especially for the era in which it was built, though not simple enough for Willard's taste. His father had always lived there, but Willard had lived in so many other places that the time in his childhood when the brownstone had been his only home now seemed like a dream he'd had before birth. When he came to New York at the beginning of the war and a suitable apartment turned up in a building near his father's house, Willard took it. It was a proximity he hadn't sought deliberately, but once he was close Willard waited as he had as a boy for his father's invitations.

The outer doors were carved in a design of acorns and oak leaves. Willard's grandfather (for whom Willard was named) had taken the acorn for his symbol and the architect had used it liberally on mantelpieces and in stained-glass windows in the master's rooms. Willard's grandmother had chosen the daisy, and pale yellow designs in stained glass and carved flowers remained throughout the house. The acorn appeared in the etched glass on the inner doors. Each time Willard rang the bell, he thought that it sounded like a bell in a tomb.

Prince opened the door and stood back to allow Willard to enter.

"Prince," Willard said. "I trust you're well."

"Sir," said Prince.

Prince was Reed's person. Prince did not like Willard and never had. It was a landmark revelation to Willard, one that came when he was beyond his father's financial control, that he didn't like Prince and never had; further that there was no need either to like him or to seek his approval. For all Willard knew, Prince was everything Reed wanted, and therefore everything Willard was not.

So far as Willard knew, Prince had no other family or

interest outside the house and Reed. Together, the two men made a household and though other servants sometimes appeared for special tasks—to wash the windows, take down the drapes, roll the rugs for an annual cleaning —Prince was the only essential to Reed and to the house. He had come to work for Reed soon after Willard's mother died. When Willard studied art history he noticed Prince's head used as ornamentation on Roman perfume bottles and carved necklaces. Age was giving the hooded eyes and sharp cheekbones even more nobility. His name might have been surname or nickname. Willard had never asked and would never be told.

HE FOLLOWED PRINCE INTO THE DRAWING ROOM, where light pressed through an opening in the heavy drapery. A large European carpet, yellow and pink, covered the parquet floor. It was not very good, but in remarkable shape considering its age. The faded rose and gold furniture lived in the same purgatory as the carpet.

"May I bring you something?" Prince asked. There was a tray on a side table with crystal decanters of brandy, sherry, and other liquors. Willard licked his lips involuntarily. He would very much have liked a highball but when he drank at his father's house the alcohol had no effect, soothing or soporific.

"No, thank you," he said. "My father is well?"

Prince made a face, as if he had come upon something unexpectedly foul.

"The lung," he said. "But it passed."

"I see," Willard said. He often speculated on what Prince and Reed talked about, if anything, during their long solitary stretches. Probably the minute details of Reed's condition.

Prince nodded and left.

When Willard was a child, he spent hours underneath the tables, playing shipwreck, and he had stared long and hard at the glass cabinet that held his grandmother's butterfly collection and a stuffed owl with furious glass eyes.

He had loved the smell of evaporating liquor that even
then pervaded the room, and the scent of the eucalyptus
leaves that Reed kept in every room of the house. Reed
believed that eucalyptus combatted ambient germs of a
low order. But what excuse did he have for the Chinese
urn filled with peacock feathers? Willard remembered
standing as tall as he could and looking up at the urn.

The clock on the mantelpiece struck the quarter hour.
His father always kept him waiting. Above the clock
hung a portrait of a young girl, one hand resting on her
hoop and stick, a cousin of his mother's, one of the first
women in Massachusetts to die in an airplane crash. He
wished he had had grandparents with vision enough to
buy good paintings instead of commissioning mediocre
society portraits.

He had brought a present for his father—the latest edition of Emily Post's book on etiquette. Mrs. Post's father, whom Reed had admired, had been the architect for
the original rustic cottages and clubhouse in Tuxedo
Park, though not the house Reed now owned. The last
time Willard had seen his father, they had drifted to the
subject of Mrs. Post, who Reed said had a reputation as
a sensible woman; he hadn't seen a copy of her famous
book. The red-and-white gift paper was garish against the
faded rose couch.

There was a sound outside the drawing-room door.
Willard looked up as the clock struck again. He stood,
adjusting his jacket, smoothing down his hair. The brass
doorknob turned slowly, the door opened by inches.
Reed's entrance was that of a premier danseur, his presence foreshadowed not by a corps of fluttering ballerinas
but by the grave Prince.

He came into the room absent-mindedly, as if he'd
mislaid something there—a letter or a cup of tea—and
looked around.

He was taller than his son, and his thinning hair more
auburn than blond. They resembled one another in profile
and form—both were slim men with slightly hunched
shoulders. Reed wore a navy-blue blazer, gray trousers,

a shirt that was almost yellow but had been restrained. He hesitated, as a cat will after begging to be let in, frowned at the windows, touched the silk ascot at his throat, then caught sight of Willard and gave a small cry, allowing his hand to rest above his heart, as though overcome by pleasure and surprise.

"Why, Willard," he said. "Is it a decent day out? Prince told me of threats. Rain. Clouds."

"It's awfully mild, Father. The only threat is being bored to death by the mildness."

Reed raised delicate pale eyebrows and smiled, unbelieving.

"You took a taxi here?"

"I walked, Father. I came from three blocks away."

"Walked. How robust you are, Willard. Sherry?"

Prince came into the room and set a tray on a low table before the couch, then took the decanter of sherry and a glass and placed them beside the tray. When he left, Reed asked, "Does it strike you that he's getting very stooped?"

"Who?"

"Prince, of course. He's more stooped than he ought to be. Bad nutrition. Early on."

"Perhaps," Willard said judiciously. He poured sherry into the tiny glass. The sticky smell of the wine, the peppermint and camomile fumes of Reed's tea, the dusty eucalyptus made him think of childhood illnesses. He sipped at the sherry and decided that he despised the taste.

"How has your health been, Father?"

"Ah," Reed said. He smiled and inclined his head. He poured tea into his cup, added a tiny amount of honey, stirred, and sat on the Morris chair by the couch. "Rather in the middle range, I would say. I had a bout of seasickness this week. Odd, don't you think?"

"On dry land, yes," Willard said.

"Oh, certainly I was on dry land. Who would take a voyage in these days or ever again. The oceans are mined, as are the deserts."

"But aside from seasickness," Willard said, "you are well."

"Before the seasickness, as you call it, I had a period of almost dull calm. I don't suppose you've ever experienced such a thing."

"It's one of your conceits," Willard said, "that I live an adventurous life. I do nothing bold."

"How disappointing."

"I read, Father. For my monograph on Whistler. I see . . . friends. That's all."

"But with these friends . . ." Reed stood with an energy that was unusual for him and pressed his back to the mantelpiece, as if to gain perspective on Willard. "With your friends, you venture to restaurants, perhaps clubs?"

"On occasion," Willard admitted. "But it's nothing, Father."

"Nothing?"

"Nothing terribly exciting. Not like an ocean voyage over a mined sea."

"How unfortunate for you," his father said. "I look back on my youth and its adventures with gratitude. How sad that your life is so dull."

"Yes, Father," Willard said. He touched the red-and-white package on the couch by his side, and he saw that Reed was looking at it.

"Now that the war is nearly over," Reed said, "you must be full of plans."

Willard stroked the edge of the book, feeling it through the thin paper. His father loved presents.

"Not full," Willard said.

"Not that much of your Europe is left standing. The Americans are awfully destructive—bombs, firebombs, that sort of thing."

"I suppose they bombed sufficient unto the day," said Willard. "The Germans were no slackers."

"But the military isn't your specialty, is it?" Reed asked.

"You know I wasn't allowed in any branch of the military."

"Childhood asthma turned the trick, didn't it? Something that might recur."

"Don't be ridiculous," Willard said. "I haven't had an asthma attack for years."

"The terrible noise," Reed said, "the clutching for breath."

"I never had an attack at home," Willard said. "You can't possibly remember them."

"You don't recall everything, my boy. Just as well. It's good you've come by. I'm thinking seriously of selling the Tuxedo house, for your sake. I spoke with Stratton the other day, and under the terms of your mother's will, the disposition of the property is entirely up to me. The pollen, Willard. The place is a menace to anyone with sensitivities. I think of it still."

"But since I never go to Tuxedo," Willard asked, "why sell the house for my sake?"

"Exactly my point," Reed said. "Why keep it? The place has held up so far, though I heard a rumor about the roof. That would cost a fortune. My fortune, not yours. And no one goes there, so why keep pouring money into it, keeping it up, that woman going once a week. You have no idea. Why bother with it?"

"If Stratton says so . . . But it seems to me . . . rather an odd decision. If it's the money. The upkeep. I might be able to . . ."

"Oh, no," Reed said. "Your mother's will made me responsible for it during my lifetime. No need for you to take it on before it's necessary."

"But if it's a question of maintaining or selling, I'd prefer you to let me take care of the maintenance. Assuming it isn't out of hand."

The steam that had been piping from Reed's teacup now formed a haze on the brown liquid. Reed raised the dainty cup to his lips and drained it. Then he set the cup on its saucer.

"Never drink cold liquids, nor hot. You must try not to become so agitated," Reed said. "A show of temperament is a liquor to the brain, enflaming it. You will do yourself damage, Willard. Perhaps a recurrence of your asthmatic condition. There is a link between body and mind, you know, stronger than you imagine.''

"You haven't taken me to task for my sprained ankle when I was eight. Nor for the time I fell out of the elm on the lawn at Tuxedo. Or have you forgotten?''

"Perhaps I have," Reed said. He glanced at the clock, then at his hands.

He loathes me, Willard thought. I make his skin crawl. I wonder if he bathes in cool water and baking soda when I leave to soothe his hives.

They heard footsteps outside the drawing-room door. Father and son looked up with the hope that the person who entered would allow them to part.

"Mr. Weaver," Prince said, "six o'clock."

The clock on the mantelpiece chimed.

"I must go, Father," Willard said.

"I'm glad you could find the time to see me," his father said. "Living so near, after all, we might have frequent visits."

"As you suspected," Willard said, "my schedule is full. But I'll make the time to go out to Tuxedo. To see what shape the house is in.''

"If you like," Reed said. "I'd welcome your opinion.''

Willard saw himself out of the house, taking the red-and-white-wrapped book with him. Two blocks west, he pitched it into a wire garbage can, and walked on.

SADIE WAITED FOR HIS CALL, ENDURING SYMPATHY from Elsa and Arlie until they left for the day. Train stopped on his way out of the office and stood before her desk, fiddling with his bow tie, which had pink butterflies on it. He had a broad open face and tired brown eyes. She knew that he was attractive to women, but she'd never liked him that way.

"Oh, come on, Sadie," he said. "Let me buy you a drink. It'll cheer you up. You look down in the dumps."

"No, thanks," she said, "I have to get home and—"

"Sort your laundry? Come on. I've known you since
you were a kid. I won't bite."

"I'm okay, Train," she said. "Really."

But when he was gone, she was sorry she hadn't accepted his invitation. Willard had promised they would
go to the movies that night, meet in front of the lions,
have a bite of supper, and see what was playing, but it
was six o'clock, long past when it was reasonable to expect him.

Sadie put a cover on her typewriter, turned out the
office lights, and locked the door behind her. She went
down the long corridor, looking in the glass office doors
for her reflection, then, when the elevator arrived, she
ran down the hall and let herself back into the office,
flinging the door open. She stood in the doorway, unable
to remember why she had returned, except that she had
a terrible fear that something important was left undone.
She walked down the hall again and took the elevator
that still waited.

The lobby was empty. It was a gold-ceilinged arcade
that ran from one end of the building to the other, usually
filled with office workers, messenger boys, and shoppers.
Willard was somewhere in the city, she thought, and
somewhere there were more people like him, who were
safe and free from wanting what they didn't have. But
even so, she thought as she began her long walk home,
she would have given anything to be on the subway,
heading for the Bronx to have dinner in Arlie's crowded,
friendly kitchen.

Six

He caught a Checker cab on Fifth Avenue and gave the driver the address on Perry Street in the Village. Willard opened the window and let the air soothe him. Near the Plaza, he saw a sailor and his girl, running to catch the light on Fifth, both dressed in white clothes that shone in the dusk, looking as though they were dancing an abandoned tango, their feet almost tripping but moving with grace, eating up the street.

When the cab pulled up at Cherry's door, Willard was tempted to tell the driver to wait for him—she might not be home or might refuse to see him—but he tipped the man and sent him away. The small foyer smelled of disinfectant and cats. He pressed the buzzer under Cherry's mailbox and waited.

Willard had met Cherry in the spring at his friend Bradley's talk on Cézanne at a midtown bookstore. She was leaning against the shelves of occult books, whispering now and then to a big, rough-looking man, a painter who was Bradley's protégé. Bradley lectured in his nasal, monotonous voice, preaching to the converted. It seemed to Willard that Bradley was less interested in art than in power. The next wave of rightness, he was saying, would take place in New York, not in Europe. And it would come from Americans. Willard stared at Cherry. He thought she was unaware of his presence until she turned and looked over at him, full face, as if she knew all about him already.

Cherry was a painter, though Willard judged her to be without promise. Even if he had been inclined to admire the distorted shapes and harsh colors she used, he could recognize the work of someone who could mimic but not create a work of art. Though in a different style, hers bore a resemblance to his own failed work.

She'd come to New York from a small town in New Jersey when she was nineteen, to study at the Art Students League. A painting had sold out of a student show, and lately Willard had bought a drawing, which he put in his hall closet. Cherry worked in a frame shop on Bleecker Street, around the corner from her apartment, and made plans for trips she never took, just to fend off the blues, she said. Next to her bed there was usually a pile of travel folders—she liked Mexico best.

And in the same way, Cherry threatened to move. The night he met her she told him she was leaving New York at the end of the month for California, where the climate and the people were kinder. A few weeks later, he saw her at an opening and when he mentioned California, she smiled as if he'd invented the idea of her leaving. "I must have been loaded," she said tolerantly. "Don't take me so seriously."

She planted flowers in a kitchen window box and demanded that visitors lean out to see how high her morning glories climbed.

The first time he'd spent the night with her, she'd called up the liquor store at ten o'clock and after an amiable conversation, a delivery boy appeared with wine and Scotch and twenty dollars in cash. "It's my bank," she explained to Willard. "Who else cashes checks at night?"

Wherever she was it seemed like night. If he came at noon or midnight, Cherry was always the same, as if she lived in a fugue, free from time, free from him.

WILLARD LEANED AGAINST THE INNER DOOR AND IT swung open. Another tenant must have left it unlocked, out of carelessness or for a visitor.

He climbed the stairs and stopped on the fifth-floor landing. The door to Cherry's apartment was ajar and he wondered if someone else was expected or had just left. He knocked on the doorjamb and waited, then knocked again. He heard a radio playing dance music—she liked to listen to music while she painted—but the sound was faint and might have come from another apartment. He pushed open the door and called her name.

Her studio was in the first room, small and square, with a window opening onto a dark courtyard. Her easel was jammed into a corner and stretched canvases leaned against the wall. Her palette was crusty and an empty glass covered with paint-stained fingerprints stood next to it on her worktable. Half-used tubes of paint, caps off, lay next to the palette, and rags torn from old blouses, checks and cabbage roses. On the floor were piles of sketchbooks and magazines, ballet slippers on top of a museum catalogue, and, in the corner by the easel, a Saratoga trunk, its humped lid ajar. The smell of turpentine brought Cherry back to him. Willard called her again, then went into the kitchen.

She sat at a small, round table, laying out cards for solitaire. Cherry wore a loose green robe, its sleeves thrust back, revealing her thin, pale forearms and hands. A cigarette burned in the overflowing ashtray. An open bottle of Scotch, a glass of melting ice were close at hand. Cherry glanced up when he came into the room, then returned to her game.

"Don't you know this is the big city?" Willard asked. "Your door is wide open."

"If I'd have known you were coming, I'd have closed it."

"That's a nice greeting," he said.

"About as nice as your hellos and good-bys."

"Okay, okay," he said, as if she had rained a torrent

of reproaches on him. "You're right. I should have called."

Cherry looked up at him fully for the first time.

"Your tie's crooked," she said. "You look as if you could use a drink."

"You once told me everyone looked as though he could use a drink."

"Except for the people who could use one less, like my old dad. You know where the glasses are."

She returned to the cards, giving Willard a view of her profile. Her hair was dark and cloudy, her eyes bright blue, and her face was round and open. When she'd been sleepless or drunk, she looked like a china doll gone to the bad.

"I've thought of you often," Willard said. "Honestly." He wished that he'd brought some token for her, though he doubted she'd have liked the Emily Post book.

"Oh, sit down," she said. "You'll embarrass me. Have a drink. You know I can't stay mad long. I'd be better off if I could."

He took a glass from the cupboard and squeezed in between the wall and the table onto a rickety chair. Closer, he could smell the perfume she wore for sex and he wondered if someone else was expected or had just left. Once she had told him that the artists she slept with walked as carefully through her studio as through a mined field.

"How have you been?"

"Charming. I took my paintings to a gallery last week and the dealer made a pass at me. The job's the same. Framing pictures of dead soldiers and sailors. You know."

"But you can pay for your own whiskey."

"Buster," she said, "I don't ask what you do with your money, do I?"

"Gin?" he asked.

"Just what you see. No wine cellar."

"No," he said. "The game."

She smiled for the first time and looked at him again, as if she remembered him now.

"Sure," she said.

They played until Willard owed her five dollars, and they were almost too drunk to see the cards.

"I surrender," he said.

Cherry stood and went to the open window. It was quiet, the middle of the night. She leaned out and breathed deeply while Willard admired the outline of her body where the soft robe fell against it. He came up behind her, cupping her breasts with his hands.

"You planning to push me out?" Cherry asked. Her voice was husky, the way it was in bed.

"Not unless you take me with you," he said.

But after they made love, Cherry began to cry. He could see by the light coming in from the studio that her sweet, old-fashioned face was as set as when he came through the door.

"I'm twenty-nine years old," she said. "What will I be doing when I'm thirty-five, forty?"

"I'm past thirty," he said, "and I still don't know what I'm doing."

"You're a man," she said, "and you're rich. You don't have to do anything. Jesus. Maybe I'll be like my mother, being good all the time."

She had talked before about the town where she was from and her mother, who'd married a drunk—he was long gone. Sometimes when she talked it was with her father's voice, and she told Willard how glad she was to be away from home and what adventures she would have when things improved.

"Why do I talk to you?" she asked. "You're as bad as the rest of them. Why did I let you in?"

She searched the crowded bedside table for her cigarettes.

"The door was open," Willard said. He was exhausted. His eyes and mouth felt heavy. Comforting Cherry, even looking at her, demanded more strength than he had.

"And I guess you wanted me," he said, touching her shoulder. Each time he was in bed with her, he was drawn to her deeply and couldn't remember what it was like with another woman, couldn't imagine wanting anyone else.

"Don't flatter yourself," she said. "When I drink enough, I'll sleep with anyone."

"Come on," Willard said. "Go to sleep. You'll make yourself feel worse."

"Oh, all right," she said. "You want another drink? A cigarette?"

"Nothing," Willard said. "I'm falling asleep."

"Wait," she said. Cherry put out her cigarette, and leaned against him as he curled into sleep.

Seven

SADIE DREAMED THAT SHE WAS WALKING DOWN A TREE-
lined street with her mother and father. Her father, who
was always in a hurry, lagged behind Sadie and her
mother. The dream was yellow and white, like a very hot
day. Her mother was annoyed with her father for not
keeping up with her. He ignored her. Sadie knew, as they
did not, that her parents were dead. When the dream
ended, she would have to return alone to the life they'd
known together.

When she woke, Sadie tried to remember where they
were going. She knew in the dream, but once it was over,
all she could hold on to was the feeling that she'd just
been with her parents.

Eight

WHEN WILLARD CALLED HER A FEW DAYS LATER AT work and asked her out to dinner, Sadie said, "Come and pick me up at home. All right? You've never met my brother Reuben."

She dashed home after work. All the way up to the seventh floor the elevator man tried to tell her a joke but forgot the punchline and had to keep returning to the beginning again. She stared at the elevator walls, which looked dingy. And the apartment didn't look much better, measured against the elegance of Willard's apartment and the palatial surroundings she imagined his father living in.

She vacuumed the living room and plumped pillows, straightened furniture and checked the bathrooms. Sadie opened the linen closet and was hit by the smell of mothballs, which Reuben called Jewish potpourri. Sadie used them everywhere, as her mother had. Now she thought, Had she ever seen a moth eating a towel or a napkin? She found the cocktail napkins, embroidered with tippy martini glasses, and closed the closet door.

Sadie put salted peanuts in a cut-glass dish on the coffee table, sat down, stood up, and hoped Reuben would remember to come. He had grunted when she asked him that morning and looked as if he was about to deliver advice to her when Train strolled into the office and Sadie was able to slip away.

"So," REUBEN SAID, "MY SISTER TELLS ME THAT you're an art historian. A teacher?"

"Not at all," Willard said, glancing at Sadie, who looked quickly into her drink. She was certain she never said that, though perhaps she had, wanting Willard to sound more legitimate to Reuben. "I have very little academic training. A few years in Paris. But I'm not at all a scholar. I don't know where you got that idea, Sadie."

"I didn't," she said, but he had already turned away from her, back to her brother.

"Paris," Reuben said, "Paris. What a marvelous place that must be. The Sorbonne? You studied there? The Academy?"

"On my own, actually. I attended lectures at both places when I felt the need. Really, Paris is an education in itself."

Willard smiled, a social expression meant to be winning. Sadie's brother was a completely different type than she, reminding Willard of shrewd Russians in Paris, who, even if they were cabdrivers or clerks, looked wise and from another age. Willard had been unable to imagine their lives.

"Though I've spent more time in France," Willard said, "I've always felt at home in Italy. That sounds awfully conceited," and again he smiled, wondering how Sadie's brother made him say such pompous things. He wanted Reuben to like him, and wished Sadie wouldn't look at him so openly in Reuben's presence.

Sadie, at the edge of her chair, smelled mothballs from the cocktail napkins. A breeze came through the open windows and the cool stillness of the room stirred.

"I've never been," Reuben said, "but I've always wanted to see Italy. What a life you must lead, Mr. Weaver. France. Italy. The Continent. And the world of art . . . looking at paintings, sculpture. It must be nice to be a man of leisure. So few men have any time to themselves. Imagine a lifetime of it!"

"I never knew you wanted to go to Italy," she said.

She wished Reuben would stop talking as though he'd never been anywhere or done anything. He'd been to Europe, after all, skiing with an Austrian friend. And he knew lots of things Willard didn't—about how New York worked and government, although Willard didn't care about those things. Reuben had interesting clients—actors, union leaders, writers, European refugees who were scientists and philosophers—but he sat like a lump, shrugging his shoulders like an old man, like their father, whose ambition was to be an American citizen and for her and Reuben to go to college. She didn't like having Willard there in his white linen suit among her mother's furnishings, which he probably thought were ugly and probably were. Her mother had loved them.

"You don't remember my scrapbooks, Sadie? I loved Latin, I was crazy to see Rome."

"Did I ever see your scrapbooks?" Sadie asked. She remembered them vaguely, thick and starchy pages between red cardboard covers.

"I threw them out," he said. "Somewhere along the line."

"Our mother never got rid of anything," Sadie said. "Reuben and I are more relaxed. Even unlaxed."

"What's it like in your family?" Reuben asked. "Keepers or profligates?"

"I don't think of myself as having a family," Willard said. "Though I suppose things stay where they are forever. My father rarely spends a dime, except on medical expenses." He frowned, thinking of the Tuxedo house.

"Your father's an invalid?" Reuben asked.

"He's sounder than the dollar," Willard said. "He enjoys pretending there's something wrong. He likes to think things are attacking him. The air he breathes, the water he drinks, and the ground he walks on."

"I see," Reuben said, glancing at Sadie, asking her to

disapprove with him of Willard's description of his father. "Another drink?"

"Well," said Willard. He glanced at his watch, then up at Sadie. "Our reservation's for eight. If you'd care to join us, Reuben . . ."

"Oh, no," Reuben said. "It's been a pleasure meeting you, but . . . I don't get out much, like the song says." He smiled in a self-deprecating way that made Sadie want to kick him.

"Are you sure?" Willard asked, standing. "You're perfectly welcome."

"Another time I'll take you up on it."

The men shook hands, and Sadie kissed Reuben when they left, self-conscious because they weren't big touchers in their family. She felt sentimental, as if, with his shrugs and self-denials, Reuben represented authenticity, the dullness she had once lived in.

They stood in the hall, waiting for the elevator, and Willard said, "You don't know how lucky you are, do you, having a brother like Reuben."

SHE SAID, FORGETTING THE DAYS WHEN HE HADN'T called, forgetting her brother, her discomfort when he was in her home, "You know me." She took his hand and put it on her bare, flat stomach. "You know me better than anyone ever has." She wanted to say, You own me, which was closer to what she felt.

THEY HAD TAKEN A CAB TO THE RESTAURANT AND THEN, outside the doors, turned and embraced.

"You're looking very lovely," Willard said. "Very sweet. Almost delectable."

She whispered, melting into him, "Let's not have dinner. Let's just go to your apartment."

He had looked down at her, still as if he were very far away, and he smiled. "The white kimono?"

"Yes," she said.

And now—"You know me."

"Ah, Sadie," he said, turning away. He reached for a cigarette from the bedside table, offered her one, lit his own. "It's not really true—I know a part of you. And no one else has known that part. You don't either."

"I don't?"

"No," he said. He wanted to tell her that her erotic life was just beginning and that no one could predict, not even she, what the variety of her experience would be, but that sounded avuncular, so he said, "It's all just beginning, isn't it?"

"I suppose," she said, missing his hand.

She hadn't said it right and he hadn't understood, but Sadie turned over, stretched, felt the strength in her young body, and thought that another time she would get it right. She would find the words and the moment to tell Willard what he surely must know: that he would be her only lover for her life, that already he was a part of her as no one else would ever be. He had taught her ways to touch him that pleased him, surely he would someday teach her words that would reach him and she would be able to describe everything—the light from the street as it fell on the Venetian painting, her delight in him, her conviction that her life had begun because of him.

He took her back to West End Avenue in a cab and told the driver to wait for him.

"I'll be away for a few days," he said at the elevator. "Possibly a week."

"A week?" She could hear the elevator creaking up from the basement.

"I'm going to Washington to see an old chum. And to have another look at the Peacock Room. You remember?"

"Oh, sure."

"I told you all about it," he said with mock impatience, "but you've probably forgotten and think it's a restaurant. I see that I bore you to death when I get on my hobbyhorse.''

"No, no," she said. "Just for a second I couldn't remember. Well—a week.''

"Maybe not," he said. As the elevator doors opened, he leaned over and, catching sight of the elevator man, kissed her forehead. "I'll call when I get back.''

She lingered, wanting more. She said, ladylike, "Good night. Have a good time in Washington," and let the doors shut off her lover from her sight.

Nine

MARTIN BOWLES, WHOM WILLARD REMEMBERED FROM school as a stout boy, stood in the Peacock Room, legs planted apart, a balding Atlas. His boyhood curls were combed into a long hank that Martin arranged over his broad forehead. Willard wondered if one was supposed to believe that the hair actually grew that way or if this was an illusion so obvious that one was meant to accept it as reality.

Willard had told Sadie that he needed to see the Peacock Room at the Freer Gallery for his work on Whistler, but he only wanted to get out of the city for a few days. He was staying with Martin, who was working for the Treasury Department in a job his uncle had arranged at the beginning of the war. He wondered what Martin would say if he told him of his life in New York, or described Sadie and Cherry. From the distance of the Potomac Willard judged that he was wasting his time.

Martin's big-boned head was tilted up to the blue-and-gold ceiling. Willard looked at the golden design, the lush fall of the painted peacocks' tails, then down to a wall mirror. He was the same, he thought, not yet altered as Martin was by time, as if his friend had lived more fully than he.

"Harmony in blue and gold," Bowles said. "What a

thing to name this room! The architect went mad when he saw all this *harmony*."

Willard knew better than Martin how Whistler had redecorated his patron's new dining room.

"Did his hair turn white at the sight?" Willard asked. "People always say that. 'All his hair turned white.' 'Went mad.' Whistler had his patron's *permission* to alter the room, to make it more suitable for *La Princesse du Pays de la Porcelaine*. . . ." he said, pointing to the portrait at the end of the room.

"In *small* ways, chappie," Martin said. "To *harmonize*. But this involved painting every surface—including the Elizabethan leather walls. Took Whistler months and lost him his reputation. Led to his bankruptcy in the end. And for what?"

"He'd say—For art."

Martin laughed and Willard remembered his crooked grin from the snow-cold playing fields of their school. Martin had hated sports; when forced to play he cheated. Willard thought he would admire Whistler's piracy more.

"I envy Whistler his passion," Willard said. "The courage to throw away everything respectable in one gesture."

"Oh, passion," Martin said. "Surely you've gone beyond that. And why Whistler? I would have guessed Ingres."

"I found a small painting," Willard said, "just by chance. And then, this being stuck in New York—"

"It's been impossible here," Martin said. "Troops in tents near the Capitol. Like engravings of the Civil War. Well, it will be different soon enough."

The dark-haired princess was dressed in kimono and obi, slouching back, challenging the artist with dark eyes, reminding Willard of Cherry.

"I envy Whistler caring this much, not for the things men usually go off the deep end for—but for a room, a look, a painting."

"If you envy passion, Weaver, you'll be jealous of the

addict with his morphine, the mother with her child—the whole gamut, and how tiresome that might become."

The princess held a fan that was exquisitely painted with a poppy and an iris against a white background, and Willard felt an almost sexual warmth, looking at the combination of colors.

Willard said, "I suppose it might."

He was staying with Martin Bowles at his small three-story house with slanting floors and too much padded furniture. The night before they'd arrived home late from a concert to find, in the icebox, a tray laden with small white china pots of chocolate mousse, left by the housekeeper. There were a dozen pots on the tray and Willard wondered who else was expected. Martin, licking his lips, made coffee for them, which they'd carried to the living room, a room mirrored on the ceiling and the walls. Willard ate one mousse, fitting a tiny silver spoon into the pot, licking off the sweet fluffiness.

Martin criticized the chocolate, saying that his housekeeper must have been thinking of nursery puddings, but he ate three and, Willard suspected, would interrupt his sleep to come down to the kitchen for more. When Willard looked up from his mousse he saw himself and Martin reflected in the mirrored wall, two idle bachelors with their solitary pleasures. Enjoyable up to a point, Willard thought, and then what would there be? He caught a whiff of eucalyptus, the scent of his father's medicine.

"Shall we move along?" Martin asked, moving toward the doorway. "I want to show you the Japanese screens. Far more interesting than Whistler."

Willard lingered in the Peacock Room for a last look, trying to reduce the kimonoed princess to a skillful composition of plane and color. Instead he saw the loved woman he did not have. He looked at the painting as if the princess were a living woman who might choose to change his life and reassure him that he had the ability to love, so different from the Little White Girl, the girl who adored him. He turned from the princess only when Martin returned, impatient to get on to the National Gallery.

Ten

WHEN WILLARD DID NOT TELEPHONE ON THE DAY HE
was due to return from Washington nor on the day after
nor the one after that, Sadie began to have a disabling
feeling of weakness, not quite an illness. Mornings she
woke sweating and nauseated, and lay in bed, waiting for
the feeling to pass and trying to remember her dreams.

She could imagine feeling differently. On the grubby
late August streets she saw girls in carefree dresses who
walked with a boyfriend or arm in arm with another girl,
and Sadie reminded herself that she might be as happy if
her flesh weren't made of mercury, her arms and legs too
heavy to lift.

The apartment was a prison, the city a trap, and she
was too weak to plan an escape. He was my only hope,
she thought.

Willard was a balloon without a string, adrift over a
white plaster city of monuments and mansions. A woman
in a white kimono stood searching the sky for him, waiting for him to drop back to earth.

THE LUNCHEONETTE STEAMED. THE LITTLE FAN
creaked side to side dutifully, blue banners waving from
it gaily to prove to the customers that it was working.

"I'm eating hot soup," Arlie confided, "because I read in a magazine that the English drink hot tea in India. To stay cool. You know?"

"Maybe I'll just have a lemonade. Something sweet."

They gave their orders to Lennie, who looked as though he might melt at any time, then settled back on the slippery walls of their favorite booth.

"I've been watching you at work," Arlie said shrewdly. "You look like hell."

"Thanks," Sadie said. "How are your girls?"

"They're away," Arlie said. "Remember? Visiting my cousin in Jersey?"

"Oh, God," Sadie said. "I forgot."

When the lemonade came, she wrapped her fingers around the cool glass, then pressed it to her forehead.

"Why him?" Arlie asked suddenly. "Of all the guys in the world?"

"Well," Sadie said, "I love him."

"Oh," Arlie said, and she returned her gaze to the hot bowl of soup before her. She wrinkled her nose in distaste and blew at it. "Well, if you love him."

Sadie felt her anger crawling up her neck. She had sat in the same booth listening to Arlie talk about her husband beating her up and she hadn't said a word.

The soup was thick, crushed beans sticking up from the surface. Sadie gripped the edge of the table, her fingers white against the green table.

"Hey," Arlie said. "What's going on here? Are you okay? You haven't been eating, right? Just like my girls. You put on a few pounds and then you starve yourself."

"I've been eating," Sadie said.

"Well, you look awful."

"Keep flattering me," Sadie said. "Isn't your soup cool enough to eat now?"

When it was time to return to the office, they walked slowly, looking across to Bryant Park where leaves crackled in the hot wind.

In the arcaded lobby, standing before the golden bank

of elevators, Sadie asked, "When you were pregnant, did you ever think of doing something about it?"

Arlie narrowed her eyes. She began to speak, but a businessman came up beside them and she turned away. When he got off on the third floor, Arlie said, "I got rid of one kid. Another guy. I didn't care for him much. Before I was married. I couldn't do it again no matter what."

"I see," Sadie said. She looked up at the gold dial and counted the floors of the building up and down.

"Oh, God, honey, I'm so sorry. But I can't help you," Arlie said. "If that's what you're asking."

"I don't even know for sure," Sadie said.

When they got off the elevator Arlie checked to see if they were alone in the hallway.

"You're in a jam, Sister Sadie. I don't want you to think I haven't noticed. But I'll tell you something I don't usually talk about, all right? You never feel for anyone else, *nothing* like what you feel for one of your own. You'll do anything for them." She looked at the door to the office and at her wristwatch. The band was fraying. Sadie knew Arlie would lose it one of these days. "I'd better get back. I've got to type something for Ash," she said.

Sadie stayed behind in the stairway, thinking, Maybe her but not me. She thought of the long afternoon ahead, typing envelopes, stuffing them and licking them. Train was helping with Jewish war relief, and he and Reuben had a stream of new clients who would never pay a cent. For whom were those people living their lives? Well, whom did they have left to live for but themselves?

She felt like an ocean liner that was pulling away slowly from its moorings. The people on shore—everyone she knew—would wave to her. Good-by, they'd shout, as she got farther and farther from them. Good-by, they'd say, some sad, some indifferent, but all powerless or unwilling to stop her progress. It made her blood boil for a second and freeze. It made her want to turn the bulky ship toward home and move it just as inexorably into the dock.

Eleven

SHE WENT OVER TO SCHOOL TO REGISTER BUT FELT SICK standing in line. She gave up her place, went for a Coke with some friends who talked about professors and majors. She knew that she wouldn't return that year.

She congratulated herself on having the sense not to tell Reuben anything: the baby, that she was letting a college education slip by, that Willard had not called her since he left for Washington and might never call again.

SADIE WENT TO A DOCTOR, NOT SONNY GOLDEN, HER father's second cousin, but a fellow on Fifth Avenue, right across from the Metropolitan Museum, which made her feel closer to Willard.

The office disappointed her with its plain chairs and gray walls. Cousin Sonny's office was more plush, but maybe that was a sign of some defect.

She bore the examination. She answered the doctor's questions honestly and avoided looking into his sea-blue eyes. Outside the office, she faced the open sky over the museum and the park. Sadie began to walk west briskly, relieved that she was out of the office, that she'd seen a doctor, which gave her the illusion that she would be taken care of. By the time she reached West End Avenue, her fog settled in again and she moved slowly across the lobby toward the elevator as if she were swimming toward shore with her last strength.

SADIE KNEW THAT SOMEWHERE IN THE CITY WAS A PERSON who would help her get rid of the baby. To find this person, she would have to relinquish her secrets: Willard had been her lover, now she was pregnant. She would have to tell everyone, and eventually, by the telling, find her way out. She would lose her secrets; worse, she'd lose the baby.

I'VE BEEN GETTING AWAY WITH THINGS UNTIL NOW, Sadie thought.

Everywhere she walked Sadie saw pregnant women, their bellies preceding them, bearing aloft shawls and dresses, their skirts billowed in kind breezes. She saw mothers and nannies pushing baby carriages. Stopped for a light, she might lean over and peek under the hood of a big carriage, expecting anything. Inside, a tiny baby, alert, alive. The babies and mothers crouched in wait, filled with an expectant light.

She wanted to ask: How old is your baby? Is it a boy or a girl? Does it sleep very much? Why is it crying? Is it happy? Is there anything wrong with it? What will you do if its nose keeps growing? Maybe you think the forehead and the mouth will balance out someday? Was it always so beautiful? Why is it staring at me?

The babies in their carriages, their eyes like miners' lamps, what were the babies waiting for? What were they watching so closely? At home Sadie hesitated before she opened her closet door. A baby might be waiting for her in the darkness, eyes shining, expecting everything from her.

She examined herself naked in the mirror—front view, profile—saw a small bulge, the swelling she might have before her period. Her waistbands were too tight. The buttons of her blouses strained. She stood still and the pregnancy progressed. Would no one come to relieve her burden?

"HOW ABOUT THIS?" REUBEN ASKED. "AN EARLY meal."

She was lying down, the phone jammed between her shoulder and her chin, pretending to be rushing off to class. Shakespeare, she'd said, knowing he would approve.

"A new find of Train's. Pink tablecloths, he told me. The works. Excellent food."

"I don't know," she said. "I've been gaining some weight."

"All Ash women gain weight," Reuben said.

"Just my point," she said, but they arranged to meet at the restaurant at Bleecker and Tenth Street at five-thirty.

Reuben never asked what was bothering her. He'd always tried to bribe her out of bad moods with a visit to the zoo, a monogrammed handkerchief, or a tiny box of Whitman's candy. She told herself to make an effort for Reuben, and never to tell him what he wanted to know.

THE RESTAURANT WAS DARK, BUT A SHAFT OF DAYLIGHT lay on Reuben's table. He had chosen of all the tables— it was so early, the restaurant was empty—a small one at the window, so he'd probably seen Sadie stop at a dusty bookstore to look at the broken sets of Browning and Hawthorne languishing in the window. As if he had to know everything, Sadie thought.

"I'm sorry I'm late," she said, waving away the maître d' who came toward her. "The bus . . . the train."

"Sometimes it's pleasant to have nothing to do," Reuben said. "To sit and wait for your sister. I ordered a sherry for you."

"Fine," she said, though she wanted a clear drink.

When the waiter had brought a tiny glass of sherry, Reuben turned his attention from the window to his sister.

"You look like hell," he said.

"It was the walk," she said. "Down Bleecker. I must have walked too fast."

He twisted his face in annoyance and said, "Nonsense. I want you to take care of yourself, Sadie. I can't do everything."

"I'm not asking you to do anything," she said.

"We haven't talked much lately, have we?" he asked. "Not for months."

"Not since Willard is what you mean." She dragged his name in, forcing his presence.

"Maybe," he said cautiously.

"You never told me what you thought of him," she said. "I know you hated him." She sipped the sherry and leaned back in her chair.

"I wouldn't say hate," Reuben said. "He seems very, I don't know. Intelligent. Sensitive in a way."

"You once told me sensitive people made you nervous."

"I don't recall saying any such thing. Does he make you nervous?"

She squinted her eyes and looked down at the table, thinking of being in bed with Willard, and she felt good for the first time in weeks, as if the life she was remembering would be accessible to her once again.

"Not exactly nervous," she said.

"You'll be twenty soon," he said.

"What does that have to do with Willard?"

"I'm saying—Enjoy the experience. But you're a young person with a life ahead of you."

"Mama had two children by the time she was my age."

"You want your mother's life? Take it from me, Sadie, he's not for you."

"Who said anything about marriage? We go to museums, Reuben, and to the theater."

"Fine," Reuben said, elaborately calm. "I want you

to have a good time. With your friends. You asked me what I thought."

"I won't again," she said, picking up the menu to hide her face. She felt ashamed because she caused Reuben worry. But when they had ordered, Sadie asked, "He's too rich? Too good-looking? Is it because he isn't Jewish?"

"Don't say things that belittle you."

Arguing with Reuben made her feel as though everything was all right, that it was weeks before when she was not pregnant, when Willard was attentive to her.

"You wouldn't marry to get away from home, would you?" he asked.

"No," she said, thinking that in fact she had been looking for refuge.

"I can't see his heart," Reuben said. "He's a stranger —I don't mean not Jewish. He's someone who's always a little bit outside."

She laughed because that was the opposite of what she knew, that Willard was inside the world and she was the one outside.

"He's in Washington now," she said. "Looking at paintings. It's just a different way of life. His upbringing is different."

"You need to finish school before you take any big steps. You won't be able to take care of yourself without an education. You won't be able to stand up for yourself."

"And why should I need to? You always see me so . . . attacked."

"All right, Sadie. I'll tell you the truth. He's on his way down. He'll never do anything worth a damn. He's older than you and he knows exactly what he's doing. And if you think anything else, you're kidding yourself. I'm telling you this for your own good."

The waiter brought their food. She took a breath, released it, decided to tell Reuben everything, took a sip of water, and changed her mind.

They finished eating and told each other what a good

restaurant it was. Reuben ordered coffee and slices of
apple tart for them both without consulting Sadie. He
stared out the window, unwilling to look at her. He had
been angry with her for moping around and depressing
everyone at work, for looking bedraggled and waiflike,
for appearing to be inconsolable. Now he felt distracted
and exhausted himself. He stared out the window. Maybe
they should go to the movies. He tilted his glasses to see
better.

"What is it?" Sadie asked. "What's so interesting out
the window?"

"Nothing," he said. "I thought I saw someone I used
to know. So. Are you finished? You didn't touch your
tart."

"You finish it," she said. "Well, it's still early. Should
we do something? The movies? A show?"

He looked at his watch and said, "Train left me some
papers to read back at the office. I'll see you at home."

"Okay," she said, sorry now that the dinner was over
and that she would return uptown alone. "Thanks for the
dinner. I mean it. Thanks, Reuben."

Twelve

REUBEN STOOD AT THE RESTAURANT DOOR, WATCHING
Sadie linger in front of one shop window, then another.
When she was only a small figure at the edge of his vision,
he turned and walked west.

The Village ended quickly and the landscape became
more interesting for Reuben. He turned north, past the
meat markets and warehouses, the docks. The powerful
gray Hudson smelled stronger than the cars or the beer-
soaked saloons. Someday he would live by the river, he
thought, uptown where he could see the bridge and the
ships day and night.

Reuben believed in bad luck and misfortune but not in
providence. He believed that he would work until he
dropped, that he might move to a river view, that he
would always take care of Sadie. He didn't regret his
future, he would not shirk his responsibility. She was part
of him, his flesh, his blood, and that was the beginning
and the end of it.

Reuben turned east at Twenty-third Street, and
crossed the island. He was feeling a little jaunty. True,
Sadie was miserable, but he'd just been handed the key
to her release, and he felt as though he were in the first
optimistic stages of love.

What Reuben had seen through the restaurant window

was Willard, standing at the window of an antique jewelry shop. Reuben knew the place—he'd bought a cameo brooch for Sadie there one birthday. Reuben had almost risen, waved his hand, had been about to rush out to the street to bring Willard back into the restaurant to share the meal with him and Sadie. He had been almost relieved to see the fellow and to cut short Sadie's misery. He's not in Washington, Reuben might have said to her, Here he is, come back to you.

Then he looked more closely. Willard was standing with a woman, and he was holding her hand.

She was as tall as Willard, and her dark hair curled down her back. She wore a green dress and a white necklace—pearls? shells?—that shone in the September evening. Reuben wondered if the necklace was a present from Willard. The woman pointed to something in the window. Willard shrugged. She laughed and said a few words, then let her smile relax into a frown. She and Willard held hands loosely, familiar lovers. Reuben had not seen such comfort between his sister and Willard. They moved away from the window. Sadie asked him what he was looking at and he said, Nothing.

He stopped on Fifth Avenue to buy a pretzel from a man who was wrapped in layers of worn clothing. Reuben stood on the next corner inhaling the yeasty odor of the bread, feeling its twisted warmth. He had figured that it would be worse with Willard. He'd thought Willard wanted Sadie.

When he finished the pretzel, Reuben stuck the paper wrapping in his pocket and walked down the street to his office. It wouldn't be so bad after all, he thought, nothing he couldn't handle when the time came.

Thirteen

WILLARD CONSIDERED NOT CALLING SADIE AND ALLOW-
ing the affair to end, for he anticipated clinging and tears,
but he couldn't dismiss Sadie or forget her sweetness and
youth, or how little it took for him to please her. He
couldn't leave her alone. Unlike another soul in the
world, Sadie loved him with an unquestioning, borderless
love. For a day or two Willard wondered what he ought
to do, then one morning he called Sadie and arranged to
pick her up at West End Avenue at five o'clock that evening. He felt worn down, as if persuaded to act against
his better judgment.

SHE LOOKED CHARMING, STANDING AT THE DOOR OF HER
apartment, her hair a deeper red than he remembered.
She wore a loose, old-fashioned blue dress that hung in
wide, soft pleats.

He bent to kiss her cheek, and said, "Sorry I'm late.
One thing and then another," hoping that his vague apol-
ogy would somehow cover the month since he'd gone to
the Peacock Room.

Her perfume, light and flowery, reminded him that he
had meant from the beginning to change her scent.

"How pretty you look," he said when they were in the

living room. He sat on the couch, she in Reuben's easy chair. "What a sweet frock."

"It's old," she said quietly.

"Shall we have an early dinner?" he asked. "What sort of food do you fancy?" He sounded hearty and cautious, like an adult trying to cajole a child who threatened a tantrum.

"I'm not very hungry," she said. "Are you?"

"Not very hungry. Just the usual amount."

Her crowded living room gave Willard the sensation that he was trapped. He shuddered and yawned. It might have been better to let the affair sink of its own weight. He dreaded speech from Sadie, assuming it would be filled with reproach. She said, "I'm sorry," and he saw that her eyes were filling with tears.

"What's wrong?" he asked.

She reached into her pocket and drew out a crumpled handkerchief. "I just have the blues today. I couldn't help remembering. It's my mother's birthday. When I look around the streets, the people on Broadway I want to tell them—You don't know a thing. Anything could happen to you at any time." She touched her eyes with the handkerchief and rubbed her forehead as if her head hurt. "Sometimes I wish I could leave here," Sadie said, her eyes on the punch bowl her mother had prized.

When she turned her gaze to Willard, he smiled at her and said, "If you're not really terribly hungry, let's go for a drive before dinner. I have an errand to run for my father anyway. The ride might—perhaps it will cheer you up," though he laughed as if happiness would be an unlikely result of their drive.

THEY TOOK A CAB TO REED'S GARAGE TO PICK UP HIS Packard Straight Eight, a silver convertible, a two-seater with a rumble seat. The car was in mint condition, even down to the leather upholstery.

Sadie laughed when she got in. "What a wonderful

boat. The seat's big enough for two of me. How old's this car?''

"I'm not sure," Willard said impatiently. "My father makes such a fuss over his car. 'Mine for life,' he says. He never uses it so it should last nine lives."

They crossed the Hudson on the George Washington Bridge. Midriver, Sadie looked back at the towered island. If she turned her head she could see the great river flowing between fat green hips of land.

"It's like leaving a party, isn't it?" Sadie asked when they were off the bridge. "A hot stuffy crowded party that you were frantic to leave but it never occurred to you just to get out."

"I've been away too long," Willard said. "I thought Sadie was always a happy girl."

"It's easy when you're around," she said, leaning her head against the high seat back. With the top down, she had to shout a little to be heard and it made her feel bolder. "Now, Reuben never tries to be cheerful. He keeps talking about the bomb. He says the world is in worse shape than it ever was and he wishes he were still a Communist."

"And why isn't he?"

"Oh, I don't know if he ever was, really, or if he just likes to talk. I never ask him, you know. I don't want to know something I shouldn't, even if he'd tell me, which he probably never would."

"I see," Willard said. This was a side to Sadie, surely to Reuben, he hadn't suspected, for he imagined they were open, emotional people, incapable of keeping secrets from each other.

Fourteen

SHE'D BEEN ACROSS THE RIVER BEFORE IN HER LIFE, BUT now with Willard at the wheel the small towns and even the shacks at the edge of the countryside were touched with glamour. The evening light edged the houses, softening the shrubbery into patterns, making mysteries of half-open doors. She took heart a little, and sat up straighter. She didn't want to miss a minute of the night ahead.

If Sadie looked hard she could see tree-lined streets and wooden houses with porches and shutters, but the towns passed so quickly that Sadie might as well have been flipping through a magazine. A hundred times, she wanted him to stop the car so that she might look into a kitchen window, touch a cat perched on a porch rail, but Willard drove so silently and intently that she was afraid to speak. If he turned his head it was only to glance at Sadie. She didn't want him to change his mind and take her back to the city. Why not be happy, she'd asked him once, and he'd laughed as though she pleased him. She would have to tell him soon.

SHE TOOK IN THE TREES, THE GREEN AND BLACK OF THE evening, the yellow air around the flowers and fences.

Sadie said, "I'm sure I'd never cry if I lived in the country."

"I see you've never lived in the country if you say that. You think it's all Norman Rockwell."

"It's true I haven't," she said. "But I have a feeling for it."

They reached a town where the houses were built against a steep embankment on one side of the highway. On the other, the land fell away in a dull plain that rose into a series of small hills, trapping the road between rises. The porches were closed in with windows that looked as if they'd been borrowed from other ramshackle places. Railroad tracks ran alongside the road to a train station that was a little like a fancy hat. Opposite the station was a row of stone buildings that looked like stores on Madison Avenue in the 90s, Sadie thought.

Willard slowed the car, crossed the road, and turned in at a heavy iron gate between massive stone pillars. Next to the gate was a graystone structure that looked like a child's castle. A smaller stone booth stood before the gate with room enough only for the man who leaned through its open window. He had a plain face, one eye slightly higher than the other.

Sadie wondered how much land the fence by the gates enclosed. She had never been in such a place before.

"It's Willard Weaver, John. I suppose you don't recognize me. It's been that long."

The man squinted at Willard, then at Sadie, looking away quickly. She started to give him her name too, but he spoke first. "Sure I remember you, Mr. Weaver," and he waved the car in.

WHEN THEY WERE THROUGH THE GATES SHE FELT happy for the first time in weeks, as though she'd been given an unexpected gift. "Where are we?" she asked.

"It's called Tuxedo Park," he said.

"What is it, though?"

A small, pretty church was on the right, but Willard

steered away from it, up to a road that led uphill into the woods.

"You'll see," Willard said. "I'll give you a little tour."

"What was that little house at the gate?"

"The gatehouse. It was a jail when the place was being built. Rowdy workmen," he said. "Now just look. Don't ask questions and I'll tell you the whole story."

Now, she thought, I'll tell him now, but she imagined that if she did the sun would disappear and the trees.

"It's a silly place, really," he said. "Founded by people like my grandfather who thought that if they had a certain amount of money and land, they would be safe forever. Exclusive and safe. Hardly an original thought.

"The real founder was Pierre Lorillard. Snuff. Tobacco. He and his sisters and brothers owned a huge amount of land, I can't say exactly how much, but Lorillard secured five thousand acres for himself, and hired an architect—father to Emily Post, by the way—and an engineer and a landscape architect. They brought two thousand men from Yugoslavia and Italy, and over one winter built roads and the fence, the first clubhouse, and some cottages."

"But why?" Sadie asked, thinking, A rich man, nothing better to do with his time.

"Lorillard said it was to be a place where his friends would hunt and fish. That kind of thing. What he really wanted was a perfect world. Patrolled borders and all the right people. But it didn't turn out that way. It wasn't Newport or New York, neither one season nor the next. It was a stopping point where people came in between the places they really wanted to be. Too hot in summer, too isolated in winter.

"My mother was given her house for a wedding present. Nothing's the same anymore. Income tax did away with places like Tuxedo Park. Half the houses are empty now. Some of the best burned down. And then there was the war."

The road rose sharply upward and Willard hugged the

curves, changing gears to meet the hill. The woods thick-
ened and it seemed that night had come all at once. When
they reached the top of the hill, the view opened again.

On the descent, they passed grand houses in many
styles: a large half-timber with stables and a servant's
house in the same manner; a stone mansion that spread
over the edge of the hill with two turrets and spires but
no flags flying; and large shingle houses, their windows
flashing back at the setting sun.

Willard slowed the car and pointed to a Gothic house
even more imposing than the others. Looking at it made
Sadie feel chilly.

"That one was built by a man named Poor. It's called
the Poor House," Willard said. She looked at him to see
if he would laugh at his joke. "I see," she said, and he
sped the car along again.

"It wasn't mere money, Sadie, that made a person
suitable to build a house here," Willard said. "The place
is run by the Tuxedo Association, and if a property owner
sells to someone unsuitable, the person's forbidden mem-
bership in the club. And if you aren't a club member you
can't own property. Of course, the Association had
deeper pockets than it has now."

The unsuitable people, she thought, Jews, people like
her.

"So what do people do here?"

"Drink and make sure no one's coming through the
gate. No," Willard said. "That's unfair. In my father's
time there were competitions all the time—court tennis,
poker, bridge, and golf, sledding, ice hockey, skating—
you'd like that—sailing. There's the Autumn Ball, the
New Year's Ball, the Horse Show, the fireworks on the
Fourth. But it was never quite right. Women wore
dresses they'd already worn in Newport. I was told that
the imported game ran away. German carp was introduced as food for the native bass, but the carp ate the
bass fry."

Sadie's views were blocked or framed by the angle of

the hills, or the thickness of the overgrowth covering all but the immediate grounds of houses. Stone fences crumbled along the road. She felt as nervous as if she were trespassing, about to be caught and sent out of the Park.

"Now it gets better," he said.

They rode along the edge of a blue lake. On the opposite shore, she saw even grander houses. In the hills roofs —tile, slate, and shingle—were just visible, roofs meant for castles and villas. The houses were dwarfed by pines and oaks.

They passed a building with tennis courts and a large terrace overlooking the lake. Willard said, "That's the club. It's not so gay as it was when I was a child. Or before I was born when this place was very lively."

"We haven't seen a living soul," Sadie said.

"This is the wrong season, really. But that's what people always say around here."

He drove her away from the lake, up another tree-crowded hill, and stopped the car. He pointed into the woods and said, "Look."

She didn't see anything at first, then made out a stone fence that rose along the hill. Stone ruins materialized through the dense shrubbery and the trees. It was like looking at a neglected cemetery, she thought. The Park was so safe and peaceful, more so than any place she'd ever been, yet she felt a terrible homesickness.

"That place was marvelous—we always called it the castle—but the old people died, and I'm not sure what happened to the son. He might never have married. So there it sits, rotting away."

Maybe he had brought her to Tuxedo Park to demonstrate that she didn't belong with him. She wanted to get out of the Park, go over the woods, the lake, along the curving road, past the barrier hills and trees, all the way to the gate. But how could she leave Willard in this place? She and the baby were Willard's, if he knew it or not. Sadie held her breath, hesitating between step and glide, between one life and the next.

WHEN THEY REACHED THE LAKE ROAD, THE SUN WAS AT the horizon, brighter and hotter than before.

"There's something I have to do," Willard said. "Maybe we'll skip it. Oh, well. Since we're here."

Reed had been at him all week, threatening to put the Tuxedo house on the market. "If the roof goes, it will take more than I have to restore it," Reed announced. "It's more than I can manage, and you take no interest." Now Willard could say he'd been out there and deprive his father of a complaint, and the ride seemed to have soothed Sadie. She seemed impressed by the Park, which annoyed him.

"Oh, well," he said, "we might as well."

They passed a wood-paneled station wagon, a red Morgan, and a solitary walker, who glared at them as he stepped gingerly off the narrow shoulder. The sun was at the edge of the lake now and they passed a shore house, gray-shingled, white-trimmed, the first house that looked like anyone lived in it.

"That's Helen's house," said Willard. "An old friend. She married a man much older than she, Johnny Franklin. And he died in a hunting accident in Cuba. Shooting dove."

"Did a dove shoot back?"

"I don't know the details," Willard said. "It was just as well. He was getting to be impossible. More impossible."

Willard turned up another hill, this time into a driveway, and stopped in front of a brick Italianate mansion with a tile roof and arched windows. The house was sheltered in the crook of the hill. Below was the lake, the terrace and lawns overgrown, though not so badly as some of the other houses. Behind them was a steep hill with stone steps that disappeared into the woods. The steps were barely visible, covered with vines and thorns.

Willard stepped from the car and shook out his key ring, selecting an old-fashioned brass key.

"And here's my place," he said. "My mother's house, really."

Willard unlocked the door and swung it open, then turned and stepped aside, gesturing at Sadie to leave the car and come in. She opened the car door slowly and got out, glancing up at the hill that rose behind the house and the woods into which the hill melted.

The entrance hall was tiled in black and white squares; it rose to a domed ceiling, two flights above. Through a Palladian window, light fell onto a curved staircase. Ahead was a large, square room filled with white-draped furniture. An Oriental rug covered the floor, folded back at the corners. Beyond the living room was a glassed-in loggia that Willard called the porch. Through its arched windows Sadie had a broad view of a lake bowled in by craggy hills.

"Were you a child here?" she asked. "I can't imagine being a child here." Willard had seemed so free to Sadie, like someone killing time between trains, but his house looked as if it had always been this way—furnished, full of a past life, waiting for him.

He stood in the doorway to the living room, his foot lifting the folded edge of the carpet.

"I wasn't much of a child," Willard said.

He stroked the painted doorjamb. Now his hand looked fragile and veined. She wanted to warm it for him, to hide it in her own, but stopped herself when she saw that he was checking the woodwork for dust.

"I thought I knew you," she said, though she hadn't exactly. "But I guess you never know someone until you see him in his home."

"This isn't really my home," he said. "This is just the Tuxedo place."

She stepped closer to him, close enough to feel the heat of his body.

"This isn't such a large house, by Tuxedo standards, nor a very good one. The architecture is very unoriginal," he said irritably. "I don't want you to be so impressed, Sadie. Don't stand there as if you were in church. Be critical."

Sadie moved away from him and frowned at the open doorway that led off to a pine-paneled library.

"I don't know how," she said. "Houses to me are where you live. I don't know the names for things the way you do."

"I'll do it for you," he said. "The best thing about the house is the generosity of the rooms. But it isn't distinguished by anything. No fabulous paneling or murals. It's big but not a real monster. And it isn't even very old."

"Is that all?" she asked.

"What do you think? Your turn now."

"I think we could put my parents' apartment in the living room."

"That's not a visual judgment. And there's a social judgment implied."

"No, there isn't," she said. "I don't mind living where I live. It's home to me."

"Well, let's get on with it and get out of here. I'm supposed to inspect the damned roof. I kept meaning to come all summer but one thing after another . . . I always mean to come to Tuxedo but I don't."

"Who takes care of it?"

"Once in a while Mrs. Misurelli comes. She's pretty good about it. But it's more or less closed up."

Willard led Sadie through the house until she lost track of where she was, and she wondered if she had missed the right moment to tell Willard. In the dining room, red drapes and a mural of Washington crossing the Delaware. ("Not a traditional dining-room subject," he said.) In the upstairs hall, he showed her a portrait of a child holding a pink rose before her, chubby legs peeking out from an old-fashioned dress.

"My great-grandmother," Willard said.

"How wonderful to have this," she said. "I don't even know what my great-grandmother looked like—no picture, nothing."

He thought, What freedom not to know, not to care.

There was a blue bedroom, papered with silver fleurs-de-lis, one with striped paper, another with roses climb-

ing the walls. Reed's bedroom was painted mustard yellow and had no curtains, only wooden furniture.

"He has a special set of allergies," Willard explained,
"that only act up in Tuxedo. Now's our chance to go to
the third floor to see if it's floating in water from a leaky
roof. It must be sweltering up there on a day like this.
But why should we go? You'll melt. Come on, Sadie.
There's more.''

Why not sell the place indeed? If his father wanted to
get rid of it, why hadn't he done so years before when it
was still worth something, and before Willard was grown
and had anything to say about it? Typically, Reed had
hung on when it was inappropriate and threatened to let
go when it was unnecessary. He wondered if Reed was
doing this to annoy him but he knew that Reed didn't
waste energy inventing ways to bother his son. He'd
come back another time or simply give up and let the
place be sold, even if the roof was sound.

OFF THE LIBRARY WAS A WHITE BEDROOM, SHROUDED
in heavy dropcloths, shadowy even when Willard parted
the gray drapery. The windows overlooked the overgrown hill in back of the house. A rocking chair without
arms began a little dance as Willard passed it to look out
the window.

At the door to the room, Sadie held herself erect. Her
lace-trimmed collar shifted slightly when she breathed.
She said nothing. She waited for her chance.

The rest of the house was ample or mean, in need of
repair or holding up fine—either way it meant little to
Willard. But simply standing here was reconfirmation of
what he ignored at other times: all light in the world was
irrevocably dimmed, all possibilities faint.

"My mother died here," he said, "when I was almost
six. She got a cut from a gardening tool. She loved the
garden. She's buried in the churchyard near the gate.
There was much less traffic in those days.''

When his mother died, his spirit diminished and his

loss went unnoticed. No one watched over him ever
again. Sometimes he forgot that there had ever been a
watcher who cared for him and delighted in him.

And this room, she thought, was held in place like her
parents' apartment. Sadie didn't explain this to him,
thinking he might resent the connection, but she said,
wanting to comfort him, "Jews say prayers for the dead.
But we never expect to see them again. Not in heaven.
We never see them again, except in dreams."

"No," he said, "I suppose I don't expect to see her
again either. You're right. This room is depressing. Come
along. I'll show you where her garden used to be."

She should have told him then and there, Sadie
thought.

OUTSIDE IT SEEMED NOISY AND BUSY WITH THE SOUND
of the birds singing in the near darkness, the wind
through the tall maples and oaks on the sloping lawn. The
faint light made ghosts of the solid forms around them:
walls, steps, trees, car.

"Who keeps the steps clear?" she asked.

"Mr. Marini," he said, then followed her gaze up to
the woods. "The gardener, though you'd never know it.
My mother went to Europe and came back wanting an
Italian garden. So she divided the hillside into beds and
Marini made the stone boundaries for them."

The beds were neglected now. Old roses bloomed and
spiky perennials whose names he had forgotten. He bent
and broke off a woody sprig of thyme, rubbed the leaves
between his fingers and held his hand to Sadie's face.

"You look like some wonderful kind of old-fashioned
rose," he said. He pointed to a rambling rose climbing
the fieldstone wall between the garden and the woods.

"I'm not much like any flower," she said. "Willard—"

He kissed her to stop her from speaking. It hurt her to
think of missing him as much as she had.

"God, this place gives me the heebie-jeebies," he said.

He released her and she guessed that he would say, Let's have dinner somewhere, let's leave.

"What I am, is . . . I saw a doctor," she said. Then louder, "Just to be positive." She couldn't be sure if he heard her. He was looking away from her now, squinting his eyes as if he saw something in the woods.

"Look at me," she said. "Willard, take a good look at me. I'll be everything to you. I'll do anything for you."

She could feel her breasts swelling against the thin dress. She felt beautiful or at least that she was all she would ever be.

Willard looked at her and guessed. He said, "Ah. So it's . . ." He took a deep breath as if he were about to dive into a dark pool. She was no longer a child, as when he found her, only young. This was all too predictable, had he only been thinking clearly.

Sadie looked at him steadily as if she would say more, but the words she had rehearsed didn't matter anymore. There was only one fact that was important, the baby.

He said, "Sadie—give me time. Let me think, Sadie."

HE DROPPED HER IN FRONT OF HER BUILDING, WATCH-ing her in the rearview mirror as he drove away. His apartment was stuffy when he entered, as if he'd been away for much longer than a day. He opened all the windows, then sat on the ledge, watching the city.

Willard looked ahead and saw himself in Europe, a bachelor of uncertain accent, neither European nor American, haunting auction houses and galleries, culti-vating friendships with curators. He would hoard his col-lection or stow it away, leave it in packing boxes, perhaps in Tuxedo, while he bought more. He might become fat and fussy, like Martin, or mad about his health, like Reed. But he would be free and he would be alone.

Against that, Sadie's grave look as she watched him drive away, and his child. And Sadie saying, "I would do anything for you," and hadn't she already? Who else would give herself to him as Sadie had—not Cherry, who

lived for herself—no one else. He thought of his father—
how would he welcome the baby, Willard's son? Willard
saw himself standing before Reed holding a child by the
hand. His father opened his arms to the child, who ran to
Reed's embrace.

After midnight, he drove across town to West End Avenue. The night doorman recognized him and took him
up to Sadie's apartment. When Willard knocked, she
opened the door immediately, as if she had been standing
and waiting for him.

He said, "There's just one thing to do. If you're sure."

When he told her what that one thing was, Sadie smiled
and came into his arms, saying, "I knew it all along. It's
so simple to be happy if you're meant to be. We'll have
this baby and another. Two at least. We'll have beautiful
babies," and she held him to her as if he were being
pulled from her. She let the last weeks roll from her, and
Sadie pushed off into the waiting air, thinking, Now
everything gets easier, now it starts.

PART TWO

One

Evenings, Sadie bathed her daughters, then dressed them in clean pajamas, flannel worn soft by many washings. Louise recognized the faded bears on her little sister's pajamas, especially the blue bear on the right cuff to whom she used to whisper at night.

They went downstairs to the kitchen, where Sadie set out their plates. Louise's had a shepherd boy playing a little flute. Her sister (named Mary Elinor for Willard's mother and called Marilyn) had a plate with a small kitten asleep on a geranium pot. Their father was allergic to cats, so the girls couldn't have a real kitten of their own. Their mother said that dogs were for the country, and she promised that if they ever lived in the country, they could have a dog. Sometimes Louise wished she had Marilyn's plate instead.

Sadie cooked plain food for the girls—chops broiled to a crisp, green beans cut in uniform lengths, carrots sliced into circles that Marilyn stabbed with her fork and ate around methodically.

After dinner the girls brushed their teeth, and Louise pulled her fine blond hair into a pony tail, and braided Marilyn's thick black curls. When Sadie finished the dishes, she polished the counters and wiped the table, then laid the damp cloths along the sink to dry.

Then the girls hid in the maroon couch in the big living room whose ceiling was open to the second floor of the little house. Sadie turned down the lights and sat in the oversize blue armchair, her feet up on the hassock. The girls hid on the end of the couch nearest the front door. The upholstery was ribbed and if their father was very late Louise went up to bed with its pattern incised on her cheek.

The girls giggled at first in their hiding place, and then grew quiet. Sadie and the girls listened to each person who passed, shuffling feet, clicking heels, and when there was a hesitation in the footsteps, their attention quickened. Sadie halted her knitting needles, and they waited for the squeak of the mews gate, the clang as it closed behind the caller, then the approach to their door, the last in the double row of tiny brick houses. If the steps ended at a neighbor's house, if another door was opened, the three sank back and waited once more.

Each day began the same for Sadie—dress the girls, talk on the phone with Reuben, checking in, he called it. Sadie fed him family talk—the girls could do this and that, were cutting teeth, could form a letter, color in a book. She gave him a little bad news—Louise had cut Marilyn's hand with the edge of a tin can, or Marilyn might be coming down with the measles. She asked him advice, as she asked Louise when they were out shopping —wax paper or aluminum foil? Ann Page peas or a better brand? If she took the girls downtown shopping, could they return in time to have their naps? Reuben tried to help but would often say, "Got to go," when her questions became so particular.

When the day was especially long—if it was raining and cold and they were all trapped together in the mews house; or if one girl had a cold and the other was full of beans—Sadie looked forward to the next year when Louise would go to the new red-brick school across West End Avenue, and Marilyn would be at the school Louise went to now. On the way to the park, Sadie stopped by the new school and told the girls that when they were big enough, that's where they'd go. Marilyn said, "Park, park," and as they passed the schoolyard with its high iron fence, Louise stared balefully at the children on the other side. Nothing would be easy for Louise, Sadie thought. Marilyn was a round, placid child, a beautiful sleeper. Sadie hadn't been pleased at first to find she was pregnant again when Louise was still in diapers, but everything that was hard with Louise was easy with Marilyn. When Sadie looked at her, she felt nothing but love.

Once the children were born, Sadie was happy, if happiness was the absence of attention to feeling. Everything in the world was beside the point except her girls—Willard's moods, Reuben's approval, Reed's acceptance, everyone and everything. She was sure that in time Willard would be as content as she. Though he loved the girls too, he was restless, she could tell. We'll all move to Europe, she offered, we'll go anywhere you like, but he said, I'm fine as we are. Her happiness slipped when the girls weren't there; late at night, she worried as she had as a girl.

Sadie had thought that when Louise started school, she'd find some kind of job or take a course, but there was still Marilyn, and Sadie missed Louise and waited for school to be over. Some of the mothers in the playground couldn't wait for their children to grow up, but Sadie knew this was the best time of her life. In the playground, Sadie settled on a bench near the mothers she liked, with her basket beside her, nodded to the mothers, and opened her book, looking up from it every few sentences to be sure the girls were all right. She eavesdropped on the mothers' talk, hoping to hear in the conversation around her traces of her own life.

When they distinguished Willard's gait from their neighbor Mr. Mordecai's shuffle and Mrs. Bowman's clip, from Mrs. Arnold's sharp high-heeled clicks (she worked in an office downtown), the wait became unbearable. His key turned in the lock, the door moved on its hinges, he stepped onto the first little carpet, the blue-

and-red one Louise liked to lie on and stare at close up, and he said, "Sadie?"

"Hello," she called. "I'm just here. Off my feet for a minute."

"Are the girls asleep? I hurried but . . ."

"Oh, the girls are around somewhere," she said, and then they sprang from the couch and he opened his arms for them, hugging them to him, crushing them against the soft roughness of his cheeks. Their mother, who had been everything to them all day, evaporated.

The girls sat on the couch, deep in, their feet not even reaching the edge of the cushion, and watched as Willard made his first martini. Louise thought the onion was part of the glass—he never ate it. While he had his drink, he sat on the couch between the pajamaed girls, asking each in turn how her day had been—had they been to the playground? to the grocery store? He had been downtown all day, he told them, working on his book about Mr. Whistler in the big building at the bottom of the island where he'd once taken Louise. He pointed to the Whistler oil that hung on the living-room wall above the blue armchair, the canal at sunset.

Willard was careful with the girls, even more so than Sadie. When they were newborn he felt a crippling fear that something might happen to them. The soft fold of a blanket might suffocate a baby; milk, imperfectly boiled, might poison. Sadie might look away and let the baby roll off the changing table. When he took them out, he checked them for handkerchiefs, mittens, scarves, hats. In summer he made sure that they wore socks with their sandals to protect their feet, and it was he who took them shopping for important clothing: their party dresses, patent-leather mary janes, velvet robes and muffs, wool coats with rabbit collars and cuffs. He never looked at the sale racks or tables, as Sadie did. It seemed to Louise that Best & Co. was a different store when she was with him.

Sadie took them shopping for overalls and snowsuits, sneakers and rain boots. She bought them brown wool gloves and attached them to the sleeves of their jackets and snowsuits by an elastic with clasps at each end. Louise winced each time Sadie secured glove to sleeve, as if the little gold teeth were biting into her flesh. "Oh, Weasel," Sadie said, "don't be so silly." Sadie made sure they had boots and oxfords, hats that covered their ears, umbrellas—red for Louise, blue for Marilyn. But it was Sadie who took them to the candy store on the corner of Ninety-fifth and Broadway just up from the mews and let them browse until they decided how to spend the nickel she gave each of them. She warned them not to tell Willard about these excursions. Like his father, Willard now disapproved of sugar. The girls were good at keeping the secret. On their monthly visits to Reed, they listened to father and son agree that processed sugar was an avoidable poison, and accepted a fat walnut and a peeled orange slice for dessert.

If it was early enough, they were allowed to stay up and watch while their mother brought out the grownup food. Sometimes Willard took them upstairs even before he'd had a drink, and he read them a story, tucked them into bed. Louise could never fall asleep until her mother had tucked her in also, turned on the night light in the shape of a goldfish, and kissed her and Marilyn good night. The nights the girls liked least were those when they waited, and then Sadie turned to them and said, "Time for bed, girls. No, no, he isn't coming, and you still have to sleep. And I mean it." On those nights Louise fell asleep straining for the sound of her father's return.

Two

EARLY, WHEN THE VEGETABLE MEN WERE JUST PUTTING out their baskets for display, when the butcher was cranking up his iron blind, and crates of iced fish were being delivered to the fish store, Sadie, Louise, and Marilyn crossed Broadway and walked up the hill toward Amsterdam.

For Louise, the school in the basement of the Presbyterian church was a secret too terrible to know. They walked down the stairs, Louise and Sadie holding hands, Marilyn following, clutching Sadie's hem, then made their awkward six-legged way down a long hallway, where they waited in line with the other mothers and younger sisters and brothers.

First thing each morning, a lady doctor, a lacy handkerchief stuck into the pocket of her gray suit, checked throats to see if the children were well enough for school. She took a fresh tongue depressor from a box that sat next to her black bag and another larger cardboard box, and tilted Louise's chin back. Tiny flashlight in one hand, depressor in the other, the doctor told Louise to open, and pushed Louise's tongue down and back into her throat. Then she threw the used depressor away. Sometimes she took her stethoscope and slipped its cold disk between Louise's shirt buttons, and listened to Louise's heart. She might hand Louise a lollipop, and say, "Sorry," or she'd say, "This one's fine," and hand Louise a small box of Chiclets from the big box, which meant that Louise had to go to school. Sadie and Marilyn stayed close by Louise during the inspection.

Louise hoped that she would be sick. Then she would turn around and march back down the hall with Sadie and Marilyn, fly up the stairs four at a time, burst into the good outside air, and rush down to Broadway, to the park or the branch library down on Columbus Avenue—anything but school, even just to be home, listening to the sounds of her mother washing dishes, vacuuming the living room, snapping the sheets to freshen them as she made the beds.

Louise asked Sadie if Marilyn would ever go to school. Sadie said that of course Marilyn would go to school soon. Louise didn't believe it. Something would come up to save Marilyn from school and if by some chance it didn't, then Marilyn wouldn't mind school, for she didn't mind much, not anything like the number of things that bothered Louise.

THE FIRST FEW DAYS OF SCHOOL, LOUISE HID IN HER cubbyhole. She'd walked into the big schoolroom and lost her breath, turned to leave, and saw Marilyn and Sadie halfway down the hall, their backs to her. She called out and tried to follow them, but one of the teachers grabbed her hand, crushing the little heart ring Willard had given her against her pinky, and she was back in the schoolroom. When the teacher wasn't looking, Louise retreated to the cubby, scrunching down at the bottom so that she was looking up at the hem of her coat, so small that she was almost not there. The teachers tried to pull her out, then coax her out; then they ignored her. The children came over and stood outside the cubby door. Through the big holes at the top of the door, she heard them breathing, some raspily, some smoothly. One called out, "I see you, I see you."

She could never be sure what they'd be doing in school —drawing or painting, clay models, singing, listening to the teacher read a story, then answering questions, or napping. The nap came so deep into schooltime that she wondered why they bothered and sometimes she stayed in the cubby rather than take out her old pink blanket, spread it on the chilly floor, and lie on it, her eyes closed, almost sleeping. After the nap there was orange juice, which tasted funny, not like Sadie's, and a cracker. On holidays they had cookies: red hearts, orange pumpkins, green trees. They sang songs about Jesus and the teachers said Jesus loved all little children. Sadie said she didn't know when Louise asked if Jesus loved Sadie even though Sadie was Jewish.

The tables at school were low, made for children, yet the teachers sat on the small chairs. The teachers stuffed used Kleenex up the sleeves of their cardigans. The teachers asked Louise what her drawings meant and if she liked school better now and wouldn't she like to make friends with Maria or Stephanie or Bruce. She didn't want to make friends with anyone, she wanted to leave.

Louise never knew when she would have to go to school and when she was allowed to stay home or when Willard would take her for an afternoon. She tried to keep track of time and asked Sadie often, How many sleeps before school? Sometimes at night Louise curled up in bed, her knees pressed to her chest, and she was back again at the bottom of the cubbyhole, pressing against its wooden walls, smelling her wet wool coat. If she didn't open her eyes and sit up in bed or hear the faint whistle of Marilyn's breathing, then Louise had to call out for Sadie to come.

The opposite of being left was being met. When she emerged into the daylight and saw Marilyn and Sadie outside waiting for her, Louise could almost forget where she had been and where she would return.

WHEN THEY LEFT LOUISE AT SCHOOL, MARILYN SKIPPED ahead of her mother, looking back now and then to be sure Sadie was still there. It wasn't until they were home that Marilyn wondered about Louise. Would Sadie remember to go back and get her, and how would she know when to go? Sadie had shown the clock in the kitchen to the girls, explaining how the clock measured time and then you knew when it was time to take a bath or go to the park. But if they couldn't see the kitchen clock, or if Sadie lost all track of time as she said she did sometimes, what would happen to Louise?

Following after Sadie, her mother pulling her along to the shops or the park or home, Marilyn looked around to be sure that Louise really wasn't there. Without her sister, the world seemed larger to Marilyn. By midwinter she no longer remembered to turn around to look for Louise.

ONE MORNING LATE IN WINTER LOUISE GOT A LOLLIPOP and went back home with Sadie and Marilyn. "You're not going outside," Sadie said sternly, as if Louise wanted to. Sadie pressed the thermometer, always cold whatever the season, into the thick glass jar of Vaseline. Marilyn squirmed when Sadie wanted to take her temperature, even when Sadie said, "Lie still! It'll break off inside you," but Louise lay still.

Louise lay in her parents' bed at the other end of the upstairs from the room she shared with Marilyn. She smelled the soup Sadie was making and heard Marilyn playing in the living room below. She watched the light travel across the little house until it disappeared. The days passed slowly and the throat that hurt touched her happiness only slightly. Louise hoped she wouldn't get better and be forced to leave the beloved place to which she might never be allowed to return.

Three

WILLARD WAS COMING HOME FOR DINNER, AND SADIE
allowed Louise and Marilyn to wait up for him. Louise
had been home all week, but now she was almost better.

The girls were on the couch in pajamas and bathrobes,
wearing the felt slippers Reuben had given them for Ha-
nukkah, shaped at the end like a dog and a bunny. They'd
fought all afternoon—who broke the silver crayon and
why Louise wouldn't let Marilyn near her on the big bed
in Willard and Sadie's room. Now Sadie listened to the
murmur of Louise pretending to read to Marilyn.

It had been a long winter, and Sadie, sick of pulling the
girls in and out of snowsuits, mittens, sweaters, and hats,
wished for a perfect summer day. Each spring they said,
Well, we might go to Tuxedo, because it seemed simple,
the house waiting for them, the pool at the club. They
went out for day trips once or twice a year, but Willard,
whose decision it was, always sent them elsewhere for
the summer—to the mountains or the seashore.

The mews gate opened. The girls looked first at Sadie,
then to the door. Louise listened, and Marilyn whispered,
"Is it Daddy?" "Sssh," Louise said and reached over to
slap Marilyn.

"Weasel," Sadie said harshly. "Don't hit your sister."

Sadie signaled to Marilyn to come over and sit by her. Marilyn sniffed and stayed where she was.

The steps sounded louder, finally stopping at their door. Then the sound of his key in the lock, turning, the door opening, and the muffled noises of the street and the windy river entering their house and leaving; Willard shut the door behind him.

"Sadie?" he called out from the small foyer.

"I'm right here," she said.

"Are the girls asleep?"

"They're—"

"Here I am," Marilyn said, and she leaped from the depth of the couch across the large room, with Louise following. Willard picked up the younger child, twirled her around, then knelt again and, not relinquishing his hold on Marilyn, gave Louise a brief, crushing hug.

"How's my sick baby?" he asked.

"Almost better, thank you, Willard," Louise said huskily.

"Ready to visit your grandfather tomorrow?"

"I'm good," Marilyn said, and he laughed.

"I'm sure you are."

Sadie allowed them to stay on the couch while she and Willard ate at the table in the corner of the living room that served for a dining room. When they'd first rented the mews house when she was pregnant with Louise, it seemed large. Now it was too small for four people, even if two of them were children.

Willard carved the chicken and put two slices of breast on Sadie's plate, though she preferred dark meat. He filled his plate, then, sitting, said, "This looks good."

"I couldn't resist the potatoes," she said. "I saw them in the market and they reminded me that—" She saw that he wasn't listening. "They reminded me of spring."

He cut into the meat, put a small piece in his mouth, chewed it over and over, then swallowed with some effort.

"You're not hungry," she said.

"I thought I was until I started to eat."

"Oh, sweetie, you look all done in. You're wearing yourself down."

"There's nothing else to do, Sadie. It's all right."

"Did you see him?"

Louise listened closely to what they were saying.

"I was there. Just now." He had stopped at Cherry's, but being with her only made him feel more restless.

"And? How does he look?"

"A little worse than last time. It's hard to measure dying, as it turns out."

"And did you talk to him? Did he speak?"

"Much as usual," Willard said. "There's nothing to report, darling. Nothing happened."

"I'm not trying to *probe*," she said. "I only wanted to know how he was. I worry about you, you know. You're there so much."

"Christ. It's awful. I sit there, waiting for him to speak to me, Sadie. I have to be there in case he'll say something—you know that." He laid down his knife and fork, folded his napkin. He could say to no one, I need his blessing. Sadie was staring at him, pinning him in place with her concern. When they were first married he caught a flu, and Sadie cared for him beautifully. For the first few days he was so grateful he almost cried. As he regained his strength, Willard could stand it no more. "I seem to have lost my appetite. Forgive me." He glanced at the girls on the couch. "Will you bring Marilyn tomorrow? I'll take Louise for the day and meet you there."

"Of course," Sadie said. "Did he ask for them?"

"No, but he seems as fond of Louise as he can be of anyone. He doesn't talk very much, he never did. Now it's difficult. I tried to get him to talk about my mother today. He wouldn't, of course. He never would." Willard shook a cigarette from a pack he took from his pocket and lit it, waving the smoke away from Sadie.

"All his life, he was much too healthy. Now—well, he's got what he wanted."

Louise coughed loudly. Marilyn was asleep, her head a dead weight on Louise's bony shoulder. Willard went to the couch and lifted her up. "Come on, Louise. We'll tuck your sister in."

"Louise's medicine," Sadie said.

"I'll do it," he said. "You stay here. You've had them all day."

"Thanks, sweetie. The pills and the cough medicine," Sadie said. "Come kiss me good night, Lulu." She put down her fork and wiped her mouth. The little girl dragged herself from the couch and reached up for the hem of her father's jacket.

"I'm sleepy," she said.

"All right," Sadie said. "No kiss. Go with your father. Sleep well, Louise. I'll check on you later." She tossed her napkin down on the table, stood, sighed, and began to clear away the uneaten meal.

Four

THEY LAY IN BED, THE DOOR OPEN A FEW INCHES, LIS-tening for their daughters.

"I wonder when winter will be over. I feel like we're under siege," Sadie said.

"Soon enough," he said.

"I was thinking about summer. Maybe we'll go to Tux-edo. That way we'd be close if Reed needed us."

"Sadie, I can't think about summer. I can hardly think about tomorrow."

"I miss you when you're not here, you know. The girls do too. I wish you'd let me help you somehow, sweetie. It's such a bad time for you."

"I'm doing my best," he said. "I don't mean to leave you with everything."

"I didn't mean it that way."

He lay in clean pajamas, staring at the ceiling, his hands crossed behind his head. She had decided long before that marriage was like breathing—as soon as you noticed the process, you stopped it at peril of your life. But now she wanted to ask him as she sometimes did, even knowing it was the worst time, did he love her as she loved him, would everything be all right again?

"And what will you do with Louise tomorrow?" she

asked. "She shouldn't stay out too long." Sadie turned
and lay on her back.

"To a museum. Then to Reed's. I may go downtown
for some papers. She's getting peaky staying at home."

"You're probably right," she said. "She'll go back at
school next week."

"Why does she have to go to school at all? She hates
it."

"She just had a rough start, sweetie. Lots of kids are
scared of school. Then they adjust. She should know
some children besides Marilyn. I may take her over to
P.S. 75 one of these days, so she can see it."

"We could easily send her to a much better school,"
Willard said. "There's no need—"

"This is a good school, a new building. If she's
bright enough she can get into the Intellectually Gifted
class—"

"We agreed long ago that these choices were yours to
make. I don't have the energy to argue now."

She could almost hear the snow falling, hitting the cars
and the empty streets, padding the sharp city.

"I don't want to argue. I don't feel that I'm depriving
them of something special," she said.

"Then be content with your decision," he said.

"Marilyn will want to go out with you. If you take
Louise."

"Another time," he said.

"I'd appreciate it," she said, "if you could take both
the girls for an afternoon next week. I have some shopping I need to get done. I thought I'd have lunch with
Arlie."

"Why don't you hire someone?" he asked. He turned
on his side and curled away from Sadie. "I'm not the
only adult in Manhattan capable of entertaining Louise
and Marilyn. You act like a prisoner. Or an indentured
servant, for Christ's sake."

"I don't like leaving them with strangers."

"The strangers would soon come to be known to
them."

"It's not the same thing. Plus Reuben is coming for dinner next Wednesday. I hope you'll be home."

"I'll be here," he said. "Remind me and I'll make a point of it."

"Willard," she said after a few minutes. "Are you asleep?"

"I was falling asleep."

"Do you love me just a little?" She sighed. "Do you love me at all? I wonder sometimes if you do."

"Of course," he said. "Of course I do. You always ask, and I always say the same thing. Why do you ask, Sadie?" He turned, held Sadie, then released her and said, "Now sleep, darling, we both need to sleep."

Did he love her? She had such an absolute idea of love, of a marble block of love that didn't change from age to age. Why shouldn't she, he thought, if Reuben's devotion was a fair sample. Of course he loved Louise and Marilyn, and she was in back of that love and part of it. But she hadn't yet realized that he was incapable of love, if the love she wanted was what she gave him.

"I know how upset you are about Reed. But I get upset sometimes too and I think . . . do you think I'm still pretty?"

This was an easier question. When Louise was born, Sadie lost her resemblance to the Little White Girl. She was heavier, solid in a way he never felt, and at times he liked to watch her move, filled not so much with desire as with simple admiration.

"Of course you're pretty," he said. "But you don't have to ask me. Look at Louise and Marilyn."

"Oh, it's all from you," she said, "all from you."

When his breathing became regular and mixed with the sound of the snow, Sadie was sorry she'd asked, as she always was. She got out of bed and pulled her flannel robe around her, shuffled for her slippers, and went downstairs. Without turning on a light, she moved through the house, checking the stove and the front door, staring out at the mews that was slowly filling with virgin snow.

Five

Sadie laid out the girls' clothing for the visit to Reed, their matching plaid skirts, knee socks, and mary janes, the cashmere sweater sets their grandfather had given them for Christmas, and the baby pearl necklaces he'd given each girl at birth. Once they were dressed, she said, "Now take your hairbrushes and ribbons downstairs. Your father's waiting." While he brought her wisps and threads together, Louise stood very still, hardly breathing. He had special gold hairpins for her, and black ones for Marilyn. When they wore their velvet dresses with lace collars, Willard tied their sashes in double bows that lay flat against their waists.

The outside air was delicious and juicy, and while Louise waited in the mews for Willard to open the gate, she let snow fall on her tongue and melt, one flake and then another.

Sometimes on their afternoons out, Willard took Louise across the park to the Metropolitan to look at paintings and statues, broken pots in glass cases, and the mummy. Louise had to be patient when her father looked at a painting, and she tried not to shift from foot to foot.

She liked the big painting of the old lady who Willard

said was cutting her fingernails, and the portraits whose eyes followed her around the room. She liked paintings of forests and wished she could step into them. But most of all she liked being there with Willard. They always looked for Mr. Whistler's paintings, and once she asked her father if Mr. Whistler had a little girl. Willard answered that Mr. Whistler was dead—didn't she remember?—but that he'd had two children. He hadn't lived with either of them, not the way Willard lived with Louise, but he loved them. Mr. Whistler didn't get along with his children's mothers.

With her mother one question led to another and another and then maybe to a shrug or a story about something that had once happened to Sadie or Reuben or a cousin Louise had never met. With Willard there always was one answer.

"Your mother was right," Willard said. "It's really snowing. We'll do a quick tour of the city museum, then be on our way."

He paused to look up at the flags of the thirteen original colonies at the museum, and read some words to Louise —Liberty or Death, Don't Tread on Me. But he didn't care for the ship models nor did he seem to admire the Victorian dolls. Louise didn't see the use of looking at a doll she couldn't touch. After they left the museum, walking back down toward Broadway, Willard asked, "Did you like the dolls?"

"Not more than anything," she said.

"Your grandmother had dolls like that. She kept all her dolls from when she was a girl," he said. The snow was still falling and the streets were nearly empty. "Next time we're in Tuxedo, we'll find them. They're in a closet or an attic."

"I'm going to keep my dolls," she said.

"Are you?" he said, and he smiled.

On the way to the subway, they stopped at a luncheonette on Broadway. Snow melted in dark streaks on the tile floor. He helped her up onto a stool at the counter, then sat next to her, ordered a cup of coffee and her hot chocolate. The trick was to let the whipped cream melt just enough but not so much that it disappeared. He lit a cigarette and let a thin stream of smoke climb to the greasy, mustard-colored pressed-tin ceiling. He blew on Louise's chocolate a few times, then sat staring at her, tapping his fingers on the counter, ignoring his coffee. He often inspected her for traces of Sadie, for Louise seemed entirely his child. Louise thought that he wanted her to hurry and she took a sip. The chocolate burned her lip and she cried out.

"You have to wait until it's cool," he said. He dipped his napkin into a glass of ice water and dabbed her lips. "No rush."

When she was bundled up again and back on the snowy street, Willard said, "Don't tell your mother about the chocolate. I don't want her to think I'm feeding you sugar, you know."

She looked up at her father and snow fell into her wide-open eyes, making her blink as she did when she was about to cry.

"Never mind," Willard said.

"Sometimes I see kids at school doing things and I don't tell," she said.

"Well, that's as it should be," he said. "No need to tell everything you know."

"And sometimes I have bad dreams but I don't tell them," she said.

"You needn't tell your dreams to anyone," Willard said, "unless you want to."

She never did. Her worst dream was a sensation—that she was walking along a wide corridor, the walls, floor, and ceiling a moving black surface that was like snow but more forceful.

"Do you have bad dreams?" she asked.

"Oh, yes," Willard said. "Almost every night."

"Do you mind?"

"I try not to let them scare me."

"Does Mommy know?"

"No," he said. "Watch where you're going, Louise.

You're supposed to avoid the high snow, not step in it. I don't want to bring you to your grandfather's with a boot full of snow."

"Okay," she said. Now they had two secrets, and Louise felt happy and scared, as she did before her birthday when she wondered if she would get what she wanted. Perhaps her father's dreams took place in her black corridor, just a little farther along, and they might meet there someday. But now not a word to her mother or her sister.

THE SUBWAY SEATS WERE COVERED WITH STIFF YELLOW upholstery that left marks on Louise's bare palms. Her father made her put her gloves on again when they emerged into the empty world at the bottom of the island. He told her to stand still, and he tugged at her coat, her skirt, the bottom of her snowpants, tucking in her scarf. Hand in hand, Louise and Willard rushed down the cavernous streets, then turned in at the Weaver Building. Willard reached deep into his pocket for the special key that opened the lobby door on a Sunday.

"I told Mr. Williams, the janitor, we'd be coming."

She nodded and asked, "Why is your office here?"

"Oh," he said, pressing the button for the automatic elevator, "the mews house is so small, Louise. I need a place for myself."

In the subway, she'd sat quietly next to her father and stared out at the black tunnels and the puddles by the shining tracks. Another train had passed theirs, and Louise saw a mother and child staring out, people she didn't know but they could see her. When the stop came, she dreaded them seeing her but the platform was deserted and Willard said, "This way."

"Would you like your own room? Would you like a room you didn't have to share with Marilyn?" he asked now.

"I guess," she said. There was a right answer and a

wrong one, and if she gave the wrong one she might lose what she had, the sound of Marilyn breathing at night.

The office was large and airy, with a view of the Battery, where the rivers met, Willard said. At the big bare windows was a wooden stepladder. Willard's binoculars hung from a nail.

He helped Louise out of her coat, and released her while he gathered the papers he'd come for. She wandered across the room, climbed the little stepladder to see above the ledge, and leaned forward, imagining evaporating through the glass like a melting snowflake, and falling into the swirl where the two rivers met. He called out, "Louise. Come down right now!" She staggered a little, startled by her father's voice.

Willard looked around the bare room for something to keep the child's attention, settling on a black portfolio that lay open on a wide table by the office door.

"Look at these photographs," he said. "Come on, Louise, look at the canyons." She turned and came slowly down the ladder. "Don't climb the ladder alone, sweetheart," and, as she reached for the smooth sepia surface, "You may look but don't touch the photographs except by the edge.

"That's much better. Now when you look," he said, hand on the child's head, "squeeze your eyes together a little. Like this."

She imitated his look.

"All right," he said. "Breathe very quietly. Listen carefully. Do you hear?"

She looked, eyes squinted together.

"Can you hear the wind?" he asked. "It's quiet, and the only sound is the wind. You're on the edge of the bluff. There's no one around, just rocks and sky. And the light. Keep looking. The wind. A buzzard flies over and his shadow crawls all over you."

She shuddered.

"You don't mind, Louise. You're watching him ride the breeze down into the canyon. Isn't it the most wonderful place?"

"Yes, Willard," she said, watching the shadows of clouds passing over the Battery, listening to the wind knocking against the windows of her grandfather's building.

"When I'm gone," he said, "this is where I'll be."

"Yes," she said.

"So you don't have to worry about me, ever."

When he was away, and she and Marilyn waited for him on the couch, or woke up and he was still gone, was this where he was—in the office? in the canyon? She opened her eyes to ask him, but he was over by the desk, opening drawers and files, leafing through papers.

He looked over and said, "Never touch the surface of a photograph, Louise. Your skin has oil on it and it harms the photograph. In fifty years, there'll be a hole where you touched it. Just one more minute. I'll find the papers I need and we'll go to your grandfather's."

He helped her on with her layers of clothing to take her out into the windy afternoon, and she asked, "Did you ever show Marilyn the canyon?"

He laughed and hugged her to him. "You're my darling. My first darling."

In the elevator going down, she felt so tired that she leaned against the wall and closed her eyes, as the box that held them fell through space. Her father said, "Louise, stand up straight. Are you getting sick again?"

She slept in the cab going uptown, breathing in cold air from the crack in the window, content to rest against his coat forever.

Six

WHEN WILLARD FIRST BROUGHT SADIE TO VISIT REED, she said that it looked as though nothing in the house had changed for decades, and nothing ever would, but now it was altered. A woman came in to clean (unthinkable in the old days), and she left a supply of bland, unappetizing meals in the icebox for Prince and Reed. The house, which once had smelled of preservation, of lavender and lemon oil, of eucalyptus and herbal teas, now smelled medicinal. Even in the furnishings—the Chinese urns, the Persian rugs, the English landscapes—even there, Sadie saw disintegration. Nothing was quite clean or whole. Everything spoke to Sadie of a kind of death about which she knew nothing. Her parents had died in an instant. Willard's father had cancer.

When she made her Sunday visits in her best tweed suit, her mother's heavy gold chain around her neck, Sadie felt like an earthworm among birds. Reed, from his spare diet of grains and juices, was even tighter to the bone than the ancestors whose portraits haunted the house. And Prince was more uplifted, pulled by an invisible thread that linked his chest to heaven.

When Willard told Reed that he was getting married, Reed asked, "Are you hurrying into matrimony or is it that you have told me last of all?"

"I'm sorry to burden you with the news," Willard said.

"I trust your marriage will not be a burden to me. The weight is on the participants more than the observers. And who is to be the bride? No one I know, I assume."

"Sarah Ash. She's called Sadie. I met her at Columbia. In a class."

Reed licked his dry lips as if moving his mouth pained him.

"Be kind," he said, startling his son. "A glass of water. I'm terribly dry. I succumbed to a Bartlett pear the other day and I lie here. Its victim." He sipped from the glass Willard handed him. "I knew of course that you were attending classes there. I had no idea that you were searching for a wife as well. Ash?"

"You don't know the family," Willard said.

"I met a Solomon Ash years ago. A houseguest in Tuxedo. German fellow. Brusque. But interesting."

"These Ashes are Russian. In origin."

"Slavic," said Reed. "I once knew a Prince Galitsin. Down on his luck but not a bad fellow."

"These Ashes aren't titled."

"I suppose it makes sense that you're marrying," Reed said, shutting his eyes and continuing to speak. "I was thirty when I married and you are past that age now. A man alone gets sour."

"You might as well know," Willard began, meaning to tell him that Sadie was pregnant, but his father gave no sign that he was listening.

"Almost like a bad smell. If a man doesn't marry. To his reputation. Though that passes too. Not a reason to marry at all. Where will it be held? It's out of the question, of course, that I attend."

"At her brother's apartment. On West End Avenue."

"How inconvenient."

Prince appeared at the door, carrying a teatray with a teapot and one cup. Willard rose and said, "Good-by, Father. I hope you feel better."

Reed said, "I shall, for a period."

WILLARD WENT UPSTAIRS TO HIS FATHER, AND SADIE
waited in the drawing room with the girls. Though there
were plenty of places to explore beneath the carved mahogany tables, between the layers of draperies and curtains, the girls stayed side by side on the couch, which
was even deeper than the one at home. Their legs didn't
reach the edge of the cushions. When Sadie was finally
summoned upstairs, the girls stayed, their eyes lighting
on every corner and knickknack in the elaborate, old-
fashioned room. Louise memorized the frieze along the
mantelpiece as if she would be tested on it later: man,
lady, dogs.

Reed didn't approve of children's books, which he
thought laden with secret messages and empty of information, and he refused to keep toys or crayons and paper
on the grounds that the girls might harm the furniture. He
provided for each visit the latest *National Geographic*
and *Life*, and the girls, like miniature patients in a dentist's waiting room, read their magazines, distracted and
apprehensive. Louise let Marilyn have *National Geographic* because she liked the bigger pictures in *Life*.

On the cover of her magazine was a woman with yellow hair and big red lips, the kind Sadie painted on when
she went out at night. Louise looked at the ads for white
convertibles with the tops down and aquamarine kitchen
appliances. The kitchen was nothing like the one at the
mews or Reed's or Reuben's.

She turned the page and came to black-and-white pictures of people who reminded her of the black corridor in
her dreams. They were flesh stuck to bones. Their teeth
were too big for their mouths, their ears for their skulls,
and they pressed together behind a big wire fence or lay
looking out at the camera, but not posing, not caring. In
another photo was a pit that she thought was filled with
snakes and bones, but when Louise looked more closely
she saw that it was filled with people, piled one on another, as if it didn't matter which way their arms and legs
went. Once in Tuxedo Louise played a game on a lawn,
holding hands with other children and twirling out in a

circle, then coming together and falling down in a pile. But it had hurt when they came together and the pile of children hadn't been still like the people in the pit.

Louise caught Marilyn glancing over and she closed the magazine but saw the people still. She let the magazine fall and gripped the side of the couch. Louise's head felt cold, then hot. Something was rocking inside her. She closed her eyes and saw the pit and opened her eyes quickly. She said, "You're supposed to be looking at *your* magazine."

"You dropped it," Marilyn said, and she got off the couch, picked up the magazine, and handed it to Louise.

"No," Louise shouted. "Don't touch it. Leave it alone."

"I will."

Louise drew her hand back and smacked Marilyn on the arm so hard that the little girl screamed and fell down. Louise cried and ran for the door.

"Sadie," she called up the stairs, "Mama," and when Sadie came rushing down the stairs, awkward in her dress-up shoes, Louise said, "I didn't mean it. I just pushed her a little."

Sadie said, "You shouldn't have pushed her at all." She took both girls to the bathroom under the big stairs, washed their faces, and calmed them, saying, "I'm ashamed of both of you," and when they both started to talk at once, she said, "I'm bringing you up to your grandfather. Be good, Louise and Marilyn. He doesn't feel well. Now take a deep breath. Now let it go," and they were at the top of the stairs.

Seven

AS LONG AS THEY COULD REMEMBER, THEIR GRAND-
father lay as he did now on his high bed, surrounded by
the brightness of white sheets and pale coverlet, his faded
hair against his big pillows. Was he breathing? At the
doorway, Louise stared for the rise and fall of his body
underneath the whiteness.

"Go on," Sadie said, giving the girls a little shove, "go
say hello."

Willard stood by the bed, and he turned at the sound
of Sadie's voice, his gaze unfocused.

"Willard," Sadie said, unnecessarily, "the girls are
here."

He turned back to his father, and Sadie made a clicking
sound of frustration. She moved the girls into the room,
taking their hands, saying, "Maybe he's having a little
nap," but as they approached, Reed opened first one eye
and then another. He looked around the room. The curtains were drawn and the only light came from the small
lamp on his bedside table. "There," Sadie said. "Come
on, Louise and Marilyn." The children stopped just short
of their father, and tried to take their hands from Sadie.
She tightened her grip, unthinking, until Louise cried out,
"You're hurting me."

Reed saw aureoles now around his visitors, and he regretted that there was no one to talk to about them. Prince was cloudy all around, Willard more definite. Sadie and the children had the same pink edge, like dried roses. Their forms—cloudy, hard, powdery—returned to Reed at night, disturbing his already difficult sleep.

Once on the bedside table he'd kept his homeopathic powders and pills, the herbs and twigs from exotic plants, that were used to coat and regulate his body. He used them for protection, along with the daily orange, the fish, always steamed and never fried, the grains that cleansed. Now, glancing at the jamboree of pill bottles, water bottle, thermometer on the bedside table, Reed saw the defeat of his method, and evidence of his imprisonment. Diseased, he was the receptacle for all he had avoided. When the long pain-broken nights receded, Reed wondered had he drunk liquor and eaten fats and meats, if he would have become sick sooner or at all? Was it possible that the strength he'd gained made dying worse? He might be dead by now and well out of it.

When Reed first became ill, he envied anyone who was still up and about. Now movement was beyond imagination. There was nothing inside to lead him back to the world of the healthy. He was curious about one last thing: when death would come and when it did if he would be terrified or would welcome relief from the rhythm of his pain and the noise of his failing heart. He had few thoughts left, and these repeated musically with small variation. Beneath his boredom was the answer to it all, that he would do whatever he had to to stay alive, even for another minute.

Reed stretched dry lips over teeth, opened his skeleton's mouth to speak. Sadie rushed to pour him a glass of water, helping him lean over to sip at it, like a bird at a puddle. When he was finished, he gave a sigh and lay against the pillows, exhausted.

"Have you come to see me?" he asked the girls. "Not too close. Some trick of light. When you're close, I can't see." They were at times more than he could absorb: their luminous skin and the blue-whites of their eyes;

Louise, so like Willard; Marilyn's violet-blue eyes. She would be splendid and he would be dust.

Louise took a step closer. Her grandfather's voice was disguised, and he was smaller than he used to be, he was like the people in the magazine, and she wondered if he would go where they were. "Willard brought me in a taxicab," she said.

He asked, "What kind of taxicab?"

Her grandfather's hands were folded one on top of the other on his gray satin bedcover. Louise decided to watch them until they moved, then she would answer. Reed sighed, twisted barely to the left, moving his pain around.

"Yellow," Louise said.

"Yellow," Marilyn repeated. "Mommy and me took a big one. A big yellow one. You could come too."

"Oh, I doubt that," he said. "I doubt that. But thank you for inviting me. All the same."

Sadie bent over to the girls and asked, "Would you like to go closer to your grandfather?" A statue come to life, Willard said, "For Christ's sake, Sadie."

Sadie lifted Marilyn, and the child's legs curled around her. She leaned over so that Reed and Marilyn could touch, then straightened and let Marilyn down.

The old man lifted his arms a few inches, and Louise would have gone to him but Willard moved between them.

"How is it now?" Sadie asked her father-in-law.

"Much the same."

"So," she said, "at least it's no worse," then she smiled and said, "People are always trying to get the sick to say they're not really sick."

"The alternative," he said and tried to bring his shoulders up into a shrug. "Worse."

Sadie laughed to give him the feeling that he'd accomplished something. She approves of bravery, Reed thought. He might tell her about the aureoles if they were alone. He resisted her kindness less as he weakened, acted less as if she were trying to bribe him. He wanted to do something for Sadie, to warn her. He sighed, coughed, closed his eyes, and listened to his beating heart.

"We don't want to tire him out, Sadie. Take the girls downstairs. I'll be right there," Willard said. When they'd gone he turned to his father who lay depleted of color, parchment against linen.

"Are you comfortable?" Willard asked.

"Prince here. Night nurse."

"Is there anything I can do, Father? I feel very helpless."

"Helpless. You are. Have you thought to sell Tuxedo?"

"I haven't given it any thought," Willard said. "It hasn't been on my mind at all, not a bit. And now, with a family. I never wanted to sell it. I thought the girls might use it, enjoy it, when they grow up a little."

Reed raised an eyebrow. "Too small," he said. "Tuxedo's so small."

"There's plenty of room in the house, I should think. Oh, I know we haven't gone there much, but who's to say we might not. I won't sell it," Willard said. "I suppose it will be up to me and I won't."

Reed raised his eyes to the ceiling and shrugged.

"Tony Misurelli checked the roof," Willard lied. "It's in remarkable shape, according to him."

Reed stared at Willard and blinked. Willard wondered if he would smile. His father tried to speak, and Willard bent to hear him.

"Tired now," Reed whispered.

Willard wanted to stay, though a minute before he wished for nothing more than to leave. He feared for his father, for Prince, even for the house. He would not have been surprised to come some day and find an empty lot where his father's house stood. When his father died, Willard would be cut adrift, without a reason to be here or anywhere. It seemed to him now that he had come back from Europe only for his father, and now his father would leave him without a word.

SADIE STOOD AT THE DOOR, WATCHING WILLARD WHO sat like a marble knight on a medieval tomb, more ghostly than his father. The girls were downstairs, where Prince was giving them skimmed milk and slices of apple.

"Willard," she said, "sweetie. We'd better talk to the girls." She glanced at Reed who slept deeply. "We have to tell them he's dying."

"What if he recovers?" Willard whispered.

"Then we'll tell them about miracles."

"We'll have terrified them for nothing," he said.

"These visits are no picnic," she said.

"Marilyn's happy anywhere. And Louise knows how to act."

"Yes," Sadie said patiently, "but how does she *feel*? What is she thinking about?"

"If you're the one who's frightened, Sadie, if this is too difficult for you—"

"Difficult? Of course, it's difficult. Not just for me."

"You always tell the girls death is natural. That bird they saw in the park."

"Big deal. Natural," she said. "It's still frightening."

"Take them home," he said. "I'll be there. I need to —I promise this will get better, darling. We'll have a long talk another time, Sadie, and we'll straighten out everything. I promise."

There wouldn't be another time, she thought. He would curl away from her in sleep, be gone in his waking hours.

But when Reed died, she thought, surely Willard would be with her again. Things would be as they were when the girls were babies. He would see that she and the girls were the best thing for him, he would come to them body and soul, just like the song, just as she waited for him to. She stood by Willard, her hand on his marble shoulder, feeling the rise and fall of his breathing.

Eight

CHERRY CAME HOME AND FOUND WILLARD OUTSIDE her building.

"Hello!" she said. "What are you doing here?"

"Waiting for you. I've been at my father's."

He made a face, bent to kiss her, then hugged her against him tightly.

"I'd say you were glad to see me," Cherry said, pulling away gently.

"And you?" He thought of asking where she'd been.

"Numb. I've been sitting around all afternoon, wasting my life. Listening to a bunch of guys talk about what great painters they are."

He reached for her again, and Cherry said, "I didn't expect you."

"It wouldn't have done any good to call," he said. "You weren't home."

"We'll see each other some other time," she said.

"You sound as if you'll be engaged tonight," he said, feeling worse than he had with his father.

"Maybe I am," she said. "Maybe you will be too. You're the one who's permanently engaged."

Cherry heard Sadie's name for the first time when she found a jewel box in his pocket. The box contained a diamond set into a thin white gold band, and, assuming it

118

was for her, Cherry jammed the delicate ring onto her pinky and teased him that she couldn't get it off now. They had ended up screaming at each other until Cherry's neighbor banged on the bedroom wall, and they sprang apart like children discovered at a naughty game. Cherry soaped her finger to release the ring. She looked so sad that Willard almost said, Oh, Christ, just leave it on. The next day the jewel was given to Sadie, but Willard imagined that the band kept a flicker of Cherry's flesh.

Willard told her that Sadie was pregnant and that he was marrying her. It would bring him stability, he told Cherry, some order to his life. He would have to settle down sometime and here was as good an opportunity as any. He told Cherry that time seemed to him like pudding —no way to measure it or confine it. But with a family, time would have definition. He needed to do this, did she understand?

She nodded, interested. She wondered what Sadie was like and if Willard would have married her if she'd been the one to get pregnant. It wasn't what she wanted, but she wondered nonetheless.

Cherry's time wasn't like pudding. It was sectioned and cut up. If she only had money, each day would flow. If she had money, maybe she would be able to paint the way she wanted.

When Willard told her Louise was born, then Marilyn, she shrugged and asked nothing. She did notice that family made him no more settled or happy. Willard was the same as he had always been, if anything a little more furtive and worried. But that wasn't Cherry's business.

Besides, she thought, she hated children. If she wanted children, she could have stayed in Hackettstown and married a farmer.

"I don't have to be anywhere," he said. "If you're free."

"Don't let's start," she said. She had been slouching, as she did when she was tired. Now she straightened up. She wanted to go upstairs to her apartment, make a drink, take off her makeup. She wanted to turn on the radio and hear some new music.

"Is it one of those painters?" he asked.

"Willard, you shouldn't ask me questions like that. Look—it's simple. I like being with them. I know they don't give a damn about me, but they're the real thing. They're all making art, the real art. I don't feel so crummy with them, it's like I was doing that work too."

In the half-light of the street, she looked worn down and he felt ashamed, as though everything in her life was his fault, the smallest wrinkle around her dark eyes an imprint of his hand.

"I'm very fond of you," he said.

"I know," she said. "Now beat it."

He let her move away from him into the little foyer, and he said, "I'll call."

Nine

CHERRY'S MOTHER CAME TO NEW YORK ONCE A YEAR to visit overnight, sleeping on the lumpy single bed in Cherry's studio. She always offered her mother the bedroom, but Martha preferred not to accept. Cherry was sorry Willard had been waiting for her that evening. Martha arrived only fifteen minutes later, and their near meeting made her feel more hunted than usual in her mother's presence.

It was part of the visit for Martha to take Cherry out for dinner, and sometimes Cherry made an effort to find a place that was special and not too expensive for her mother. This visit, Cherry chose the French restaurant down the block.

"You're looking fine," Martha said. Cherry's hands shook a little as she lit a cigarette, Martha noticed, and steadied when she took a sip of the house wine.

"Well, things are taking a turn for the better," Cherry said. She licked her lips and postponed taking her next sip of wine. She pushed her hair back from her forehead. "I'm going to be ready for a show soon."

"I see," Martha said cautiously.

"Not this season. This season's almost over. But maybe next. There's a guy named Bradley, well, a critic. A very important critic who's interested in my work."

Why did she feel as though she was lying to Martha when she was telling her the truth for once? Bradley said he would come and look at her stuff when he had time, and meanwhile she was working toward his visit. But it was wrong to say he was interested.

"When this critic comes and sees your work, will this mean you'll have a show of your paintings?"

"Well, not right away. These things take a lot of time." She knew her mother was thinking, It's been a long time, Cherry. "Of course, the important thing isn't a show at all. That would be nice. But if he comes and sees something in the work, it'll be, it'll mean that—"

"Well, everyone always said you were very talented," Martha said. She had tried for years to find a way to tell Cherry that she thought she was brave to go to New York to be a painter. Unambitious herself, Martha had worked for safety all her life, and her child's precarious existence was more a cause for wonder than the disapproval Cherry imagined.

"Yes," Cherry said, "but talent—"

Martha had raised Cherry in a small, windy house she rented down the street from the school where she was secretary to the principal. Hackettstown lay at the bottom of a valley, surrounded by large, prosperous dairy farms, and cattle farms for rich New Yorkers and Philadelphians. Though Hackettstown was under two hours from the city, Martha and Cherry rarely saw each other, acting as if the Hudson were an impassable moat. Martha had lived around there all her life, moving when she married from the village of Long Valley to Hackettstown, just over the mountain.

The rhythm of the school year dominated Cherry's childhood, though it was interrupted by her father, who blew in every once in a while, looking good and talking about better times and long shots paying off. He left when the regularity of Martha's existence got too crushing for his spirit, or when she produced the money for his next deal. Martha was a plain, private woman who had never expected to marry, and when she did was not surprised by the bad luck that followed. Cherry had watched her mother for years for signs of heartbreak at the loss of her one and only love.

Cherry took a sip, then drank the rest of the wine in a gulp. The glasses at this place were too small, she thought, glad she'd had the courage to order a large carafe.

"Talent isn't much," she said. "It's work. It's concentration. It may even be luck," and she gave her mother a brilliant smile that usually pleased people but made Martha frown. "I mean, luck to get a gallery. But to be a great artist, even a good artist. That's something different."

"I see," Martha said. "I hope you'll let me know. I'll come to the city willingly, you know, Cherry, to see your show. It would please me very much."

"Oh, sure," Cherry said. "If anything happens. But nothing will, probably. Though I don't know. Sometimes I think it'll all work out."

When she left Hackettstown after high school, she told Martha that she'd seen the last of her. Now she wished she had left more quietly. When she remembered the look on Martha's face, she wished she could take back her words.

"Gladdy always asks about you," Martha said, "and she says it's a pity she never gets to the city. She says you were the most talented girl she ever had in class. And the Searles ask too."

Not too often, Cherry hoped. Martha rarely had fresh news to give. When her mother was around, Cherry's existence seemed as humdrum as if she were in Hackettstown still.

They ordered their dinners, consulting on the meaning of the dishes. Martha hadn't meant to squander greetings from her small circle so early in the visit. She tried not to stare at Cherry, at the line of makeup around her neck; at her nails, irregular, bitten, the polish chipped. She didn't want to be critical of Cherry.

"Sometimes I miss Hackettstown," Cherry said.

"I would never have thought that. I wonder if I'd miss it."

"You'd have to leave it first," Cherry said, laughing, then stopped abruptly. "Do you think you ever will?"

"I'll be retiring one of these days," Martha said. "I've saved enough . . ." Cherry sipped her wine, uncomfortable. She liked to gulp her drinks and bolt her food, as she'd been warned not to as a child. "I've been thinking of taking a retirement trip. To Europe, maybe."

"But what would you do there?"

"Travel around. Take one of those tours people take. See the sights and eat in restaurants. I don't suppose I'd do anything unusual."

"It costs an awful lot of money," Cherry said.

"I thought you were all in favor of people going full steam ahead."

Cherry pushed away her half-empty glass. If she kept drinking this way, she'd finish the carafe before dessert. She wanted to say it wasn't as if going to Europe on a retirement trip would make any difference in Martha's life. "I guess Europe's as good a place to start as anywhere. Paris, Rome, London," naming cities she hadn't been to either and doubted if she'd ever see. "You'll have the time of your life."

"I expect I'll be sort of overwhelmed by everything," Martha said.

Cherry said, "You might have a good time."

They ate silently, as if they were at their kitchen table. When she'd finished picking at her veal stew and eating a few leaves of lettuce, Cherry poured the last of the wine into her glass.

"If I save up enough," Martha said, "I'd like you to come with me, dear. I won't be leaving you anything in the way of property, and I'll use up my savings and pension by the time I go."

"I don't want to know about this," Cherry said.

"I don't believe in parents being a burden on their children," Martha said. "I don't believe in it at all."

As if she could depend on me, Cherry thought. She

barely supported herself, and the thought of her mother needing help made her feel like running.

"Maybe I'll be able to take you to Europe sometime," Cherry said, "first class."

Martha tucked in her head and smiled a little. Cherry, profligate, finished off the wine. "You shouldn't argue, you know, because you never know what might happen and it doesn't cost you anything to hope."

She was quoting her father word for word, she realized, her face growing warm. She even got the intonation right, slurred the words a little.

Martha said, "There's hope and there's hope, Cherry. Sometimes I wonder what will happen to you when I'm gone."

"Maybe you'll outlive me," Cherry said.

"I think of that too," Martha said, though she knew Cherry meant it to be a joke. She couldn't imagine how the girl lived. Martha kept, framed, a drawing of a barn that Cherry had done the summer before her last year of high school, and while Cherry got the tilt of the old barn right (it was struck by lightning the next year and burned), that didn't seem like enough to build a life on. Cherry's current paintings were puzzles to Martha.

Cherry, defeated, added up what the meal would cost her mother, plus the bus fare from New Jersey. Martha wasn't getting her money's worth.

"Would you like to go to a museum tomorrow? Or shopping up on Fifth Avenue?"

"Oh, I have everything I need," Martha said. "I was planning on an early bus home."

She paid the bill and the women stood, lifting their heavy winter coats up onto their shoulders. Cherry wore a black fur she'd bought secondhand. In the brief walk back to Cherry's apartment, Martha decided against giving a twenty-dollar bill to Cherry, as she'd planned. In her long black coat and her red scarf with silver streaks, Cherry looked so much like the New Yorker she had hoped to become, that Martha decided she'd do her daughter a favor and keep the money.

REUBEN ATE SLOWLY, BRINGING SPOON TO MOUTH AS IF the soup were iron ore, too heavy to lift. He watched as Cherry and the older woman left the restaurant. He wondered briefly if Cherry were in some sort of trouble. She didn't look well. If Willard gave up on her, he might find someone younger and more demanding, and that would be worse for Sadie.

People did what they wanted. He was in a profession where people asked advice all the time, and Reuben gave his opinion, if asked. Then Reuben stepped back, because people did whatever they pleased, and that was the truth of it. No one really wanted to listen to advice. People wanted an ear, and then to do as they pleased.

Over the years, Reuben had developed a fondness for Chez Marandel, down the block from Cherry's. Never a lover of chicken livers, he ordered broad, fresh noodles with chicken liver sauce as often as it appeared on the menu, or a simple steak and bright, tasty carrots. Reuben invited his brother-in-law there to lunch, and asked him what region of France the food was from. Belgium, Willard replied. The pink tablecloths lasted a few years. By the time Reuben brought Marilyn there for her third birthday, the décor had sunk to red-and-white checked cloths and napkins, bottles hung against the wall, tourist-bureau maps of French wine country.

Often, after a meal, Reuben strolled along Bleecker Street, looking in the shop windows at pink fish lounging on crystal beds, elegant-feathered pheasants hanging by their feet, at a bright-eyed pig's head, and loaves of twisted bread thrown in a pile, used books, antique furniture, keeping an eye out for trinkets for Sadie and the girls. Also he looked for Cherry. A private detective the firm used on occasion gave him her name and address. He might have told Sadie about Cherry but couldn't see the use of it. Once Marilyn was born, he considered talking to Cherry, but what was there to say? Would knowledge of her lover's second child change a thing? And who was to say it would be news to her. People didn't often act from noble motives, and why should she care about

Sadie? It made a little sport for Reuben to see if their paths would cross. And if he did see Cherry, trudging head down to the frame store; walking lopsidedly, a little drunk, midafternoon; dressed up in the evening—Reuben stepped aside and made way for her. He wondered—stranger things had happened—if ever he would be the watched, not the watcher.

Ten

A few weeks later, Sadie took Marilyn and Louise for an afternoon walk in Central Park. Sadie pointed out tight forsythia buds, and the way the melting ice and snow coated the stone walls of the park tunnels. She stopped at a florist and bought a bouquet of violets and a bunch of daffodils. "It's spring," she told the girls, "smell the air, it's fresh and clear." Sadie sang "I'm forever blowing bubbles" for the girls as she put them to bed.

Downstairs, she turned on the radio but couldn't find what she wanted—Les Brown and His Band of Renown or Paul Whiteman. The nearness of spring made her feel too restless to wait for Willard as she usually did.

Sadie dialed first Willard's office and then Reed's house. Prince answered and said, "It's Mr. Weaver. Good you called. He passed this afternoon." "This afternoon?" "I thought you knew," the most she'd ever heard Prince volunteer. "I didn't," she said, "and Willard—he's there?" "He won't move, not at all. I asked him to. I told him—Eat something."

"I wish you'd called," she said. Reed finally got out of there, she thought. "I mean, where is Willard?"

"In his father's room. Drinking whiskey. Old whiskey."

She imagined Willard and a glass, a decanter, in the half-dark of Reed's room, Willard unable to move.

"I'll be there right away," she said.

But as she prepared to go, Sadie saw herself alone in a taxi, on her way across town to bring Willard home. She saw the empty streets, the last walkers in the park. Reed's house, dim as ever; Prince, hushed and at a loss; Willard in the dark room.

He would accuse her of deserting the girls, or would they be downstairs, bewildered and wrapped in blankets, like refugees? What she wanted was to enter the room, for him to look up at her as Louise did, as Marilyn did, and reach up his arms. Then she would enfold him with love, as strong as the love she had for the girls.

The girls had been asleep thirty minutes. Why rouse them, bother them, drag them across town? Why frighten them? She might ask a neighbor to stay with them, but what if one of the girls woke needing her? She remembered the first minutes after she heard about her parents' accident. Here it was, death again, just the same as it had been.

When she reached Reuben, he asked what she wanted him to do.

"I don't know. I feel like I should be in two places, here and there."

"Who knows what condition Willard's in. A man who's been drinking, lost his father. I'll go."

"Oh, I don't think it's that bad," Sadie said. "Prince said he'd been drinking, but Prince probably thinks one drink is a lot after all that herbal tea. You come stay with the girls."

"Absolutely not," Reuben said. "It's late, you have no business running around. What are we talking about anyway? He'll be home in an hour. That's it, I don't want to talk about it anymore."

Sadie hung up the phone and put on water for coffee. She had to wonder, when it was too late, was it a better thing that Reuben was going? Maybe Willard would have been happier to see her, or maybe he did need a man to lead him away from Reed's deathbed. Maybe it was her place as his wife to go no matter what. But these were guesses, and Sadie was sure only that she had just done the wrong thing.

Eleven

THE CHURCH IN TUXEDO PARK WAS BUILT AT THE fence, very near the gate. In the early days, Tuxedo servants from the Park and the village worshiped there, entering by the side door on Sunday evenings, enjoying a separate service. Sheltered by tall pines, the stone Gothic church was chilly even in spring when the earth was thawed and the lawns of Tuxedo were covered with violets.

The church, like everything else in Tuxedo, needed attention: a coat of paint, dusting and polishing. The memorial window didn't glow; the stained-glass figures of a saint and his flock of sheep were cloudy.

The door opened and slammed shut. A man and a woman stood at the back of the church. The man was slight, with a boyish, handsome face, dressed in a suit years out of fashion, his hair slicked back and combed carefully. He had a clear expression, as if he had nothing to hide. The woman was blond and as tall as the man, plainly and somberly dressed. She had a distinguished face, with a long thin nose and a heavy jaw. Looking at her, Sadie felt young and crude. The man met Sadie's eyes and looked startled, touched the woman's arm and nodded. They sat a few pews behind Sadie and the girls, who'd never been in a church before.

The night of Reed's death, her brother had helped Willard in, and Reuben stayed in the mews house for days, missing work, sleeping on the couch, taking Willard out for air once a day. He kept the girls quiet and even in bed Reuben seemed to be there, hovering. Willard fell asleep clothed the first night. She'd reached over to stroke his back but he didn't stir, as if she didn't exist.

The morning of the funeral, Reuben was gone before the girls were up. He returned in his black lawyer's suit, hair combed as flat as he could make it. He said, "It's time, Sadie," as if she were holding things up. He led them outside to the black Cadillac limousine that waited outside. The girls wouldn't get in and Louise started crying. She didn't like the black, she said. "Don't be silly," Sadie said. "How did you think we'd get to your grandfather's funeral, by subway? The subway doesn't go to Tuxedo Park."

The girls kicked their mary janes on the plush seats, slipping their white-gloved hands over the upholstery, and breathing on the chrome door gadgets, watching their distorted reflections cloud over and emerge clear.

Reuben led Willard out to the car. He had him by the arm and Reuben's lips were moving. Sadie wondered if he was saying, "Just a little more," as if to an invalid. Reuben had done everything—on the telephone he'd made arrangements for the church, for the house, for the burial. The Cadillac pulled away from the mews noiselessly, heavily, down the slant of Ninety-fifth Street, past the red-brick school, over the river to Tuxedo.

From far away, Sadie thought, Tuxedo looked perfect, even when you knew the houses were crumbling and closed. Even then it looked as though there might be something going on—an extraordinary party that she hadn't been invited to. It was a place that reminded her of the opera, with people speaking in arias.

The organist struck the same chords again and again. Sadie took Marilyn's gloved hand and held it. They could repeat chords all day, she thought, the man didn't have any friends. Or if he did they were dead or in Palm Beach or wherever.

She reached across her husband and touched Reuben on his dark sleeve. "Prince," she whispered. "How's he getting here?"

Reuben shrugged. "Who knows?"

"Didn't you offer him a ride?"

"Sadie. Be quiet. This isn't the time."

"But he should *be* here."

Reuben shook his head.

The chords changed (thank God, she thought), and she told Louise, who was standing on her knees looking at the church, to turn around and sit. A minister appeared, younger than she expected. The hymn, he announced: "For all the saints who from their labors rest." After the singing, during which the organ drowned the faint voices of the congregation, the minister coughed and spoke.

"Revelation. Twenty-four. Verse four. 'And God shall wipe all tears from their eyes; and there shall be no more death, neither sorrow, nor crying, neither shall there be any more pain: for former things are passed away.' "

The church was cold. Louise puffed and saw her breath. Sadie heard a little sound. Marilyn was humming. Heaven. He was talking about it as if it existed, Sadie thought. She couldn't remember a word from her parents' funeral, only the ride out to the cemetery in Queens and back, the relatives who appeared at the apartment like a swarm of bees and whom she missed when they left her alone with Reuben. She closed her eyes and summoned up Reed's spirit: he was still in his house, he refused to leave.

Pale Willard, dark circles beneath his eyes, looked up at the end of the sermon. He yawned and looked around, leaned toward Sadie. "People may come to the house afterward," he said, his warm breath near her ear. She nodded, leaning toward him. "Don't let them stay long," he said. "Don't offer a second drink."

She nodded again, turned to look at him, but he masked his face with his hand.

FLANKED AT THE CEMETERY BY THE SMALL GIRLS, Sadie squeezed their hands to keep them in place. Louise squirmed. Marilyn leaned sleepily against Sadie's leg. Sadie looked around at the tombstones and read the black mildewed marble letters, trying to find a place between the angels for her and the girls.

Twelve

THERE WAS HOT COFFEE WAITING AT THE HOUSE, AND crustless sandwiches and cookies. Bottles of liquor stood on a table in the library, and a full ice bucket. Reuben went right to the liquor. Sadie made up plates of food for Louise and Marilyn, who were chilled from the cemetery and shy in the house that they remembered only vaguely.

"Sit over here," she said. "Come on. You haven't eaten since this morning. Take off your coats. Come on, darling. Put the sandwich down, Marilyn, before you take off your coat."

Willard poured himself a Scotch, carried it into the living room, and settled near the girls, watching them eat. Sadie put a plate of sandwiches by him but he didn't look at it. Sadie took a sandwich into the kitchen, where she ate, wiping her lips with her fingers. She heard someone at the front door, and stopped short. She washed her hands in the sink. When she got to the door, the man and woman from the church were shaking hands with Willard, being introduced to Reuben and the girls.

They turned to Sadie as she came into the entrance hall, and she felt like an interloper. Suddenly she was close to tears. We're all alive, she thought, and we just put Reed in the ground.

"This is my wife, Sadie," Willard said. "And Jimmy Baker, Helen Franklin."

"Hello," Sadie said, "I hope you'll come in for—"

"Oh, dear, no," Jimmy said. "We mustn't really. But we wanted to come, to see Willard, to—"

"Oh, Jimmy, just a short one." Helen's voice was stronger than Sadie would have expected from her pale, thin throat. "We don't see Willard at all these days, and we've known him forever, Sadie. Since we were children."

Marilyn and Louise looked up at Helen, then at their father.

"It's hard to imagine him as a child," Sadie said.

"You think I sprang full grown?" Willard asked.

"He was much the same," Helen said, and she laughed. "Jimmy stays the same, Willard gets better looking, and I grow old."

"Come," Sadie said, "a drink, and we have all this food."

"Well," Jimmy said, and exchanged a glance with Helen. "Just one small one. I'm expected elsewhere. But there's something about funerals that makes you want to drink."

"There's something about being awake that makes you want to drink," Helen said. "And no one's expecting you anywhere for three days except me. Honestly, you've lived too long in Tuxedo. Remember, Willard, how terrified he always was of being trapped at a Tuxedo party?"

In the pine library, while Sadie carried in trays of sandwiches and Willard made drinks, Jimmy asked the girls if they went to school and where, and how did they like Tuxedo Park, had they been all over the Park, they hadn't seen very much, had they, if they hadn't seen the lakes.

"We've come a few times for an afternoon," Sadie said, "but do you know, we've never stayed overnight. It's silly, I guess, this big house and all."

Helen said, "We all get stuck in place like a game of

statues. I hardly ever leave the Park. Except in winter. I give a big party and flee to town most of the week.''

"You don't leave because you're under an enchantment," Jimmy said. "You're the sleeping princess of the Park. When the spell's complete you'll stay all the time. You'll be the duenna at all the balls.''

"I'd have to be very sleepy for that.'' She laughed and said, "We're all enchanted here. When I do leave, I think, Why, it's marvelous out here in the world, why don't I do this more often?''

Sadie sat on the couch with the girls, listening to Helen, Jimmy, and Willard talk about people she didn't know. She tried to put an intelligent look on her face and to react just as Willard did—surprised at some pieces of news, pleased at others, as if she knew what was being said. He was coming out of it for Helen, she saw, acting as anyone might, not half dead with grief, only subdued. She had thought that only sudden death could stun that way, but Willard was reacting as though his father's death was unpredicted.

Sadie noticed Jimmy swirling the ice in his glass delicately, and said, "Have another drink? More to eat?''

"Goodness, no,'' Jimmy said.

"We really should run along,'' Helen said. She began gathering her things, and Sadie was about to press them again, invite them to come to the city for dinner, when Willard said, "For Christ's sake, Sadie, let the poor people go.''

They all stood for a moment, embarrassed, even the children, until Sadie said, "Oh, you're right, sweetie. But next time maybe,'' laughing as if it were a silly habit she couldn't stop herself from, offering hospitality.

When Jimmy and Helen were gone, Willard asked the girls if they were finished eating. Marilyn held out the end of a sandwich and he took it from her.

"Good,'' he said. "Do you know the gardens in back of the house?''

They nodded. He had hardly spoken to them for days and they listened carefully.

"You may go there," he said.

"It's almost dark," Sadie said.

"This is Tuxedo, not Riverside Park. They're perfectly safe. You may go into the gardens," he said, "but not into the woods. Not down by the road. Not anywhere near the lake. Only the gardens. And, Louise, you must look out for Marilyn."

"Yes, Willard," she said.

"Good," he said. "Come here." He kissed them, straightened their dresses. "It's warm enough to be without coats."

"Oh, Willard," Sadie said. "It isn't."

"If it gets cold," he said, "just come back in."

Without looking at Sadie, they ran for the door, flung it open, and went outside. She caught a glimpse of hill and woods. "I don't like it," she said when she couldn't hear their steps any longer.

"Stop looming," Willard said. He went across the living room, past the grand piano, and returned to the library. Reuben and Sadie followed him so closely that when he stopped before the drink table, they bumped into each other. As though we're afraid he'll get away, Sadie thought.

"Drink?" Willard offered. He looked around the room, parted the curtains. He poured himself a brandy. "Reuben? Sadie?"

"I could use another drink," Reuben said, and moved heavily past her.

Willard splashed some whiskey into a glass for Reuben, and settled in an armchair close to the fireplace.

The armchairs and couch were covered in a faded chintz. Sadie wondered who had planned the room. Reed's house in the city had the same inevitable quality. It didn't mean that the houses were beautiful, only that they were whole in a way that the mews house wasn't. It must be a question of time, Sadie thought.

"Willard," she said, "I have a crazy idea." She knelt by his armchair, her back to Reuben, touching Willard's hand. "Let's stay here, sweetie. Just us and the girls. We haven't ever stayed here, and they'd love it."

"Why would we want to stay here?"

"To be together," she said. "I feel as if I haven't seen you in days. And this has been so awful for you, you're all done in. It would be an adventure for the girls. Reuben could send the car back for us in the morning."

Reuben sipped from his glass. Willard swirled his brandy.

"A whim," Sadie said. "A little wish. Please, Willard."

He said, "I wouldn't want to send Reuben away, would I? I wouldn't want to be impolite to Reuben, would I?"

"It would be less polite if you didn't offer me the car," Reuben said. "Then you'd be on the border of rudeness. Don't worry about me. I'll find my way home."

"You've been a champ, Reuben. We'll all go back together. We came together and we'll leave together. Anyway, the nights are still chilly, and we'd all catch cold," Willard said. "I'm surprised you didn't think of that first, Sadie. It's just the kind of thing you always think of."

She wished for a way to remind Willard that here, in his mother's garden, he had heard the news about their first child. She wanted to tell him that she had given him everything and was happy to continue, but give her a sign, a word. Willard rested his head against the high back of the chintz armchair. He looked like Reed now and would look more like him with age; the fine lines in his pale skin, the thinning hair. There would be less of Willard with time, she thought, less to love, less to hate.

"I'll be outside," she said. "I don't hear the girls anymore. I don't want them getting lost."

Willard grabbed her wrist when she stood, and pulled her down to him again, kissing her cheek and releasing her. "One minute more. Then I'll go."

Thirteen

THE WOODS ON THE HILL ABOVE THE HOUSE LOOKED AS though they held darkness at their center, a pit for little girls to fall into, the blackness of the pupil of an eye.

They climbed up the hill, ignoring the cold (it was not so warm as Willard had promised). As they trampled the old stone steps the smell of herbs sprang up, a reminder of all they didn't know about this place. Burs stuck to their ankle socks. A branch scratched Marilyn's hand, and it was hard for her to keep up with Louise. At last, at the edge of the woods, Louise stopped and they looked up to the top of the rocky hill to a castle, empty and lonely. When their father was a child, he'd played with the castle boy. No one lived there now.

"Dark," Marilyn whispered.

"So what?"

Marilyn followed Louise up toward the woods. She would rather have been in the house, even with its musty smell. When the bare outlines of the overgrown garden ended, Marilyn hesitated and Louise said, "Come on."

"Hold my hand."

"That's dumb," Louise said. "We can't walk," but she took her sister's gloveless hand in hers and walked on. Soon Louise was holding only one finger, tugging at the round little girl. "Come on." Marilyn turned to look back at the lighted house. Louise tugged at her again.

"We're almost there," she said; then she tripped over a mossy rock and fell, bringing Marilyn down with her. They lay still for a minute, testing the temperature of the ground, breathing the sharp, moldy scent of the forest floor.

"Look," Marilyn said. She pointed to a rusty urn taller than she, a few feet from where they'd landed. Louise scrambled up to it, and stood on tiptoe to see over its edge. She looked down into a long empty hole, and saw icy black water, the moon reflected at the bottom. Marilyn came up beside her, jumping up to see over the edge. She tried climbing up the side and Louise said, "Don't. You'll get hurt. You'll fall."

"What's in there?"

"Just water," Louise said. But it was more, something to do with her grandfather's open grave and the blackness that she walked through in her dreams. She backed away, pulling Marilyn down the hill.

"The castle," Marilyn said.

"Come on," Louise said, "I want to go back," hurrying through the oncoming darkness, thinking of the water.

SADIE SAT OUTSIDE ON THE STONE WALL BETWEEN THE house and the ruined hill garden. If she turned, she could make out their forms as they moved down the steps toward her. She would scold them, she thought, for going into the woods, though she knew, as Willard had said, they were safe on this hill. It was theirs, or would be some day.

She pulled her jacket around her as the stone grew sharp and cold against her flesh. How little Willard would let her do for him. The girls were sneaking up behind her, whispering and giggling.

She stayed as she was, head bent, arms pulled in to her sides, waiting for their small hands to touch her, surround her.

Fourteen

ONCE A YEAR CHERRY SHOWED HER PAINTINGS TO A painter, critic, or dealer, to someone who counted. The private occasion in her studio marked her progress since she had no gallery and had been in a group show only a few times. For the showing, she looked at her work and chose what was good enough to be seen. She cleaned the studio, washed glasses, bought a fresh bottle of Scotch.

Each year she used the words to feed herself for another stint of waitressing or working at the frame shop. She accepted the critical opinion of whomever she invited as her agenda for the year: more sense of the canvas, less color, more drawing, more color, less shape. She didn't care what Willard thought because he didn't like any New York painting. It was aggravating that he didn't appreciate what the New York painters were up to, but wonderful that he was indifferent to Bradley. Every painter she knew, even people who never read anything but the ads in the subway, made their way through his articles on abstraction and mainstream painting. She had been in New York almost ten years and finally Bradley was coming to see her work. She wished she had more to show.

She had seen him around for years, but he acknowledged her only when she was with Willard. The men talked, mostly about people they knew in Paris, Bradley nodded to her, then it was over. But when she called him up to ask him to come to her studio, he recognized her name before she could slip in Willard's and he said he'd be happy to drop by.

He used her phone as soon as he arrived, talking for twenty minutes to an important dealer (she thought she recognized the first name) about a painter Bradley liked. His big head tilted to one side, Bradley pantomimed thirst and she brought him a Scotch on the rocks, which he set near her drawings. Now, as he looked around, she regretted calling him. He was not a large man but he seemed so in her studio, and the room with its easel and Saratoga trunk looked amateurish and insignificant. He was smoking a cigar that he told her was Cuban and very good, but it made her gag like the ordinary cigars her father smoked.

He looked at the paintings lined up against the wall, stepped back as far as he could (he almost backed into the front door), squinted, covered one eye, looked again. Then he opened the portfolio of drawings and looked briefly at them, sighing but persevering, as if to demonstrate that he was an honorable man.

Finally, he looked around for a place to set his cigar and she held out an ashtray for him. He took one last puff before surrendering it.

"So," he said, "first of all, you're painting too small. You can't accomplish that kind of patterning on this scale. Forget it. Also, your ideas of painting are too literal. You think it's Milton Avery but it's really . . . oh, maybe, Chagall, only with a squint. Those little lines." He smiled at his joke and she hated herself for smiling back.

"Seriously, Cherry," he said. "There are so many painters and you look at what's being done now. It's vision. I mean, tremendous changes in the whole way of perceiving what painting is. Changes that come from the historic roots of art."

"So?"

"So you're not getting any younger, are you? And
you're not a very good painter and you never will be. I
wonder what's kept you going this long." He looked at
her studiously.

"I want this. More than anything. I went to art school
for a while," she said, "long enough. So I've worked
without a teacher, but—"

"I know," he said. "I know your whole life story. You
don't have to tell me. You were the best in your class in
your little podunk town. You wanted out. Your mother
and father objected, they wanted to keep you there but
you insisted. Just a year. So they staked you. Your father
owns the hardware store, right?" He looked again at the
paintings, and he turned his gaze to her, appraising her
face and body, her tongue licking her lips, her nervous
cigarette smoking.

"Right," she said. She would pour herself a drink at
the count of ten. He was an ugly man with bad teeth and
a sharp nose, his forehead like a ledge, and his vanity
greater than his intelligence. But still she looked to him
for something to keep her going.

He moved toward her and though she knew she should
step aside, Cherry stood her ground. His large belly, sur-
prisingly hard, pressed against her. He put his face
against hers and pushed his tongue into her mouth and
she thought that she should have expected this. He took
her breast in his hand and squeezed, as if he were testing
it. His tongue was grainy as a cat's, and Cherry gasped.

"Ah," he said, and he looked around the room. She
thought now she might push him away, but he tightened
his grip on her arm and pushed her toward the old studio
bed. She said, "Wait," and tried to pull away. He
pressed her to him, taking her hips in his hands and
squeezing, again as if he were testing her quality. He
changed direction, pushing her toward the wall. Cherry
caught a glimpse of their backward tango reflected in the
window. He propped her against the wall, trying to reach
her through her layers of skirt and slip and underwear.
Somehow, he had opened his pants, while he covered her

mouth with his, so she couldn't breathe or call out. He lifted her skirt, jamming his erection into her so that she groaned. She wondered if he would tear her and hoped she might bleed to death. He was finished in a moment and let go of her so suddenly that she staggered in place. He moved away swiftly, saying, "My knees. I'm not so limber as I once was." Then he disappeared into the bathroom.

She was sitting in her work chair when he came out of the bathroom, looking at his watch and saying, "My God, I didn't realize . . ."

"Just get out," she said.

He looked around again and she said, "Over there," and pointed to his briefcase and *Times*. He reached past her to his cigar, now dead in the ashtray, and she leaned away from his arm. He said, "Ah, Cherry. Come on. Don't be childish."

She looked at him and looked away. Then he was gone. After a few more minutes, she went into the bathroom and showered for a long time, came out in her robe, and poured herself a drink. She stared at the paintings against the wall. She squinted at them, blocked portions with her hands.

Cherry stayed in the studio for hours, smoking and drinking, squinting at her paintings until the sun went down. She went into the kitchen, looked in her empty refrigerator, closed the door against its bright light, went back into her studio. The phone rang once that night and not at all the next day. She stared down the black instrument, daring it to ring.

When Cherry thought about it, she had to admit that she had had sex with people for less reason and with the same lack of desire, but this time she'd been sober. She hoped that whatever else happened to her, she would never tell anyone what had taken place.

Nights, alone in her apartment, the paintings still lined up, Cherry thought of her mother, two hours into New Jersey, alone in her half of the Spruce Street house. She thought of the distance between them and drew a line between the dots. Sometimes the line turned into a rope, pulling Cherry toward her mother, sometimes it lay slack. Her mother was always her anchor. She could never have left home without her mother's permission. She saw this now for the first time, though she'd always before imagined herself a rebel. Now Cherry wanted her mother to step forward and deny the years Cherry had been away. She wanted her mother to call up and say, This is enough, dear. Please, come home.

ON A PLEASANT SATURDAY AFTERNOON, CHERRY TOOK the bus to Hackettstown. After a few hours, she saw Budd Lake, the white club building and the restaurant and ice-cream stand, the changing room for visitors. It wasn't open yet, she saw. It took until Memorial Day for people to admit that it was spring.

After the lake there were scrawny farms, their roadside stands still full of winter debris, and then the bus took her down into the valley. She wondered if she should have called her mother but now it was too late. The bus climbed up the big hill, then swung down again, leveling out at the Sunoco station, the beginning of town. There was the Presbyterian church and Main Street, the wallpaper store with its door wide open. Lilacs bloomed in front of the old houses crowded between stores and churches. The same faded cardboard cutout of a banana split was propped in the window of the Cottage Luncheonette.

The bus stopped in front of the corner drugstore, and Cherry went inside for a pack of cigarettes, arming herself against seeing someone she knew or being recognized by someone from high school.

She walked slowly down the other side of Main Street, looking in the hardware store window at the display of seeds and terra-cotta pots and in the sewing store at the bolts of summer cottons.

Cherry hesitated before her mother's door, then rang the bell and went in, calling, "It's me." In her mother's bedroom, the bed was made tightly, the dresser covered with framed pictures of Cherry at all ages up to eighteen. The house was clean and neat as ever, the kitchen linoleum waxed to a shine even in the places where it rose and split. Cherry went into her bedroom and set her handbag on the dresser. She took out a silver flask Willard had given her and had a drink, then rinsed her mouth with Listerine at the kitchen sink. Back in her room she brushed her hair with an old hairbrush. In the corner of the dresser mirror was a snapshot of her mother taken years before. It was as if they knew only each other—there were no photos of them together or of anyone else.

She heard the front door and went out.

"Mom," she called out. "Here I am."

Martha's face broadened into a smile, and she said, "Well, this is quite a surprise, Cherry. I hope everything's all right?"

"Let me take the bag," Cherry said, reaching for the grocery sack her mother held.

"No, no. It's more trouble to hand it over than to carry it to the kitchen."

Martha put the groceries down on the green Formica table and turned to Cherry. "Well," she said, "what a surprise," giving Cherry a kiss and looking at her critically. Cherry had put on little makeup and she wore a skirt.

Cherry said, "I just felt like visiting," as if it weren't the only time she'd done so except for Christmas since she'd left home.

She watched as her mother unloaded the same brands of canned vegetables and soap she'd always bought.

"Look," her mother said. "I bought two fresh peaches. You usually don't see them just now, but the A&P had them. Even though they're so dear. Now I'm glad I did because you're here."

Cherry tried to remember another time when her mother had ever said anything extra to her.

"That's nice," she said. "I like them too." She sat at the table and pushed aside a can of string beans. She laid her head in her arms and closed her eyes. When she left home, she swore never to cry again in front of her mother. They'd had such fights at this table. She remembered crying until her eyes were slits and gulping for air through her tears. She wished she would cry again like that, but she looked up dry-eyed.

"I'm sorry," she said. "I'm kind of tired, and I've been having a bad time."

"That's fine," her mother said. "I don't mind." She wiped her immaculate counters, then asked if Cherry would like a cup of tea or a sandwich.

"No, thanks," Cherry said. She wondered if she felt this miserable because she was home or if she'd come home because of the misery. She tried to remember how she'd felt that morning in her own apartment and it seemed worse.

"You're welcome to stay here, you know," her mother said. "Until things look brighter."

Cherry laughed. "You never used to talk about things looking brighter."

"Well. Maybe people change."

"I didn't bring much with me. I didn't bring a toothbrush."

"Well, I guess you can buy a toothbrush at the drugstore, Cherry. If you'd like to stay. It seems a shame to go all the way back to New York for a toothbrush."

Cherry felt like crying with relief that she'd retreated here safely and didn't have to think of going back. She was glad when her mother looked at the clock and announced that she was going to take a little nap before supper.

SHE WALKED TO THE DRUGSTORE, FORCING HERSELF TO take it slowly. In the city she walked fast and saw everything in a blink. She stopped before the open door of the wallpaper store and stared at the piles of sample books. When Cherry was in her first year of high school, her mother let her pick new wallpaper for her bedroom as her birthday present. Cherry had strained her eyes looking over the sample books, worried that her choice would be wrong and would show people something shameful about her. Now she wondered why she hadn't just chosen paper she liked, and who she thought would see it anyway. She had only one friend who came to the house, Angela, and she'd gotten pregnant that year, and moved to Wilkes-Barre.

In the drugstore, Cherry bought a blue toothbrush and a tube of Colgate. Her mother used salt. She bought a Revlon lipstick, Melon Red, though she rarely wore lipstick. Around the corner, she stood in front of the liquor store window, staring at the pyramid of gin bottles, wondering if it was really gin or water and if the liquid evaporated inside the bottles. She decided she'd better not bring any more liquor into her mother's house, then went into the store and bought a half pint of Scotch. Cherry was glad there was a new clerk in the store. The old one must have died, she thought. For a while Martha blamed the clerk for Cherry's father's binges, saying he shouldn't sell to a drunk.

As she walked back down Main Street toward home, Cherry considered calling Willard to tell him she would be away for a while, but she thought that maybe she would only stay for a night and why bother. The only place she ever called him was at his office and he was rarely there these days, more often with lawyers or his brother-in-law, discussing his father's estate, he said, or spending time with his daughters. Everything had changed, she thought, her painting, her life in the city, Willard. Since his father's death, he talked more about his family, and she guessed he'd stick with his wife and daughters, become a family man, though she couldn't see it for him. Still, it was none of her business. The way it worked with him was that she kept her distance. She listened if he talked, but she never asked.

Cherry walked by the phone booth at the Cottage Luncheonette. On her mother's block, she saw a maple bright with new leaves, and Cherry forced herself to stop and examine the light as it passed through the green. She was completely happy then and even after the intensity of the happiness passed, Cherry was able to keep feeling good all the way to her mother's door.

Fifteen

SADIE FELT AS THOUGH SHE HAD NEVER LEARNED ANYthing before in her life—how had she learned to read or to count? Starting a car, steering, one foot on the brake, pressing in the clutch, to put it all together and move the machine forward and backward without jerking and stalling, without causing Mr. Garcia to brace himself against the dashboard—these were accomplishments. Her lessons were forty-five minutes long, and Sadie emerged from them drained and exuberant. She was moving again, though she couldn't place when she'd stopped moving nor what she was moving toward.

Mr. Garcia's school was on Broadway at Ninety-ninth Street, and he generally drove them up Riverside Drive to Grant's Tomb. She admired his driving, his small feet so casual on the pedals, smart in their wing tips; his pudgy hands resting like pads on the steering wheel. He knew to stop at lights, to check the rearview mirror. She had decided to learn to drive on the way home from Reed's funeral and she'd found Mr. Garcia in the Yellow Pages, the AAAA School of Driving. He taught her very slowly and patiently, and she wondered if he did so to get more money from her. She didn't care. He was her professor of the automobile and she had to trust him.

A few weeks into the lessons, he told her she was ready

for Broadway. "Well, I don't know," Sadie said, but Garcia held up one hand and said, "I am the judge."

It was particularly quiet at the tomb. The fruit trees in the park were blooming, the grass was getting green, and the sky was very clean and blue. Lights, Sadie thought, and people. "You'll go up that street," he said, "take a right, and drive down Broadway to the school. To your home, if you like." She imagined it: pulling up before the mews, maybe Willard and the girls outside, astonished that she could drive. There were so many old people in the neighborhood, though, who walked around hunched over, frail old people whom she might overlook. There were dogs and cats, the red-brick school down the street was full of children. The tomb, which she had circled that morning, looked safe and familiar. She wondered when she had become such a coward and tried to summon up courage.

Mr. Garcia was gazing at himself in the sideview mirror. His hair was perfectly in place, but he smoothed an eyebrow, forcing it in line. He turned to her and sighed. "The time is really up," he said. "Perhaps for the next lesson, if you don't have the feeling for it now."

She felt ashamed and relieved. "It's silly of me. Only a few blocks." She wanted to tell him that she was not always this way, that she took care of two little girls, had the whole responsibility for them and didn't shirk any task that arose, but he said, politely, "I think you are ready, but you must have confidence." Garcia's sweet cologne was sickening in the warm car.

"I need more experience," she said.

They got out of the car to change places so that he could drive them downtown, but Sadie stayed outside when Mr. Garcia took the driver's seat.

"I'll walk," she said. "It's such a nice day and I'm not expected home for a while."

"Such a long walk," he said, adjusting the mirror for himself, but he started the car and put it in gear, ready to leave her.

"Well," Sadie said, hesitating. When she'd first seen

Mr. Garcia she'd worried he might put a hand on her or pinch her, but he always kept his distance. She got into the car again, hating herself.

When she opened the door to the mews house, she heard the last chords of the "Trout Quintet" and the low murmur of the radio announcer. Willard was lying on the living-room couch, a half-eaten sandwich on the table beside him. He was reading the paper. He looked up when she came up next to him, and he scowled.

"I've kept you waiting?" she asked.

"Not really," though he glanced at his watch. She remembered that once when she was pregnant with Marilyn, he guessed that she felt exhausted, and, without asking, had taken Louise out for the day. They'd gone to a museum or the zoo, Sadie couldn't remember, then to a fancy French restaurant on the East Side, not the kind of place you usually take a child. Louise arrived home clutching a pink swizzle stick.

"You're finished with this?" Sadie asked, and picked up his sandwich plate. He followed her into the kitchen where she made herself a chicken sandwich, applying mustard to one side, mayonnaise to the other, layering pickles, lettuce, tomatoes.

"How can you stand all of that?" he asked.

"I like a big sandwich. Something on your mind?"

"I'm very concerned about the girls."

She looked up from the sandwich, wary. "Why? They're so—" She wanted to say that they were perfect.

"I worry about their safety. In the city."

Reed had died without a word for him. For the first terrible weeks, Willard felt as oppressed by his father's death as by his life, but now it was as if someone who had been holding him back released him without warning, and Willard was flying. He might lead any life, with Sadie and the girls, or without them. To lose them would be to lose both their devotion and the burden of them. He hadn't touched his Whistler monograph for months; now he decided it was a silly occupation, and he might be free of that too. He felt such warmth in his body, surges of

energy that made him impatient with everyone. He was
sure for once in his life that he would find an answer. He
had no clear plans but quick visions. He wished that
Sadie and the girls might remain just as they were now;
then he would have the time to see what it was he wanted
to do.

"There are a million dangers. Children are kidnapped
every day. There are strangers all around who could
mean them harm. And they aren't free in the city. Between the dangers and the germs, they're too restricted."

"You sound like Reed," she said.

"Some of his ideas were sound," Willard said.

"So you want Louise to go to private school?"

"I'm talking about something larger," he said. "Not
just private school, their whole little world. I'm not sure
I want them growing up with these vistas."

Sadie put her sandwich on a plate and pushed the plate
away from her. "What do you mean, vistas?"

"I think we should be willing to experiment a little,
darling. For them. Give them a chance at something better. I'm thinking of moving the family to Tuxedo Park.
For the summer, that is, then perhaps elsewhere. I have
an idea but it isn't fully formulated."

"You hate Tuxedo Park," she said. "You told me it
was provincial and small minded, and that it was going to
the dogs. And what am I supposed to do there? What
would I do all day there?"

"You don't have to come," he said.

Sadie was suddenly vigilant. She asked, "I don't have
to come?"

"You could come out when you liked. You could continue your lessons."

"My driving lessons? This isn't a career, Willard. I'll
have my license soon. Mr. Garcia says I'm ready for
Broadway."

"I suppose he knows his business, but driving in a car
with a teacher beside you is an entirely different matter
from being on your own. I've discussed the whole matter
with Reuben," he said. "He agrees that it makes sense

to move the girls to a safer place, and for you to have more free time. You might take some courses. Complete your degree . . .''

"Just a minute," Sadie said. "Before you have me getting my doctorate, tell me again what's supposed to be so great about Tuxedo Park. Make me understand.''

"In the Park," he said, looking patient, "no one enters without the guard's permission. There are cars on the road, but they go very slowly. There's a fence around the place, as you know. The whole place is safe as a bank vault. It's practically a playground. And you'd be much freer. We'll get a governess—''

"Hey, what's going on?" She laughed and kissed him. "Are you trying to get rid of me?''

"Of course not, darling. But the girls love the idea, you know. They're already looking forward to it.'' He smiled and went to the kitchen door. "I know you don't understand, but you will in time. There's no need to get upset. I'll be home this evening and we'll discuss the matter further.''

Sadie waited in the kitchen until she heard the door to their house open and close, the gate to the mews open and close, then sat down heavily at the kitchen table and looked at her trembling hands. She didn't feel very often as though she understood Willard or stood a chance against him. If she didn't agree, she would be left behind, for how could she stop Willard from doing anything.

Sixteen

SHE WAITED A DAY AND THEN A WEEK, HOPING WIL-
lard would change his mind about the Tuxedo summer,
as he and the girls had started calling it. She overheard
them talking, Louise and Marilyn asking if they could
swim in Tuxedo, play in the woods, did they have ice
cream in the club and would he let them have some, but
she didn't ask questions. Sadie pretended the summer
wasn't going to happen, and Willard, after offering her
the chance to travel for a month ("Europe should be
marvelous in June"), changed his mind and urged her to
go with him and the girls to Tuxedo Park. "I'll feel better
about you there than in the city," he told her one night
after they'd made love. "I'd worry about you without
us."

One afternoon, while Willard took the girls for haircuts
at Best & Co., Sadie met Reuben for lunch in a dark
Spanish restaurant near Eighth Avenue. He'd ordered
paella for them both.

"Don't you look relaxed," she said, sitting down.
She'd run from the bus; sweat trickled down one side of
her face.

"I've ascended to a certain level of maturity," Reuben
said. "I don't try to change things. I accept them as they
are."

"Such as?" She ordered sweet vermouth on the rocks
and reached for the bowl of green olives.

"Such as ever since you had Louise you're fifteen minutes late. I thought it might double with Marilyn, but it's
held steady at fifteen."

"I didn't know you were counting," she said.

"Don't get huffy," he said. "It's the truth. Nothing to
apologize for."

"Who's apologizing? I'd like to see you or anybody be
on time if it meant dressing two little girls and organizing
them and pinning down Willard . . ."

"Willard?"

"Oh, the master of evasion. When he'll be home. If
he'll take the girls. Which classy penal colony he's taking
us to."

"Your husband has things on his mind," Reuben said.

"Such as?"

Reuben made a face to show her he didn't want to talk
about it anymore.

"Legal palaver," he said. "The estate is complicated.
We've been helping him with it."

"You and Train?"

"And the family lawyer. A character straight out of
Dickens."

"What about Prince? What happens to him?"

"Willard didn't tell you? Reed gave him a pension, or
a sum tantamount to a pension, and that's that. Willard
offered him something from the house, all those years of
taking care of it, I guess he thought it was right. I thought
I explained this to you—the house and its contents will
be auctioned off, and the proceeds go to form a trust for
the girls. The building downtown goes to Willard and he
may sell it soon. The Tuxedo house is Willard's for life
use, then it's theirs—the same arrangement Reed had."

"What did Prince choose? Or is he still making up his
mind?"

"Willard gave him a week to clear out. He chose that
mirror in the hallway, the one with the gold around it.
Fake, Willard said."

"After all those years of service, a week's notice and he's out on the sidewalk with a mirror?"

"I gather he has relatives down south. North Carolina, maybe," Reuben said. "Don't get sentimental about Prince, he always treated you like something the cat dragged in. Willard worse, I gather."

"He never liked him," she conceded, "but I thought that Reed—"

"Such an innocent," he said. "Always thinking the best of people. Ready for paella?"

"Not really. Oh, I don't care. I hate women who complain," she said as the steaming pan was set on the table. "I sit in the playground all day with women who complain."

"You shouldn't be wasting your time in the playground," he said. "Go back to school. Get someone for the girls. A nursemaid."

"I don't want the girls with strangers," she said, "is that so odd?"

"Who said anything about odd? You don't eat mussels, do you? If not, I'll take them all."

She watched Reuben eat and pushed the seafood around in the saffron rice until it looked as though she'd eaten.

Over coffee, she said, "Reuben, I need your help."

"Anything," he said. "Name it."

"I don't want to go to Tuxedo for the summer and Willard won't listen to me. Help me. Please. It'll be horrible for me. A bunch of anti-Semitic snobs. That big house. Please."

"I don't understand," he said. "I thought you liked the country."

"Oh, God," she said. "You too? I like New Jersey. I like cows. But there's a *fence* around the place, Reuben. I can't talk to Willard. He's fixed on this idea of sending us out there. Which side are you on, Reuben? Whose brother are you?"

"There are no sides, Sadie. You married someone

from Tuxedo Park," he said, "why are you getting so upset about spending some time there?"

"All right, all right," she said. "I'll bet you won't even visit."

"Of course I'll visit," he said. "If I'm invited."

"Invited! I'm dreading going and you worry about being invited."

"Why are you dreading it?" he asked. "If you really didn't want to go, Willard wouldn't make you, would he?"

"No. Of course not. He's just been so miserable since Reed died," she said. "Leave it alone, Reuben."

Later, she walked her brother to his building and watched him disappear into the crowd of businessmen and office workers in the arcaded lobby. She didn't have the energy to visit Arlie, even for a minute. She would tell Willard she'd changed her mind about Tuxedo Park. Sadie looked at her watch, saw that she was late to meet Willard and the girls, and she ran to the corner, looking desperately up and down Fifth Avenue, telling herself that if she found a big yellow cab everything would work out fine.

Seventeen

WILLARD WASN'T SURPRISED THAT CHERRY WASN'T home. He'd been trying her when he could in the last few weeks, but he'd been busy settling Reed's estate and supervising the move to Tuxedo, and he lost track of how long it had been since he'd spoken to her.

He should leave a note for Cherry, but he couldn't stand the thought of taking out notepad and pen, deciding what to say. He kept walking away from her street, down Bleecker toward Washington Square, and he relished his movement. At the triumphal arch in the Square, Willard looked up at the figures stuck in marble and imagined that once Sadie and the girls were in Tuxedo Park, he might do anything.

He wondered, moving uptown along Fifth Avenue, how he would find Cherry and how hard he should try. Once Sadie and the girls were settled in Tuxedo, he would go by the frame shop and her favorite bar to see if Cherry was all right.

WHEN WILLARD LET HIMSELF INTO THE MEWS HOUSE later that night, Sadie was asleep on the couch, a book lying on her chest. He traced the line of her cheekbones and when she opened her eyes, she seemed not to know who he was. He imagined for a second a life without Sadie's recognition, and he took her hand in his. She said, "I tried to stay awake."

"So I see," he said.

"I thought . . . one of our last nights in the mews house. For a while."

"Sentimental," he said.

"I am sentimental. A sentimental girl. I've always told you so."

PART
THREE

One

LOUISE LEFT HER BED, CAREFUL NOT TO DISTURB MARilyn, who slept as usual with her limbs flung, her mouth open. She tiptoed to the open door of her parents' room and watched the still forms until she was afraid that Sadie would feel her there and awaken.

Downstairs, Louise opened the refrigerator and saw eight eggs, a loaf of bread, a bottle of milk. The vegetable bins were empty, the inner walls of the refrigerator gleamed. Louise settled on the living-room couch, which Sadie had covered with summer slipcovers. She tried to memorize the print that hung next to the bookshelves of the temple of the sibyl, who knew everything, Willard said. Each time Louise looked, she saw something new in the print, this time a woman leaning into the fountain. She looked around the room, trying to memorize everything, to hold each object in place when she closed her eyes, but each time she lost something—the old rocker, the silver-framed photographs of Sadie's parents and Reed, the iron lamp in back of Sadie's armchair. If she could lose these things so quickly, what would happen over the summer in Tuxedo. She closed her eyes again and thought of the gate, the road, the lake, the house, and the castle above the garden. It was a whole world, large as the one she already had.

When they returned in the fall, Sadie said, everything would be just the same except that Louise would start at the red-brick school across West End Avenue, so Louise half wished that something would happen to prevent their return. She wondered if the sibyl knew what would happen.

Louise took off one of her socks and tucked it behind the couch cushion, then curled up and fell asleep again, waking when Sadie came down the stairs and found her there.

THEY DIDN'T LEAVE UNTIL AFTERNOON. MARILYN cried because Sadie wouldn't let her wear her party dress in the car, and then because she couldn't bring her tricycle. "Willard's bought you a bicycle with training wheels, Marilyn. It's waiting for you in Tuxedo." The girls' suitcases wouldn't close, and Sadie insisted Louise bring fewer stuffed animals, which caused tears, and led to an extra suitcase for stuffed animals. Sadie annoyed Willard by packing a picnic basket with peanut butter and jelly sandwiches and two thermoses, one with milk, the other hot tea.

"For Christ's sake," he said, "it's under two hours' drive."

"When you travel with children, you have to be prepared," she said, as though he never had before.

They dragged all their luggage and paraphernalia out to the sidewalk. Willard had inherited the Straight Eight as part of the Tuxedo property, and Sadie and the girls stood and watched Willard put the convertible top down and try to pack everything one way and then another, filling the floor of the rumble seat, and the space behind the seats. A few bundles still remained on the sidewalk and he looked over the car, exasperated.

"The girls can sit up with us," Sadie said. "This car's like an ocean liner. We can all fit."

"No! I want to go in the rumble seat," Louise said.

Willard frowned at her and said, "Will you go there alone? Without your sister?"

"I don't know . . ." Sadie said.

"Yes," Louise said. "I can do it."

"Fine," Willard said. "That solves our problems. Now hop in. Fine. Thank you, Louise," and he loaded the rest in the rumble seat next to the little girl. She was dwarfed by the pile of luggage, her head coming barely over the side of the silver car.

When the car was loaded, Sadie stepped back, proud that he'd gotten everything in. She would keep an eye on Louise, and not mention that she'd rather have her up front, where she could hold her.

"You did a wonderful job," she said.

"Okies," he said. "Couldn't you have managed with less?"

"Should I start unpacking now?" she asked. "Come on. Let's jump in ourselves and go. This whole thing was your idea."

It was a clear, crisp city day, and all the shops they passed along Broadway looked new and inviting, as if she'd never seen them before. Sadie thought, That's New York for you, showing you what a dope you are to leave.

She told Marilyn, who'd climbed into her lap, "Say good-by to it. Doesn't Broadway look nice, Willard?"

"Very nice." He was concentrating on driving, staring ahead, checking in the rearview and sideview mirrors.

"But I'm sure Tuxedo looks very nice too," Sadie said.

"That's the whole point of Tuxedo. To look nice," he said. In a few blocks, he noticed a woman walking a German shepherd, and he said over his shoulder, "You know, Louise, in Tuxedo there are no strange dogs. I mean, all the dogs have owners and the owners are responsible for them. So you're safe."

Sadie laughed. "I didn't notice they were in danger from dogs," she said. "For heaven's sake. Don't put ideas in their heads."

"In the city," Willard said, "everything is arbitrary.

Do you know what arbitrary means, girls? It's when nothing makes sense." He looked at them in the rearview mirror. "There are all sorts of strays—dogs, cats, even people. And if children walked around unattended—"

"They'd be strays too!" Louise called out.

"They never do walk around unattended," Sadie said. "What are you talking about?"

"This is a hypothetical case," Willard said patiently, "something that might or might not—"

"I know what a hypothetical case is," she said.

"It could happen very quickly. When you aren't looking. Rabid animals strike fast."

"There hasn't been a rabid animal in New York State since nineteen twenty-six," she said. This was the sort of fact Reuben used to come up with to win arguments, and by the time she'd checked, it was too late for either to care if he was lying or not. Willard said, "There are other problems besides rabid animals."

"We're going to Tuxedo," Sadie said. "You've won. Relax."

"I'd like one," Louise said. "A white one."

"A gray one," Marilyn said.

"White what? Gray what?" Willard asked.

"Rabbit," Louise said. "Can't we have rabbits and a dog if we live in the country?"

LOUISE SAT UP AS STRAIGHT AS SHE COULD AND TRIED to memorize everything along the road—houses, churches, post offices, stores, billboards, cows, flowers. When she and Marilyn got tired of singing and counting things they saw, Sadie gave them sandwiches to keep them happy. At last, Willard announced that they were in the town of Tuxedo. Louise recognized the narrow houses along the road, like the ones she drew in school, but tilted because they were built against the steep hill. On Marilyn's side was a big building with a roof that sloped down like a mountain. Willard said, "That's where I'll take the train to go into the city."

"Should we shop for food now?" Sadie asked.

"Oh, Mrs. Misurelli will have dinner prepared."

"You didn't tell me," Sadie said.

"You didn't ask."

Sadie turned and told Louise to stay in her seat because they weren't there yet.

Willard greeted the guard and drove through the gates.

"Will he always let us in?" Marilyn asked.

"Unless you do something terrible," Willard said.

"Of course, he will," Sadie said. "He just wants to be sure that people don't get in who shouldn't."

"Like who?" Louise asked.

"People who shouldn't be here."

"But who are they?"

"I don't know," Sadie said. "I don't know anyone like that. But that's the idea. Look, girls. There's the lake."

"Can we go in one of those boats?" Louise asked.

"Of course," Willard said. He hated sailing but he supposed that, like a number of other things, he would do it for the girls.

When he stopped the car in front of their house, no one moved until Sadie opened the car door and got out. She said, "We're here because we're here. Come on, there's things to do. Key?"

"The door is open," he said. "We only lock it when we're away and—"

"Mrs. Misurelli," Sadie guessed. "I know."

She opened the door and looked into the domed entryway. Light came into the house from over the lake, through the glass porch, and from the woods through the Palladian window. It was a wonderful time of day, Sadie thought, the full afternoon, not edgy and worrisome like morning or pressing on you like evening.

Sadie began setting bundles and suitcases on the ground, saying, "Louise, sweetie? Do you want help getting out of there? Do you want your animals? Would you give me a hand? Marilyn, I see something of yours here," until the girls stood by her reluctantly, peeking at Willard, who still sat in the driver's seat.

"All right," Sadie said, "take something that you can carry, don't take too much, and let's go in and find you rooms."

"When's Daddy coming in?" Louise asked.

"When he's ready."

"When's that?"

"Only he knows. Let's go, girls, let's find some rooms for you."

THE TRUTH WAS, HE THOUGHT (RELIEVED NOT TO HEAR their voices or worry if anyone had to eat or go to the bathroom), he might not be able to endure this. The Park was stuffy in the summer, close and humid, and the house annoyed him, it always had.

Willard unloaded the last bundles from the car, remembering when he'd traveled all over Europe with one small bag, loathing Sadie's idea of packing, the unruly pile of belongings that she considered necessary for life. He parked the car in the garage, and entered the house through the musty basement, passing by the laundry room, the carpenter's shop, the wine cellar, and the big downstairs kitchen. He climbed the narrow steps between the basement and the upstairs kitchen, listening to footsteps up above and, faintly, voices. Sadie and the girls were invading the house.

He had underestimated Sadie. Her gift for domesticity was innocent but devouring, and it wore him down. Still, Tuxedo might be a match for her. Devouring, domestic, innocent, he repeated on his way to the pine library to savor the silence.

THE GIRLS FOLLOWED SADIE UP THE POLISHED, CURVing stairs. On the landing, Sadie asked, "Would you girls still like to share a room, just like at home? Or maybe you'd like to share a room *at first* and then later on—"

"I want my own room," Louise said.

"You do? You're sure?"

"I've never had my own room." She kept her eyes on her mother, not wanting to see if Marilyn looked as if her feelings were hurt.

"Well," said Sadie. "That's true. And how terrific now, Marilyn, you get your own room, you know? Just like Louise. And if you get scared, which you don't have to, but if you do, why, then you could stay together. Like you do at home."

"Where will you be?" asked Marilyn. She looked smaller to Sadie in the Tuxedo house.

"Well, that's a good question," Sadie said.

They followed her to a room with blue wallpaper figured with silver fleurs-de-lis and a canopy bed. Across a small alcove were two bedrooms, one facing the garden, the other the lake. The garden room had wallpaper with pink roses and gray ribbons, the lake bedroom was more severe, with cream and slate stripes. Neither looked like a room for a little girl.

"Now if you slept here," Sadie said, "one of you in each room, I mean, you'd be near me and near each other. Right, Marilyn?"

"Near Willard too," Louise said. Marilyn looked shocked at the idea of having her own room. Louise touched her sister's foot with her own and said, "You choose first because you're the baby."

Marilyn walked through the rooms, circling the beds slowly, looking out the windows. The striped room had a wicker rocker and a crinkly yellow bedspread.

"Stripes," she said, and Louise let out an explosion of breath because she'd wanted the rose room so badly. She ran into her bedroom, laughing and wondering if Marilyn had seen something she hadn't in the striped room.

Two

AFTER A WEEK, IT WAS AS IF THEY HAD ALWAYS BEEN there, though, like a visitor, Sadie was shy about opening drawers and closets.

One day she took the girls with her upstairs to the third floor of the house, announcing as they walked Indian file down the narrow corridor that this was depressing. "Six rooms," she said, "six servants. Can you imagine? I hate even having a cleaning lady, you know that, don't you, dolls? Look at these small rooms, one after the other. This one's all right, three windows and this is the best view of the lake, isn't it? Better than downstairs, well, that's a little joke, isn't it? I wonder what the servants were like, and did they have lives of their own. One day off and where could they go? Everyone here is supposed to complain all the time about the servant problem, I wonder if I will. Here's a joke I read in a book about Tuxedo: Q: 'How many servants do you have, Harry?' A: 'Oh, twelve. Six going, six coming.' "

"Who is Harry?" Louise asked. She opened a closet door and found two wire hangers on the floor.

"Don't touch anything," Sadie said, "you never know. It doesn't matter who Harry is, it's a joke."

Marilyn climbed gingerly up on a bare mattress that

rested on a painted iron bedstead. The plaster wall behind the bed was cracked like a spider web.

"When's Reuben coming?" she asked.

"Maybe the weekend," Sadie said. "I asked him but he didn't really say. Definitely for July Fourth. We'll see fireworks, sweeties, did you know?"

Willard slept late in the mornings, lay on the library couch reading all afternoon, dined in the club at night, then had insomnia. Sadie waited for him to invite her to the club. He took the girls there for swimming and for lunch, sometimes for dinner, leaving Sadie. She made more and more elaborate meals, never knowing if she'd be left to eat them alone. Though she never asked him to stay home, she told Willard in detail about each dish.

She took walks or drove at a snail's pace around the Park's curves, sometimes turning up unmarked roads. An old man dressed in plaid pants, a vest, and a sweater with holes at the elbows demanded her name and asked what she thought she was doing there. Behind him, past the steep circular driveway and wild hedge, rose a gloomy timbered cottage. She didn't expect the Park to be a friendly place but his assurance and contempt made her shake.

Willard pointed out that it was illegal for her to drive, but it got her out of the house (where she thought he wanted her to stay) and even if there were moments of fear when another car passed on the narrow road, Sadie liked driving. She wondered what would happen to them all if one day she drove the Straight Eight through the gates of Tuxedo Park and never returned, like an enchanted character in a child's storybook.

The girls slept with their doors open, and music drifted up to them when Sadie sat on the glassed-in porch, watching the end of the sunset over the lake. She tuned in the radio to dance music, and drank a highball. She considered going down to the club (she could see the roof just beyond the trees) and asking for Willard. She might approach the place from its broad terrace and find him herself. He might see her as if she were a stranger, be

interested in her and then realize that she was his, she
was Sadie. But she knew that her appearance in the club
would be like driving up a driveway thinking it was a road
—an honest mistake—and being humiliated for it.

Whom did he talk to, she wondered, and what was the
talk about? Perhaps the women were very pretty and if
she wore the dinner dress she'd picked up at Saks just
before they left the city, perhaps Willard would take her
to the club.

But this was all wrong, too. The new dress would be
too new, too fashionable, the exact wrong thing to wear.

At other times, the dance tunes and the highballs gave
her another dream:

It was a question of hours or days or weeks. If she
knew each element in the formula, she could make a cal-
culation and name the exact moment that Willard would
remember her. Why not be happy? she'd asked, falling in
love with him, and nothing had changed for her. He was
all she wanted and she was as full of him as in the time of
the white kimono and their long afternoons in his bed.
She still felt her good fortune in being his wife, remembering when she believed that he was meant for someone
else, and she to be alone and miserable. Perhaps the re-
moval from Manhattan to Tuxedo was Willard's way of
giving them a new start after Reed's death, and she had
failed to understand this too. She had never been able to
predict the smallest thing about Willard: when he was
hungry or thirsty or wanted to make love. When she
discovered what was wrong with him, she would do
anything in the world to make it right for him.

Three

Sadie found a seat by the window, and she laid her pale blue shrug on the seat beside her, hoping no one would want to sit next to her. There were few people on the train. Businessmen going into the city late, already absorbed in the *Times* or the *Wall Street Journal*. Women, in pairs, looked out the window or talked about shopping, the theater. Sadie felt alone and idle. She'd thought about bringing one of the girls with her, and decided it would be easier alone, but at the last minute before the train left the Tuxedo station, she stood and looked around, afraid that she would never see the girls again.

It was a relief to be in the city, one of the crowd of bodies in the subway and on the streets, in line for her driving test. She'd passed the written test in the spring, and Mr. Garcia, as he'd promised, had sent down a nephew with a car for her to take the driving test. She chatted with the woman in front of her, who asked where Sadie lived when Sadie said she'd come into the city to take the driving test. "Tuxedo Park," Sadie said, and the woman looked at her warily, saying, "That's pretty exclusive, isn't it?" and Sadie laughed a little high laugh, saying, "Not if they let me in," but that was the end of the conversation.

Mr. Garcia would have been proud of her, although she failed to look behind her while parallel parking. The man giving the test wore perfectly round glasses and a pale blond crewcut. "There could be a kid back there," he said, "or an old lady or a dog. Someone infirm."

She parked the car where the nephew waited, and thanked him. She was sure that she failed. She didn't have the strength to go uptown to the train, much less to shop for the girls as she'd planned. They didn't look right in Tuxedo Park. Their clothes were too new or too old. She would try Bonwit Teller, where she never shopped. The year after her mother was killed, she went alone to buy a new winter coat and chose one in a bright blue. Reuben had tried to convince her to exchange it. "There's nothing wrong with the style," he said, "just the color. An overcoat should be neutral." But she'd kept it, loyal to her mistake, and all season she wore the coat like the Scarlet Letter, to show that she had no one to help her pick out clothes anymore.

"You did everything okay," the inspector said. "Just watch it on the parking."

She filled out her papers, stood in another line, and left the municipal building a licensed driver.

IN THE AFTERNOON SHE STEPPED OFF THE TRAIN AND was happy to be back in Tuxedo. She had meant to shop and to check on the mews house, have lunch with Reuben, pick him up at the office, say hello to Arlie. Instead Sadie walked uptown through the Chinese and Italian neighborhoods, then over to Washington Square where she sat until it was too late for lunch and she no longer wanted to shop. The thought of checking on the mews house made her throat tighten. She decided that she was uneasy, and the discovery of the right word for her indecision and unhappiness made her feel better immediately. She found a cab and caught the next train to Tuxedo.

Instead of calling Willard when she got to the station, she decided to walk.

Wally, the friendlier guard, was at the gate, and Sadie waved as she passed by the gatehouse as quickly as she could in her city high heels. The sun was warm on her back as she crossed the open green by the church, but the shade of the hills and tall trees soon chilled her, and she was glad for her shrug. The ground was rough, and there was no place to take off her high heels. She walked on, increasingly aware that her left shoe was rubbing a place on her small toe.

At the top of the hill there was a clearing at the Round House lawn. Sadie stopped, hoping Jimmy wasn't looking out his windows and watching her. He came by in the evening sometimes for a drink with Willard. Once when Willard wasn't home, he asked if he might have a look at the old garden behind the house, and he told Sadie the names of the irises, lilies, roses, and herbs that he found among the weeds and overgrowth. "Black thumb, black thumb," she said, waving her hands, to disavow any interest in the garden. Jimmy smiled and told her, "This was a wonderful garden once. I adore gardening, it's the only thing you should ever count on me for."

She sat on the soft grass in the shade of a giant pine, and took off her shoe carefully. The stocking was split and the flesh on her toe was raw and swollen. She couldn't put her shoe back on again. She looked around and decided that the lawn, though green, was not so pretty a color as early spring grass and that the summer flowers and trees were not so beautiful as they looked from a distance. She stood, gingerly, and began to walk. The road was rough and hard, and her toe hurt even without the shoe. She tried to think of something to take her mind off her toe. She wished she could drop the paper, her shrug, pocketbook, and shoes by the side of the road.

Mrs. Misurelli doesn't like me, Sadie thought. She had never seen it quite so clearly before. Mrs. Misurelli, when Sadie finally met her, turned out to be only a few years older than Willard, and a descendant of one of the original workers imported to build Tuxedo Park. Mrs.

Misurelli's face was drawn and hard, with penciled-in
eyebrows, like a kewpie doll's. Mrs. Misurelli didn't
seem to like Willard either, Sadie admitted, but she believed in his authority, calling him Mr. Weaver and Sadie
only Mrs., as if she had no other name. She probably
didn't like the girls either, Sadie thought, remembering
Mrs. Misurelli's expression as she dusted Louise's collection: a geode, split by lightning, Louise insisted; a tiny
pine cone, Marilyn's gift; a bird's nest with one brown
feather and the fragment of a blue egg. Mrs. Misurelli
talked about *my people*, and Sadie mistook her gossip for
friendliness. Now Sadie decided that it was another sign
of her contempt for Sadie, who made it worse by being
willing to listen to scandal about people she hadn't even
met. It occurred to Sadie for the first time that Mrs.
Misurelli gossiped about her and Willard and the girls to
anyone who would listen, and that Jimmy was one of
Mrs. Misurelli's people.

Her progress was slow, impeded by her sore toe, the
steepness of the hills, and by the mosquitoes. Sadie
slapped at them and brushed them away as she trudged
along. Tuxedo drivers drove on any side of the road they
chose, as if they had the only car in the Park. There were
too many blind curves on the narrow road.

There were six cars in the club parking lot, all but one
at least five years old, and there was something solid and
splendid about them. The newer model was a dark green
British sports car, and Sadie suspected it was at the beginning of a very long life. Replace nothing, repair everything, give nothing away, she thought as she rounded the
clubhouse curve. The clubhouse wasn't even seventy
years old and it looked like an ancient ruin. Through the
leaded glass of the club's bay windows, Sadie made out
rippled figures, and when she was past the curve and able
to see the terrace, she saw women in big-skirted, cinch-
waisted dresses and picture hats, men in sports jackets
and white trousers. One of the women turned and looked
in Sadie's direction, and Sadie hurried on, her face hot
and embarrassed. Here in Tuxedo she felt invisible, even

Mrs. Misurelli hardly noticed her. Only with the girls did Sadie feel real.

She heard a car in back of her and turned to see a Cadillac lumbering up the hill behind her. As it passed, she raised her hand to wave and in the instant the car lurched around the curve, her eyes met those of the driver, a red-faced man in a golf cap, and his passenger. They looked away from Sadie deliberately, as if they weren't moving smoothly in their big car while she stood pinned between the road and a ditch. Then they were gone and Sadie looked down, trying to decide if she was in poison ivy. Another car was coming. She was in a bad spot, on a curve, but she recognized the Straight Eight and stepped forward so that Willard would stop for her. The silver car passed within inches of Sadie, so close that it brushed her newspaper, and she jumped back. Louise and Marilyn were in the rumble seat, and Sadie thought Marilyn called out, "It's Mommy, it's Mommy."

She walked on slowly, trying not to put too much weight on her left foot, and she shifted her possessions from arm to arm. Another car was crawling up the hill behind her. She wasn't in the way, she thought, surely they don't want me to move over any more.

The car stopped next to Sadie. "Are you all right?" The driver was Helen Franklin.

"I'm fine. Thank you," said Sadie.

Another car came toward them up the hill, and Sadie heard its horn.

"You'd better go," she said.

"Oh, no," Helen said. "Jump in."

"I can walk," Sadie said.

"Don't be silly," Helen said sharply. "Please get in."

"Okay," she said, and scrambled in just in time for Helen to get moving before the green sports car passed her.

"I was married to a drunk driver," Helen said. "I don't linger on these roads. Home?"

"Oh, please," Sadie said. She settled gratefully in the car.

"Jimmy told me you may tackle the old hill garden. He says it's really quite remarkable what's survived there."

"I don't know anything about it," Sadie said, thinking it was remarkable that anything survived in Tuxedo Park.

"You mustn't be offended because Jimmy told me about visiting you," Helen said.

"But I'm not offended," Sadie said.

"Everyone gossips around here, it's just like any small town, really. It's harmless but persistent gossip. And Mrs. Misurelli's cousin Beatrice comes when I have a large house party. So there's another source of information."

"There's nothing to know about me," Sadie said. "I can't imagine anyone being interested."

"Marini took pretty good care of the garden," Helen said, "until he slacked off at the end."

"Maybe that's because no one paid him," Sadie said. Helen laughed and said, "You catch on quickly, Sadie. I don't know about Marini's case, but people impose on the villagers. Noblesse oblige. They act as though the people in the village mightn't just walk away from the Park, take a train into the city or somewhere. Get another job."

"And do they?"

Helen drove the car up Sadie's driveway, stopping before the door. She turned off the car and looked at Sadie. She had a classical look, Sadie thought, like a Greek statue—ivory skin, golden hair.

"They don't leave very often, no," Helen said.

"Well," Sadie said, her hand on the car door. "Thank you for the ride. I'd still be trying to climb the last hill, I guess, if it weren't for you." She stepped from the car, feeling the cool ground beneath her feet, and closed the door awkwardly with her elbow, clutching her shoes, shrug, and bag.

"I'm glad we had a chance to talk," Helen said. "I've been meaning to call on you. We're so pleased that Willard's here, and with an adorable family. Who would have thought it?"

"Yes," Sadie said, unsure what Helen meant. She wondered if she should invite her in but the moment passed and Helen had already begun to pull away.

THE GIRLS WERE IN LOUISE'S ROOM, DRESSING LOUISE'S collection of dolls, an activity they took up and abandoned for no particular reason that Sadie could ever tell. Willard had brought out his mother's dolls and had ceremoniously given the collection to the girls, warning them not to play with them because they might break. She knocked on the open door, went in and kissed Louise, then sank to the floor, pulling Marilyn against her.

"What happened to your foot?" Louise asked.

"Never try to walk uphill in high heels," Sadie said.

"Oh, Mommy." Louise sounded like the mother of a naughty child.

"But a nice lady gave me a ride, so all's well that ends well." She leaned back against Louise's bed and Marilyn leaned with her, saying, "Willard took us swimming in a big pool."

"Was it warm enough?" Sadie asked.

"Yes. But we came right home after."

"I see." Sadie thought of asking them if they'd seen her in the road but decided not to make an issue of it. She watched Louise dressing her red-headed doll in a pinafore, slacks, sweater, vest, coat, and hat.

"Is she leaving the country?" Sadie asked.

"She's cold," Louise said. "She lives in a house with no heat."

"Why no heat?"

"Oh, all the heat was turned off and the water and the lights when everyone went away. Now there's nothing in the house."

"Poor house," Sadie said.

THAT NIGHT WITH HER FAMILY SEATED AROUND THE oval walnut table, the white inner curtains blowing

slightly in the evening breeze, Sadie decided that she had
imagined the whole thing. Both girls were listening to
Willard explain the mural of Washington's heroic journey
across the Delaware. The front door opened and closed.
Mrs. Misurelli's journey through the Park, across the
tracks, to the village began.

Willard couldn't have driven past her, nearly run her
over, then not mentioned it. He hadn't even asked how
she got home.

Louise stared hard at her sister, and made a disgusting
face, thinking of *The Hunchback of Notre Dame*, which
Reuben had taken them to see. Marilyn gazed, unmoved,
as if she were blind, then in a flash stuck her tongue out
at Louise.

Marilyn looked out the window behind Louise at a
robin on the lawn. The robin seemed cross, for it pecked
at the ground, rested, then pecked again, a little harder
each time. "Marilyn," Sadie said. "How would you like
to see your Uncle Reuben?" Sadie asked.

"When is Reuben coming?" Willard asked.

"For the Fourth of July," Sadie said, addressing Marilyn. "There'll be fireworks and we'll have a wonderful
time."

She had overheard two Tuxedo ladies talking in the
drugstore about the celebration. There would be a dance
at the club and a supper, but Sadie was more interested
to hear that the fireworks wouldn't be displayed on the
Fourth itself but on the day after, to save money for the
Association. The ladies discussed who was coming up for
the weekend and how much better everything had been,
before the war, before the Depression. Before the Jews,
Sadie thought. There were a few Jewish families in the
Park, allowed in when the Park was even more on its
uppers, as Jimmy had said. She had been so uncomfortable discussing Jews in the Park with him that she hadn't
asked all she would have liked, but only learned that the
Park had, early on, rejected priceless Jews, famous Jews.
Too bad for everyone, she thought. Nothing was what it

once was, the ladies agreed. Sadie bought two shades of pink lipstick, both wrong for her.

"I was thinking of inviting Helen Franklin. She gave me a ride home. If she isn't busy, of course."

"As you wish," Willard said. "I always enjoy seeing Helen."

Sadie stopped herself from taking another helping of dessert. The waistbands of her skirts were getting tight. She wondered if she gardened if she would look as trim and neat as Jimmy.

Louise coughed, pointing to her throat as if she were choking, and Sadie told her she could leave. When Louise left, Marilyn did also. Marilyn was growing even more silent in Tuxedo, she thought, and she called the girl back to her and hugged her. "Don't stay outside too long, doll," Sadie said. "It's your bedtime more or less."

THE EVENING WAS LAVENDER AND YELLOW, AND Louise forgot all about the dining room. Marilyn stayed solemn, and dragged her feet, telling Louise not to go so fast, as they mounted the garden steps.

Marilyn wanted to stop Louise so they could go into the basement, get the Mason jars with punched lids that Sadie made them, and fill them with fireflies. She remembered an illustration in a book of little children carrying firefly lanterns through dark woods, and she thought Louise and she could use some too. She'd heard Sadie say once during her morning call from Reuben, "Everything's perfect, except I'm falling apart." Sadie was laughing, but Marilyn noticed that her mother often resembled her old rag doll, not coming apart at the seams but never quite looking sewn up. Her shirt stuck out from her skirt, her hair escaped its pins.

When Louise was fast and haughty, Marilyn knew better than to argue about fireflies because Louise only got worse, gritting her teeth until she exploded at Marilyn, as if everything were her fault.

So far they had explored around the castle, and tugged

at the boarded-up windows to no avail. Released from
their mornings with Sadie and afternoons with Willard,
they lay on the warm flagstones of the castle terrace
watching the clouds. They played statues or hide-and-
seek in the overgrown rose garden. When Marilyn rubbed
her hand on the castle walls, the brick crumbled and her
hand came away dusty. She felt like crying, as if her skin
had been removed and the nerves beneath exposed.

"Come on," Louise said. "You're a slowpoke."

It was true, Marilyn thought, but Sadie always told her
that that was her nature.

"It's dark," Marilyn said. She didn't like the castle the
way Louise did. Louise walked along the parapet with
her arms out like a tightrope artist, chanting, "Oh, we've
got to get into the castle." All Marilyn could think of was
Louise falling off and rolling down the hill like Jack and
Jill.

"I know it's dark," Louise said.

In the woods, they rushed past low-hanging branches.
Marilyn wished her legs were long and skinny like
Louise's so she could keep up.

At the end of the woods was the castle lawn, a meadow
now, and a fountain at the end of the garden. The marble
statues looked half melted from exposure. The castle was
much higher up than the Weaver house and commanded
a view of the lake and the road, of some of the larger
houses along the lake shore, and, in winter, of Jimmy's
Round House. "Come on," she said when Marilyn
paused to rest; Marilyn followed her sister. By day they
had inspected the windows—high above their reach—
and the doors without finding a way in, but Louise
marched around to the back and threw herself on the
ground. She pressed her fist against a small door in the
foundation, no wider than she, and, after a moment,
the door gave into the chilly castle.

"It's a coal chute," she told Marilyn. "Mrs. Misery
showed me the one in our house. So there."

"Let's go home," Marilyn said.

Louise withdrew her arm and said, "*If* you come back here with me tomorrow, then we'll go in. No matter what."

"Tomorrow?"

"You know what I mean. When we can."

Marilyn looked around at the deepening shadows and said, "Okay. But let's go now." Louise scrambled to her feet and said, "Last one home's a rotten egg."

When they emerged at their edge of the woods, Sadie was standing at the bottom of the garden hill, looking straight up at them.

"Oh, there you are, girls," she said. They could tell by her tone of voice that she hadn't been thinking about them at all. Marilyn, breathless, ran down to Sadie and hugged her.

"Where's Willard?" Louise asked when she reached the bottom of the hill.

"Oh, he's probably down at the club," Sadie said. He'd driven past her in the big silver Packard, in the direction of the club, but that was also the direction of the gate and the rest of the world.

LOUISE WOKE UP IN THE MIDDLE OF THE NIGHT AND couldn't help herself with any of her tricks: she counted to twenty-five; she tried to imagine she was in a bright place with flowers and everyone was happy. Sadie was just across the way, but Louise couldn't cross the blackness. She listened to the wind and to a bird calling. When she closed her eyes, she saw black tunnels again and had the feeling that something was pressing on her chest.

Four

WILLARD LAY ON THE COUCH, ONE HAND BEHIND HIS head, the other holding up a book that he was falling asleep reading. When the girls knocked at the library door, he called out, "Come in." They greeted him shyly, took their places on the couch, Marilyn nearer to Willard, Louise closer to the window. It was a warm day, and the window was open a crack. Louise could hear birdsong and, at a distance, the scrape of her mother's rake against stone. Sadie had begun to clean out the garden on the hill, and Louise could hear her whistling.

Willard coughed, closed his book, and brought the portfolio of photographs to the coffee table and opened it.

"Do you see," he asked, "how precious a tree is in this terrain? How the tree clings to the edge of the cliff. We have lots of trees here in Tuxedo and they have to undergo Tuxedo winters and Tuxedo summers. But out there, it's like this," pointing to a twisted mesquite standing alone on the horizon. "Elemental. Do you understand?"

Both girls nodded.

"Good," and he turned the prints slowly, pointing out an armadillo, which made the girls giggle; a rattlesnake, which made them flinch; scorpion, tarantula. He took out a close-up of a rock ledge and laid it on top of the other photos. Pointing to the distinct layers, he said, "This is from the time before men walked. And this from a time when there were birds too large to fly, and this . . ."

Louise preferred pictures of flowers or animals like cows that she could see along the road. Marilyn hardly heard what Willard said. It was too many words for her. Louise listened to Willard and tried to see what letters his words would make. Willard told them things in the library. During one of their afternoons he told them that Tuxedo was founded by their great-grandfather, but Louise didn't know whether to believe this. It seemed to her that the Park, like the city, like the lake, the two city rivers, and the castle, must always have been just as it was now.

All over the house were treasures from the past and Willard explained them to the girls: French bronzes of sylphs with airy fabrics slipping from their shoulders; Piranesi prints, which Louise recognized from the one of the sibyl's temple at home; watercolors of the Berkshire pines that Willard's grandmother painted in her youth. There were trunks filled with old linen, and the floors were covered with Turkish rugs their great-grandparents had bought on a grand tour of the East. Louise couldn't decide whose things the treasures were, or whose house it was, the way the mews house was her own.

Now Willard put the portfolio back on the side table. "Suppose," he said, "you were walking in the desert. And you saw two rocks. What would you do?"

"I would look at the rock," Marilyn said. "I would see if it was a nice rock. A very very old rock."

Louise could tell that this wasn't the answer Willard wanted. He was keyed up, unable to stay in his chair. He lit a cigarette and stood at the window.

"I'd want to know about those rocks," Louise said. "I'd be curious." Willard said that great men made changes in their lives through curiosity.

"You would be curious?" he asked, turning from the

window. He threw his cigarette in the fireplace. "And what would you do with your curiosity?"

"I would look at the rock," she said. "Very hard."

"And would that be enough for you?" he asked. "It's very hot in the desert and the sun's beating down on the back of your neck—"

"She's wearing her hat," Marilyn called out.

"I know," he said. "Don't interrupt. Louise. You've stopped walking. You're looking at the rocks. What do you notice?"

She wanted to say that she didn't know but she didn't want to be a baby like Marilyn.

"Maybe I would pick the rock up," she said cautiously. "And bring it home with me." She wanted to say that she would give the rock to Sadie who had been reading a book on rock gardens.

"Ah," Willard said, and Louise knew she had given the wrong answer. Sometimes he sent them away early and they were unable to be happy in their free time, thinking of Willard disappointed in them.

"Well," he said. "And what if there had been a rattlesnake under your rock?"

Marilyn's mouth was hanging open and she looked so stupid that Louise almost hit her then and there.

"A snake?"

"Don't you see?" he asked. "That's what I've been telling you. You must always be very careful. *Very careful.*"

Louise said, "I'd like to be excused, please."

"One minute. If you want something, then you must take it. Especially if you're a collector. A collector of rocks or paintings, anything."

"No," she said. "I'd just leave the rock where it was. Because of the snake."

"But maybe there isn't a snake. Then what would you do, if you missed your chance at the rock? And there might be something precious under the rock—an Indian necklace or a piece of pottery that was never broken. And you'd have missed it."

A movement at the window caught Louise's eye and she saw her mother standing outside, a hoe in her hand, trying to see through the screen into the dark room. If Willard turned, he would be able to see Sadie. Marilyn would cry if he said anything to Sadie.

"I have to go to the bathroom," Louise said loudly. "May I now? May I?"

Willard said, "Of course you may go if you wish. You don't have to announce where you're going each time you leave a room. You, too, Marilyn. You may go too."

Louise knew he was disappointed in them, and she knew it was her fault. She should have said something else or acted differently, but she couldn't imagine how things should have gone.

Five

"MARILYN! LOUISE!" REUBEN CALLED OUT FROM THE steps of the train, "You big sweeties. Coming to meet me?" He was wearing his summer seersucker, a white shirt, and a red bowtie. He crouched and kissed the girls, crushing them, then shaking hands with Willard, saying, "The squire! Country life agrees with you, I see," though Reuben thought Willard looked like hell.

"Mildly," Willard said, turning to the car. "Shall we?"

Reuben breathed in the air, which smelled of pines and summer flowers and exhaust fumes, the smell of childhood holidays, the endless trip north when, to entertain Sadie, their father talked about the Russian village where he was born and about cousins and aunts and uncles Reuben and Sadie would never meet. Reuben remembered arriving in the clear darkness of an Adirondack summer night.

When the car had passed through the gates, Reuben began rummaging in his pockets, asking, "Where could they be? Lost? Are they lost?"

Willard glanced over and asked, "Something the matter?"

Reuben winked broadly and said, "Two little packages. Might have left them on the train."

When they got to the house, Willard excused himself, telling the girls to take care of their uncle. They walked up the stairs to the bedroom they'd chosen for him, and Reuben asked, "Do you like it here, girls? Do you miss the big city at all?"

"No," Louise said. She felt shy with Reuben who was larger and louder in the country.

"Your room," Marilyn said, and she pointed down the hall to an open door. She tugged at his arm to get him moving. The night before, Marilyn and Sadie had picked black-eyed susans to put in Reuben's room, a small blue bedroom. Willard had taken over his father's room, for nights when he couldn't sleep. Reuben set down his suitcase and exclaimed over the flowers, the view of the hill, and the print of an Indian maiden. He patted his suit pockets while the girls watched, until he brought out two little boxes, one wrapped in pink paper, one in white, and gave one to each niece. Marilyn opened hers quickly, crumpling the paper and dropping it to the floor, and Louise held back, careful to save the paper. Each girl had a necklace, her first initial set in diamond chips. Louise held up her *L* to make the tiny stones catch the light.

"Thank you," she said. "Marilyn, thank Reuben."

Marilyn let him put the necklace on her, and she fingered the surface of her *M* over and over.

"Uncle Reuben," Louise said solemnly when he'd fastened the gold chain around her neck, "you'll always stay in this room when you visit, and we'll call it Reuben's room."

"I'm honored," he said, "but, you know, I miss you in the city. Everyone on Broadway asks about you girls, where you are. And where's Sadie? they ask. So won't you be happy to come back?"

Louise stroked the necklace and said, "The kids here go to school on top of a hill. They don't have a playground. Just a big field."

"Are there a lot of nice kids here in Tuxedo?" he asked.

"We don't know," Marilyn said. "Because we just play with each other."

"I see," Reuben said.

"Mrs. Franklin says she'll introduce us to some kids soon," Louise said.

"And who is Mrs. Franklin?"

"An old friend of mine," Willard said. He stood at the open door to the room. "Why not come downstairs and have a drink before lunch. I can't imagine where Sadie is."

A BORED GIRL WATCHED FROM THE CASH REGISTER while Sadie selected anchovy filets, olives and peanuts, graham crackers, marshmallows and chocolate bars, as if war might come again to keep her from such inessentials.

Jimmy waited outside in his black Studebaker. It was just like Willard, he thought, to have driven off and left Sadie with shopping to do and no car. If he hadn't happened along, she'd have been stuck.

Peanut butter, peaches, dozens of eggs. Mrs. Misurelli had left food for the weekend, but Sadie kept shopping. Tuna fish. Until her cart was filled and, eventually, the back of Jimmy's car.

Driving up the hill, she felt peaceful and excited. She looked over at Jimmy, who looked gloomy.

"Holiday weekends," he said. "The Park is invaded."

"Oh, I don't know," she said. "It makes a change. Don't you like a little break from working?"

Jimmy had a small business, not really a business because businesses were forbidden by the Association, but a private landscaping service.

He shrugged. "No work, no money. Anyway, it keeps me out of trouble." He glanced at her. She seemed sad and distracted, not much of a holiday girl herself. "Look. I know of an old graveyard, way out in the country. Eighteenth century. I go there to dig vinca and lily of the valley. Would you ever want to come? You could use some for your garden. That is, if it's all right with Willard."

"Oh, he won't care. It would be wonderful," she said. "I'd love to do that. If it's really all right with you. I used to buy flowers all the time, in the city, but I never had such pleasure as now. I go out every morning to see if anything's happened." She laughed. "Usually nothing has."

Though he liked going on such expeditions alone, Sadie looked so happy that he couldn't resist extending himself even more. "It takes time with a garden like yours. To clear away the rubbish and find the good perennials that have survived. You know, I remember a certain rose garden. Very deep into the Park. The house has been gone for a decade, but the roses may be there in some form. Would Monday be all right? We'll scour the area and fix you up."

"Perfect. Are you sure you won't come for dinner? Meet my brother?"

"Maybe another time. Or I might, Sadie. I can't really say," he said. "I usually celebrate the Fourth in my solitude."

"Another time," she said. She was sure he wouldn't come. He was too polite to say that he would be doing something much better than anything she might offer, going to the kind of party to which she would never be invited.

Jimmy left the heavy bags in the butler's pantry and waved good-by, leaving noiselessly. When the door closed behind him, she stood for a moment in the domed entryway, wondering what it would be like to leave also, then Sadie followed the sound of voices to the glass porch. Reuben looked so solid and homey, so familiar, that her throat swelled with feeling. When they kissed, she felt his beard, already scratchy at noon, and thought of Jimmy's fair skin and Willard's ivory jaw.

"Hello, stranger," Reuben said.

"Hello, stranger yourself. Listen, Reuben, you're talking to a driver. I went into the city and I passed my test."

"Mommy," Marilyn said, "Uncle Reuben gave us letters," and she tried to wave her necklace at Sadie.

"That's beautiful, darling."

"Well, was the test hard?" Reuben asked.

"You didn't tell me," Willard said.

"Why, I guess I didn't," she said, flustered by Willard's attention. "The test wasn't bad. There was one part where—"

"We've been waiting for you, actually, Sadie. Lunch is ready, isn't it?"

"Well," she said. "I guess it is. And the table set. Yes." She'd meant not to tell Willard anything about the license or the test unless he asked. "Fine," she said. "So let's get the trays from the refrigerator and see what Mrs. Misurelli's idea of lunch is."

During the meal, she told Reuben that she was beginning to garden though this one had been neglected for so long that it would take her time to find the old patterns and plants.

"Well, don't count on anything. You've never grown a thing in your life except mold on bread," Reuben said. "We're a family of black thumbs."

"My thumbs are pink," Marilyn said.

"It's a figure of speech," Sadie said. She had done it again, given herself away. "Like saying someone's an angel."

THE GIRLS TOOK REUBEN UP THE BIG HILL TO THE school. When they passed the castle Louise thought about showing him the coal chute to see if he could find another way in. She still hesitated, unwilling to fling herself down the black chute. But if she told him, he'd tell Sadie—they told each other everything—and Louise would have no secret left. As they passed the castle, Louise looked sternly at Marilyn but she was picking buttercups along the road and didn't glance up at the castle.

The school was at the top of the big hill, two turns off

the lake past the Weaver house. Willard had explained to Reuben over lunch that once it had been a grand home, more or less Gothic, with too many towers and silly balconies. The original family sold it to a young couple who divorced and sold it again to a New York stockbroker who attempted to sell it to a doctor for use as a small nursing home. The Association bought it and leased it to the school.

The closed doors and windows of the school made it look like a napping monster, and Louise said, almost whispering, "Sometimes we come up with Mommy after dinner. To see the sunset. She says it's the only place where you can see the sunset."

"Well," Reuben said, "do you take walks with your father?"

"We take lessons," Marilyn said.

Reuben laughed and said, "A good thing. And on what subjects in particular?"

"Rocks," said the little girl, the buttercups clenched in her fist. "The Park. Our great-grandmother lived in the Park but her house is gone. And he's teaching us about cactuses and scorpions. And tarantalas."

"Tarantalas? You mean tarantellas? Is that the dance?"

"Tarantulas, stupid," said Louise. She had the feeling that they shouldn't be telling this to Reuben, and she fingered her diamond *L* guiltily.

"Tarantulas. Oh la la," Reuben said in a smeary French accent. "Shall we perambulate?"

Down on the road, he said, "Well, you've been learning a lot."

Marilyn said, "Mommy doesn't like the club."

"No, Sadie knows how to drive, and now she's in the garden all the time."

"I see," Reuben said. "And your father? Does he go out driving too?"

Louise said, "Just with us." She didn't know how to answer Reuben's questions. If she told the truth or made up a story, she would still be wrong.

For the rest of the walk to the house, he told them about their grandmother whom they'd never met, his mother and Sadie's, who came from Russia when she was ten, only a few years older than Louise, all alone, with a small silver cup sewn into the hem of her skirt. He would give the cup, he said, to the first girl who married.

"Me," Marilyn called out. "Me!" She danced a little down the hill until Louise shouted, "You can't get married until I do, stupid, because I'm older than you and I'm never getting married. Never." Marilyn began to cry, and Reuben picked her up, though she was getting big for that, and fished around in his suit pocket for some half-melted Hershey's Kisses, and gave one to each girl.

Six

ON SATURDAY MORNING OF JULY FOURTH WEEKEND, Sadie began to work on the second tier of the garden, weeding and clearing. When she drove by nurseries and spotted flats of bedding plants—phlox, dianthus, pansies, petunias, daisies, columbines—she was tempted but she stayed faithful to Jimmy's advice. First she'd clear and see what was there.

She was down on her hands and knees, pulling grass from a section of wood-stemmed thyme, when she heard a car coming up the drive. Helen stopped the car a few feet from Sadie. She was wearing a white broadcloth shirt and baggy khakis that Sadie decided cost a fortune.

"Good morning," Helen said. She reached to the back seat of her car, stepped out, and handed Sadie a *Times*. "You forgot this. I was sure I'd see you along the road but I didn't."

"Thanks," Sadie said. "I forgot all about it." She took the paper and spread it out on the stone retaining wall. "Have a seat," she said.

Helen sat on the paper. "I've always been terrible at gardening. I can't even pick a rose without strangling the bush."

"My brother's here for the weekend," Sadie said. "He tells me I'm from a long line of black thumbs."

"It's marvelous to be encouraged by family, isn't it?"

Sadie laughed and asked, "Do you have a lot of company for the Fourth?"

"I intended to but they canceled, thank God."

"Well, in that case," Sadie said, "how about coming for dinner? Tonight? I know it's awfully late to be inviting anyone around here but—"

"I'd love to," Helen said, standing, as if this was why she'd come. Willard, who had heard their voices, came to the door. Helen waved to him as she drove away, and Sadie crouched down to weed. Willard watched her from the door, then went back inside without a word. She was getting fat in Tuxedo, Sadie thought, but New York would melt it away in the fall.

GEORGE WASHINGTON STOOD IN THE BOAT, DETER-mined, iron-jawed. Across the dining room, impassive on a summer cliff, Indians stared at his icebound struggle. After all, Sadie thought, she and Willard had known each other a long time. She thought that Willard's hair was thinning and that age became him, as had youth. She wanted only what she had always wanted—his love and approval and attention. Her table was a success, laid with a flowered cloth, candles in faience holders, roses from Helen's garden in a silver bowl, and china adorned with pale pink roses and jagged green leaves. Her children were clean, fed, and upstairs asleep.

Something in the too-symmetrical pattern made by four adults around an oval table reminded Willard of a drawing of Cherry's from years before. It made him melancholy to think of her here where she would never be and where he didn't want to be.

Reuben thought that he would have to be more vigilant than ever. He thought of the paper chains the girls made to decorate their rooms and decided to fashion his care on that model: firmly linked, fragile in appearance.

Helen thought, How odd marriage is. Though this is all none of my business.

"I'm glad you're back in Tuxedo," she told Willard. "Your family brings new life to the place. Are you pleased to be here?"

Willard said, "Tuxedo's all right. Now I see it as a social experiment that failed. It drips with failure."

"Real-estate venture or social experiment?" Reuben said. "Whatever, it's still ongoing, which is more than you can say for Brook Farm."

"Tuxedo was most importantly an experiment in self-government," Willard said.

"Oh, pooh," said Helen. "It was just another way of being exclusive."

"Perhaps at the beginning," Willard said, "but that's over. Soon the customs will be forgotten: the Horse Show and the balls will fall away. But the Association will still struggle to maintain control."

"And what difference if it fails?" Helen asked. "When did you become so solemn about Tuxedo? You've always hated it. You always said it gave you asthma."

"That was my father," Willard said. "Who claimed it gave me asthma. Tuxedo only makes me feel tired. Enervated."

Sadie thought, Tuxedo's only perfect, no matter what they say, except for me. Her uneasiness in Tuxedo was, she thought, hers alone. She didn't imagine that anyone else felt that way. The garden was changing her time there, maybe other things would change as well in time.

The trick was to stay married. If she could manage to be quiet, to simply stay connected with him, then he would settle down. They had their children, the strongest bond two people could have. She sipped her wine, watched the fading light over the lawn, observed the shadows of giant elms extending to meet one another. How lucky she was to be alive, Sadie thought. Had she been born elsewhere she might be a memory. She might have gotten her way and gone to Florida with her parents had Reuben not volunteered to stay with her. Here she found something uplifting every day—her discovery of a marble bench in the garden; a fat robin that had stopped very near her on the lawn and hunted for a worm, accepting her presence. She thought she saw a deer in the garden, though it came and went so quickly she couldn't be sure.

"Tuxedo can be terribly depressing, of course," Helen said, "whether you see it as a failed social experiment or a slightly inconvenient suburb. The best houses are empty, and the occupied ones are in disgraceful condition. No one puts any money into the place, or no more than they have to. The place should be kept up, you know, but it won't be until the old guard sells or dies, and new people come in. We are in a weakening condition."

"Why don't you live elsewhere, for heaven's sake," Willard asked, "if you feel that way?"

"I have lived elsewhere," she said. "I come back."

"Well, surely it isn't fond memories binding you to the spot," Willard said.

"You and Willard were childhood friends?" Reuben asked.

"When he visited the Park, we were friends. But you weren't here a good deal after your mother's death, were you? It's a wonder the house has held up," Helen said.

"It was my father," Willard said. "He didn't know how to do anything but keep it as it had always been. Sadie?"

She was staring out the window, listening to the sound of their voices. Sometimes in the evening when Willard had the girls she could hear cocktail parties in the house down the road, loud braying laughter that climbed the hill to her terrace. Now she was inside a party.

"Coffee and dessert on the porch," she said. "Go on. I'll be out."

SADIE URGED RASPBERRIES AND HEAVY CREAM, RICH coffee and brandy on them.

My God, Willard thought, who could care so much about food. He had provided her with Mrs. Misurelli so that they wouldn't have a constant fuss about meals, and still Sadie packed the house with tin cans and provisions as if they were under siege.

They sat on the glass porch, on the old, heavy furniture that Sadie wanted to replace. Willard wanted nothing changed in the house. Lights were visible around the lake, at the club, and in the grand houses. Helen's gray house had faded with the sunset into the lake shore, leaving her glowing, floating windows. She was extravagant, he thought, to keep so many lights on. He tried to imagine Cherry in Tuxedo but was unable to bring her there. Cherry knew him without house, wife, or family. He watched Helen, Sadie, and Reuben, reflected in the porch window. They didn't know a thing about him. He was a balloon, he thought, tugging at the long, fragile string that confined him there. He closed his eyes and tried to be in another place: dry canyon, high mesa, uninterrupted sky. He would live in a dry place, he thought, and when he died, he wouldn't rot but would become part of something cleaner.

Helen said, "Defend our honor, Willard. Reuben says that the Association couldn't possibly be saving money on fireworks. How much could they be saving anyway? It's the principle of the thing."

"Who would do such a thing on July Fourth?" Reuben asked. "Very un-American. I have clients who would be frightened to be making such a joke."

"Helen knows everything about Tuxedo," Willard said. "She's the resident authority." This was the classic Tuxedo subject, the parsimony of the rich. This was a conversation that might make one feel part of the community, but it made his skin crawl. He could no longer be what he had been.

Helen left soon after dessert, saying that she was sleeping badly these days and liked to start on it early. She insisted on walking home alone.

They stood at the front door of the house, watching her make her way down the stone steps cut into the lawn.

"What a nice woman," Sadie said. "It's a shame she never remarried."

"She's had a lover forever," Willard said. "Packy Schwerner. He's married to an enormously rich woman. An oil heiress. The arrangement seems to suit Helen better than her marriage did."

LATE THAT NIGHT, ALONE IN BED, SADIE DECIDED THAT he had told her about Helen's lover to hurt her feelings. She had never been tempted to be unfaithful to Willard, and she knew that she was more lucky than virtuous. People were addicted to all kinds of things—heroin, money, sex—but these pleasures were inconsequential to Sadie, nothing compared to family love. Like all passions, such pleasure would pass, like a momentary illness.

When she was pregnant with Marilyn, she'd lain in bed with Willard, and told him that she would love him forever.

"What would it take," he'd asked, "to make you stop?"

"Mountains," she answered, "earthquakes. Or if you ever look at another woman," and now she could recall the touch of his hand on her swollen breast.

"Look? Only a look?" He kissed her. Later, when she was almost asleep, he said, "You'll never catch me looking, Sadie, I promise, darling."

Perhaps Helen wasn't having an affair with a married person named Packy Schwerner. Nonetheless, Helen's secret was now interposed between Sadie and Helen, where earlier that day friendship had seemed a clear and simple probability.

DOWNSTAIRS, THE MEN DRIFTED TO THE PANELED LIbrary. On the coffee table was a decanter of Reed's excellent brandy and four snifters. Reuben let his belt out a notch. He shifted in the chintz armchair and sighed.

"How is the city?" Willard asked. "Not so quiet as Tuxedo, I hope."

"These are grim times for my clients," Reuben said. "It's Halloween every day." He looked at the table behind him, at the portfolio of western photos and asked, "Some work you're doing? Whistler?"

"Christ," said Willard. "I've given up on Whistler for the nonce. I'm content to go down in history as the owner of an insignificant Whistler oil, rather than as the author of an insignificant Whistler monograph."

"None of us know how we'll go down in history. It isn't up to us exactly. That Helen's a nice woman. What was her husband like?"

"He was a skunk. Of course, Tuxedo marriages . . ."

Willard liked this time of night, when Sadie and the girls were asleep and he was alone. Often he had wished for someone to talk to, but Willard always felt that despite all that Reuben had done for him when Reed died, Reuben didn't quite like him.

"So different from mortal marriages?" Reuben asked.

"I heard a story at the club that might interest you. With a legal twist. A husband died—he died in Mexico, you see—" Willard felt relaxed and keyed up at the same time. "The estate was significantly smaller than expected, you see, and people thought he'd provided for himself, and then he took his chances . . ."

Reuben shrugged. "Anything can be arranged. But why make such trouble? Why not just separate?"

"Perhaps," Willard said, "there was something else binding him."

He thought of Sadie's face as he passed her in the car, the cry of the children, his immediate denial as he drove on—It couldn't have been Sadie, she's taking a late train. It was the hour of the night when it seemed possible to say anything. "Tell me, Reuben, do you honestly believe that people can change?" His question sounded earnest and naïve, but he wanted Reuben's response.

"They can't help it," Reuben said, his smile broad and bland. "Try to stop it."

"Yes," Willard said. "I suppose that's true, but do

you believe that there can be deliberate change, to make good certain deficiencies or mistakes.''

"Keep it simple," Reuben said. "My best piece of free advice. And worth every penny." He reached behind him and brought out Marilyn's rag doll that had gotten wedged between the couch cushions.

"Human beings are more resourceful than you can imagine," Reuben said, resettling himself, the doll across his legs. "You don't know everything about another person. Ever. The trouble comes when you tinker with someone else's life."

So, given that he could no longer do what he had done —he had tried it in Tuxedo and now he saw it clearly— he might cut the fragile string, Willard thought, so long as he left the girls behind. The girls were more precious than life, yet he would survive without them, they without him.

When they stood to say good night, Reuben noticed that one of Willard's shoulders was slightly higher than the other, making him look like a man caught mid-gesture.

WILLARD SLEPT THAT NIGHT IN HIS FATHER'S YELLOW bedroom. He stretched out his full length between heavy ironed cotton sheets, with wordless joy. Then the image of Cherry disturbed his peace, and he imagined her most scornful look as she asked: Did you really think I left in order not to be found?

THERE WAS TALK THE NEXT DAY OF WATCHING THE fireworks from Helen's terrace on the lake, but nothing came of it. Sadie gardened, and Reuben pulled a dining-room chair outside to sit and watch her. The girls went into the woods to play, and Sadie bragged about how free they were in the Park and how safe the woods were and that Willard, who was eavesdropping half-heartedly from the library, had really beautiful instincts in bringing them there for the summer.

"They'll never forget this summer," Sadie said.

They had cold fried chicken for dinner, then waited for the dark. At last, the first crackle was heard, and they gathered on the lawn overlooking the lake. The green lawn shone phosphorescent in the half-light. Reuben went inside to find a jacket, and missed the first brilliant bursts. Sadie, Marilyn, Willard, and Louise lined up on the sloping lawn, holding hands. The patterns of white, lime green, the blue and red of the flags, the shots of yellow and clouds of stars, were all well done, Willard said, instructing the girls to judge fireworks by the intensity of the colors.

Marilyn held on to her parents, her mother's hand small and rough, her father's bony and smooth. She wanted to crawl inside both of them and disappear. She looked to one side and then the other, leaning forward to see Louise. Then Marilyn shut her eyes and through her thin lids saw light and dark as the fireworks exploded and disappeared, and the lake came and went from view. In the distance, she heard applause and shouts from the club after each burst of light and sound. She heard the wind blow into her ears and rush past, and the light filled her head. She was transparent, no more skin and bones, all light and sound. Marilyn wished they could stand there forever in the dark, the four of them together.

Reuben came out in time for a pinwheel. Standing behind the family, his hands on Sadie's shoulders, he said, "Bravo. Splendid. Who cares if they are a day late?"

Seven

CHERRY WAS TAKING A WALK, PAST THE HIGH SCHOOL and the softball field, and the old-age home, out to the edge of town where the dairy farms began.

Back in her room at home, she'd looked through the art books with the awful reproductions that she'd studied so carefully in high school, as if New York and the Metropolitan Museum were not two hours but two centuries away. She still loved best paintings of people—saints and families, Vermeer's solitary and dreamy women, Homer's boatmen, Ingres's porcelain-skinned beauties, and most of all Manet's couples, on a country picnic, on a park bench with a palm behind them, in a café garden with geraniums in the background and a waiter hesitating to interrupt. She looked for hours at Turner's London, everyone's Venice, at Monet's meadows covered in wildflowers. As she walked she saw paintings she might make of flowers, close-up portraits—of the man in the liquor store whom she decided she didn't like, and of her mother, who was probably waiting for Cherry to leave.

She realized now that she had never wanted so much to be a painter as to be in a painting. She'd wanted, then more than now, to be part of a group in a club in Paris, a laughing woman on a red banquette. She'd wanted to leave home, and her art teacher told her she drew well.

She did draw well, Cherry thought, but it wasn't every-thing. She had no burning vision to bring to the world. She had tried and failed. Having failed, she was not eager to try again. She blamed herself for what happened with Bradley. She was a bad painter, so he assumed that she'd invited him there with something else in mind. He saw her as a hanger-on; how stupid to think he would waste his time on her work.

She had enough savings to pay the rent in New York for another month. Then she would decide if she wanted to move back there and find a job. She had had too many jobs since her move to New York to value the one she'd just quit by postcard. The knowledge that something else would come along was of little satisfaction to Cherry.

She wondered if her mother knew she was drinking in her room at night, if she had found Cherry's hiding place for the pint, up on the top shelf of her closet. She won-dered when she would start to get bored. She knew it would come sometime, that she'd wake some morning and have to get out of Hackettstown, but that day wasn't here yet. If she didn't get bored, then she'd find a job in Hackettstown. She might become an old maid, like her mother, worrying over the fungus on the roses, drinking tea at night in bed. Some days that didn't seem so bad to Cherry. She could become the town whore, which would amount to the same thing as living as she did in New York. Or she might marry one of the men whose faces she could barely remember once they'd passed her on the street, and it would be as if she'd never left. She might forget everything.

Some evenings, when the day lilies, sturdy and gor-geous, nodded and pointed to her while she walked, when she could look up and see the pastel streaks of the fading sunset, Cherry felt a stirring she associated with sex. In those moments, she wanted someone to touch. But the sexual act, which had always before seemed to her com-ical or pleasurable, now seemed grotesque and violent. She recalled now the litany she recited when the question of sex came up: *Well, it's late and it might be all right,*

or, Well, why not, you never know, or, I don't feel like
being alone tonight. Of course there had been times when
she'd thought she would explode if the man didn't touch
her just as she wanted. She still felt that way sometimes,
but the sexual act now seemed an odd way to go about it.
All she saw when the lily moments came were Bradley's
bad teeth. She didn't remember the sensation of his penis
inside her, or anyone else's. What a funny thing, she
thought, remembering wanting a lover inside her. What a
funny thing to want.

Her mother wouldn't kick her out, nor would she ask
any questions. Martha asked Cherry questions only if an
outside force came along and demanded it—a guidance
counselor or teacher or the mother of a friend. Martha
framed her questions neutrally, keeping a bubble around
Cherry. "Is it so, Cherry, that—" and she left Cherry
free to lie. Her father had taken a more active interest in
her. Once he hit her so hard she saw white.

Cherry checked the doors and windows of the house
each night, and when Martha first saw her doing this, she
asked what on earth for, and Cherry said, "Oh, you
know. City habits," and she didn't explain. Now that the
summer weather was here, she had to leave windows
open at night. But the alleys of Hackettstown frightened
Cherry in the dark. She wouldn't go out at night. If she
stayed past the summer, she thought, when the days grew
short, this might become a problem, though the problem
would be solved if she had a gun. She didn't know how
to shoot one but she decided after chatting with people
around town that a shotgun would be her weapon of
choice. Simple to load, easy to fire, its spray would cover
her lack of skill.

"One thing about a gun for protection," the clerk in
the hardware store told her, "you got to mean it when
you raise it to a man." She was sure he'd been in her
high-school class. He looked broader now and sported
thick black-framed glasses, but he was the same. She
couldn't remember his name or what classes they'd had
together, and he never asked her anything about herself.

He never said, "Are you Mrs. Wilde's girl, Cherry? The one who went off to New York to be an artist. Back, I see." And since she hadn't asked to start with and neither had he, the subject wouldn't come up. She went into the hardware store frequently to buy small things for the house—a new can opener, a better spring for Martha's screen door.

She knew that you'd better mean it if you threaten a man with a gun. If it came to it, could she take a life because hers was threatened? Out on her evening walks, Cherry sometimes passed carcasses—birds half eaten by cats, woodchucks shot and flung over barbed-wire fences, dogs run over by cars. It might happen in an instant, she might pull the trigger and fire. She would have no time to weigh her decision, to figure out whether to shoot or not, whose life was worth more. It might be a mistake to think it would be better to take a life than let herself be taken.

She tried to think it all out—the paintings and the flowered summer air, the beauty of the softball games Martha persuaded her to come out after supper and watch, if she would be willing to kill a man. But Cherry never landed anywhere with her thinking, she came to more questions and retraced her routes over old ground, as if she'd dropped something minute in the dust and would have to search very hard to find it.

Eight

WILLARD'S DESK WAS COVERED WITH A LAYER OF DUST, fine as pollen on a flower. He set documents from his lawyer and documents pertaining to Reed's estate on top of the dust. On Reed's death, Willard inherited his mother's estate, and Willard was working out a scheme with his lawyer to provide an income for Sadie by giving the girls what Reed had left to him. His other income would thus be kept intact. It was simple for Willard to come to decisions about what he wished in the long run. He waited to feel pain at his task or fear for his future, but neither sensation arrived to keep him company while he worked.

LATER, HE PICKED UP THE PHONE AND DIALED CHERry's number. He had been phoning her for weeks at all hours of the day and night. Back at Tuxedo, he had phoned from the library, aware that at any moment Sadie or one of the girls or Mrs. Misurelli might pick up an extension.

He imagined that Cherry might actually be in her apartment, counting the number of rings, refusing to pick up the phone. He imagined her on her bed, the phone in its usual place, on the floor by the sink. The first ring startled her and she lay motionless, as if in an increasing state of paralysis until she could not answer the phone even if she wanted to. Or she might be nude, lying with a look of contempt on her face, staring at the ringing telephone.

Still other times Willard imagined that the apartment was empty, not only of Cherry but of everything she owned. He thought of the phone ringing in the abandoned bedroom, the sound covering the walls and the dusty floor, the outlines of places where her things had been.

She had never given him a key to her apartment. Her self-control, or indifference, had made it easy for them to continue. They got together when he turned up at her door and she happened to be home, or when they met by accident on the street, at a museum or a gallery. She wasn't always glad to see him. If he rang her bell, she might call down the stairs and tell him to go away. She never called, not when he was a bachelor and had his apartment, never at the mews house or at Tuxedo. In a city of millions, it was remarkable that they met so easily and frequently, Willard thought. The accident gave their time a sanctuary and permission that reminded him of his school holidays in New York, as if the person he'd chosen at random to follow, turned around and lovingly greeted him by name. After years, the coincidences seemed less remarkable. He came to accept them as part of being with Cherry, until now when she was no longer there.

CHERRY HAD TOLD HER LANDLADY THAT SHE WOULD BE spending most of the summer with her mother, and it took little persuasion on Willard's part to pry the address from Mrs. Vine. "Cherry didn't tell me don't," she said. "But—"

Willard said, "I'm sure it's all right," giving Mrs. Vine five dollars, slipping out of the apartment house.

Nine

HE HAD NOT TRAVELED OFTEN IN THIS DIRECTION. Once he and Reed had spent the weekend near Morristown with distant cousins. Willard was sent to see Washington's winter quarters with his bored oldest cousin. Each time Willard worked up interest in a painting or piece of furniture in the place, she tugged at his sleeve and asked, "Finished?" as if he were a slow-eating dog.

Hackettstown might have been in the Midwest or the South, but for a distinguished Federal building trapped between a gas station and the dry cleaners.

He found the house on Spruce Street with little difficulty, went up the two front steps and across the shallow porch and knocked, first on the wooden screen door, then on the front door. Willard stepped back and waited.

The door was opened by a woman who looked like Cherry, but out of focus and smaller.

"Hello," she said. "May I help you?"

"I'm Willard Weaver, a friend of your daughter's. From New York. Mrs. Wilde?" The woman nodded, and Willard asked if Cherry was home, feeling like the high-school boy he'd never been. She stared at him, taking his measure, and he was relieved when Martha said, "She's out taking a walk. Would you care to come in and wait?"

She settled him in the kitchen with a cup of tea, told

him to take off his jacket if he liked, and they spoke about the weather, which, they agreed, was mild this summer. Now that Willard was there and could see the green Formica table, the little-used front parlor with antimacassars on the arms of overstuffed chairs, the worn kitchen linoleum, the Currier & Ives calendar from a local insurance agent hanging on the wall, he admired Cherry's courage. She had transformed herself into a woman with opinions on the Fauves and Hans Hofmann. Everyone came from somewhere, he thought, but he hadn't ventured this far from his mark.

"You're a schoolteacher, Mrs. Wilde?"

"No," Martha said. "I'm secretary to the principal of the school here. I never have taught. Did Cherry tell you I was a teacher?"

"I have a dreadful memory," he said.

"One more year," Martha said, "and I train my replacement. Then I retire."

"Fine," he said, wishing he had a more friendly manner.

"And your profession, Mr. Weaver?"

I am idle, he wanted to say, remembering a charming genre painting called *Two Idlers*, of a man and a woman lounging on a front porch. On a burnt-bamboo table between them a pitcher of lemonade sweated.

"I suppose you might say that I'm a student. An old student."

As if she'd learned all she wanted to about him, Martha drank her tea.

WHEN SHE CAME TO THE FRONT DOOR OF HER MOTHER'S house, Cherry heard voices in the kitchen. Often her mother's friends dropped by. They sat at the table and drank cup after cup of bitter tea, slowly depriving a flowered plate of its butter cookies. With her mother's friends Cherry felt the same as she always had, rebellious and sulky, though she told herself to ignore them, they were harmless old women now.

In the kitchen, she saw her mother, stiff-backed and uncomfortable, an empty teacup in front of her, no plate for cookies, and Willard.

ALONE, FOR MARTHA LEFT THE KITCHEN QUICKLY, SAY-ing she had things to attend to, they viewed one another cautiously.

He waited for Cherry to come to him. They were not always affectionate, but they had always been physical. Now she stayed by the kitchen door.

"This is kind of a big surprise. Just passing through Hackettstown?" she asked.

"No," he said. "I took the bus."

"I see," she said. "So you met my mother."

"We've been talking," he said.

"What's up? What's the idea?"

"You were never home. I called. I wondered how you were. No word from you," he said.

"I'm all right."

"You look fine," he said.

"Do I? I was just thinking I was looking like wallpaper or something. Getting smaller."

"Well, it's a small town, isn't it? You don't have to be so big here."

"I guess," she said. "How are you doing?"

"I've been in Tuxedo," he said.

"I asked how you were, not where you've been. I don't want to hear about it."

"For the moment, Cherry, it's the same thing, how I've been and where."

She felt unwillingly like touching him, moving his fad-ing blond hair from his bony forehead, smoothing his pale eyebrows. Prissy and self-contained, she sat where Mar-tha had, folding her hands on her lap. The kitchen looked more depressing than usual with Willard there. He had always killed her with his looks, which she never got used to. She'd assumed that was because they didn't spend enough time together for her to get used to him, but now, in her mother's kitchen, she knew that it was because he was beautiful in a way that didn't become ordinary, like one of the people in the Manets she liked.

"Are you planning to stay in Hackettstown for a long time?" he asked.

"I don't know. Honestly."

"This change," he said, "seems so sudden. I had no idea."

"Neither did I."

"I admire you for it," he said. "I consider and consider, and I get nowhere. Everything is always the same for me. The children grow, with or without me. My wife has taken up gardening."

Cherry felt as she used to when she played charades. Just tell me what it is, she always wanted to call out. She was glad he didn't ask her why she was in Hackettstown.

"Some people have it," Cherry said, "and some don't. The M&M company's moving to Hackettstown. Maybe I'll get a job. Maybe I'll get a job making decisions for them."

She felt as though she had never smiled in her life, but through that feeling she saw a clue to something else.

"Your mother said she was retiring soon," Willard said.

"You had a nice talk with my mother?"

"We exchanged some words," Willard said. "Is there someplace I could take you for dinner?"

"When do you go back to New York?" she asked.

"I hadn't thought about it," he said, a little surprised at himself. "I only got as far as finding you. Then I assumed something would happen from there."

CHERRY CHANGED INTO AN OLD SUNDRESS, PINK WITH pale cream flowers, and, for the first time since she'd come home, she put on rouge and lipstick.

She knocked on the door of her mother's room. It was seven and, as usual, Martha was in bed with a book, a pot of camomile tea by her bedside.

"I'm going out to dinner," Cherry said. "And I'll need the car, if that's all right."

"Fine," Martha said. She put a finger in her book, the new John O'Hara, and closed it, turning at an awkward angle to look at Cherry. "I hope you have a pleasant time."

"He's just someone I know from New York."

"Leave a light on in the parlor. And the porch light. That way you'll be able to see, coming home."

Martha hated leaving lights on and Cherry paused before she spoke, absorbing the gift. Her mother might be thinking she'd left New York because of Willard, she realized.

"Okay," she said. "I don't think I'll be late. He's a friend. That's all. And I'm sorry about borrowing the car. I should get a job and have a car of my own, I guess."

Martha opened her book and squirmed to make herself more comfortable.

"I don't mind," she said. "I would tell you if I minded," and Cherry left, thinking it was the nicest thing she could do for her mother just then.

SHE DROVE HIM IN HER MOTHER'S FORD TO THE LONG Valley Inn.

She took him the long way, over Schooley's Mountain, past the Drakestown schoolhouse where Martha had gone, slowing as they passed a big Black Angus farm. At the end of its long, straight, tree-lined driveway was a white clapboard house. "Do you know the people?" Willard asked. "No," Cherry said. "I went there once to an auction. It's a big house. But I'll bet you've seen bigger." It was the only house she'd ever wanted, but she wasn't going to tell him. She drove more quickly through the thick, darkening woods, along the curving mountain road.

"Pleasant countryside," he said. She knew he was watching her and could only have seen the scenery as a passing blur.

"I wish she'd had this car when I was in high school. Of course, I'd probably have stolen it and gone to California, or gotten knocked up in the back seat. These houses are Dutch," she said as they pulled slowly into the village.

She drove over the stone bridge and past the general store. Across the wide road from the store was the inn, a long building with a porch running its length. Wooden rockers lined the porch, and window boxes filled with red geraniums, white petunias, and blue lobelia hung from the railing. The inn had two entrances, one to a barroom where men sat in a darkness broken only by neon beer signs and a television that glowed with the baseball game. The dining room next door was papered in a pattern of eighteenth-century lords and ladies dancing.

They ordered drinks and dinner from the waitress, a skinny woman who clutched a cardigan across her chest but didn't button it. Cherry asked, "Why are you really here?"

"I missed you," he said. "I was curious."

"Why?"

"Wouldn't you be curious if I left town without an explanation?"

"You come and go as you like," she said. "You just got used to me being in one place. Sometimes a person has to make sudden moves. Otherwise you get stale. Stodgy."

"I hadn't noticed you becoming stodgy," Willard said.

The waitress brought their double Scotches, and Cherry was glad there wasn't anyone in the dining room besides them. It was a relief to drink openly and she gulped the Scotch, getting high quickly, loosening up too fast. She ordered another. She couldn't believe he was there.

"Maybe not stodgy," she said, "but too settled."

"Not good for your art?" he asked, and she looked at him to see if he was making fun of her.

"I've given up art," she said.

"Everyone needs a rest sometimes," he said.

"This is different," she said, wishing she would stop talking. "I've given it up for good and now I have to figure out something to do. Maybe I will steal my mother's car and go to California, after all."

They left half the food on their plates, the thick slabs of roast beef and scoops of mashed potatoes. Neither touched the relish tray of cottage cheese, pickles, and olives, crackers wrapped in cellophane.

The inn was her father's favorite spot. He liked nothing better than spending most of a Sunday in the bar next door, joining Cherry and Martha for dinner. Often they'd sat at the table where she was now sitting with Willard. For his serious drinking, the kind that ended in the police station or the emergency room, he went to a tavern out on Budd Lake. Cherry thought it was strange that someone like her father—so noisy, so much going on when he was there—could be gone, and it was as if he'd never been there.

They declined dessert—Welsh Farms ice cream with hard sauce—but had coffee. They decided against brandy.

Willard looked at his wristwatch, signaled for the check. She didn't know when it happened, but the balance had shifted; she didn't want him to leave.

"There's a ten o'clock bus," he said. "Would you mind dropping me back in town?"

There are rooms upstairs, she wanted to say, and motels along the highway.

"The bus stop's near my mother's house," she said.

They were silent during the long cool climb up the mountain. Before Cherry was ready, she was pulling up in front of the drugstore at the bus stop.

"Do you need a ticket?" she asked. "If you do, you're out of luck."

"I have a round-trip ticket," he said.

They sat in the dark. She waited for him to make a move toward her. Her heart was beating hard against her ribs, and she didn't know if she wanted more for him to touch her or to leave.

"I'm not going back to New York," she said. She saw herself years from now in the same spot in front of the drugstore, scrubbed clean like her mother, saving her pennies.

He reached for the door handle and asked, "Would it be all right if I came next week? I have some business to take care of in the city and then I'll go to Tuxedo. To clear things up."

"If you like," she said. "It's fine."

"Unless you'd rather I didn't," Willard said.

"No," she said. "I don't mind the company."

He left the car and she thought of waiting for the bus with him, but instead she drove away. She drove around for a while in the north part of town where the fancy houses were with deep yards shaded in ancient elms. When she got back to the bus stop, Willard was gone.

Ten

JIMMY PAUSED, WIPING HIS FOREHEAD. HE SETTLED back on his haunches, waiting for Sadie to finish weeding her section before they moved along.

"Do you have a terrible time waking up in the morning?" he asked.

"No," she said. "I open my eyes and I'm awake for good."

"Not I," he said.

When they worked, Jimmy asked her freely about everything—how she and Willard met, when they married, what she thought of this person or that, but he liked the conversation to go a certain way. If it became too serious or dwelled too long in the area of the impossible —things one could never have, desires that couldn't be fulfilled, opportunities missed or mistakenly taken up— he quickly made his excuses to leave or set his face in a bored, polite look. Sometimes after Jimmy left, Sadie felt robbed, as if in talking freely—she told him about her parents' accident, remembering feelings and details as she talked—she'd given away something she would rather have kept. But Sadie shrugged off all doubts about Jimmy. She wished she'd known him all her life. He looked so youthful, even adolescent at moments, that Sadie was surprised to see lines and wrinkles in his fine skin, and a hint of an old man's mask resting on his features.

Jimmy made most of his living designing and maintaining gardens for absentee owners, but it was a meager living. Along with his sisters (one lived in Paris, the other in California), Jimmy owned the Round House, all that remained of his grandfather's mansion, which had burned long before ("Imagine four of Willard's house strung together by a not very tasteful architect"). Originally built as a summer house for large dinner parties and informal receptions, the Round House stood at the edge of a cliff. "I never kid myself that I'll get out of here or that things will get better," he told Sadie. "I live here and now, it's all I have and it's more than enough, thank you. I can't bear hopeful people."

The Round House was hell in the winter, impossible to heat and the Park was so lonely. No gardening to do, only days to scratch off the calendar, waiting for spring. He had his cats—Winken, Blinken, and Nod—but they stayed by the woodstove and refused to stir even to sleep by his feet at night.

"This is the trick of summer in Tuxedo—everything looks just as it should but it doesn't last." Jimmy lifted his head to listen to a piercing cardinal's call and he sighed. "I dread the mornings so much that sometimes I can't bear to sleep at night."

"The children don't like to go to sleep either."

"Give them long enough and they'll hate waking, too. You won't have to face this, but in the winter, when I wake up in the Round House, not a soul for miles but some old cranks who are too cheap to go to Palm Beach, I think, Christ, why bother?"

Sadie looked up from her work. Helen had told her that the story around Tuxedo was that the love of Jimmy's life had committed suicide when Jimmy was at Bowdoin, but Helen doubted the story. It was hard to believe that he was so miserable to see him in the garden.

They had decided that the three tiers she'd finished

could use some annuals and had bought out the nursery of their supply of white petunias.

"Maybe you won't be here this winter," she said. "When you've finished retrenching."

"What a pleasant outlook you have. But I regard that as dangerous talk. Loose lips sink ships," he said. "Here, I think we're ready to move along."

Sadie knew about Jimmy's drinking from Helen, who told her that he had smashed three cars and had his license suspended, gotten into a fistfight in a bar down on Route 9 with one of the locals, been caught urinating on the church. All was forgiven, fines were paid, but there were inroads, Helen warned, into every friendship Jimmy had. He drank in a spectacular way, not the steady consumption of most of the Tuxedo people Sadie had begun to meet through Helen. He binged and got violent and lost something from each binge—money, another friend, his car, or a piece of furniture he broke or sold to keep going.

But Sadie had never seen him that way. As they gardened she was entertained by his talk about liquor. He liked the transparency of gin and vodka, the crispness of a martini, the homey integrity of bourbon, and on and on. At times she thought he could intoxicate himself just by talking about alcohol. She watched his thin face light up, saw him straighten his muscular neck to a different, more social angle, as if Sadie, who was weeding side by side with him, had become someone new.

In everything else, she learned, Jimmy was frugal and careful. He grew vegetables, planting them among flowers so that necessity was disguised, he said. He had a larder filled with glass jars of preserves for the winter, contents, date, and his name on the handwritten label. His clothes were good and old, not threadbare but kept up carefully. "I can't afford anything as short-lived as style."

He and Helen told Sadie who was who in the Park, introduced her to people, sent her to the right shops for this and that, and told her that her presence was wonderfully refreshing, a real treat for them, and she believed them. Though there, too, she could go too far with Jimmy. She could imagine him gesturing stiff-armed to say, Don't *lean* on me, thank you.

He glanced over at the children who were playing nearby on the lawn. "Well, it will be years before they have any real problems. Oh, I know childhood is a time of terror and nightmares and all that. But it's so nicely suppressed. Even I was happy as a child."

"They like it here," Sadie said.

"Oh, *children* like Tuxedo. Why shouldn't they? Louise looks so much like Willard, it's shocking."

"Why shocking? Anyway, Marilyn's the perfect combination, I think. Louise looks a little scrawny to me."

"So did Willard at her age. I remember him, poor little orphan boy."

"But he wasn't an orphan," Sadie said. I was, she wanted to say, I was the orphan.

"Well, he looked like one," Jimmy said.

She liked their afternoons so much, the sun on her back as they worked, the children's voices coming over the lawn. Willard had called the night before. He would come out at the end of the week with papers he wanted Sadie to look at. Though she did want to see him, when he was here, her peace would end. "Oh, well," she said aloud and when Jimmy looked up she said, "Nothing. I was just thinking that nothing really can make you unhappy on a day like this."

"Aren't you afraid of lightning striking? Although of course you're right. I should stop being so gloomy."

"I didn't mean that at all," she protested, "really," and Jimmy handed her a pack of petunias, saying, "More work, less talk."

JIMMY LEFT FOR COCKTAILS AT HIS FRIEND SUZANNE Widerberg's ("Suzanne has enough trouble to make four people unhappy any day of the week"), and Helen came by, as she and Sadie had arranged that morning by phone.

They'd planned to look for items for a charity drive, but the evening was too pleasant to go through Reed's suit pockets, Helen said.

The women half-sat, half-lay on wicker lounge chairs on the terrace overlooking the lake. Hollyhock and delphinium bloomed upright and mature. Bright clematis covered the stone parapet. She and Helen held large clouded glasses of gin and tonic in which slices of lime floated like happy fish.

"I fell in love with him," Helen said, lying back, closing her eyes, "almost at first sight, almost before I saw him. I married when I was terribly young. Nineteen. Twenty. Well, not all that young, but I was naïve about a great many things and that made me younger."

Sadie wondered if she and Helen had been naïve about the same things. The girls were in the house and through the open windows, Sadie could hear them playing cowboy. Louise was threatening to tie up Marilyn and leave her for the wolves.

"I had heard about him," Helen said. "It was a much gayer time, before the war."

"The Depression, gay?"

"Between the wars there *was* a kind of gaiety. Oh, well. I was young and much richer than I am now. I didn't know a thing." Helen looked stern and glamorous, and Sadie felt like a child next to her. Sadie had the feeling that Helen knew everything, not only about her own life but about Sadie's. Helen knew everything about Willard, Sadie was sure, and, in time, she would tell Sadie. Until then, Sadie had to be patient. She shifted, and the wicker creaked beneath her.

"And the Park was different then, Sadie. It looked marvelous but it was probably getting ready to go bust quietly. Some people already had. I didn't know a thing about it. I heard people talking and I ignored it, I thought it was boring and temporary."

"You met your husband here?"

"At the spring Horse Show. Have you ever been to a horse show? I suppose they're wonderful if you're show-

ing or if your child is riding or—someone must like it,
they have them all the time. But I always thought how
uncomfortable the seat was and when would it be over."

"And was your husband in the show?" His full-length
portrait hung in Helen's living room, and Sadie imagined
the large florid man in a hunting jacket, about to mount
an enormous horse.

"Heavens, no," she said. "He hated horses. He loved
hunting and fishing, but he drew the line at the costume
sports—tennis, riding. He was pacing up and down in
back of me, and drinking from a marvelous flask he always carried."

"He offered you a shot," Sadie guessed.

"No," Helen said. "But he spoke to me. I don't think
he'd noticed me before. Boredom drove him to me. And
if you'll fetch another drink—one for you, I see, as well
—I'll tell you more. I feel like an ancient crone, telling
fairy tales."

More like a fairy godmother, Sadie thought. Inside, her
feet quickly cold on the tile floor of the glass porch, Sadie
mixed another round of drinks. "There aren't any deer
in the canyon," she heard Louise say to Marilyn, "no
deer, stupid, no bunnies or cows. Just snakes. Come
on."

"Marvelous," Helen said when Sadie returned with
the drinks, "thanks. Johnny was between one thing and
another when we met at the Horse Show. He was having
an affair with—" and she named a grande dame to whom
Helen had introduced Sadie in the post office "—but that
was all but over, coming to nothing. What have you heard
about Johnny, or are you too polite to tell me?"

Willard had told Sadie that Johnny was a drunk and a
blowhard. Sadie blushed, sipped her drink, and said, "I
heard he was a sportsman."

Helen laughed, "Yes, and a ladies' man. He liked
women."

She sounded proud of it, Sadie thought. Was this the
way grownups talked, much less the way they really felt?

"I knew about most of them and not every affair bothered me. But if the woman had been a friend—that was rock bottom. There was a point when I wondered what to do.''

"Do?'' Sadie asked. "What's to do?'' If Willard had an affair and she found out, what could she do? Did he like women? Was he a ladies' man? She had the girls and their welfare to think of, and the rest, all the shine that had been on Willard when she saw him at the skating rink, when she saw his blonde outside the classroom, wasn't the point anymore. True rock bottom was the telephone ringing, the Florida police saying her parents had been in an accident, nothing short of that could hold her attention, that and the girls. He was married only to her, had chosen only her as the mother for his children, what else mattered?

"When I was jealous, I'd think about divorce or having a fling myself, although that seemed too extreme because I was still so in love—it all meant something else to me. The options were unattractive. He was the love of my life.''

"But he loved you?'' Sadie asked. Helen lay, ivory skin, gold and silver hair against the aged brown wicker, who could not love her? Who could look at another woman?

"Oh, he loved me,'' Helen said, "but life goes on for someone like Johnny.''

Sadie hoped that Helen would stay for dinner as she had frequently since Willard had gone to the city. When she stayed, the evening drifted into night, the girls cared less who got the bigger lamb chop, the larger slice of pie, and often they went up to bed without Sadie having to urge them.

"Once I followed his car,'' Helen said. "I was quite mad. I lost him somewhere in New Jersey, in one of those towns just over the bridge. And I got lost coming back here and wandered all over, around and around on the same damn streets in Leonia or Fort Lee or wherever it was, still hoping I'd spot his car. When I finally got back here—we were spending June in Tuxedo that year—I thought, Well, that's the end of something."

"So you were divorcing when he died?"

"Good Lord, no. He was a man of forty-two, Sadie, and when he walked into a room everyone looked up, men, women, dogs, children. Everyone brightened up, even people who didn't like him. He had a big booming laugh that made you feel witty. Anyone could tell you. Willard never liked him much, but he would agree with me."

"Have you noticed the days," Sadie asked, "how they're so perfect lately? These colors at night, the pink and the blue and the purple."

"And your white petunias," Helen said, frowning at being interrupted.

"But why did your husband want to be married at all?"

"I suppose he wanted me. We were married ten years, you know, Sadie. He might have changed with age, of course. But in the years I knew him Johnny simply became more like himself. Drank more, spent more money, shot more ducks. I should have just loved him, accepted him as a natural phenomenon. People in the Park still feel sorry for me because of his bad habits and because when he died I did have a tough time. But no one else really knows a thing about it."

Sadie thought: She's talking about me. She's telling me that he is having an affair, of course he's having an affair. Sadie felt herself pushed back into her chair as if hands were pressing her down.

"Of course," Helen said, "it might not have been such a rosy picture as I paint. If he'd lived. You know that I have a lover, don't you? Willard must have told you."

"Yes," Sadie said, "he told me." Her heart was beating in her throat.

"You'll meet Packy sometime," Helen said. "I'll be interested to hear what you make of him. We're on the same hospital board, that's where we met. It's fine so far, but the thing is—nothing lasts forever, Sadie. Nothing."

Sadie forced herself to stand. Helen was saying that

now she loved Packy and Sadie thought that Helen was trying to give her another message, something more about Willard. But it couldn't be true. She must have drunk too quickly, Sadie thought, or eaten too little that day. Louise stuck her head from the library window and waved to Sadie. "I suppose," Sadie said. "I'd love to meet Packy. You'll stay with us for dinner, won't you, Helen?" It didn't do any good to speculate. The thing to do was to keep moving as if everything were going according to her plan, not hoping for anything, and accepting the present. The way she saw Helen and Jimmy living.

Eleven

WILLARD CAUGHT SADIE AT A BAD MOMENT WHEN SHE looked out an upstairs window and saw him drive up in a shiny black sports car. She had meant for him to arrive later, at cocktail time, with the garden looking wonderful and she in a loose chemise that flattered her. Instead he appeared when she was on her hands and knees cleaning out Reed's closet for Helen's charity. She waited where she was, pushing overcoats and sweaters into neater mounds until he found her in the yellow bedroom. He glanced through the door at the clothing, then at Sadie, and raised an eyebrow.

"I would have asked before I actually gave anything away," she explained.

"Burn it," he said. "For all I care."

"They're awfully good clothes, but it's for a good cause. Helen says that—"

"Where are the girls?"

"Helen took them to an auction in Harriman. We didn't expect you for hours."

She stood, and went to Willard to kiss him, but he held her away from him, saying, "I'm dirty from the trip."

She followed him downstairs and outside to the new car. He lifted a small leather attaché case from the passenger seat.

"I need to have a few words with you, Sadie," he said. "At some point. Maybe now, with the girls away."

"They won't be gone long," she said. "It's almost time for their snack."

"I have some papers for you to sign," he said. "Relating to various things . . ."

"Things like what?" She backed away from the car a few steps and frowned at the petunias, blooming as if they were a little too eager to please. "Where did you get the car?" There was barely room in it for him, she thought, much less the girls, much less her; he must have borrowed it from someone.

"At a car dealer."

"But where?"

"What *difference* does it make? Manhattan. Why don't we go into the library now? To get started."

"Didn't you want to take the train back?"

"What are you talking about?"

"Why did you buy a car?"

"Christ," he said. "There's no need to talk to me in that tone. You have a car here. That's all. I decided I wanted a car." He shifted from one foot to the other and turned to leave the room.

"But it isn't the right car, Willard. It's too small."

"Too small for what?" he asked.

"For our *life*," she said. "What were you thinking of?"

"When you're ready, I'll be in the library. I didn't come to Tuxedo to discuss cars. I have a serious matter to bring up, and we might as well get a few things out in the open."

"I think buying a car is serious. I mean. I've never bought one."

Willard turned and went into the house.

"I'll be there," Sadie called to the open door. "Just let me finish what I was doing."

Sadie went to her bedroom where she searched for a comb and her pocketbook and the car keys, and tiptoed

downstairs, hoping Willard was still in the library. She
listened for him and heard the afternoon breeze.

Heavy, solid, the Straight Eight might want to roll
down the driveway, she thought, and with a mind of its
own pass the club and the tennis courts, the swimming
pools behind the hedges, the shuttered mansions, pass
the Round House, pass Helen's house, roll into the lake
and sink without a trace.

ONCE SHE WAS BEYOND THE GATES, SADIE'S MOOD
lifted. There was plenty of time to talk to Willard anytime
she chose and to finish the closet, to shop and cook, even
to weed a little before dinner. She had been wrong to feel
so pressed by him. Jimmy wanted her to help him separate his irises and he would let her have some bright
yellow ones that looked like butterflies, he said. She
might move her big white bearded iris onto the terrace
next to the house and plant astilbe, he suggested, which
would look good next summer behind the iris. But we
might not be here next summer, she'd said. There was
time to stop by the Round House and lend Jimmy a hand,
and all before dinner.

Summer was at its peak now, she thought, why stay
inside and talk to Willard.

THE LIGHT WAS DAPPLED THROUGH THE TREES THAT
lined the road. Sadie drove past the train station and the
farm stand that offered corn and tomatoes, and the IGA,
a few miles down the road. Soon she was beyond the
cramped houses and scruffy cottages on the edge of Tuxedo. The road opened and on both sides were meadows
filled with sunflowers and daisies. Every so often, she
saw a house set back from the road and she turned to
look for signs of life: wash on the line, a child on a swing,
a tractor moving slowly in the distance.

Ahead, she saw a house just before a bridge. The house
was gray and weathered, and surrounded by overgrown

lilac and hydrangea. The front lawn was almost as high
as the windows. At the front door she thought she saw
the tips of purple flowers of some kind, and she reached
in her bag and found a handkerchief. She spat on it, and
wiped the windshield. She couldn't tell irises from daisies, she thought, with the windshield this way. Sadie
rubbed at one spot in particular, but the handkerchief
only seemed to spread it. Louise's fingerprints, she
thought.

Sadie looked from the smudge to the road and saw
something like a shadow or a rock in the center of the
road. She braked and the heavy car swerved, pulled to
the side, and stalled out suddenly. Her forehead struck
the steering wheel and she cried out in pain.

By the side of the road lay a long-haired yellow dog.
She'd hit it straight on—it hadn't tried to run, she thought
—and its blood was pulsing out onto the hot road. Intes-
tines spilled from a bloody wound. The dog's eyes were
open and a pale tongue fell limp from its mouth.

Everything was quiet now—no wind, no car noise but
the clicking of cooling metal, no sound of birds. At death
the dog had let everything loose and the stench made
Sadie back away. She looked at the car, which hadn't
even been dented, then at the dog, wondering what it was
doing all the way out here by an old, deserted house. She
wondered why the house was empty, why the dog had
decided to stand in the road just at that moment. The dog
didn't have a collar, but it might be someone's dog. Its
muzzle was grizzled; someone's old dog. A dog's one
year was seven human years. The dog was older than
Marilyn and Louise combined. Sadie wanted to say that
she hadn't meant it but when she opened her mouth to
form the words, to speak to herself and reason it out, she
cried, her shoulders and body wracked with sobs. Sadie
listened to herself crying as if she were separate from
herself, and she waited on the road for help that didn't
come.

When she tried to start the car, the engine purred as if
nothing had happened. She parked the car by the side of

the road and returned to the dog. She reached down for
the dog, gasping at first and then grew used to the scent
and the burden. The blood seeped into her blouse, and
she told herself it was all right, it was just blood, just
what was inside of us all. She carried the dog across the
derelict front yard of the old house, weeds and stickers
grabbing at her legs as she went, and put it down by the
front door. She looked around for a shed or a barn or
garage, but there was nothing. With her hands, she tried
to dig a grave but got no farther than blackened fingers.
She needed help, she thought. She felt calm now and
better for her tears. She picked some grass and threw it
over the dog, then brushed at her blouse where the blood
was already drying.

JIMMY WAS DOWN ON HIS HANDS AND KNEES AT HIS IRIS
bed. He turned at the sound of her footsteps and
frowned. "What's wrong?" he asked. When she told him
about the dog, Jimmy said, "Oh, my dear, I'm sorry, but
the blood and all—I thought something awful had happened to one of the girls."

"The girls are with Helen," Sadie said, "at an auction
in Harriman."

"Here," he said, "I'll drive you home and then I'll go
and bury the dog."

"I'll come with you," she said. "You can drive and
I'd be grateful if you did. But I did it, Jimmy, don't you
understand? Doesn't anyone around here understand
about responsibility?" She was about to cry again.
Jimmy said, "I think we should both have a slug of whiskey. Come along, Sadie, this will be grim work."

"It already has been," she said, "Willard's home and
he—" She looked at Jimmy and saw him stiffen up, embarrassed. She followed him into the Round House.
She'd never seen it before in what had to be its ordinary
state—dirty glasses and full ashtrays, towels and clothes
slung over the furniture.

"Today's the day for us to see each other's dirty laundry," Jimmy said. She swallowed the whiskey, then followed him to the shed where he selected a shovel. By the time they were in the car Sadie was relieved that he had taken over and grateful that she hadn't said more.

"I BLAME MR. GARCIA," SHE SAID.

The children were asleep. Dinner was over. She and Jimmy had managed to get her in the house without anyone seeing her, but now, in the library with Willard, it was as if the death had just happened.

"That's a little farfetched. Didn't Mr. Garcia tell you not to run things over?"

"Not specifically," she said. "For a minute, Willard, I thought I'd hit a child, and I thought that if anything ever happened to Louise or Marilyn, I couldn't bear it. I think about poor Suzanne Widerberg—"

"Poor Suzanne?"

"Her oldest boy has a fatal cancer," Sadie said. "Didn't you know?"

"I didn't," Willard said, shortly. "I don't want to gossip, Sadie. You have to listen to me. We must talk."

"It isn't *gossip*," she said. "It's just talking about other people. I mean, Suzanne shows that it doesn't matter how rich you are or how fortunate, there are important things. More important."

"Well, of course, there are. I don't know why you had to get a license to start with," he said.

"Because you brought us to *Tuxedo*," she said.

"So the dog's death is my fault," Willard said. "His blood on my hands. You always try to *involve* me in everything, Sadie, entrap me in your mess. You want me to do this and that with the girls, and be home because you're cooking, oh, I don't know, some dish out of berries and nuts. But I don't care about these things. They don't matter to me at all."

"Don't talk about blood," she said.

Her face was white and the bruise on her forehead was turning colors. Willard was afraid she would be sick. He

saw, for the first time in a long time, Louise's face in
hers. He remembered that he had married her because he
had decided a family would be good for him, not because
she was pregnant.

"You'd better go to sleep early tonight. Take a bath.
We'll talk tomorrow," he said, almost kindly.

"I don't *try* to involve you," she said. "You are involved. Don't you see that?" But she wondered as she
fell asleep if she'd really said it or only wanted to.

"IT WAS AROUND HERE," SADIE SAID, "SOMEWHERE
around here. I was feeling a little distracted, you know,
because Willard had just come back and he hasn't been
here for weeks. Is it weeks? Or only a week? I don't look
at the calendar in Tuxedo the way I used to in New York.
He came driving up in that little black car—it does seat
the girls, I was wrong, but it won't seat the girls and me,
not together. It was somewhere around here. I was looking at the flowers, aren't they wonderful?"

"Wonderful," Helen said, her eyes on the road.

"I wasn't going any faster than I am now, just driving
along, this old car is like a boat, and looking at the flowers
and the houses, here on the road, past where there's any
stores or anything, and I remember I saw some—"

"Stop!" Helen screamed, bracing her arm against the
dashboard, and Sadie jammed on the brakes.

"What is it? What's wrong?"

Helen pushed her hair back off her forehead and said,
"Well, you certainly have good reflexes. No one can say
that you don't."

"What do you mean?"

"I wanted to test you," Helen said. "To see if you
have quick responses. That's why I suggested the drive."

"So you wanted to see if you could get me to crash
again?"

Helen shrugged. "There's no car in back of us. Nothing around."

Sadie listened to her heart beat.

"You're a good driver," Helen said. "Just not terribly experienced. You didn't see the dog soon enough. It didn't register. But it won't happen again. You have to drive, Sadie, if you're going to be in Tuxedo. Unless you have a chauffeur."

"Oh, sure. I can see that any day now." She stared out across the meadow and listened to the hum of bugs and birds, and she said, "I think Willard's fed up with me."

"Maybe you're fed up with him."

"Me? Oh, no. Never. I'm just waiting for him to want me again. I know it'll happen. Sometime. He doesn't know how happy he would be if he just accepted me. And the girls. Accepted what he has. He had a very unhappy childhood."

"Who didn't?" Helen asked.

"You did?"

"Oh, God, it's too nice a day. Turn the car around, Sadie. Let's go."

"You're not saying what you mean," Sadie said. "Do you know something I don't?"

"No," Helen said. "I don't know anything you don't."

If she pressed, Sadie thought, she would only make matters worse, like scrubbing at a stain and rubbing it in instead of out.

Twelve

"ARE YOU READY TO TALK?" WILLARD ASKED.

"No," she said, looking up from the News of the Week in Review.

"You don't even know what I want to say. You've stalled all weekend—that stupid accident, driving around with Helen, fussing over the children. Honestly, Sadie."

"The accident just happened. Accidents happen. Maybe you're right and I shouldn't have gotten a driver's license, maybe I shouldn't drive—"

"Now listen to me. Forget about the dog and the children. Just listen."

She loved the long summer evenings in Tuxedo, even the lonely ones. The library looked cozy with the children's toys around and the *Times* strewn about. She looked up at him and said, "Go on, sweetie. I'm listening."

One of the things he couldn't bear any longer was being trusted by Sadie, almost as overpowering as being loved by her, and so Willard forgot the kind ways he was going to use to disguise his announcement and he said, "We're going to get a divorce. I think we can do it amicably. I have a settlement worked out for you, and I've provided for the children. Once you look at it, show it to Reuben, I'm sure it will seem fair."

"You can't be saying this. Why should we get a divorce?" She heard a ringing in her ears, and her voice, nasal and querulous. "What's fair about that?"

"What's fair about staying married this way?"

"This is the only way I've ever been married. This is the way I'm going to stay married."

"You don't know what you're saying," he said.

"Of course I do," she said. She laid aside the paper, folding it carefully. "We have two little girls. This would be very bad for them."

"I know," he said. "Of course, I know that. It will be awful for them. And it will be worse for me without them. Don't make me say all this, Sadie. At this point, though, I'm willing to let you have them. Sadie, be reasonable. There isn't enough between us for a marriage."

"No," she said, surprising him by her firmness. "That isn't true."

"Why don't you see what I do?" he asked. "How much better and more possible everything would be if we were free?"

"Not that kind of freedom," she said. "I don't think you understand me."

"But I do," he said. "I've been watching you for years."

"Have you? Then you know that I've been waiting for years, for always. And that I can keep waiting."

"Waiting for what?"

"For you," she said. "That's all we do, the girls and me, we wait for you to love us—"

"I do love the girls," he said.

"I'm sure. But you're not really here. Not one hundred percent the way we are. You don't know yet that you didn't make a mistake with me. You think, oh, that you were trapped. But it isn't so. This is right. This is the way you and I were meant to be. If you don't see, we'll wait for you. That's what it is in a family, Willard. People stay together always."

"Sadie, stop it," he said, as gently as he could because she looked right now stolid and immovable, and he wanted only to push her away and to leave. "I want you to understand that nothing will bring me back."

"And you should know," she said, "that nothing will change my mind. I know you'll be back."

She could not see beyond him. She thought of herself at nineteen, falling in love with Willard and looking ahead to years of love with him, not to this, and how unfair it would be if her vision were wrong, if her unhappiness before she found Willard were not equaled by happiness with him.

"Sadie, it's wishful thinking. Give up. I've seen you do this before. This is an imaginary marriage. Pretending that everything is going to be fine when you know that you're miserable, that—"

"I'm not miserable," she said. "I have my beautiful daughters. I have a husband I love. I have—"

"You know, I used to admire your capacity for life," he said. "Your little routines and deeds, your shopping on Broadway and taking care of the house and the children, Reuben calling every morning, you checking the damn house three times before you go to sleep. And I thought you were right—this was what I never had, and if it drove me crazy, well, that was my fault. But I hate it. I simply hate it in a way that you can't possibly understand because you're living just as you wish, as it's natural for you to live, one person on top of another. But I was never meant to be in this life with you. It was a terrible mistake. I hate you, Sadie. Not always. Most of the time I can just ignore you. Tolerate you. You're on the edge there, some noise at the edge of the girls."

She looked down at her lap and began to cry. "You're wrong. You just don't know it yet. And when you see how wrong you are, you'll be able to be happy with us. And with things as they are. And until then—"

"Until you give me a divorce you're on your own," he said. "A maintenance allowance. But nothing more. See how much you enjoy life then. But if you give me a divorce, we can work this out. You'll have an income for life. My lawyer will explain it to Reuben." He was breathing heavily as if he'd been running but he was holding himself back from moving. He wanted to go across the room and hit Sadie, but he stayed, back against the wall, near the door, as far from her as he could get.

"You've never really understood a thing about me. I don't know why you'd cling to this marriage with such tenacity. You're a young woman. You could marry again, someone who would—"

She put her hands over her ears and said, "I won't listen to any more. I don't want you to say things you'll regret, things that you can't take back."

He went over to the couch and looked down at her steadily, counting to ten, then said, "You are being intolerably dense."

"This is the way it is, Willard," she said, almost in a shout. "Nothing will change it. This is your family. I'm your wife. This is what you've done."

He took her by the hair and tilted her head back, forcing her to look at him. He said, "You don't understand this yet, do you? I've lived with you long enough to know how you avoid things, how you twist things around. It's useless to talk to you. It was too much to hope that you'd see reason."

"Oh, Willard," she said, suddenly quiet. "You still don't know how I love you." He wouldn't let her turn her head, but if he had, she would have kissed his hand.

"Then I'll have to try something else, won't I?" He pressed his hands against her ears until she could hear the ocean, then released her so abruptly that she slumped back. He went to the table and gathered up his papers, putting them carefully in his briefcase. "I'll have to find another way to demonstrate my seriousness."

"Willard," she said. "We can talk more. We can find out what's making you unhappy and then—"

"Good night," he said. "Try to remember—if you can keep anything straight for long enough—this might have gone very differently."

IT WAS HOT ON THE STAIRS. SHE HAD HEARD JIMMY tell Sadie that in August you begin to feel winter, and now it was August. One, two, three, Louise counted the August days on her fingers. Soon they would go back to the mews house, and she would have to go to school.

Louise hunched down, burying her face in her nightgown. Their voices echoed through the living room. Sadie was louder than Willard. He was only a rumble but she tried to make out the words. She didn't hear her name, though she thought she heard *girls*. She wondered if she and Marilyn had done something bad, and Willard and Sadie were trying to decide what to do with them. A little girl at the club who'd set her parents' house on fire told Louise about boarding school and being sent away, and though Louise thought that almost anything was better than the brick school, boarding school sounded worse, unless she could take Marilyn with her. She doubted Sadie would part with Marilyn.

She thought she might fall through space trying to catch her parents' conversation. She heard: *Willard, family, no, wrong*. She didn't get full sentences, only words. She would strain to remember and understand her parents' conversation all her life. Later that night (though Louise wondered afterward if it really happened that night or if in memory separate occasions blurred together), Sadie climbed the stairs and found Louise, lifted her up, and carried her to bed. Louise, half asleep, half awake with excitement, thought she could hear her mother crying across the open hallway, an eerie, thin wailing like the wind.

When light crept around the edges of the trees and the hills, Willard came into Louise's bedroom. He was dressed in a wrinkled white suit, and he scratched her cheek with his beard when he kissed her. She breathed in his smell of cigarettes and whiskey, his stale odor of being awake too long.

"Louise," he whispered. "Can you wake up, baby? I have to talk to you but I don't want to wake Sadie or Marilyn. Don't talk loudly."

She turned and curled toward him.

"I don't expect you to understand," he said. "And I can't really explain. I'm leaving, darling."

Louise forced her eyes open but she let them close again. In her dream she was about to touch a lake.

"I can't tell you where I'm going."

"Where?" she asked.

"I can't," he said. "Maybe I don't even know."

She tried again to open her eyes, but it was like the old dream of the black hallway where she ran and ran and didn't move. Her eyelids wouldn't stay apart, her eyes wouldn't focus. She thought her father's eyes were filled with tears.

"I must ask two things," he said, stroking her hair. "First, that you trust me and take my word that I love you and your sister very much. You must know that. Don't you?"

He waited. She tried to speak but her lips were sealed shut.

"I want you to undertake something for me. Even if you don't really understand what I'm asking. And it must be our secret. You mustn't tell another soul. I want you to take care of Marilyn and Sadie."

She stirred and frowned. Sometimes in the city Sadie got a babysitter to take care of them, but how to take care of Sadie?

"You have the most sense." His voice was growing softer now, he was leaving her. "Who else might I ask? Your mother? Marilyn?"

He was smiling solemnly and asking her agreement. To her lifelong shame, Louise nodded and said, "Yes." She nodded and agreed that Sadie and Marilyn were not the same flesh as she and her father. And by the time he disappeared, leaving her in her blackest sleep, he set her apart from them. They were no longer what they had been: the people she loved most, aside from Willard; the people whom she could not tell from herself.

Thirteen

WILLARD SPENT THE REST OF THE HOT DAY IN THE CITY
at his lawyer's office. Long past rush hour—he lingered
over dinner in a nearly deserted restaurant on Ninth Avenue—he drove his new car through the Lincoln Tunnel,
past the crowded industrial towns into the countryside.
The summer was full, and the green landscape embraced
him. Ordinary houses—faded clapboard, crooked
porches—shimmered along the road. Gardens glowed in
strips of color that ran together as he passed. He wanted
to cry out in pure happiness. He tried not to think ahead.

He thought: It's Sadie's fault. A simple divorce, but no
more simple than the marriage. I give her a year, then
she'll see the light.

Should he have been more clever and found a way to
make Sadie leave? Or was this after all what he wanted,
more suited to his nature. He remembered his daughters
as if they were beloved landmarks he'd passed miles
back. Love is what you decide love is, he thought, beginning and ending as you choose. The children would go on
without him, but Cherry—without him, what might happen to her?

By the time he reached the house on Spruce Street, the
porch light was out. One light still burned in a back room,
he could see, but he didn't know if it was Cherry's or her

mother's. He smoked a cigarette, hoping that Cherry would come out, and when she didn't, he drove away.

He slept that night in one of the bachelor's rooms on the second floor of the Long Valley Inn, turned toward the breeze from the stomach window. Before dawn, when he relaxed into dreamy sleep, the Welsh Farms milk trucks woke him. Willard couldn't remember where he was for a moment, and he felt suspended and happy, relieved of time and place.

Later in the morning, he drove back to Hackettstown and found Cherry on her mother's porch, leafing through a *Woman's Day*, the only magazine her mother took.

She said, "Cute car. Let's drive somewhere." She disappeared for a moment in the house, then reappeared holding her purse. Cherry got in his car without looking back, without locking the house, without a thought.

CHERRY DIRECTED WILLARD OUT OF TOWN AND DOWN another road, to Budd Lake. One side of the lake was filled with swimmers and rowers. The other shore held small cabins with screened-in porches. "Keep going around here," she said. They passed a cluster of green-painted cabins, a white clapboard restaurant, and a beach marked PRIVATE. She said, "Here. Stop here."

The cabin was hidden by overgrown shrubs and weedy lilacs, and it sat a little too close to the lake, giving it the look of a boathouse. Cherry took a key from her purse and opened the padlock on the front door.

"Come on," she told Willard, who remained in the car.

"What is this place?" he asked.

"I'll show you," she said.

She opened the door and smelled the dampness and the animals that had lived and died there. He came up beside her and peered in at the darkness.

"It wasn't this bad last time I was here," she said.

"When was that?" he asked.

"A couple of years ago," she said. In the first room there was a table, and she straightened a glass vase that had fallen over, the kind florists' flowers come in. "It was never much."

She turned to look at him. He still stood in the doorway, not setting foot inside.

"Well, I'm really something," she said, her face set and angry. "I was thinking I might be able to come here. I thought if I moved out of my mother's, I would live here."

"Is it your mother's?"

"My father's," she said. "He of the all-time disappearing act. He bought it one time when he breezed through and Mom got stuck making payments. You wouldn't think she was that much of a sucker, would you? I shouldn't complain—I get in a jam, and I'm back like a bad penny. And she never has said a word, asked me a question. And she never complains. Everything's fine, she says. It's always fine. She listens to *Brigadoon* when she gets blue."

"What kind of jam?" he asked. Cherry sounded like Louise when she talked fast to keep from crying.

"My own business," she said. Moving, she bumped the table and the vase fell over again.

"I haven't asked—" he said.

"You never ask. We've known each other for years and you never ask a thing. The perfect romance, right? No holds, no questions."

"You haven't wanted anything different."

"Who said I did?" She opened the door to the screen porch, letting hot air into the damp little room. "I knew if I asked a thing, you'd be off like a shot. Don't shake your head. You have it so neat and clean—your wife and daughters stashed in one place, and me in another."

"And what did you want? Something else?"

"How could I?"

"Oh, wanting, Cherry. Anyone can want."

"Anyone but me," she said, her face crumpling. "No, you're right. I didn't want anything else. For long enough." She turned back to him, composed and grave once again. "Let's get out of here, I think something's

growing on me," but she padlocked the door carefully
behind them.

ON THE WAY TO THE LONG VALLEY INN, ON THE LONG
road downhill, she rolled down the window and stuck out
her hand, her fingers spread, slicing the air like cheese.

"He probably brought women there," she said. "What
a joke. Martha making the payments. My father was a
real charmer. We really used to cheer up when he came
to town. He came and then he went. Like you, Willard."

"I'm not a real charmer," he said.

"You have your good points. You're better-looking
than my father. You don't drink as much. You're
richer."

At the inn they were taken to a corner table. Across
the room was a large party of women, jolly and loud,
secretaries or office workers celebrating a birthday or
retirement. One woman wore an orchid corsage. In the
opposite corner by a window sat a man and a woman and
two teenage boys, carefully studying the menu.

When they had drinks in front of them, Cherry stuck
her finger in her scotch and twirled the ice, then sucked
her finger.

"What kind of jam are you in?" Willard asked.

"It's over," she said. "Maybe sometime I'll tell you."

"Tell me now. Or tell me what you want. Cherry, I
feel as if I'm holding my breath. Waiting. At Tuxedo—"

"Don't tell me anything," she said. "I can't hear it."

He looked away, then took a sip of his drink. She
watched him, remembering his taste and touch. She
thought, Not yet, that she was not ready to return to the
world of the living.

They ordered a second round of drinks, and the waitress brought them the relish tray, the glass dishes of cel-
ery and carrots, cottage cheese and pickled beets. Cherry
played with a cellophane package of crackers, flicking a
finger against the crisp surface. She looked past Willard
at the women, who were toasting someone now, laughing

and clapping their hands. She recognized one of them, though she couldn't remember her name. The woman worked at the five-and-ten, and she'd been a class ahead of Cherry in high school.

The family closed their menus and looked off in different directions, the father for the waitress, the mother at her reflection in the window, the boys toward the bar from which the faint noise of the jukebox and the TV could be heard. They didn't look happy or particularly enviable, but Cherry wanted what they had, and being alone felt shameful.

"Cherry—" Willard began.

"No," she said. "Don't talk to me yet."

She had started to guess or to hope that he was about to do something for her. The hope buoyed her spirit so that she wanted to tell him everything that had ever happened to her, up to and including this moment, this sip of scotch, so that Willard might, uncharacteristically and miraculously, take over and align her events into a long column and total them for her. In that sum she might see her next step. But she didn't want him to know about Bradley, for now that seemed like a mistake that had taken place a long time before, an abuse to which she should assign a low value in her column.

The woman across the room was staring at Willard and Cherry, trying to place Cherry, wondering who Willard was, Cherry thought.

Willard sipped his drink and waited.

Cherry thought, Why not? If she could have him, it would be the end of everything as it was now. Her shrug (which he thought meant she had decided not to talk after all) and her sigh (which he thought expressed her new sadness, worse than her old irritability) were outward signs of excitement. She might be able to pull herself from the fire. She had waited so many years before she finally caught on that her father wasn't coming back. She waited until it was too late for him to make it up and too late for anything to substitute for him, but now she might turn it on its head and change everything once and for all.

She said, "I can't stay here. I've been back here long enough to see that. And I've given up on my work. It sounds so stupid to say that." He nodded, encouraging her. "I'm no good at painting and I never was. There, we agree on that. And I'm thinking of cutting my losses, but I don't really know how to go about it. The first step."

She placed her clasped hands on the table. She wondered if she cried would her tears be honest? She could do anything she wanted. She wouldn't look at Willard because he might look away from her with his trapped-animal look, the one he often had in the morning if she suggested a walk or coffee, his almost-home look. She didn't want her chance to disappear in a moment of guilty feeling.

Finally he said, "Cherry, are you saying—" and he stopped because his voice was shaking. He feared for her and for himself, and the fear went into him through and through, the way Cherry once told him she felt when he was inside her, complete.

"Don't offer to set me up somewhere," she said. "I want, I want—" The ice was melting in her drink. She held back from reaching for it.

"Something better," Willard completed. "You want something more."

"Yes," she said.

"Don't think about it anymore," he said. "Let it be my responsibility. All of it is, anyway. You shouldn't trouble about the details of my life or of yours. See it—largely."

"We'll be together?"

"Of course," he said, even a little impatiently, as if anything short of that goal were unimaginable.

She sighed and unclenched her fists. She leaned toward Willard, ready now to touch him. He said details and meant wife, children. She thought of the children, whose pictures he carried in his soft leather wallet. She wouldn't say a word. The woman from the five-and-ten was leaning over, whispering to the skinny woman in the hat next to her.

Cherry stood and walked over to the table of women.

"I know you," she said to the fat woman. "And you know me, right?" She stared her in the eye as she'd been told not to look at a strange dog, right in the eye, but the fat woman met her gaze.

"If you say so," she said.

"Cherry Wilde. So you can stop looking at me now."

"I was looking for the waitress," the woman said.

"Just cut it out," Cherry said, and she returned to her table. Her heart was beating hard, and she laughed when she saw Willard smiling.

"All right," she said, "all right," as if he'd chided her.

"I can see why you won't be able to stay in Hacketts-town much longer," he said. "We'll have to find some-place bigger for you. Maybe on another continent."

"Another planet," she said. "I don't care. Is this real? Am I going to be happy?"

HE WENT TO THE DUSTY MEWS HOUSE AND PACKED hastily, leaving even his Whistler. When Sadie changed her mind and granted the divorce, he would return and make a more thorough job of it. In the meantime, his lawyer advised him, he must leave the appearance of in-tended return, or Sadie might attempt to seize his assets. The divorce now seemed important but not crucial. What was crucial was leaving.

Willard found a letter from Martin Bowles waiting at the mews house, where the post office delivered some letters, forwarding others to Tuxedo. Surprising both himself and everyone else, Martin wrote, he had married recently, a Virginia widow with four children and more horses, much acreage. The domestic adventure suited him so far, he reported. Willard thought of his bachelor's pots of chocolate mousse and the mirrored ceiling, Mar-tin licking his lips and reaching for another, the forlorn luxury that had led Willard from the Peacock Room back to Sadie. He thought of writing Martin and saying, To no one's surprise I have failed as a husband and father. To my immense delight, I am escaping once again. His childhood, which usually looked wrong-headed, seemed lovable to him. He had been free, and in some of the most beautiful cities on earth. Now he would be able to return and he would go into new territory. He would travel west with a companion as restless as he was. How simple, he thought, happiness was in the end, only the ability to accept things as they were, and to want only what you had.

At the open door of the girls' bedroom, he felt crushed by grief, and wondered—not for the first time—if he shouldn't go back to Tuxedo and take the girls with him. Then he set down his suitcase and closed the door on the abandoned dolls and coloring books. He thought, This, too, must be accepted, this failure and loss.

SHE WAS WAITING ON THE SIDEWALK AS SHE SAID SHE would be, smoking a cigarette and pacing around one small suitcase. Down the street boys had opened a fire hydrant and were jumping in and out of the rush of water. Beside her on the sidewalk was the usual row of garbage cans, covered with boxes, loose clothing, and broken furniture. As he neared, Willard spotted, stacked neatly beside a garbage can, Cherry's canvases, easel, and paintbox. Beside them was her Saratoga trunk.

She watched him pull up and saw him taking inventory, recognizing the finality of the garbage pile. When he was close enough, she picked up her suitcase and stuck it in back of the passenger's seat. "I'm traveling light," she said.

He smiled and asked, "Is the apartment empty?"

"Not a scrap. No souvenirs." She walked around the car and got in, taking her sunglasses from her purse and putting them on. "Let's go," she said. "But how far will we go?"

"A few thousand miles to start with. I'll know when we get there," he said. "Or maybe you'll tell me."

Fourteen

THE PHONE RANG WHILE SADIE DRANK HER COFFEE AT the dining-room table, and George Washington gazed past her, oblivious. When it stopped, the silence of the house rushed in on her. She thought how many things sound like a phone when you wait for a call; a bird, the wind, a car horn. But when you don't care to pick it up, there it is, unmistakable.

She heard the ringing again when she was in the downstairs kitchen, clear through the floor and the carpets, through the wood and ceiling plaster. In the corner were the suitcases they'd brought up for the summer at Tuxedo. An old refrigerator was turned to the wall.

The basement kitchen was for the house as it was meant to be, with a large family and staff, and hundreds of guests throughout the year. She'd been using the small upstairs kitchen all summer. The iron stove—eight burners, two ovens, a broiler and a griddle—was layered with dust and grease. She ran her hand along the surface and her fingers came away coated. She wiped her hand on her pants.

When the phone stopped, Sadie heard a sound like music—the rain. She looked out the small windows eye level with the lawn, and saw the stern black trunks of the elms and maples. The world was beautiful, she thought,

but it had nothing to do with her. Her shoulders hurt.
When she knelt, her knees crackled. Sadie felt a hundred
years old, shut off like a turtle inside her skin.

In the servants' dining room, glass-fronted cabinets
were filled with sets of dishes, decorated ironstone English patterns, cheerful Italian faience. There were mouse
droppings inside the cabinet and flies lying on their backs,
feet up.

Sadie fired Mrs. Misurelli as soon as she concluded
that Willard was gone. She sat grieving, hunched down
and defeated. She remembered from her parents' death
that grieving wouldn't end when everyone else got tired
of it. The girls should have been starting school—Louise
asked her, "Now do I go to the red-brick school?" She
should have been repacking their suitcases for the trip
back to the city. Then a call came, and Sadie went into
the city to see Willard's lawyer; while Helen—who came
by every day, sometimes with Jimmy—took the girls
across the river to visit her cousin who raised Labradors.

"Poor Sadie," Helen said when Sadie explained that
the lawyer had some kind of message from Willard.
"Poor darling." Sadie didn't want anyone feeling sorry
for her. Sadie envied Helen for not being miserable and
disliked her sharply for the poor Sadie. But on the other
hand, she thought, let's attempt to be fair—if not now,
when?

Firing Mrs. Misurelli brought little satisfaction. All it
meant was that Sadie had to clean the house, and cook in
the stuffy upstairs kitchen in the last heat of summer,
cursing Mrs. Misurelli for hiding spices, Willard for having married her, and Reuben for calling constantly, for
circling the remains of the marriage.

SHE DIDN'T LET THE GIRLS SEE HER CRYING. SHE TOLD
them Willard would be back but when she didn't know.
Didn't he always turn up, no matter how late he was?
After ten days, she told them not to wait for him because
that would mean it would take longer for him to return.

She told them not to bother her right now, then regretted it and sought them out, interrupted the games they'd taken up when she shooed them away. For a few nights, Sadie let them sleep with her in the fleur-de-lis room, but she stopped that soon enough, realizing what a comfort it was to her.

Her lungs hurt from breathing, her heart from beating, her stomach from not eating, her skin from holding her together.

What a construction her life seemed, a thin façade built paper brick by paper brick from loving Willard. The girls were evidence of her feeling for him, which was what it always had been.

She should have known but she didn't want to say it aloud. She wanted no one else's opinion on her marriage. She wouldn't discuss it with Helen. Until Sadie could lift her chin and laugh again, she would not talk to Helen. She was wary of Reuben, who kept saying they had to discuss the future. She would have liked to spend time with Jimmy, but he apologized and avoided her. Her distress embarrassed him, she knew. Silence, gardening, drinking; his were not bad methods, she thought, but it was too soon for her to employ them.

If one of the girls saw Sadie now, it would frighten her. If Reuben knew, he would take her from here. If Helen came, she would pity her more. But it would be hours before Helen and the girls were back. Sadie had thought she'd be at the lawyer's all day but the meeting had taken only forty minutes and then she'd taken the first train back to Tuxedo. Tactful and kind, Helen had robbed Sadie of a reason to walk up the stairs with her shoulders back, to take from her face the mask of disappointment.

Time, which had been one steady flow since the girls were born, was her enemy again. Not since the summer when Willard had courted her had Sadie felt this press, as if, all things being equal, she might as well stare at the clock, watching seconds pass.

Sadie took *The House of Mirth* (a gift from Helen who said, "Tuxedo's in it") and lay on the couch in the library. She read a few words at a time, then looked out the window, hoping for Jimmy or Helen. The phone rang again—Reuben, but she wouldn't answer. She looked at the clock. She'd been up eight hours, in six she could sleep again. She read more words and missed a sentence. She forced herself to read the sentence again. A page later, relaxing into the world of the book—Lily Bart wasn't going to have a pretty fate, Sadie guessed—Sadie sneaked a look at the clock. Seven minutes had passed. She was still caught in the quarter-hour.

Helen and Jimmy, and Willard, had told her that Tuxedo was an in-between place, between high seasons, between better places. Now she believed it. The burst of the annuals, the proud window boxes and stretches of day lilies and roses, the swaths of lawn had seemed permanent to her. Tuxedo in summer was a spectacle that she'd watched from her terrace with Helen, from Jimmy's gardens, along her own slow walks, while the children swam in the little lake. The temperature was still mild, even in the rain, and the flowers were not yet faded, but the peak had passed. Tuxedo was an in-between place if you had somewhere else to go. Looking out the library window at her garden, Sadie forgot summer and believed that it had been like this forever: half-light, pale rain, greens glowing before winter came to get them.

WILLIAM PEABODY STRATTON, WILLARD'S LAWYER, had a dark little office on lower Park Avenue, and when Sadie's eyes grew used to the dimness, she saw past the piles of journals and leather-bound volumes, and before the wall covered with lawbooks, Stratton, who bulged over the sides of his high-backed chair. He wheezed as he spoke, which distracted her, but she understood what he told her.

Willard wouldn't accept any communication from her until she was willing to grant him a divorce. At that time, they would work out alimony, a settlement, maintenance for the girls, and custody. Until then she wouldn't know where he was.

"Doesn't this constitute desertion?" she asked.

He wheezed, lit a cigarette, and coughed, then smiled a thin smile for a fat man. "You should, of course, consult your own attorney. Having drawn up this plan, I'm not in the best position to advise you of its defects. You're free, naturally, to go to Surrogate Court and try to prove that your husband is absent and hasn't been seen or heard from, that attempts to locate him have proven futile, then have a Temporary Administrator appointed to protect Mr. Weaver's assets and use them to meet his obligations. But since he hasn't actually deserted you and his children in the usual sense, nor is he unavailable to the court—it would be wasted effort, I'm afraid."

"I don't care about the assets and the court. I won't give him a divorce. So now what happens?"

"Happens? In the financial aspect, you receive an allowance, a keen argument against desertion, by the way. You may continue to rent your present New York house or move elsewhere. He isn't recommending what you do. His idea, Mrs. Weaver, is that you decide for the divorce. And when your brother makes contact with us—"

"My brother?"

"Your lawyer is your brother, as I understand it. Mr. Weaver was confident that your brother would be in touch with me about this arrangement."

"There's no need," she said. "I can tell him."

"He was confident that you would want your lawyer, your brother, that is, to look over the plan."

"Well, if I don't call in my brother, does that mean Willard comes out of hiding and scolds me?"

"Mrs. Weaver, nothing will make him come out of hiding, as you say, except granting his wishes."

"I didn't think he'd do this," she said. "Not leave the girls."

He watched her impassively. She felt a desire that she

knew was impossible, to convince Stratton that Willard was in the wrong.

"If my brother calls," she said, trying to be as cool, "don't tell him anything. He doesn't represent me. Can you be that confidential for me? Or do you have to check with Willard?"

He met her eyes and smiled, and Sadie thought he was seeing her more clearly than anyone had in a long time.

"Though you aren't my client, I can keep this matter confidential for you," he said.

"My brother doesn't know everything," she said. "So if he calls, remember he doesn't speak for me. Only I do."

"Certainly. Though I'd advise you to seek legal advice elsewhere in that case."

"Tell Willard," she said, "that this isn't going to work."

"Mr. Weaver and I are not in communication. Not for such messages."

"Tell him that I don't believe in divorce. I don't believe in *this* divorce. Our family is staying together."

"We will arrange for deposit of the allowance," he said, "and if you wish to receive it monthly, quarterly, or—"

She stood abruptly, gathered her gloves and purse, touched her hat. She said, "Monthly. Tell him what I said."

"Should you change your mind—"

"I won't. You don't understand and neither does he. I won't." She opened the office door. "What about Tuxedo? Can I stay there?"

"He didn't specify . . ."

"But you wouldn't evict us, would you? I don't think so."

"Since he didn't make his wishes clear, I wouldn't take any such action. It doesn't interfere with Mr. Weaver's wishes that I can see—at least for the moment."

"Only with his ideas about me."

SHE CLOSED THE BOOK, AND WHEN THE PHONE RESUMED its patient ringing, she picked it up and settled in the chair by the window.

"Sadie!" Reuben was alarmed and annoyed. "Where the hell have you been? I thought you'd come by the office, have lunch or something."

"Well, I came right home," she said.

"I've been calling," he said, still annoyed.

"Maybe I was out in the garden."

"So what did Stratton have to say?"

"Willard's gone. That was about it. When he wants to come back, he will. And in the meantime, he's given me a kind of allowance, you know. I said I'd take the money monthly, like a salary, what do you think?"

Reuben made a quick, harsh sound of disapproval, and said, "You shouldn't have spoken to him alone. Look, we can get him back here anytime we like, Sadie. We'll file in court for—"

"No," she said. "I don't want him home like that."

"Home? Who said anything about home? We'll get a decent divorce settlement is what we'll get."

"You don't understand," she said. "I don't want that either."

"You want to wait for him to saunter back in? Ask for his pipe and slippers? Look, Sadie, another man might take a holiday from his domestic situation, but not Willard. If he's gone, that's where he wants to be. So I wouldn't make any bets on him coming back."

"Willard doesn't smoke a pipe," she said.

"Sadie, I warn you. The longer these things drag on, the harder it is to get a good judgment when the time comes."

"Maybe," she said.

"All right, all right. You're too upset to talk about this rationally. We'll discuss it when you get back to New York. When do you move back?"

Reuben had given up only momentarily, she could tell. "Move back?" she asked.

"To New York City. It's time the girls were in school, and you got out of that place."

"But I don't intend to leave Tuxedo," she said. "Why should I?"

"Not leave? Don't be silly. If you're afraid to be alone in the city, I've been thinking. There's room in the apartment." Involuntarily, she thought: She would take her old room. Or move into her parents' room, the girls into her room. If she kept imagining the move, it would be as good as done. "Or we could find a bigger apartment. Then you'd have someone to keep an eye on you and the girls."

"You'd move from Mama and Pop's?"

"If I had to," he said, and she remembered him saying, We'll do what we have to do, meaning he would take care of her until she grew up, and that was that.

"You've lived alone for so many years now. You have your habits. Anyway, Willard might come home at any time. If we were all moved in with you, what position would that leave us in?"

"A great position for a divorce," he said. "Which is all you want if you have a brain in your head."

"Reuben, I can't do it."

"Won't," he shouted. "You can but you won't. Grow up, Sadie. Admit that you're making a decision. I shouldn't have let you marry him."

"*Let* me."

"You're ruining your daughters' childhood."

"Oh, you're wrong."

"You don't understand what you're doing," Reuben said. He didn't sound protective, he sounded furious. "You were a fool to marry him and now you're worse than that. You're no longer a child, Sadie. You have your own children to think about."

She said, "I need to be in a place where—"

"Sadie, you don't understand the first thing about Willard. You think he's gone off in the wild blue yonder to be alone? To broaden himself with travel?" Reuben stopped talking and he listened. He couldn't tell if she was crying or if it was the sound of all the air between Tuxedo and his office on Forty-second Street. "Sadie?"

"I won't go back to the city," she said. "Help me, please. Don't do this to me."

But what about me, he wanted to say. He had been waiting for her to return to him, waiting for the end of the marriage, and now his triumph was taken from him.

"You want to garden? Join the club? Supervise your daughters' debuts? What are you talking about?"

"It's just a house," she said, "in a place that's safe. There's a school here and I can use Pop's money for the tuition. I can live here cheaper than New York—"

"Don't be stupid. The upkeep on that place must be a fortune."

"I don't see anyone around here breaking their banks painting and repairing. We'll be all right."

"All right, all right. We'll discuss this more. I'll give you one winter," he said, "and then you'll be back."

You give me a winter, she wanted to say, and who are you to give me a winter?

She said, "Reuben, please. I'll call you later. Or in the morning. I think I hear Helen's car. Bringing back the girls."

"Have you told your friend Helen?" he asked. "I notice she doesn't spend the winters there, you know. The girls need people, even if you don't."

"Oh, Reuben, you sound just like the people you hate. NLU. NOCD."

"What is that supposed to mean?"

"Not Like Us. Not Our Class, Dear."

"Precisely," he said. "My sentiments exactly. You're being stupid. Stupid and obstinate, and—" Should a brother say his sister was breaking his heart?

"I'll call you," she said. "I'll call you."

LOUISE AND MARILYN RAN INTO THE LIBRARY, BOTH talking at once, and Helen followed; all three were red-cheeked and windblown.

"We went around a little lake, Mommy, and the row-boat was so big but Louise got to row. I'm too little."

"Maybe next year," Helen said.

"And Dandy has lots of dogs. *Lots,*" Louise said, frowning at her mother.

Sadie could imagine how she looked to them in her city skirt and blouse, a smudge on her face from the down-stairs kitchen. She was so tired. She put a hand to her head and felt the hat she'd worn into the city.

"There was one darling puppy," Helen said, "but we agreed that you'd have to see her before—"

"Before?" Sadie asked, alarmed.

"You said we couldn't have a dog because we lived in the *city,*" Louise said, reviving the argument of the day. "You said we couldn't."

"Oh, cookie," Sadie said, "could I persuade you and Marilyn to take your baths?" She held out her arms and both girls came to her. She hugged them, saying, "Run your baths, okay? Just like I showed you. I'll be up in a minute."

"Well," Helen said when the girls had left, "it was quite a day."

"You were wonderful to take them. I don't know what I would have done. You know, I've never had a dog."

"Never?" Helen asked. "That's terrible. We used to have lots of dogs. Not so many as Dandy, of course. But she's always been crazy about dogs."

"Does she have any nice old dogs? House trained? Not about to have puppies? Company in the winter?"

"Is this a dog for New York?" Helen asked.

"For right here. We'll stay. I decided. So long as Willard's away. There's no sign of when he'll come back. According to his lawyer. I mean, I know he'll be back. Some men need time away, a holiday. Maybe it wasn't easy for him, having the family, or—"

"And what will you do?" Helen asked.

She didn't have the expression on her face most women would, Sadie thought, not eager or waiting for gossip.

"Well, stay here. That's all. Just continue what we've started. That's why I'm thinking about a dog. I know it sounds crazy. I just got off the phone with Reuben, telling him and he thinks I'm crazy too."

"Why, I think it's terrific," Helen said. "I was wondering what you'd do, and hoping—I was thinking of wintering here too. Now it'll be real fun, won't it? I haven't had a winter in the country for ever so long."

Sadie didn't believe Helen for an instant. She believed that Helen would stay but not that she'd been thinking of staying. Helen was staying to help her, she guessed. Sadie said, "And Jimmy will be here."

"He can't go anywhere else."

"Of course, with us, it's temporary," Sadie said. "Just until Willard gets back. Then we'll go to the city again. Or somewhere."

"Plenty of time," Helen said, and when Sadie looked at her sharply, she explained, "Plenty of time to make up your mind when Willard comes back. But in the meantime, Sadie, it's marvelous in the Park in winter. So quiet. Like being in a little pen-and-ink drawing. I'll call Richard Pankhurst in the morning, if you like. The headmaster at the school. For Louise. And I'll call Dandy. She might have a line on the right dog, even if she doesn't have one herself."

Sadie thought of her brother. What was he doing now? Heading home from the office, opening the door of the dusty, old apartment, eating sour cream and potatoes for supper? Helen was telling her about ice skating on the lake and the Winter Ball. When she finished with supper and putting the girls to bed, she'd call Reuben and beg his forgiveness. He and she were all that was left of their parents, how could they quarrel?

When Helen left—she hugged Sadie before she left, which took Sadie by surprise, and said she'd find her the perfect dog—Sadie went upstairs.

The girls were both in the big tub in the bathroom between their bedrooms. They had used too much water and splashed soapy water onto the tiled floor while they played tea party. Absently, Sadie put her hand in the water and let it drift, smiling at the giggling girls. She looked down into the water at their arms and legs that floated in the water as if disconnected from their bodies.

"Let's get organized, cookies," she said. "Time for supper soon. And don't run around wet. It isn't summer anymore. Or not for long."

Marilyn stood in the tub, and Sadie leaned over with a big towel and picked her up. The little girl clung to her mother, laughing. Sadie looked down at Louise, who remained in the tub. Louise looked back at her, cool and appraising.

"Okay, Louise," Sadie said. "You too. Come on, get out. Don't dawdle. Get right in your pajamas, you might as well. And we'll have something nice for dinner, soup with noodles."

"Noup with soodles," Marilyn said.

"Whatever you like," Sadie said. She found a towel for Louise and wrapped it around the girl when she got out of the tub. Then Sadie went to the door.

"Are you going too?" Louise asked.

It would have been easy to deliberately misunderstand Louise, but Sadie turned to the dripping, solemn child, and said, "Never. Not unless I can't help it, and even then . . . Just never. Okay?"

Louise nodded and began to dry herself in earnest.

LATE THAT NIGHT, ALONE IN HER BEDROOM, SADIE picked up the phone to call Reuben. She listened to the dial tone, replaced the receiver, and pressed her hands against her forehead. What Reuben would never understand was that she had no choice. To move back to the city, she would have to believe that her married life was over. And to be practical, it was cheaper to live here, at least how she would live, no club, no trips abroad, no long journeys to wear out the car, just living here as if it were anyplace, only safer and better. She could not see herself being able to live now in any apartment or street of the entire city without Willard. The Hudson was the Styx to Sadie and she knew there was only one way to cross it. She would wait for Willard right where he left her, and he would have to be dead before she could believe in a place or time past Tuxedo. She would not give up, would not call Willard back for a divorce. Reuben would come around, he always did, or there would be some way to make it up to him. She wondered if she was strong enough to live this life alone, if she was loving enough to outwait Willard.

She would see if she could last a year, she thought, then reconsider. In a year, he'd probably be back anyway and would respect her for keeping the family together. He had never been an ordinary person with ordinary feelings. She took her hands from her eyes, smoothed down the sheets around her, and turned off her light.

Fifteen

BUYING A SIDE OF BEEF WAS THE KIND OF THING THAT Sadie would never do in New York, but living in the country it seemed right. When Sadie returned to the mews and brought all their things to Tuxedo, she hadn't understood how they'd lived in such a small, dark house. In Tuxedo there was always the glow of broken shade, a patch of light across the lake.

They had a dog now, a spayed female mutt named Dandelion after Helen's cousin Dandy, who found her wandering along the road. Dandelion was red-haired with floppy setter ears, and a terrier ruff around her shoulders. She had shaggy white paws and broad black nostrils. At night she roamed from room to room, her long nails clicking on the wood floor, dividing her loyalty among Sadie and the girls.

With a dog, they would need extra bones and meat. Helen said she would take some of the beef and gave Sadie a list of cuts she preferred. Jimmy finally agreed to take some ground meat and a few steaks if there was any left over after Helen and Sadie filled their freezers. "One hoof," he said, "no more."

One afternoon in October, Sadie left Marilyn with Helen and set out with Louise for the slaughterhouse on

Route 17. The first leaves were turning and it was crisper at noon than at any midnight in summer.

Louise watched out the car window and counted mailboxes, which went by too fast, and then porches. She hated it when Sadie drove, leaning forward, frowning, her shoulders hunched up to her ears. Louise was always sure they'd miss their destination or that Sadie would get distracted and drive into a tree or a house. She had not been able to believe her luck when Sadie told her they weren't going back to the city. She wouldn't have to go to the red-brick school. Going to the Tuxedo school, even if it meant wearing an ugly uniform, wasn't as bad. She could see the castle from some classroom windows. But she wondered each morning when she woke happy to be going to the Tuxedo school instead of the city school, if she was wrong to be glad, and if the loss of her father was meant to be an unfair exchange for this little happiness.

"Okay, Louise, look out now, it's anytime now, the ad said after Sparksburg, okay there's the Sparksburg sign, entering, leaving, okay." Sadie kept saying, "One and a quarter miles, one and a quarter miles, do you think we've gone one and a quarter miles yet?" until Louise said, "I don't know a mile, Sadie."

Sadie asked her all kinds of questions that Louise couldn't answer. Did Louise think the car sounded all right and should Sadie trust the mechanic, who certainly seemed to love the Packard but was he charging too much to replace the brakes? Maybe they could get along with the soft ones for a while, like putting up with a hole in your shoe just until you got to the shoemaker. Was it better to pay him in full at the grocery store? Did Dandelion seem to notice any difference between the dog food they fed her now and the more expensive stuff?

The butcher's was a low cement-block building set next to an abandoned garage, its metal red-horse sign flapping in the wind, and a trailer that was up on blocks, a few pieces of bleached-out clothing stiff on the clothesline.

Inside, there was the smell of cool meat and fat, as if they'd stepped into a giant refrigerator. The people working there dressed in white, and kept their sleeves rolled up. They looked alike, eyes close together and flat broad noses. Sadie guessed it was a family business. She squinted at a big diagram on the wall of a cow with letters and numbers covering its hide. She would have to tell the woman behind the counter how many pounds ground and which to be steaks, how thick the steaks should be and if they wanted stew. She wanted to turn and run.

Sadie fluttered and laughed, talking to the woman, telling the woman that she'd never done this before and needed lots of help, they were new to the area. What did the woman care? Louise wondered why she had to be the one to come along, why Marilyn was supposed to be too young.

She scuffed her feet along the floor and leaned against Sadie until her mother asked her to stand up please. Sleepy, Louise walked around the place, pressing up against the glass of the display cabinets, looking at a pig's head, its eyes wide open, and wheels of bright yellow Cheddar, dozens of eggs, slabs of bacon. She looked through one cabinet and watched a man slicing chops from a large slab of meat. He reminded her of Willard when he drew a picture for them; the same concentration and precise movement. She wondered where Willard was all this time and if they would go back to the city when he came back, if he would think she'd done a good job with her mother and sister. It was hard watching out for Sadie, who got a new idea every day, about the dog and where they would plant the vegetable garden in the spring. Louise tried to come up with answers to Sadie's questions and not give in to her feeling that Sadie shouldn't be asking her. The smell of fat penetrated Louise's nostrils and she worried that she would be coated inside and out with the white solid stuff, clogged until she choked.

Next to the man, on a butcher block, was a pile of pink and white snakes lying shiny and silent. She stared, waiting for them to move, wishing she could ask what they were. The butcher looked at her and winked, and she hurried back over to Sadie, who was saying, "Oh, well. I guess we could eat a lot of meatloaf." Louise said, "Come here. I want to show you," and when Sadie didn't answer, but kept looking from the diagram of the cow to Helen's list, Louise said, "Mommy, Sadie, you have to come look." "Just a minute, Weasel," Sadie said. "No," Louise shouted, "now," and she pulled at Sadie's skirt until Sadie looked down. "For God's sake, Louise, whatever is it?" she asked, and let herself be led over to the cabinet to look where Louise pointed. "What is it?" Louise asked, close to tears, "what is it?" She thought she saw one of the snakes move and ducked behind Sadie, feeling stupid and little, like Marilyn or some baby. Sadie leaned forward to get a better look, and Louise tried to pull her back.

"Louise, what is wrong with you?"

"What is it?" Louise asked again, crying, ashamed of herself.

"For heaven's sake," Sadie said, "it's what we're all made of. It's what's inside us all. Now calm down so we can get out of here."

She waited by the door, her back to the butcher, who might wink at her again, trying not to hear Sadie's voice as she finished up ordering. Louise vowed not to eat any of the meat, and she thought, Not what I'm made of, not what my father's made of.

PART
FOUR

One

IT SEEMED TO MARILYN AND LOUISE THAT AS THEY grew, the world became smaller. There was the Round House, with its overflowing gardens and ceiling-high mirrors, though the Round House changed as Jimmy sold off his furniture and paintings, and the pastel interiors and faint scent of carnation in Helen's house, which were always the same. The castle was Louise's. The gardens that grew to cover the hill and surround their house were Sadie's. Blindfolded, they could draw maps of Tuxedo Park showing gate, lake, house, castle. To go to school they went up the hill, and to enter the world they went down the hill, past the club, around the lake, through the gates, out to the road that led everywhere.

Though their house seemed endless and mysterious when they first arrived at Tuxedo, each corner became familiar, and had its season and use. The glass porch was only for summer, though sometimes it was warm enough for Marilyn's birthday party in October; the library for year round. In winter, Marilyn and Louise shared Reed's yellow bedroom, landlocked in the center of the house. The radiators were broken in their corner bedrooms and Sadie said she would wait to repair them. Some third-floor rooms were closed off, too, when a window broke or the plaster cracked. Sadie taped up cardboard over the

missing pane and closed the door. Furnace and roof—if
they went the house would go, and Sadie woke up at
three on winter nights, listening for the shudder of the
furnace's cold-air return, and the slide of tile from the
roof. During their first January thaw, the roof leaked,
ruining the plaster ceiling of a servant's room. But with a
few tiles replaced, the roof was sound again. Early on,
the bathroom with the Oriental mural froze, and Sadie
had the pipes disconnected and locked the door to the
room.

She listened at night for sounds that would cost her
money. She had the allowance from Willard, the trust
from her father's business, and what she earned helping
Jimmy garden in season. Each month she and Louise sat
down with the bills, and Sadie divided them into those
that had to be paid, those that would be paid partially,
and those they could put off. Louise was shy about going
into stores where they owed money, though Sadie told
her everybody did it and that in fact they paid more than
most.

In spring (just after Louise's birthday), the girls took
their rooms back. Louise's rose room looked out on the
hillside garden, where her mother's rugosa roses covered
a weedy bank. On summer nights, the smell of roses in
the air, Louise stared at each repeat of the wallpaper:
petals, stem, bud, and each assumed a different shape
and shade. In the yellow winter room, she fell asleep
trying to remember the roses.

Marilyn's memory began when Willard left and Sadie
decided to use the downstairs kitchen. Only when Louise
pressed her could she recall the summer before the fall
when they didn't go back to the city and Louise didn't
have to go to the red-brick school. Louise coaxed city
memories from herself, then foisted them on her sister,
insisting that she must remember the time he took them
to a museum or the park or to a toy shop or brought
them velvet ribbons. How he used to tie their sashes for
them when they wore their party dresses.

"But I don't remember," Marilyn said.

In summer, the big kitchen was cool, and Marilyn could see blue sky through the lawn-level windows, though she liked it best in winter, when the big stove made it the warmest room in the house, and the windows showed snow packed against glass and only a corner of ice-blue sky. Marilyn sat in the rocker in the corner of the servants' dining room, one step up from the kitchen. Sparky, a smoke-gray cat who turned up one winter day on their doorstep and never left, lay like a fur stole across the table while Louise did her homework. Dandelion slept on the floor, her feet twitching in a dream chase. Marilyn was content. She had no wishes.

Louise was restless in the winter, and though she went ice-skating and sledding, was taken out on iceboats on the lake, and played ice hockey with the school team, she complained that she was trapped. The blanket of snow that her mother told her protected the plants choked her. During snowstorms, she paced the house until Sadie told her to stop. "You're making me nervous," she said, "you'll drive me crazy."

In winter, the Park was reduced to a few elements. Snow covered the earth, obscuring cared-for and neglected gardens alike, the horizon of snow broken only by low stone fences. Trees were bare, and loaded after storms with piles of snow precarious as a big spender's savings.

No one plowed the circular driveway to the castle or worried about snow damage to the slate roof or about ice storms that smashed windows and flung sticks and branches inside. Once snow piled against the door and lower windows, Louise couldn't get in. At home her mother watched her, in school the teachers. In the castle, she could sit unobserved, admiring her own stillness and waiting for something to change.

Early on, she found the closet where Sadie stored his clothes, books, boxes of photographs and reproductions, and his manuscripts. When Sadie wasn't around, Louise went through the boxes and suitcases, even the pockets of his jackets and coats, and took what she liked up to

the castle. She set up a corner for his green silk muffler;
the portfolio of western photos; a few books on Japanese
prints, which reminded her of trips to the museum with
him. She wanted to take the Whistler, but Sadie set it up
on the mantelpiece in the library and would have missed
it. Louise worried that in winter the rats in the castle
would eat the photographs, starved as they were in the
cold.

LOUISE WALKED REGINA WILSON HOME ONE AFTER-
noon when there was nothing better to do. Regina, a fat
girl with pale freckles, lived near the castle, in a gabled
cottage that Jimmy called the unhappy house. No one
lived there for more than a few years. More often than
not it stood empty. Owners divorced or left the Park in
distress. One man committed suicide, not in the house
but still, Jimmy said, and another, a stockbroker, had
gone to jail for kiting checks. "These things happen,"
Sadie said, but it was true that they happened more often
in the unhappy house. Before Regina's mother, the house
was owned by a couple from New York, who'd had the
place redecorated, chintz everywhere, and put it on the
market while the gardens and the lawn were still torn up
for landscaping. Between owners, the place was littered
with buckets and empty clay pots, geraniums knocked
over by dogs or the wind, or perhaps one of the unhappy
sellers.

Louise and Regina had worked after school on a special report for History on Elizabeth the First. Louise
meant to go straight home, but Regina had persuaded her
to walk home with her. She talked about her mother, who
was retrenching, "trying not to buy so many clothes, you
see." Regina's mother spent all day on the phone, smoking cigarettes and laughing in deep, quick barks, and at
two she switched from coffee to sherry, at four to Scotch.
When she first came to the Park, Mrs. Wilson tried to
become friends with Sadie, who had a reputation as a
good scout, who didn't steal husbands or boyfriends, was

reliable to round out a table and helpful with advice about gardening. Sadie might be pitied in comfort, for her trouble was insoluble, and no one need feel they should try to help. Sadie avoided Mrs. Wilson. When Louise visited, Mrs. Wilson hung up the phone and focused her mascara eyes on the girl, asking her about school and why Sadie never visited her, and who exactly were Sadie's friends, leaving Louise tongue-tied.

Louise dragged her feet through the snow, too tired to do anything but listen to Regina's tinny voice and follow her around the lake. When they reached the unhappy house, Regina called out, "Bye. See you tomorrow."

Louise wasn't sure she would have gone in if she had been invited. Still, it was cold and gray, starting to do something between snow and rain, and Louise caught a glimpse of Regina's foyer, decorated with red ribbons and lights for the Christmas season. She usually didn't mind Regina, but when the door closed on Regina's chunky form, Louise swore she would never speak to her again.

She retraced her path around the lake, looking up to try to make out the castle high above. It was dusk, when Sadie worried if the girls weren't home. Louise trudged on.

Feet cold and wet, wool coat smelling wet, Louise came into the house and called out, "I'm home!"

"Here," she heard faintly from the kitchen.

Louise took off her boots and stuck a finger through a hole worn through one sole. She hated to tell Sadie because she would have to hear about how poor they were and how they couldn't afford new boots. She set the boots on the brown paper bags Sadie laid down for that purpose, soles up, hoping Sadie would notice the hole on her own. She peeled off her wet coat and draped it over a hall chair. Louise could see Sadie's face wrinkle when she saw the damp upholstery.

Sadie was in the big kitchen rocker, and on the floor all around her were cookbooks. Marilyn was at the table, rolling out pastry. She wore a bath towel around her waist and there was a streak of flour in her hair.

They both looked up at Louise and smiled, warm and oblivious to how cold her feet were, to the snow, to anything but what they were doing. Marilyn stood on a wooden box to roll the dough, and Louise wanted to kick it out from under her.

They were happy in their cores, she thought, something they couldn't share because they had no idea they had it. They had the ability to go through a day as if it were a maze with a prize at the center. They made ceremonies of baths and cups of tea, food and flowers for the table, spotting a songbird or seeing clouds that looked like charcoal smudges. Perhaps her father meant her to care for their happiness, as if it were an affliction.

Sadie was sad sometimes, but all people got that way, she reassured Louise. "Don't worry, dolly, everyone alive goes through this," she'd say, looking at her daughter in despair, wandering around the house in layers of old clothing, her hair unwashed for days, smoking one cigarette after another and boiling chicken for stock. "Just be happy you're still a little girl."

"So late," Sadie said. "A good day at school?"

"Regina and I worked on a report. Then I walked her home," said Louise.

"Nice of you, a day like this," Sadie said comfortably, returning to the cookbooks.

"What are you making?"

"Maybe a meat pie," Marilyn said. "We wanted to do something we've never done before. So Mommy's reading the books and then we'll make something up."

"When will this be ready?"

"I don't know."

"When will dinner be ready, Sadie? I have a lot of homework to do."

"I don't know, Weasel. It's only five, and we just started. Why don't you make yourself a snack? It'll be late but fabulous."

"I don't want a snack," Louise said. "I want dinner."

"Well, dinner won't be ready for a while. So just eat a little something and calm down."

"I hate this," Louise said. "I just hate this. Why doesn't anything ever happen on time?" She sat at the table and burst into tears, which she hated also. She put her head down, avoiding the flour, and wept out of her own core, which wasn't made of happiness. Sadie came over and rubbed her back, saying she had no idea Louise was so hungry; then she made a jelly sandwich while Marilyn stood big-eyed at Louise's side.

Louise said, between bites of the sandwich, "I'm sorry."

"Oh, don't be sorry," Sadie said, already back at *Fannie Farmer*. "My goodness, when I was your age, I cried all the time."

"You cry all the time now."

"Not all the time," Sadie said.

"Not so much," Marilyn said.

"Okay," Louise said when she'd finished. "I'm going upstairs. Wake me when the pie's open and the birds begin to sing."

Upstairs, beneath the cold blankets, Louise tried to see her father's face, bony like hers, hair like hers, but all she could see was herself, and when she tried to hear his voice, all she heard was herself crying.

Two

HELEN KEPT A SMALL APARTMENT ON EAST SIXTY-eighth Street, a *pied-à-terre,* she told the girls, and spelled it for them, to which she retreated when Tuxedo was gloomy. If Helen didn't like a day, she called it gloomy, whether it was dark or bright. If Helen liked something, it was adorable, and the opposite of adorable was ghastly. After one try at sticking it out—Sadie's first winter—Helen moved to her *pied-à-terre* when the season turned both ghastly and gloomy after New Year's, reappearing only for an occasional weekend.

While Helen was away, Sadie kept an eye on the gray house. After a power failure, she checked to see that the furnace was back on. If work was being done to the house —painting or papering—Sadie dropped by and reported the progress to Helen by phone. Sometimes when Helen was gone Sadie walked down the road with Dandelion and, while the dog waited outside for her, went upstairs to Helen's bedroom. In the dressing room she opened the door to Helen's closet, breathing in the faint sachet of Helen's perfume and letting the colors of the clothes that hung on padded hangers give her peace. Sadie was startled when she glimpsed herself in Helen's full-length mirror, dressed in an old overcoat of Reed's, a scarf wrapped to her ears, a wool cap pulled down over her forehead.

Before she left for Manhattan, Helen always gave the best Christmas party in the Park.

Year to year, the decorations were the same. Pine boughs were always draped across the front of her gray house, the boughs dotted with pine cones painted silver. She gathered and painted new ones each year, she explained to the girls, because, "They lose their newness."

Inside, wood fires burned in every fireplace, and white azaleas in terra-cotta pots were crowded onto the windowseats of the bay windows. Helen ordered a Scotch pine each year, twelve feet tall, three feet shorter than the living-room ceiling. She hung the tree heavily with decorations that had been in her family and her husband's. One year, at Packy's urging, she used only small white Austrian candles to decorate the tree, and lit them for the party. She said they were beautiful but it made her so nervous she never had them again.

Helen had an album of photos of her Christmas parties, and her mother and grandmother's Tuxedo albums of their Christmas parties and toboggan runs, skaters in long skirts and carrying fur muffs, boys in short pants hauling wooden sleds up the hill, iceboats on the big lake, and grinning tennis players shaking hands across the net. "That was at the old club," she said. "It burned down."

"Who's this?" Marilyn asked on rainy days when Helen showed her the albums, pointing to one or another figure.

"Oh, he was a darling man," Helen said, and if she didn't know exactly who it was, she said he was a guest. It was hard for Marilyn to accept that the vigorous, smiling people in the photographs were either dead now or in their late eighties. Helen gave up explaining and spoke of them as if they were liable to walk in the door any time looking as they did in the pictures.

Beneath the tree was a crèche carved from an oak on Helen's grandfather's upstate farm. She'd kept the crèche since she was a child, and she explained the meaning of the figures to the girls. Marilyn loved to pick up Baby Jesus and kiss him when no one was looking. Sadie

worried at first about going to Helen's Christmas party,
about her girls growing up without Jews, and she wondered at herself, how easily she had slipped into the celebration. But she decided that because there was no way
to get rid of being Jewish even if she or the girls wanted
to—hadn't history shown the world the truth of that—
then there was nothing to worry about.

Surrounding the crèche were presents to and from
Helen, always two each for Louise and Marilyn. They
made presents in art class for Helen and Jimmy. Each
Christmas, the girls collaborated on a drawing of family
incidents from the past year for Sadie, who framed the
drawing and hung it in the library. One year after a
Thanksgiving that everyone agreed was gloomy, Sadie
found a yellow kitten by the lake and brought it home.
Sparky hated it. Sadie kept it in a box by the kitchen
stove and tried to feed it with one of Marilyn's doll bottles, but the kitten died in two days. Marilyn wouldn't
have anything to do with it from the start. When Louise
asked if they should include the yellow kitten in the
Christmas drawing, she asked, "What kitten?"

Helen hired Ben and Beatrice from the club for her
party, and sometimes Darian, who lived in the village and
whose grandfather had helped build the Park. The same
people came to the party each Christmas, some of them
Park people who had sold or closed up their property.
Louise asked Helen if the family who owned the castle
ever came, and Helen said it wasn't a family, just one
man, and he lived in Geneva and played chess all the
time. Louise read *Daddy Long Legs* and imagined the old
man giving her the castle, saying, It's yours—property
belongs rightfully to those who love it best.

If her wish were to come true, it would happen at Helen's Christmas party, Louise was sure. Park people
came to the party whom Sadie and the girls never saw at
school meetings or in the store, post office, or library,
never passing them on the narrow Park roads, as if they
existed only at the party. Mrs. Hunter, who never remembered Sadie from party to party and never nodded

back when Sadie said hello to her at the post office or the store, came, and each year Helen introduced her anew to Sadie. Helen laughed and said, "She's always been a terrible old snob, don't pay any attention to her."

There were guests from New York and Long Island, from the boards Helen served on, and from her schooldays. Relatives came on occasion from Savannah, where Helen's mother was from, and stayed the holiday week.

The guests at the Christmas party came to expect not only the same decorations, the same food and drink, but each other. They also came expecting the same weather. What they wanted was a snowstorm that would begin when the last of them passed through the gates. It would coat the ground and the trees but leave the roads passable. The storm would progress until it was a feast of whiteness, so that if a guest should look out the window, he would feel as if he were inside a glass snowball in a world that was nothing but snow. The storm would end in plenty of time for the roads to be cleared for the walkers and the cars, and especially for Christmas midnight to be toasted under a black winter sky whose clarity was broken only by the stars.

Though such a snowstorm didn't always arrive, it was its snow and wind that the guests recalled about Helen's party. If questioned, no one could name the year when the snow was perfect, but each guest would swear that it had happened the year before or the year before that one, just out of reach of memory.

Three

"DO WE HAVE TO GO?" LOUISE ASKED.

Sadie was in her black dress, looking in the mirror and holding up earrings. She glanced at Louise, already as tall as she.

"Yes," Sadie said. "We have to go because Helen expects us. And we *want* to go because we always have such a good time."

Sadie had long ago stopped trying to dress up or down for the Park, knowing that not only was she too poor to do much about clothes, but that she didn't look any worse than her neighbors. "It's the country," everyone said, and wore clothes from the year or decade before. Sadie wore her black dress to winter parties, and her blue one to summer gatherings. Helen had given her rhinestone earrings for the party.

"You could say I was sick," Louise said. She tugged at the sash of her wine-colored velvet party dress. The lace collar—real lace, Sadie said, handmade—scratched her chin. The dress was the best of a package sent by some Long Island cousins whom the girls had never met. Louise didn't want to meet them, and was grateful only that her hand-me-down wasn't from Park people.

"I could say you had the flu," Sadie said. "And tomorrow Helen sees you on the ice at forty miles an hour.

Then what? You've hurt her feelings. And you always have a good time there."

"I don't. I hate parties. I hate dressing up."

"Me too," Marilyn said.

Marilyn was becoming fatter, and Sadie hoped that puberty would bring her a Weaver body. Marilyn's party dress, blue velvet with a lace collar, was from Helen's niece in Savannah.

"Helen always has those neat cookies," she said. "And the little sandwiches and biscuits and ham from her cousin's place." Louise rolled her eyes. "Am I old enough for punch?"

"One glass," Sadie said. "If you get loaded, Louise and I will have to carry you home." Marilyn's face clouded over, and Sadie said, "Oh, I'm sorry, dolly, I didn't mean it that way."

"If you'd let me diet," Marilyn said.

"You're too young," Sadie said. "You're still growing and you need everything you can get."

"Growing," Louise said. She snorted and left the room.

Sadie decided that the rhinestone earrings made her look like a silly woman wearing earrings rather than a woman wearing silly earrings. Her mother's diamonds were too small with all the black, so she settled for her pearls, also too small, and an enamel pin of a Christmas tree.

"Christmas spirit," Sadie said. "Bless us everyone."

SADIE LIFTED A GLASS OF CHAMPAGNE FROM THE SILVER tray Beatrice carried. She glanced around the room, noting that Packy Schwerner and the guests from the city stuck out from the Park people, not just as if they were from another place but from another time. Beatrice sometimes served at Helen's dinners, and early on when Sadie went into the kitchen to fetch something, she and Beatrice began to talk, and Sadie confessed that she was the one who had fired Mrs. Misurelli, Beatrice's cousin, and now Sadie didn't know how to find someone to come once or twice a month to help with the enormous house. She apologized to Beatrice, who had sallow skin and patient eyes, saying she'd fired Mrs. Misurelli at a difficult time for her, but before Sadie could say more Beatrice said, "Milly's a bitch, Mrs. Weaver. Who could stand her?" Beatrice sent her sister-in-law Anna, who came when she needed extra money, which suited Sadie, though she never felt at ease with Anna as Helen did with her servants. Sadie wondered if this meant some lack in her, if Anna could detect that she didn't belong in the Park.

From his nickname, Sadie had expected Packy to be big and blond, like Helen's late husband, not a hawk-faced European. He wore a black tuxedo and looked more distinguished than any other man at the party. Sadie watched Helen, who turned her head now and again to place Packy, her expression softening as if it gave her pleasure to know where he was.

He had stationed himself by the Christmas tree and was scanning the crowd, not because he wanted company but to see how the land lay.

"Sadie!" he said as she approached. "I thought you'd never get here!" Packy's accent was faint, more like a speech impediment than an indication of his origins.

"It's not easy to get two girls dressed. Two girls and me. And out in the snow," Sadie said. He always made a fuss over her, and he reminded her in the most general way of her family. He wasn't Jewish but was Russian-born, great-nephew of an official high up in the Kerensky government.

She followed his gaze to the teenagers and children gathered around the piano in the next room, singing Christmas carols. Louise was next to Regina. Marilyn was harmonizing with a Savannah niece.

"Well, life seems very pleasant just as it is this Christmas," he said.

"I thought you were all for change. Last year you were urging me to sell my husband's rugs and take a trip."

"There is no being for or against change, Sadie. You should know that."

"Oh, I do," she said, "a prisoner of fate, that's me."

The children were being organized by Suzanne Widerberg Fletcher, who had recently remarried and who was pounding on the piano—"Oh Rose So Brightly Glowing" was the first song.

"Terrell wanted a white Christmas this year," Packy said. "She is coming this way."

Perhaps she was the reason Helen was keeping an eye on Packy, Sadie thought. Packy's wife was tall and blond, much flashier than Helen. She had long, almost silver hair, and tanned skin. She wore a long, black velvet dress; between her breasts was a yellow diamond, so large that Sadie assumed it couldn't be real until it flickered convincingly. Terrell was a Texan, a restless woman. After years of feeling sorry for her, Sadie decided that she probably gave Packy as much trouble as he gave her.

Sadie regarded Helen's affair with Packy as different from other Park adultery, sacred because Helen loved him. She listened to gossip, rapt as a child hearing a bedtime story, and was always surprised at inconclusive or unhappy endings. "But how could that have happened?" she'd ask, and Helen would say finally, "Oh, Sadie, for Christ's sake, these people are no more safe or secure than you. It's one of your fairy tales, believing that they are."

"Isn't it all like a postcard?" Terrell asked, coming up beside them. Her voice was small, as if she had to squeeze it up from the depths. "Well, Sadie, another Christmas."

"I haven't seen you for years. Two? Three?"

"Oh, don't let's count," Terrell said. "Who's the fellow in the turban?"

"That's Jimmy Baker. You just can't see him under the bandages. Winter's hard on him."

Even now after seasons of gardening together Jimmy seemed unknowable to Sadie, someone about whom she had pieces of information rather than knowledge. He had been sickly as a child—weakness in his joints, asthma—and now he hated the cold. In winter the floor-to-ceiling mirrors of the Round House were covered with ice, and Jimmy moved his armchair and bed within six feet of his woodstove. Whatever secret life he had didn't interfere with what she believed was his real life, the one she could see. Sadie regarded Jimmy as someone just like her, without love for however long.

Jimmy must have heard his name mentioned, because he turned and waved, disentangled himself from the people he'd been talking to, and came over, shaking hands with Packy, kissing Terrell, fussing over Sadie.

He explained to Terrell and Packy, touching the white bandage on his head, that he'd been sober for weeks before Christmas and had fallen off the wagon the night before. He was driving home as cautiously as anyone could—"If cars could tiptoe"—when he lodged his Studebaker between a tree and a rock, and was suspended above the lake. If the tree and the rock had been six inches farther apart, he might have made a watery end.

"But I am not Ophelia, you know. Nor was meant to be, etcetera. And the good Dr. Barber said, 'Thank God you were drunk.' "

"He couldn't have," Sadie protested.

"Words to that effect. I bounced around like a big baby."

"Too bad Wes and Lilian weren't drunk," Sadie said. "They both have colds today, I heard. From rescuing you."

"A small price to pay for being Good Samaritans," Terrell said. "Jewels in their crowns. I love your turban."

"Is that a real diamond?" Jimmy asked.

Terrell laughed as if he'd said something much funnier, and her laughter made the others laugh too.

"Well, there it is blinking like a traffic light, so of course you'd ask. It's real but not very good. There's a flaw. What an eye you have, Jimmy. I wear it to make everyone happy—you know what people think of Texans. My sister gave it to me for Christmas."

"Last year," Packy said.

"Or the year before."

Helen was across the room, attending to an elderly lady who had just arrived in a burst of snow. If Terrell cared about her husband's affair, she didn't show it. Helen once said that Packy lived at the end of a golden thread that was too fine to see but strong enough so that he might be reeled in at any time.

What a pair of eyes I am, Sadie thought, watching other people. She was looking at Packy and Terrell for signs of affection, which were there. She was trying to see with Helen's eyes, she thought, though she wondered sometimes if she knew really what Helen thought. They were such close friends, almost like family, Sadie watching Helen's house, Helen taking the girls for treats, yet Helen was free to come and go, and Sadie stayed put. In her worst moods, Sadie felt like a beggar with her nose pressed to the window. Helen's graciousness grated on Sadie at such times, and she wondered if life was as easy as Helen made it seem.

SUZANNE WIDERBERG FLETCHER TOOK A BREAK AND the carolers drifted over to the buffet. Georgie Woodward slid onto the piano bench. He was thin, tall, balding, and tried to keep a lit cigarette in his mouth as he played, squinting into the smoke. He played "Stormy Weather," and couples danced. Georgie had been overheard referring to Sadie and her daughters as Our Hasidics, as opposed to the Others up the road in the Catskills. Sadie wondered what else he said that wasn't repeated to her, but she danced to his music with Packy. Fathers danced with daughters, sons with mothers and grandmothers. Sadie would have liked to dance with Jimmy, but he showed no interest, and so she went from Packy to other Park men, some of whom she'd turned away when they'd shown up to console her after Willard left. The only

Christmas party Sadie really disliked was the one to
which Helen had invited a man for Sadie, a member of
the Explorers' Club, who had, at the last minute, been
unable to come. Sadie had been troubled that night by
the extent of her relief and regret. She knew she had lost
her youthful prettiness. She had a new face, her hair reddened and coarsened by the sun, her skin tanned in summer, windburned in winter. It was an earthy face, she
thought, not the airy one she'd presented to Willard at
nineteen.

Around midnight, everyone gathered near the piano
and sang Christmas songs. Beatrice served coffee and
brandy, and people began murmuring, Another party
over. The snow had stopped and it was time for the chilly
Christmas toasts given under the stars. The guests left
gradually, kissing Helen and each other, bundling into
furs and heavy country wools, slipping off evening shoes
and donning boots, waving desperately to people they
saw every day, returning to the house for something to
clear their windshields and to say it was a marvelous time
and that the tree was more beautiful than ever, except
the year with the candles. "Good-by," "Good night,"
they called out, Packy and Terrell among the first to go,
until there was no one left but Jimmy and Helen, Sadie
and the girls, and the tired servants. The girls and Sadie
put on their coats and said good-by, told Helen it was the
best party ever, and started down the clear road.

On the slow walk home with the girls, Sadie felt complete. She loved the scheme of the Park—the houses
grouped on the close little hills above the lake, private
behind trees and rocks, blazing with lights on the party
night and looking welcoming if they were or not. When
Sadie looked at her house, she remembered Reed wanting to sell it and Willard refusing just to spite him. The
way things had turned out seemed the only way they
could possibly be, and remembering on what slim
grounds Tuxedo was still hers, Sadie shuddered and forgot again.

Four

IT TOOK A WHILE FOR WILLARD AND CHERRY TO FIND A place to spend each Christmas, but at last they settled on London, where Willard's friend Martin Bowles had moved after his divorce from the Virginia widow. They took a suite in a big Bloomsbury hotel, close to the Courtauld, within an easy walk of the British Museum, and Willard took a long lease on space in a warehouse in Southwark. Over the year he sent back the paintings, urns, and textiles he bought abroad. It was a big open space with light falling from a bank of high windows in a neighborhood that smelled of the Thames. "Too bad we can't live here," Cherry said, though the orderly squares of Bloomsbury suited her better. In Southwark she studied the windows of sweet shops as if she would be tested on the names of each unfamiliar candy.

Bowles had an apartment in Cheyne Walk, and included Cherry and Willard in his Christmas dinner. The other guests were in the government, mostly bachelors, and Cherry and Willard never saw them the rest of the year. Bowles had settled into a comfortable bachelorhood and each time they met, Willard was reminded that Bowles was what he would have become without Cherry.

"We could live here a million years," she told Willard, "and it would never be our city."

"If we took a flat," he said, "or a house."

"Maybe. But who wants a flat or a house?"

Neither had a capacity for domestic life; they preferred hotels, not the best hotels but those that were large enough for privacy and small enough for good service if one tipped well enough. They disliked residential neighborhoods, and liked to be close to central London. Willard could spend long hours in museums and galleries, but too much time there made Cherry nervous. She preferred her walks and her hours of dreamy shopping. She discovered stores where one might buy elaborate luggage and outfits for long journeys, the kind she would want if she were posted to a jungle. Cherry bought very little because she ended up carrying it along on the next trip abroad, sending it to Martha, or leaving it behind for the chambermaid.

They hadn't thought ahead when they left New York. They drove west, a long ride that gave Cherry time to try to recall famous painters and photographers in Taos and Santa Fe. Willard told her about the canyon photos he'd left in Tuxedo, saying he imagined that he would like to die in such a clean, dry place. They drove down past Washington and through Virginia, then across the South and into Texas. After Dallas, the country changed from blazing summer green to yellow left behind by the sun. She learned again and again on the long August drive— from breakfast to dinner to where they would stay the night and when the drive would end that day and when they would start out in the morning—that she was dependent on Willard. The car was his and the money. She became quieter and didn't ask for much, her complaints about the heat and length of the journey silenced by an image of herself standing alone by the side of the road, though he was always kind.

They stopped in Santa Fe and stayed in La Fonda for a few weeks, tired of the road and the heat, grateful to be in the mountains. One day Willard rented a pink adobe house behind a high adobe wall on Palace Street. The house was small and sparsely furnished. In the little courtyard garden, flowers bloomed that Cherry had never seen before, and she liked to take her coffee there in the early morning and watch the lizards on the wall. The light was empty, unimpeded, and all the colors of the house and town were strong and consistent with the earth. She felt light-headed (the altitude, Willard said) from the beauty of the town, as if at last she were inside a painting.

She learned where to shop for food and the man at the Sombrero liquor store soon called her by name. Willard gave her money to run the household. Cherry had never liked cooking, and was proud of her ingenuity when she hired the maid Maria who came with the house, to bring them a week's worth of rice and beans and to roast a chicken for them every few days. The woman kindly brought them more, food Cherry didn't know existed.

At a bar, Willard bumped into a real-estate agent who lived in an adobe house in the hills above town, a house better than the one on Palace because it was owned, not rented, and was filled with rugs, old Santa Fe drawings and Indian pottery.

The agent took them out one day to a ranch where they drove through bumpy, flat terrain, past six gates, and climbed rocks to look at petroglyphs. Afterward, they found pot shards just where the man said they would be, in the runoff, and they filled their pockets with the glazed chips. Willard was gleeful and careless, claiming every shard he spotted whether it was good or not. She had never seen him greedy before, glowing and taking it all in, the cleansing sun, the rocks with the ancient, obscure drawings, the endless terrain. She wondered if he played like that with his children.

After that, Willard bought Cherry dungarees and hiking boots, and took her for walks in the mountains high above Santa Fe. He told her that he had come to the right place, and when she tired of going daily to the mountains, he continued to go each day, returning an hour after sunset.

Little by little, having used up the shops and cafés, Cherry stayed home, leaving only to get more books from the library, and more liquor. She moved from bedroom to garden to living room in time for her first drink. She was careful now when she started to drink, and she counted her drinks, trying not to cheat, even on the size of the glass.

SOMETIMES UP IN THE MOUNTAINS, JUST BEFORE IT WAS time to head back, to come in, he always called it, Willard felt a terrible reluctance. He didn't want to simply camp out overnight in the mountains, and though the agent showed him property now and again, he didn't want to buy. What he wanted to do was to desiccate, to become part of the earth beneath his feet, dust on the rocks. Once he stayed too long and had to race the darkness along the mountain trails, and his heart beat very hard, independent of the rest of him he decided later as he drove the little car back to town. So his heart was fearful, he thought, and not ready yet to give up the house on Palace Street and Cherry.

FIESTA MORNING, WILLARD STAYED HOME AND SLEPT, and Cherry walked down to the square. Fiesta commemorated the Mexican victory over the Indians, and between Cherry and the Sombrero were floats and crowds of Anglos and Mexicans. Her way was blocked also to Harry Hunton's drugstore, and she needed aspirin badly.

She pressed through the crowd, passing a little girl with braids, dressed in a cotton frock and a cowboy hat. All around Cherry were children with dogs, cats, ducks, even one boy with a bird in a cage decorated with ribbons. In a stroller in front of her was a dachshund wearing a kerchief. They were waiting for the pet parade to begin. A truck, the Pila Atomica float, crawled by to blasting music and the chants of the people crowded on the flatbed. There was a sign: WHAT YOU SEE HERE/ WHAT YOU HEAR HERE/ LET IT STAY HERE/ WHEN YOU LEAVE HERE.

A white convertible passed, filled with Mexicans play-ing guitars and wearing sombreros and singing. Across the fender, like a deer shot in season, was an Indian boy wearing a piece of fur over his shoulder. Around the square were the closed-faced Indians who sat there most days selling their jewelry and pots. Cherry made it across the street, bought a paper and a bottle of aspirin, then pushed her way out of the square again to Palace Street.

That night Willard made a fire in the little fireplace. She was telling Willard about Fiesta, trying to remember What you see here, What you do here, What you hear here, What are you here, Do you stay here?

"There was a kid there today wearing a cute little cow-boy hat and she had a scarf over her dog's head and damn if the dog wasn't sitting in a stroller. I'll bet she won the pet fiesta prize."

"And?" He looked up at her warily.

"I used to march in the parade in Hackettstown. It could have been me. Or it could have been one of your kids." She began to cry a little, which she hadn't done in front of Willard since they'd left the East.

He felt his face flush. When she cried he felt as he had when the girls were infants and cried; his knees turned to water and his stomach ached. He asked, "You're not happy here?"

"What do *you* want?" she asked, looking up at him, her lipstick smeared, making her look as though her mouth drooped to one side. Don't you want to see them? she wanted to ask. Aren't you sorry?

He thought of the desert and the mountains, more beautiful than he had imagined. He was able to think of nothing when he was out there. He might stay forever.

"I don't know," he said impatiently. "Why do I have to make up my mind?"

"For no reason," she said. "No reason at all. The house is ours. It won't snow for a while."

"Yes," he said. "The snow. Well, we'll see, won't we?" and when she agreed he felt the same relief he did when Sadie turned from him and let him be.

He drove, by himself or with Cherry, to the pueblos west of Albuquerque, stirred by the simple shapes against the unending sky, by the thought of continuous habitation. Cherry looked restless in the pueblos, and always asked to stop in Albuquerque, though as she said, Albuquerque wasn't much. "It's new to me," she said. "Well, you wouldn't know. I never saw one new thing until I left home."

One day, months later, he returned from a walk and found the house nearly dark. He wondered for an instant if Cherry had left him. He opened the door and in the light from a dying fire, saw sharp silhouettes, rising from every surface—tables, chairs, sofa, rug. He called out, "Cherry," afraid to take a step, and when there was no answer went to their bedroom and found her there asleep. A smell that was like liquor but more like fuel rose from the bed. She lay so still that he held her wrist to feel her pulse. He saw her try to move her lips. There was a glass covered with greasy fingerprints on the floor.

What she had done was to cover every surface with the shards they'd taken from the ranch. She'd set up each broken piece of pottery with its sharpest end sticking up, carefully, methodically, so that the house was no longer a simple, easy place but a mined surface, like the cruel edge of a wall with broken glass cemented in for an intruder's hands.

She slept through the night and in the morning when she woke he was gone. The living room was undisturbed. She didn't know if he had been home or not, and she rushed down to the square, hollow-eyed and frantic, to look for him in the bars and cafés. But she knew he was in the mountains, nowhere that she could find him.

When he returned late that afternoon, the house was clean again, everything as it had been, and she had gathered the shards like fruit into a bowl that she'd bought in the square. She put the bowl in the middle of the table, which she'd set for one. He smelled beans warming on the stove. By the door was her suitcase and her coat, everything she had.

"You should stay if you want to," she said, appearing
from the bedroom. "I could go back and—"

"You shouldn't drink like that."

"I try so hard. I try every day—"

"From now on, I'll take care of you. I'll help you try.
Look, I told you I would. I don't always break my word.
You mustn't think that. You couldn't. And if it's this
place—we can go back to New York together, if that's
what you'd like."

"We can leave?"

He was not yet ready to be alone, not ready to let
Cherry go or to relinquish his conviction that he was
essential to her. He thought of the desert, more beautiful
than he had imagined. He had never seen so much before,
nor felt so much. He might stay there and not care for
how long, but he could not bear to send Cherry away so
helpless and defeated. Love is what you decide love is,
he thought. He could not give up everything yet, not
Sadie and his daughters, and Cherry.

"We can go wherever we like," he said.

"Even New York?"

"Of course," he said. "It would be easier if my wife
gave me the divorce. But if you want—" He thought of
the girls. He might see them again. He felt both dread
and joy, wondering how he would face them.

"I don't want to go there," Cherry said. "Not yet at
least."

"Fine. I meant it—we'll go where we like and stay as
long as we like."

He heard his words not so much as evidence of their
freedom but as a glimpse into their future; and in that
future he would cling to Cherry as if she were the essential one, his life raft, the only thing he wouldn't change.

ONE CHRISTMAS THEY LEFT LONDON ON IMPULSE AND
rented a stone villa in Grasse. Willard remembered the
fields of flowers and the villa on the steep hill from a visit
he'd made before the war. The house was damp and cold,

worse than London, and the furniture was hard and without charm, and they quarreled over who would have the
one comfortable chair by the fire. They both refused to
pick anything up and tripped over piles of books and
clothing. They hadn't brought much with them, but what
they had gained in volume as the holiday went on. Cherry
didn't speak French and couldn't enjoy shopping without
talking to the shopkeepers. She cooked as little as possible, preferring to eat anywhere but home. Willard read
Bernard Berenson and Delacroix's diary, and ignored
her. He had done his part by thinking of this place and
varying their season. Both were depressed by cheer, and
the English went at Christmas with too much zeal for
Willard, who didn't want to think about holy children and
blessed families.

By chance, they met a landscape painter named Georg
Bartos who rented a dilapidated house nearby. His girlfriend had just left him and he fell into the habit of coming
to the villa at the end of a short work day to complain
about his loneliness and to argue about painting. His misery made theirs seem lighter, for after all they were
together and would be leaving Grasse for Italy when the
short lease on the house expired. Things had been right
before and could be made right again.

One night Willard went to sleep early with a cold. Bartos and Cherry finished a fourth bottle of wine and staggered around the shuttered town, ending up at his house.
Bartos—lanky and dark, pale and always dressed in
black—told her about the war in Hungary. She told him
why she left New York, describing Bradley's hands on
her, and she wept. She hadn't ever told Willard, and so
she wept doubly for having told Bartos and because she
was afraid of what would come next. She spent the night
with him, as she knew she would. In the morning, Willard
awakened and saw that she wasn't there. He felt calm, as
if he'd been waiting for this to happen all along. He made
a pot of coffee, and drank it while reading *Figaro* from
the day before, then he packed his bags, wondering why
he was taking one night's infidelity so seriously. He was

on a train to Paris before Cherry awakened and ran home. He returned to Grasse a week later, and found her drinking red wine in a spotless house. "I thought I'd clean up instead of killing myself for losing you," she said.

"You wouldn't have," Willard said.

"Maybe," she said. "I wanted to."

"I'll make her give me a divorce," he said. "We'll go home if you like."

"No," she said. "I like our life fine. Why would I want to go back to New York? What did it ever do for you and me?"

He might think he would return home, settle things with his wife, resume the care of his daughters, but Cherry knew better. What he wanted, she had come to believe, was what he had and what she could help him with—exile and restlessness. He was angry with his wife for not divorcing, he grieved for his children and turned away when he saw girls like his on the street, when he realized that they must be growing unrecognizable in two years, three years, five. But those feelings were nothing compared to what he would feel if they ever had to return. What he couldn't accept, she thought, was that his escape had been so successful.

They were careful with each other after that, more like a courting couple than like people who'd been together for years, and even after they became comfortable again, one or the other might say, "It's like Grasse" as if it were a memory of reunion, not of separation. They said Santa Fe when they were ready to leave a place. It surprised them for a long time that they were enough for each other.

Five

REUBEN USUALLY CHOSE THE WEEK BETWEEN CHRIST-
mas and New Year's for his holiday. Each year he
stepped off the train with the same baggage, his father's
leather suitcase and his own black figure skates in one
hand; in the other, his briefcase, which held papers and a
week's supply of Cuban cigars, and a shopping bag of
food. The *Times* was tucked under one arm.

Reuben tried to resign himself to Tuxedo. "What is,"
Reuben repeated to himself on the train ride, in time with
the wheels, "what is." He no longer urged Sadie to
change, though he watched for a shift in her stance, listened during their morning call for a cry for help. He'd
met a woman soon after Willard left, a nice woman who
edited a left-wing journal down in the Village, a divorcee
with a little boy. She lived on Riverside Drive opposite
the Soldiers and Sailors Monument. There was no question of living together or of marriage. She had doubts
wrought from experience, he had Sadie. But she made a
difference to him.

During the in-between week a hush fell over the Park.
By and large it was an interim devoted to expectation and
recovery. When Sadie walked around the lake, she
passed houseguests bundled up and striding gamely, as if
undergoing an ordeal. The girls thought the time between

Christmas and New Year's was so long and quiet because they were waiting for the ice to thicken sufficiently for Reuben to skate.

He filled the library with clouds of cigar smoke, and kept a fire smoldering in the grate. He dropped newspapers over the coffee table and the floor. In the evening he kept a glass of whiskey, iceless, within reach, in the daytime a cup of tea.

He examined the library, a collection left behind by the Weavers. Willard's mother's books on Italian gardens and roses. Ruskin, of course, *Crown of Wild Olives, Sesame and Lilies; Cynthia's Chauffeur* by Lewis Tray, illustrated by watercolors of Gibson girls and mustachioed men, one captioned, "Still those radiant eyes remained invisible." *Who's Who* for 1908. *King's Notable New Yorkers 1896–99.*

"I don't expect the ruling class to be brainy," he reported to Sadie, "but this—"

"THAT CIGAR!" SADIE SAID. SHE LAY ON THE COUCH, covered with a quilt.

"This cigar!" he said, holding it up to see the ash still perfectly intact. "One of life's consistent pleasures. So, girls. What do you say?"

They had been out when he arrived and burst into the library to find their uncle waiting for them, calm as a walrus.

"So, girls, what do you say?"

"Not much," Louise said, "just trying to make a buck."

"You, too, Marilyn?"

"Just a buck."

"Hah! I admire such enterprise," and Reuben reached into his pocket, shifting with a great rearrangement of paper, armchair, and flesh.

"Oh, Reuben," Sadie said, "don't you think the girls are getting a little old for this?"

"Maybe they are," he said, "but I'm not."

He withdrew two small packages from the pocket of
his old tweed sports coat, anonymous boxes from the
diamond district, slightly smashed. When they opened
the boxes, the girls always found identical jewelry—
pearls hanging from delicate gold chains, tiny rings with
rubies or opals, lockets enameled with forget-me-nots,
which they treasured. He always brought the same present for each niece, not making a difference for coloring
or age, except at birthdays, when they received their
birthstones.

"You're very traditional when it comes to jewelry. Re-
actionary almost," Sadie said.

"Next year," he said, "ruby stars. You'd prefer to
advertise my so-called leanings?"

On New Year's Eve, the girls were allowed to stay up
as late as they could. Louise remembered New Year's at
the mews house, being put to bed early and wanting to
stay up, while in Marilyn's memory things had always
been just as they were. They ate downstairs in the
kitchen, Reuben wearing an old baggy cardigan and telling the girls about their grandparents who fell in love at
Aida, at the Met in standing room. For supper, they ate
the city food Reuben brought with him: lox, cream
cheese, bagels and rolls, herring salad, thin-sliced roast
beef, whitefish, and grapes wrapped in tissue, and they
drank champagne from the dwindling wine cellar.

After dinner, the girls were sent upstairs to change into
their nightgowns and robes, and returned to the pine library to wait for the New Year. Reuben and Sadie drank
brandy, and he told her about the real world: McCarthy,
HUAC, television, *Brown v. the Board of Education of
Topeka, Kansas.* "Oh, yes," she'd say, "I think I read
something somewhere." The girls, after all, watched TV
when people invited them over. Louise, restless, half-
listening, watched the time pass on her uncle's wristwatch. The room filled with the smoke of his cigar and
Sadie's Luckies, and the girls fell asleep.

When midnight came, Sadie went to the french doors
in the library that looked out onto the shallow balcony,

opened the doors, and the night air fought the smoke for the room.

Sadie woke the girls and told them to go upstairs, saying, "It's already next year, past your bedtime." They were usually happy to be in their beds, but often just before she drifted to a deeper sleep, Louise was sure she'd missed an important transition.

THOUGH THERE WAS PLENTY OF TUXEDO ICE TO SKATE on, Reuben insisted on taking them out of the Park New Year's Day. On walks around the Park and on drives, Reuben pointed out birds and trees. "Birch," he'd say, "spruce, willow, chickadee." But he named them without love, like an indifferent tour guide. Outside the Park he admired nature more. When he drove them through the gates, Sadie caught her breath, frightened that they would never return, and she closed her eyes and walked through the house, checking doors, windows, stove, the embers in the fireplace that might leap out and destroy everything.

An old chum, Bugs Klein, owned a cabin on Hunter Lake, which had, Reuben said, better ice.

Marilyn began New Year's Day with a feeling of expectation, as if the familiar trip would reveal something new, or that a discovery made along the way would change the coming year.

"You never know," Reuben always said, "unless you care to eat at one of the big resorts, you never know what you're getting," and so they stopped at a known evil, a diner halfway between Tuxedo and Hunter. Between the parking lot and the road was a row of sick-looking pines that Sadie was surprised to see alive year to year.

"The pumpkin pie sign!" Reuben said. "Still up from Thanksgiving."

"Thanksgiving before the war," Sadie said.

"Thanksgiving before we were *born*," Marilyn said.

"Well," Reuben said, "let's don't eat and say we did."

The fresh air felt good after the heated car. They stomped their feet, adjusted their coats, and entered the diner. Its silver surface was pockmarked inside and out, but shone in the cold sun. The only other customers, a pair of men in red-and-black hunting jackets, sat at the counter, hunched over cups of coffee.

The four squeezed into the booth in the corner, with windows on either side of them.

"Order what you like," Reuben said. "I'm picking up the tab."

"Our big chance," Sadie said.

They ordered the same things each year but studied the menus intently.

Maybe when we're all dead, Sadie thought, we'll come back here, and there'll be a new pie sign and a pie from real cherries, English muffins toasted on both sides, cream with the coffee, and breakfast twenty-four hours.

Marilyn was frowning at the menu. She was picky and at times wouldn't eat anything green or anything but white food.

"Okay," Sadie said. "What'll it be?"

"BLT down," Marilyn said.

"Wonderful," Sadie said. "I'm having a western sandwich. Same as breakfast, which they don't serve after eleven."

"Smart," Reuben said, "you should always get eggzackly what you want. For me, the traditional hamburger. Louise?"

"Grilled cheese. You know that."

They ate slowly, except for Reuben, who finished his food in record time and sat tapping his watch face in time to the jukebox.

"You eat like the IRT," Sadie said. "You know, one of these years, we'll bring Dandelion along. She likes a little trip."

"She'd like the music," Reuben said.

In the shining aluminum case was half a cherry pie.

"Canned cherries, this time of year," Sadie said.

"You always say that," Louise said. "I want whipped cream on my piece."

"Four pieces," Reuben signaled to the waitress.

They ate the sticky sweetness in silence, savoring the redness and the sameness, then Reuben ordered two coffees to go and they were on their way.

BUGS URGED REUBEN TO STAY AT THE CABIN FOR AS long as he liked, but they never even stayed overnight. They opened the house and smelled mice and mothballs, checked that the water pipes weren't frozen, and went outside. Reuben and Louise carried the skates from the car while Sadie and Marilyn brushed snow off a boulder by the edge of the ice. A large area had been cleared for skating, almost halfway across the lake. On the other side, the lake was ringed by pine-covered hills, which looked solid and black in the afternoon light. Where the snowplow had pressed hard, they could see a pattern of circles on the ice.

"Is the ice really thick enough?" Louise asked.

"A machine did the clearing," Sadie said. "Heavier than the four of us together."

"I'll test the waters," Reuben said.

He wore a short gray jacket for skating, an extra pair of red socks, and he lit a cigar before he started out. Marilyn had crocheted a bunchy red scarf for him and he wrapped it around his neck and pushed off.

Louise and Marilyn leaned against the rock and laced their white figure skates with wool pompoms at the toes. Inside each pompom was a jingle bell that sounded with each movement of the skate. Sadie pulled on her old skates slowly, and listened to the sound of the wind and the chimes of the girls' bells. The sky was cutting and blue. Her skates needed polish and the blades needed sharpening. New Year's to New Year's she meant to fix them up.

Reuben skated with surprising grace. He made his way to the middle of the lake. His cigar smoke rose peacefully into the air. He clasped his hands above his head and shouted to the girls on the shore, "Come on in. Hard as a rock."

"Are you coming?" Louise asked Sadie impatiently.

"One minute. You and your sister go on. I'll watch."

"We'll wait," Louise offered, wanting to get going.

"No, sweetie. Just go. I want to sit in the sun for a minute."

Marilyn looked out at the expanse of ice and piney hills, then turned to her mother.

"You'll be fine," Sadie said. "I'm right here."

Louise shrugged and stepped gingerly on the ice, bent her knees, and took off. She skated as though she wanted to be racing, but scraped the tips of her blades on the ice. Halfway to where Reuben was practicing figure eights, she caught on and glided to him. Marilyn fell a few times in a resigned way, as if she half expected it, and started up again. When Marilyn fell she pursed her lips, the way Reed used to when he was in pain, Sadie thought. Sadie fiddled with her laces, stalling.

WHEN SHE REMEMBERED THINGS ABOUT HER MARRIAGE, the events seemed interesting, no longer painful or remarkable. She wondered what she had been doing before she went to Rockefeller Center to skate. She closed her eyes and saw herself sprawled in one of the big brocade armchairs on West End Avenue, bored, eating an apple, reading a novel—*Mill on the Floss*. And she'd gone skating to get out of the house, worrying if she'd be back in time to make dinner for Reuben, wanting to leave so badly that she didn't care. She had considered not going skating but staying home and getting an early start on a term paper.

Now she had plenty of time, thanks to Willard. In staying where she was, in gardening and living quietly, she gained the respect of the community and freedom. She wondered often if he'd known what he was doing, leaving it up to her and his lawyer whether to call in Reuben or not. He assumed that she would involve Reuben. And had she, the divorce would have taken place long since, and Willard might be back in New York.

Everyone assumed that he had disappeared mysteriously and those who knew a few more details forgot them in time. When Jimmy and Helen teased her with Park scandals, she wondered what they would think of her secrets. They thought she was incapable of keeping even one.

When she got the first letter, it was around this time, between Christmas and New Year's. The girls and Reuben were at the drugstore, having lunch, but still she went to her room and locked the door, her hands trembling. She stared at the handwriting, the foreign postmark, the stamp of a wildflower. She rubbed her fingers on the soft airmail paper. She read her name: Sadie Weaver, Tuxedo Park, New York, USA. Did he know from Stratton that she had remained in the Park, she wondered, and did that mean that he spied for other news of them. She had won, he would be coming home. She looked at her room, trying to see how it would look to him.

The first letter began *Dear Sadie, You will be surprised to hear from me when I took such elaborate measures to be contacted for only one reason—our divorce. But I thought I might speed things along by disabusing you of a few of your fantastic notions.*

Sadie, I followed you. You said once that it was a coincidence that brought us together. I want to disenchant you and to make you see that there is no such thing as fate where we are concerned. I followed you to the rink because I had nothing better to do.

He wrote: *You may wonder that I take the trouble to write, having taken so much trouble not to be in a conversation with you. Whatever you imagine you gain by obstruction, you will lose. You mistake stalemate for peace.*

But what did he know about peace? She hated the letters in which he recanted on their life: *We both thought the children would bring a change.* But the children had changed everything. *I have a new life, one that suits me. No one could be more astonished than myself that I am content.* Who cared? How mean to rub it in.

He was wrong if he thought that she would admit that their marriage had been a mistake or that it could be ended. There were the girls, there was the house and this life. She would give anything for him to come back, but if he would come back only for a divorce, then let him never return. She believed that he would return, that sooner or later he would want to be with them again. She looked at everything in the present—house, children, garden—and wondered what Willard would think. For she had a new life, and one that suited her, the same one she'd been leading since that afternoon skating, when she'd fallen and he'd helped her up.

She hadn't been skating long when she fell. Looking up, she saw Willard. The moment before she saw him, the moment as she fell, were different sides of a gap in the earth. Before, nothing could be changed and everything had been lost. With him, there was possibility. She wondered if everyone had moments which in recollection looked fixed as stone, everything before and after fluid and vague. It was a moment when she was without body or mind, without volition. And that's what fate was, if he knew it or not. It didn't matter if he thought it was a manipulation on his part—Willard was there that day because he was part of her fate, her one and only life that could be led no other way.

"What's the matter?" Reuben called. "You stuck to the rock?"

"I'm coming," Sadie called back, "Coming," and got to her feet and to the ice, pushing off awkwardly toward the others.

THEY RETURNED TO THE PARK IN THE DARK, THE GIRLS asleep in the car. It seemed to Sadie after each New Year's skate that they had been away a long time. When

Reuben stopped at the gate to wave to the guard, she felt that they were in the future, which they relinquished on passing through the gate.

Yet once inside the Park, she no longer cared what was future, past, or present. She unlocked the house and woke the sleeping children, relieved to be safely home.

PART
FIVE

One

AS THE SUN GRAZED THE TOP OF THE CASTLE HILL, Louise was dreaming that she was loved and had no body. She pulled herself, swimmerlike, to her side and opened her eyes to see the rose wallpaper. She raised herself on one elbow and, yawning, looked out the open window.

In the edging light Louise could detect movement, not the breeze brushing the ferns nor the hummingbird on the beebalm, but the careful movements of a doe and her fawn inside the new fence Sadie had put up the day before.

For as long as Louise could remember, Sadie had been trying to keep away the deer, who ate both flowers and vegetables, and the woodchucks and rabbits. She tried new kinds of fencing around the vegetables, planted defensively, spread dried blood, black pepper, and mothballs. She stuck empty pop bottles in the ground, their necks protruding, to make a weird music. Nothing worked.

Louise smiled as the deer grazed along a row of tender lettuce. Long before her mother dreamed of gardening— she always told people she was an accidental gardener, as if that was something special—Louise hated standing in underheated shops on Broadway while Sadie and the

florist discussed flower arrangements. Nose to nose with
a bucket of bird-of-paradise, Louise worried that they
wouldn't do all the chores on her mother's list.

Louise held her hands before her for an instant. If she
clapped, the deer would leap the fence. She tightened her
hands as if in prayer, then slid from bed, and dressed.

Down the staircase, past the living room, which in its
summer incarnation wore faded chintz slipcovers that no
longer fit, past the vases of daisies and roses that dripped
petals onto the tables, leaving new rings next to the old.
The sunlight traced its path along the silver frames of
photographs of Louise and Marilyn, Sadie and Willard,
Reuben lighting a cigar, Reed scowling at the camera, a
portrait of Sadie's parents. Louise used to search the
fuzzy features for her own. "What do you care about
them?" Marilyn asked.

And out into the world. At moments like this, at the
start of a day and when she was all alone, Louise couldn't
remember why she was unhappy. She closed the door
quietly behind her—sometimes a click woke Sadie,
sometimes it took shaking—and walked up through the
garden, fitting her gait to the irregular stone steps.

Grudgingly, she admired the garden. At the dinner
table, she defended the simple squares and rectangles in
the village and along Route 17, utilitarian gardens with
neat rows and tidy beds. After ten years, her mother's
garden climbed and sprawled, and combined perennials,
rare and common, with vegetables, herbs, and showy annuals. Hybrid tea roses were isolated in the front, shrubs
at the top of the garden to blend in with the woods. The
soil, once hard and depleted, was rich and friable. Tuxedo people visited Sadie for her garden and invited her
over to look at a flower in bloom or diagnose a plant
disease.

Louise turned at the top of the hill and looked down at
the house. She hated it when Sadie recited her favorite
motto that she'd clipped from *Family Circle* and taped to
the wall so long before that the tape was yellow and brit-
tle: *Live as if you had a thousand years and as if you*

knew you'd die tomorrow. The words made Louise feel as though time were pressing in on her from all sides, and that death was a wall that she would run up against in the dark.

The woods smelled of mold and rotting pine needles, mushrooms pushing up through the forest floor. Maybe Willard was dead, or he would have come for her long ago.

She went into the castle by the front door, having found a key upstairs in a paneled room she called the den. She'd chosen a room near the den with a view of her house and terrace. Sometimes she saw Sadie and Marilyn. When Louise was on the terrace, she looked up to see if anyone was looking down at her from the castle.

She was dreamy, people said. Her Latin teacher, a thin young man named Kaiser, whom everyone said was teaching in the Park because he'd had a nervous breakdown, called on her during Vergil class, saying, "Please perform your matudinal libations elsewhere," joking so that the other students would think Louise was combing her hair rather than staring out the window pulling a lock of her hair. He met her startled gaze, saying, "Book Two, lines twenty-three through twenty-four. Please illuminate us as to their meaning. You are prepared, are you not?" She was always prepared for Latin and English, sometimes in History, never in Biology or Math.

Sometimes she worked so hard at Latin that she thought she could see brave Aeneas, his father Priam on his back. She could find cases and voices, and the pattern the words were in. But even when she was translating well and Mr. Kaiser looked pleased, his thin hands beating a tattoo in rhythm, she knew she understood nothing. Her body was reciting and Louise was watching. She was the smarter sister, everyone said, but Louise's intelligence, like her father, seemed just beyond her reach.

MARILYN STOPPED COMING TO THE CASTLE WHEN SHE was old enough to choose where she'd play. Now she came only to fetch Louise, saying, "Sadie needs help," or, "Dinner's going to be ready." Sadie didn't know that Louise was in the castle at such times, and assumed she was in the woods or at the lake.

A few days before, Marilyn stood at the door to the tower room and said, "Someday someone's going to catch you here." The wallpaper in the tower room was gray and imprinted with silver ferns. It was a square space that Louise had moved a small desk into, an armchair, a hassock, a mirror, and a table for looking at Willard's photographs.

"Not unless you blab," Louise said.

"You think you're invisible or something," Marilyn said. "Come on. Sadie's waiting."

SADIE CLAIMED THAT HER HOUSE PLAYED TRICKS ON her, hid keys, flooded when guests were coming, broke windows to get her attention; old smells reappeared on rainy days—Reed's medicines, lavender from Willard's mother's closet, something unpleasant just at the top of the stairs that would not leave no matter how Sadie scrubbed, and the small sad odor of mice and birds.

But the castle always smelled the same to Louise, the moldy odor of woods and memory, of promise. Though she had been through every room, she thought of the castle as endless.

She'd forgotten *Anna Karenina* there two days before, and found it right where she'd left it, face down across the fat arm of the armchair, another advantage of the castle over home. "Relax and make a mess sometimes," Sadie begged Louise, "you should take a lesson from your sister."

Louise skipped the political theory, horse racing, and rural bliss in *Anna*, but she wept at the scenes between Seryozha and his mother. Louise picked up the book, opened and closed it, checked the spine for damage, and put in her place a leather bookmark Helen had given her.

She hated it when she did things carelessly; it was as if someone else did the wrong things, but Louise was held responsible.

Louise reached behind a pile of books and magazines and brought out two oval French candy tins, opened the lids carefully, and spilled the contents on her desk. Another advantage of castle over home was that she could keep things here and know that no one would find them.

For a year Louise had been searching medicine cabinets in the houses she was dragged to for tea, dinner, parties, to play with visiting nieces and nephews, and unpopular schoolmates or new ones who didn't know any better than to invite her over—and she'd been taking triangular green pills, round yellow ones, red capsules, pure white tablets; anything with a label that read For Sleep—and she hid the pills in the candy tins. Some of the red ones froze over the winter and she threw them away. She never took the round yellow pills that Sadie got from Helen for emergencies because she knew they would be missed.

Louise didn't swallow the pills often. She learned to nibble at them like Alice, rather than take them whole. The red ones knocked her out, the yellow ones made her tongue-tied, but having her collection made her feel protected. She had a secret that she didn't have to share, not even with her father.

Book in hand, she was ready to go home for breakfast. She stood at the side table looking at the photographs of canyons and bare rocks, of the big sky, trying to trace a trail. When Mr. Kaiser told the class the story of Penelope, Louise sat up a little straighter. That was she, plagued not by suitors but by other distractions. And that would be she—loyal, unforgetting, and resourceful. She looked at her watch and saw that almost two hours had passed since she left home. What had she thought of? What had she accomplished? And how had the time slipped by without her noticing?

SADIE AND MARILYN SAT SIDE BY SIDE, COOKBOOKS AND magazines spread before them. Sparky lay across Sadie's lap. Jimmy was in the rocking chair, a cup of coffee in his hand, and Dandelion lay nearby, her tail dangerously close to the rockers. Louise looked down on them from the kitchen stairs. Marilyn was completely absorbed, notepads in front of her, one for the menu, one for ingredients. Her plumpness was gone and her skin glowed, so good, Louise thought, she'd never get a pimple. Disorganized in every other way, Marilyn was a wonder when she planned meals. Sadie was frowning at *Stella Standard*. Louise wanted to sweep the books off the table.

"Weasel princess," Jimmy said. "How are you? Sadie tells me you walk at dawn. Much safer than at night, I'm sure."

"I never see anyone," she said. "Except old Mrs. Christopher and she doesn't see me." She went to the stove and lifted a cloth that covered a baking pan.

"Try one, darling," Sadie said. "Angel biscuits. A new recipe."

"That's okay," Louise said, dropping the cloth. "I'm not hungry."

"Oh, go on and have one," Marilyn said. "We need you to taste. Jimmy thinks everything is wonderful."

Jimmy caught Louise's eye and winked. She felt better and settled at the table with a plate of two biscuits, and picked at the butter with a knife someone left lying on the *Times*.

"There's strawberry preserves around somewhere. Last year's were exceptional," Sadie said.

"I don't want any," Louise said. "How's gardening?"

"Oh, it moves along," Jimmy said. "Painting the roses red. I have enough work to keep me busy all summer. If only the summer were year round, I wouldn't have a thought."

"Something always comes up," Sadie said, looking up over her glasses. Louise liked her mother best when she wore her reading glasses, because they made Sadie look more serious and reliable. Sadie looked down again, and tapped at the recipe she was studying.

"Summer's just begun," Louise said. "There's lots of time left." She bit into the biscuit and allowed herself to close her eyes as Marilyn and Sadie did when they wanted to really taste. Preserves would make the soft biscuit perfect. Dandelion looked up adoringly, waiting for Louise to drop her biscuit.

"Youth," Jimmy said. "Summer, I've found, creeps along from Memorial Day to the Fourth of July. Then Mary Justice's birthday. Tonight. And suddenly it's Labor Day."

"That's not true at all," she said. Louise put down the biscuit, stood, and stretched to her full height. "There's almost all of July and August left. It isn't *true*."

Jimmy rocked, managing to look as if he might stay there all day or leave at any moment. She concentrated on his nose and cheeks, from a distance like a boy's, up close a broken map. He wore a T-shirt and khakis, and the long, stringy muscles and veins in his tanned arms bulged. Louise didn't care what he did, but Sadie always tried to make him stay longer.

Sadie looked at Louise.

"Well," Jimmy said, "it's the way it strikes me. How quickly time goes. But it does go more quickly at my age than yours, dear." He set his coffee cup on the table carefully.

Louise sat down and ate part of her biscuit, her eyes filled with tears. She bent down and fed the rest to Dandelion, though she was still hungry.

"I think I hear the postman," Sadie said.

"You have ears like a fox," Jimmy said. "I didn't hear a thing."

"It's hours too early," Louise said.

"My, my," Sadie said mildly, "I can see some people got up on the wrong side of the bed."

Marilyn said, "Look at this one. Georgia Peach Soufflé."

Louise picked biscuit crumbs from the table and licked them off her fingers.

"There's more," Jimmy said, gesturing to the stove.

"No, thanks," Louise said. "I'm stuffed. Maybe I'll go see if the mail's there."

She was sorry if she'd hurt Jimmy's feelings. He was the one adult she could stand in the whole Park. Jimmy and her mother were invited for dinner in the Park as if they were married, but Louise was happy that they had no life like Helen and Packy who embarrassed her by acting as if no one else were in the room. Now Sadie was on her high horse about what a good mood she was in, and Louise could feel Marilyn looking at her to see why she was cranky.

"Sit, sit," Sadie said, "I'll go," and she patted Jimmy on the shoulder as she passed him and would have touched Louise if the girl hadn't ducked before Sadie could reach her.

Louise followed Sadie. Her mother had left the front door open, and Louise saw her framed against the rich colors of the garden. Light and color streamed behind Sadie as she stood frozen, a blue airmail envelope in her hand.

"Sadie?" Louise said.

Caught off guard, Sadie looked old, and the flesh of her face hung flaccid, her bones seemed to protrude, then she changed back to the everyday Sadie.

"Chickie," Sadie said. "What are you going to do today?"

"Marilyn and I are riding our bikes to the lake."

"I'll make you delicious sandwiches from the roast," Sadie said. She slipped the letter into the pocket of her apron. "And tonight we go to Mary Justice's."

Two

LOUISE'S BIKE WAS BLUE, AND SHE'D NAMED IT BLUE Heaven, for a song her mother used to sing in the mews house, "Heaven, I'm in heaven and my heart beats so that I can hardly speak . . ." Marilyn remembered "When you wish upon a star," which Louise said was an inferior Tuxedo memory. Louise loved the bike and often planned to run away on it, though she'd never gotten beyond the gate. Marilyn's bike had once been red but she'd left it out on so many hot days and rainy nights that it was dull pink.

"Go home, Dandy," Marilyn shouted, at the bottom of the drive. "Go home." The dog looked as if her heart had just cracked, and she wagged her tail to let Marilyn know it wasn't too late for her to change her mind. "Go home," Marilyn shouted until Dandelion seemed resigned to standing at the top of the drive for the rest of her life, waiting for the girls. "Should we go the easy way or the hard?" asked Marilyn.

"Let's go the hard way and come back the easy," Louise said.

They climbed the hill, standing on their pedals to grind their way up. It was a clear day with a high blue sky and a breeze that ruffled the leaves. At the top, they stopped

and looked out at the overlapping trees and houses onto
a blue corner of the little lake.

"I'll race you down," Marilyn said.

Louise was surprised because Marilyn usually liked to
go downhill slowly, pulling against gravity.

"Okay," she said.

They lined up their front wheels.

"On your mark," Marilyn said, "get set. Go!"

They pedaled furiously downhill. Marilyn tried to keep
up with Louise, who was cutting from one side of the
road to the other, ignoring the curves and the sharp slant
down.

Marilyn glanced over at Louise, whose face, usually
closed and masklike, was twisted in a maniacal grin, her
hair pulled back by the wind, looking as if she were the
queen of happiness.

Marilyn barely stopped in time at the wooden gate to
the lake path, pressing her brakes so hard that she could
smell rubber. Louise held out her arm trustingly as she
crashed into the gate, which wobbled back and forth until
she jumped from her bike and held it steady.

"Whew," she said. "I win."

"I guess," Marilyn said. She had lost by seconds. Now
she couldn't remember why she'd bothered to race
Louise.

THEY LEFT THEIR BIKES IN THE HIGH GRASS ALONG
the fence and walked down to the lake. The gate and the
stone path were part of a house that had burned. In the
spring irises and daffodils outlined the foundation; when
there was much rain, the lake almost covered it. Louise
wondered how people had lived there.

"They built that huge pile," Jimmy told her when he
showed her how to get to the lake, "without listening to
an architect or engineer. They liked the spot." He'd visited there as a boy, unwilling companion to the son of the
house, "a real stinker." The father had gone bankrupt
and sold the house, which burned down after an autumn

holiday years later. No one was hurt except a small poodle who'd been left behind accidentally.

The girls stripped down to their bathing suits and walked out gingerly on the planks of the splintery dock, spreading out towels to lie on. The towels were repaired and rebound, and Louise wished for the lushness of Helen's towels. Helen had only white towels and replaced them all once a year. Louise prayed that her mother wouldn't ever accept the old ones from Helen. Marilyn lay on her stomach in the sun and studied the mends to determine their period in the life of the house.

Louise said, "Someday I'll only have new things."

"I like old things," Marilyn said.

"You're in the right place. Lucky you."

They lay flat, passing suntan lotion back and forth over the gaps in the dock.

"Swim?" Louise asked.

"Not yet," Marilyn said. She liked the sound of the water hitting the pylons, the brackish lake smell, and the smell of her skin, slightly salty, slightly sweet from the lotion. She felt happy until she recalled the energetic glee on her sister's face as she careened downhill.

"Well, I'm going," Louise said.

"I'll watch," Marilyn said. Once Louise had almost drowned here, swimming alone. She told no one but Marilyn, and made her swear never to tell.

Louise slipped into the water and made her way out. Marilyn could see the Schwerners' house across the lake. Packy had arrived the day before. Louise told Marilyn once that it would be disgusting if Jimmy and Sadie married because it was disgusting to be married to two people, and Jimmy and Sadie weren't like that. Like what, Marilyn had asked, and Louise repeated, Not like that, and Marilyn concluded that her sister knew something, but not much more than she.

LOUISE LAY ON HER BACK, BREATHING HARD, HER hands clasped behind her head.

"You should have come swimming," she said.

"I hate moving. I'm happy here."

"You're happy anywhere. You'd like the water too if you would force yourself into it. You're a much better swimmer than I am. You have a real stroke."

"Me and Esther Williams. Maybe before we go home."

"Is Reuben coming tonight?" Louise asked.

"No. He hates Mary Justice for some reason."

"Too rich," Louise said. "Good old Reuben."

"You *like* him," Marilyn said. She wondered if Louise and she would ever live apart and if they would talk every morning.

"I like him," Louise said. "But everything is always the same."

"We're lucky," Marilyn said sleepily.

"You always think that," Louise said. "You and Sadie think everything's great as long as the house isn't burning down. You don't have any standards."

There was a long argument between Louise and Marilyn. Since Willard left, Louise had wanted to know, more than anything, more than geometry and Latin, the history of art and war, how to do needlepoint stitches or how to put out a fire, where he was. She was sure that somehow Sadie was hiding him, though how Louise didn't know.

But Marilyn thought that since he was gone, they should be happy with what they had now. Louise wondered what her sister saw in the present that pressed on you but vanished when you tried to touch it.

"Are you still thinking of, you know, going to find him?" Marilyn asked.

"Maybe. I'd need money. And anyway I'll be leaving pretty soon."

"Years," Marilyn said. "I mean, maybe he doesn't want to come back, Louise. Maybe you should leave well enough alone."

"He can't come back. Otherwise he'd be here. He *wants* to. And it isn't well enough. You know that."

For a long time they'd talked about Louise going west after their father, probably when she was sent to college, and that Marilyn would stay home with Sadie until she was married. Louise thought this plan was fine, though sometimes she looked around the house and the Park, and felt sharp regret that she would have to leave it.

"It's too long to think about," Marilyn said. "What will you wear tonight?"

"I only have one dress that's clean and the hem isn't falling down."

"I'll fix your hem."

"Never mind. Do you want to swim?"

Marilyn looked up at the water and said, "I don't think so. It looks too—"

"Wet? Let's eat. I don't want to go uphill carrying the hundred-pound lunch Sadie packed."

On the way back, they walked their bikes around curves, then mounted and rolled home easily. They took their bikes down to the garage and leaned them against the Packard. Through the garage, past the carpenter's shop, the tool room, the laundry, and the wine cellar, they breathed in the stillness of the lower house.

The smell of the morning's biscuits still hung in the air, and the perfume of a peach someone had taken one bite of and left on the table. Marilyn picked up the peach and finished it, its juice running down her chin.

"Milk?" she asked. "You want a cookie? I filled the jar this morning. I always get hungry when I go swimming."

"You didn't go swimming," Louise said.

"I had to watch you swim," Marilyn said peacefully. "Oatmeal raisin with a few chocolate chips."

Louise stood up a little straighter and examined her knees. "I'm not hungry," she said. "Where's Sadie?"

Marilyn shrugged and said, "Maybe on a job. Maybe she and Jimmy went off somewhere." She opened the refrigerator to find the milk.

LOUISE WENT UPSTAIRS AND STOOD IN THE FOYER. THE
house was silent. She pictured Marilyn in the kitchen,
looking through a magazine that had been there for
months, page by page, eating cookie after delicious
cookie. All her life Louise had watched out for Marilyn,
feared for her and envied her.

SADIE AND HELEN LAY ON WICKER LOUNGE CHAIRS ON
the terrace. If either looked up, she might have seen the
blue lake and a sailboat drifting past. Between them on
the burnt-bamboo table was a pitcher of iced tea and two
glasses, half filled with tea, lemon slices, and ice. Their
cigarettes and Helen's gold lighter lay near the puddle
around the sweating pitcher.

"This is bliss," Helen said.

"Heaven," said Sadie. "Who would have thought as a
young person that it would be so wonderful just to lie flat
and do nothing?"

"That's all adults ever did. Lie flat. Drink. Smoke.
How boring, I thought. Drove me mad."

The sounds of tennis came up the hill from the club,
and really, Sadie thought, the game was beautiful to listen
to, if dull to watch. There was something she'd been
meaning to talk to Helen about, a disturbing rumor about
Terrell and Packy putting their house on the market and
leaving the Park for good. There was something else bad
but she would keep it to herself—the letter that had rat-
tled her this morning.

The sun made her feel languid, in a way she still associated with Willard. Her long celibacy had left her feeling
virginal once more, unable to imagine lovemaking. And
yet, lying there in the sun with the heavy smell of her
roses, the birdsong, even the rhythms of the tennis game
down the hill, she had the feeling that she oughtn't be
untouched. Then the feeling became dispersed as Sadie
thought of the pleasures that were around her, and forgot
why she'd felt even for a minute such an urgency.

Helen and Packy were the best couple she knew, and

an object lesson for her. Helen tolerated his marriage,
and he approved of everything she did, as if any simple
statement were evidence of what a talented and inventive
person Helen was. Perhaps they didn't see each other
enough to exhaust it, Sadie thought. She could not think
of a time when she'd been watched and approved of in
that way, not even in the early days of her marriage.
When she remembered the mews house, it was as the
place where the girls had been babies, not as her and
Willard's first house. Then he brought them to Tuxedo,
then he left. At times it seemed that they had always been
here, that he'd proposed in Tuxedo and the girls had appeared.

  She shifted, the wicker creaked. Old Mrs. Hunter had
stopped Sadie in the drugstore that morning and told her
that Terrell was going to sell. She decided that the source
of the rumors about Packy was unreliable and her own
secret so imbedded as to be irremovable. True, the market was getting better for Tuxedo houses, but why would
Terrell want to sell now after so many years in the Park?
Sadie concentrated on the sound of the hollow balls sailing through space only to land and be struck again, regu-
larly and reassuringly.

LOUISE STOOD AT THE DOOR AND WONDERED WHERE TO
start. Sadie's room was filled with photographs, half-
mended clothing, seed and garden-tool catalogues,
home-maintenance books, old *Vogue*s—Sadie studied
the magazine, one lasted for months. There were three
dressers and a desk, plus boxes of files and envelopes
stuffed with little pieces of paper, and a wooden filing
cabinet Helen gave to Sadie when she cleaned out her
garage. Louise pulled open a file drawer and saw papers
half out of envelopes, files that looked as though they'd
been stepped on. One was labeled *Louise*, and she found
her birth certificate and x-rays from a New York dentist,
a kid's crayon drawings. In another file, she found crumbling newspaper clippings. Sadie talked about saving clip-

pings, now Louise saw what happened to them. A mess was a perfect place to hide things, Louise thought. The room reminded her of Sadie's refrigerator, packed with jars and bottles with half an inch of unidentifiable food that might have been put in yesterday or six months before, might be delicious or might kill you, and only Sadie knew which was which.

"Louise?"

She turned and saw her mother at the door.

"What are you doing?"

Her mother's voice sounded cold, and Louise thought: If I say the wrong thing, I could lose Sadie too.

"I was looking for the bills," she said.

"What bills?" Sadie looked distracted now, as she did whenever it occurred to her that her daughters needed anything.

"The bills, you know. For the house."

"It would have been more polite to ask me, dolly." Sadie rubbed her forehead. "You haven't wanted to do the bills for so long, remember you said you didn't want to anymore?"

"I changed my mind. I need some responsibility," Louise said. "How am I supposed to grow up around here?"

"Well, you should have asked me. But it's all the same, we live on this and that. The Packard needs new tires. It's such an old car, everything's more *expensive* for it. But of course we can't afford a new one."

"I wish we could pay off everyone."

"I do too, Weasel, but we can't. I won't repeat some of the things Helen's told me about people with real money around here. These people think the world owes them something—a summer or a house."

"Most Park kids my age have checking accounts."

"I'm sorry this discussion started. First of all, you wouldn't have anything to put in your checking account even if I let you have one. Second of all, don't start on the Park. It's just a place. And we're lucky to be here."

Louise let her face darken, frowned, and with her heart

pounding walked to the door. She thought of slamming it behind her, but she turned and said quietly, "Are you sure?"

"Sure we're lucky? Sweetie, you have no idea how much better we've been able to live—"

"Not that. Are you sure Willard didn't tell you where he was going?"

"Willard? No, of course he never told me."

"He must have told you something. Left a note or something." Louise started to cry, and her voice was shaking.

"Oh, pumpkin," her mother said, "he just left. I mean, the lawyer's arrangement, yes. But I wouldn't know where to look, you know, to find him."

"I would," Louise said. "I know."

Sadie was startled, and the same frightened, aged look came over her face as it had at the front door that morning.

"What are you talking about, Louise—you've heard from your father?"

"No," she said. "Not directly."

"Indirectly?"

"Not in words. Nothing. I just know I can find him." She was tempted to confide in Sadie and tell her that Willard was in the West, but she hated herself for wanting her mother's approval of her plan.

"It's no use looking for people who don't want to be found." Sadie lifted a pile of clothes from her desk chair and sat down heavily. "You can look all you want, Louise, and he still won't be found. And anyway, you don't want to find him. You want him to come home."

"You're happy he's gone. Now you can run everything."

"You're wrong. You're so wrong. I'd give anything in the world for him to be back and all of us happy again," Sadie said, sounding tired and matter-of-fact.

There was nothing else in the world but this, Louise thought. She stared at her mother, feeling as though there was a train inside her that was getting closer and closer. She turned and left the bedroom.

"Don't forget Mary Justice's party," Sadie called out, listening to Louise's footsteps and the slam of the front door.

LOUISE HID IN THE CASTLE, CURLED IN THE MOLD-smelling armchair with her book. How contrary Anna Karenina was, feeling one way, acting another. Vronsky was balding but Anna should have been nicer to him. Louise put her book down; it was giving her the same irritable feeling she had before storms.

Her mother was right. Louise didn't want to go find him, she wanted him to come home. She was as bad as Sadie and Marilyn, worse because she thought she was different. She wouldn't leave the Park no matter how much she pretended to want to. What would she do out west, what would she do in the world?

She took up her book again, falling off to sleep and jolting awake. Anna thought Death! and Louise sat up straighter. The knots Anna was tied in, her terrible boredom, then there it was—Death! Sadie and Marilyn were far away, different after all, for she was sure they had never thought of death with longing, as she did. She had believed that one day she would leave the Park and find not only her father but someone else to love who would love her back, someone she couldn't imagine. Now it seemed that this might never come true.

Three

MARY JUSTICE LIVED ALONE IN A STONE MANSION SET on the highest peak in Tuxedo. As Jimmy told it, Mary's husband, Hal Justice, found out that Mary was sleeping with her hairdresser, who had gotten into the habit of coming out to Tuxedo on weekends as Mary's guest. Hal questioned Mary one summer's day when Jimmy happened to be in the garden below, weeding. The crux of Hal's objection was that the affair was so common and conducted under his nose. Jimmy claimed he asked, "Why not someone I don't know?" "But, dear, you know everybody I know," Mary said. "Not unless you introduce them to me," Hal said. Hal died four months later of a heart attack. This was his first surprise for Mary. The second was that he'd remade his will in favor of the children of his first marriage, leaving Mary with the house in Tuxedo and the apartment in New York. The children were never at home. Mary organized their year between European schools, long visits to Justice relatives in California, and summer expeditions. The hairdresser lived with Mary for a year after Hal's death —by then he was the owner of his own salon—then moved back to New York and disappeared from the Tuxedo view.

When Sadie heard the story she tried to imagine if the

hairdresser was in love with Mary or she with him. Why had Mary risked her long marriage for an affair, unless it were a great love? But when she looked at Mary, she couldn't imagine her in the thrall of a passion that would make her ruin her life. She wondered what Mary thought when she looked at her.

Sadie coaxed the Packard up Mary's hill and parked at the foot of the lawn. Mary spotted the girls as they got out of the car. She shrieked and made her way through her guests to them.

"Sadie! and the fabulous girls. Park princesses. The enchanted girls. Sadie, don't your day lilies look beautiful? That spot by the wall has never been so lovely."

Sadie frowned critically at her handiwork, and Louise was afraid she would go over to straighten out a drooping stalk. The previous fall Sadie had divided the tangled day lilies and spread them along the entire length of Mary's stone fence, and in summer filled in with annuals and planted biennials for the next year. The effect didn't please her. Sadie and Jimmy called such work Hollywood gardening.

"Water it," she said. "It's a little dry. But lovely, yes. Happy birthday, Mary. The party looks wonderful already."

"I want to hear all about these girls," Mary said. She was a golfer and her skin was tanned and grooved. Her voice, whiskey-deep, caressed the girls. Marilyn, usually shy, was about to speak when Mary spotted a new guest, and said, "Oh, good, she did come," and walked back into the crowd.

"Who's she kidding?" Louise asked. "She doesn't really care about us."

Sadie shrugged, and pointed out tables and chairs set up across the lawn, surrounding a tent with tables of food. Salmon-pink tablecloths flapped in the breeze. Mary Justice had gotten someone (not Sadie and Jimmy) to fill large terra-cotta pots with fluttery salmon petunias. A few girls lounged by a table, trying to look comfortable. "I think I see some young people over there."

"Regina's there," Marilyn said. "I thought she was gone."

"Maybe it's her ghost or something," Louise said. "Go up and pinch her and see."

"Now, Louise."

"Now, Sadie," Louise mimicked. When she had stopped being friends with Regina, Marilyn took up with her. All the things about Regina that annoyed Louise passed Marilyn unnoticed, which annoyed Louise even more. She hoped Regina and her mother would leave the Park so the next inhabitants of the unhappy house could move in.

"Don't always act as though I'm trying to boss you. Be polite," Sadie said.

Though it was early, the lawn was covered with people, men in white or seersucker suits, women in big dresses and picture hats. Louise recognized many people, but there were strangers too, not houseguests but new people who were buying up the old Tuxedo houses and tarting them up, Jimmy said, making carriage houses and servants' quarters into weekend cottages. Some of the new people were children of old Tuxedo families, but some were just anybody, people in advertising and show business who were now allowed to join the club. Louise had spotted them in the drugstore and along the lake road. The women wore big sunglasses and had hair that swooped obligingly on either side of a middle part, like Jackie Kennedy's, even though everyone said it was a shame Jack Kennedy had won, and they dressed like her too, as much as Tuxedo life allowed. And there was an even stranger young couple who drove a foreign car, not like the sports cars or ancient station wagons most Park people did. Once, when Louise was on her bike, pedaling very slowly past their house, trying to get a glimpse of them, she heard loud rock-and-roll coming across their lawn, not the kind on the local radio, sung by Italians and Poles, but black people's music. Louise caught sight of the man in bell bottoms and a ruffled shirt, his hair curled like Jesus', next to a geranium pot. The woman next to him was tall and skinny, and she wore the tiniest skirt Louise had ever seen, and a nearly transparent blouse, her long hair draped over her breasts. Louise drew her breath in sharply, and had a vision of herself, just like that, grown up and with a stranger. Then she thought she was ridiculous, it was nothing she ever would do.

It turned out that Marilyn knew all about them. In fact, she and Regina had been inside their house. They were almost English because they lived in London some of the year and they'd come to Tuxedo because they thought it was a hoot. Though she liked looking at them, Louise wasn't sure she liked them being in the Park. She thought of the Park as having around it not only its fence (now untraceable among the trees) and its gate, but an invisible shell. Outside the shell was the world, which had no limits and was unmappable. Louise wondered if the castle would ever sell. The old man in Geneva wouldn't sell it surely, not even if a million people in miniskirts offered him a fortune.

Sadie was looking small and lumpy in her summer dress, and Louise wanted to take her away from the party. She looked so cheerful, so hopeful that Louise wanted to warn her—It's just another stupid party, Sadie, don't look so eager. Sadie spotted Jimmy, who waved from a group by the bar, and she said, "All right, girls, don't leave without telling me," and walked away.

"I'm going to the bathroom," Louise said. "Will you wait here for me?"

"No. I want to talk to Regina. Just look around for us."

LOUISE STEPPED THROUGH THE OPEN FRENCH DOORS into the house, quickly passed through the living room, and went upstairs to Mary's room. The bedroom was blue and white, with lace-covered pillows on the bed and the velvet chaise longue. Off the bedroom was Mary's sitting room and bathroom. Early on, Mary had one of the few TVs in the Park—the girls used to come and watch "Howdy Doody" and "Kukla, Fran and Ollie" when Mary was away—and the small sofa in front of the TV was covered with pillows needleworked with mottoes that Mary liked: No Good Deed Goes Unpunished; I'd Rather Be Lucky than Good; Formula for Happiness— Good Health and a Short Memory; Never Mistake Hospitality for Endurance.

Mary's bathroom was paneled in cherry, and the fittings were brass, shaped like scallops. Louise locked the door behind her, then turned the knob of the second cabinet. Sometimes Mary locked it, but more often she forgot. The cabinet's many shelves were crowded with pill bottles, inhalers, sunburn lotions and poison-ivy and insect-bite ointments. Some of the bottles were empty, the contents having evaporated long before.

Mary had pills from the Tuxedo pharmacy and one in New York. For sleep, as prescribed: the red ones. As prescribed, every three hours: the whites, greens, and yellows. Diamond-shaped pills and tiny round ones twice daily. A few of the prescriptions were from years before and the bottles held half a pill and colored dust.

Mary's supply of red ones had been renewed, Louise saw. She took five and shook the bottle to rearrange the contents. She pocketed a green and a yellow, flushed the toilet, and washed her hands. She inspected herself in the door mirror, and lifted her hair above her head, knotted it tightly in her hand, and opened her eyes wide and blank, like the models in *Vogue,* until her eyebrows hurt.

On the way downstairs, she passed one of the Widerberg boys. He winked, and she wondered if he knew what she'd been doing or if he, too, was after Mary's bathroom cabinet.

WHEN SADIE JOINED HIM, JIMMY INTRODUCED HER TO Dick Emerson, who was back in the Park visiting his parents. He and Jimmy had been friends as boys.

"I thought I read your father's obituary," Jimmy said. "Or am I simply losing my mind?" Jimmy was laughing and tossing back his head the way he did when he was drinking, and he wasn't noticing that his friend was backing away inch by inch and looking around as if he'd like to be talking to someone else.

"My uncle," Dick said. "Their names are alike."

Half-listening, Sadie looked around for the girls and saw Marilyn with her friend Regina. Helen and Packy were sitting off by themselves at one of the tables, both dressed in white linen trousers and pale blue shirts. Sadie sipped the drink Jimmy handed her, remembering what she had been ignoring all day. First thing in the morning she had discovered that the deer could get into her garden. No one understood how it made Sadie feel to see her ruined garden. It brought her back to the moment when the elevator door shut and her parents were gone, and she hadn't kissed them good-by, a thing as final as that.

"The Park's changed since our day," Jimmy said, "the generation of the eighties is gone, the people who built the place. They were remarkable, adventurous—philanthropists, generous. I don't have to tell you, Dick. But now—the Park's filled with stockbrokers' wives, commuters. There's no real social life, only these gruesome cocktail parties. It's so meanspirited here. So gossipy."

"I don't know," Dick said. "This party could be twenty years ago or ten, and people have always gossiped here, Jimmy. It's all the same."

"You just think that because you've escaped," Jimmy said, as if Dick had angered him. Sadie wondered why Jimmy was talking this way. He hardly saw anyone she didn't, and he'd said only the week before that the new people would spend some money and make their situation better. "And why are you looking so gloomy, Mrs. Weaver?" Jimmy asked.

"Nothing, Jimmy. It's nothing. You don't want to hear it. Deer in the vegetable garden. Eating the lettuce."

"I gave up growing lettuce in the Park years ago," he said, as if that settled the matter for everyone and forever.

"I suppose," Sadie said. "But I tried so hard this year, I thought I had the fence the right height." Dick mentioned fences he'd seen in game parks, fifteen feet high.

"Electrified," Sadie said. "Lights and guards."

Packy had been with Terrell at her ranch in Mexico all spring, and Sadie thought how lucky Helen was that he'd come. "It's been so long," Helen had told Sadie, "I'm dying to see him," though now she looked indifferent, lighting a cigarette, taking a sip from her drink. "I don't want to go near the damn party," she'd said on the phone, "but if I don't, it'll set off a chain of reprisals."

"If one spends any portion of the year in New England," Jimmy was saying, "it should be summer. So romantic and doomed. Winter's too crisp by far. Even in this moldering place."

"This isn't New England. Strictly," Dick said.

"More New England than not," Jimmy said. "And the gardens!"

"Oh, gardens," Sadie said. "What a struggle with gardens. Sometimes it seems so useless—fighting worms and bugs and birds. Deer. Mold. But it can't be useless, otherwise—"

"We all *know*, Sadie. Everyone knows everything you do that's brave and wonderful, and everyone knows what a time you've had. We've all had times. But we don't mention it."

Sadie's face grew red, and she looked down at her glass, trying to think of a way to calm Jimmy down. He'd never turned on her before, though she'd seen him be nastier to other people. Some people didn't seem to mind, but it felt disastrous to her.

Dick smiled thinly. "You shouldn't drink so much, Jimmy. You make a fool of yourself by saying things you don't mean. You might start some trouble some day you can't finish." Jimmy grabbed Dick's arm and held it until Dick stared him down. "Let go," Dick said. "People are noticing." Dick finished his drink, turned, and walked away without looking back.

When he was gone, Jimmy looked furious, his nostrils

pinched in. He turned to Sadie and said, "Don't look so shocked, Sadie. We've known each other too long for that." They stood side by side like people waiting for a train, until Jimmy drawled, "Well . . ." and wandered off.

"WELL, MY DEAR," PACKY SAID, "WHATEVER IS THE use of coming to a party if you look at your watch and demand to leave the instant we get here."

Helen said, "It's been forty minutes. A polite visit."

"But the breeze is so pleasant, and Mary has dressed the tables so fetchingly—would you like another drink?"

"No."

"Will you spoil Mary's birthday? and our visit?"

"Our brief visit? Our last visit?"

"Not the last, Helen. The house is on the market, not sold yet. This might drag on for years."

"So I might still have you when you come to look after your wife's property? Don't be so sure I'll always be here waiting, even I—think I understand Terrell better than you do. She'll lose patience. Oh, hell. Sadie's looking at us now. Don't turn around. She'll come over."

"And what is so wrong with that?" Packy asked.

"I don't feel like talking to her this minute. That's all."

"You are in a difficult mood, Helen."

"You've always frightened me before when you ask such a question, Will I spoil our little time? Won't I keep it perfect? I've been so stupid. Stupid as Sadie."

"But we all love Sadie," Packy protested.

"Oh, well," said Helen, "love."

"I forgot to tell you, this will take your mind off things —I saw her husband. The missing one."

"She's only had the one. Where on earth did you see Willard?"

"No very special place. The Victoria and Albert. Terrell—"

"Collects Majolica. I know. Are you sure it was Willard?"

"He looks quite like his daughter. He was with a rather tired-looking woman. Dark. Nothing like Sadie."

"I've always wondered," Helen said. "Whom he was with. Well, poor Sadie indeed. You didn't try to collar him or speak to him?"

"What should I have said? Return home immediately, sir, your wife and daughters are waiting? I only met the fellow once. Briefly. If he's going to frequent places like the V and A the only miracle is that he's stayed hidden so long."

"Fifty minutes now," Helen said. "Can't we go?"

"All right, my dear," and he stood and offered to help Helen up.

"If I have to drag you home, then it's no good," Helen said, holding out her empty glass to Packy, and standing on her own. "We'll stay."

LOUISE SETTLED BEHIND A TREE, HER BACK TO THE table where Packy and Helen were sitting. Once they began to talk, she felt too embarrassed to move. Packy mentioned Willard, and Louise thought her heart would explode. When they walked away toward the bar, she stood up carefully, as if she'd been injured and was unsure of her legs. She had been so sure that he was in the West. She looked over the crowd, trying to find Sadie or Marilyn. She spotted her mother first, talking to Helen and Packy. Marilyn was with Regina over by the food tent. She waited for them to come over to her, but neither did. She tried to move but she felt glued to the spot. There were too many people at the party. She looked toward the house and over the lawn. The doors were blocked with people, the lawn clogged with food, drinks, more people. She thought that if anyone talked to her, she would be sick. Louise began walking carefully, as if she might break, practicing invisibility.

She was almost at the road when she heard Marilyn call her name. Marilyn and Regina were sitting on an old garden bench nearby.

"They look fine now," Regina said, "but wait."

"We're watching them drink," Marilyn said.

"Who?" Louise asked.

"Them," Marilyn said. "I'm mostly watching Jimmy, and Regina's watching her mother."

"I thought your mother——" Louise said.

"She was," Regina said.

"I wish Jimmy could go to one of those places," Marilyn said. "I think he's going to get into a fight if he doesn't stop." She giggled, and said, "Watch him. See, he's talking to people and they smile. Then he talks more and they sort of freeze."

"How long do we have to stay?" Louise asked.

"Until we eat," Marilyn said. "And then the cake, of course."

"The food is always good at this party," Regina said.

"You both sound like old ladies," Louise said. "You sound like you've been coming to this party for a hundred years."

"Well, I have," Regina said, "ever since we came to the Park."

"You never notice food anywhere," Marilyn said. "So just take it easy."

"Oh, God," Louise said. "That's all anyone ever wants around here, to take it easy and for everything to stay the same. But sometime something's going to happen."

"Things happen all the time," Regina said. She had taken to dressing in several layers of clothes, long skirts and baggy blouses over oxfords and heavy knee-socks, even now at the height of summer.

"What are you talking about?" Marilyn asked.

"Everything just goes on and on," Louise said, "and people think they know what's what. But they don't. There are secrets."

"Jimmy's coming," Marilyn whispered.

"So what?" Louise said, and she tried to walk past Jimmy.

"My, my," Jimmy said, catching Louise by the arm.

"Mary's party must be infecting her guests with her spirit. Very dissonant."

"Nothing infects me," Louise said, twisting away.

"You must tell me your secret sometime," Jimmy said. "Now come to that table by the tree—your mother is getting food for you."

"Well, that's a change of pace," Louise said, but she began walking with Jimmy, who relaxed his hold.

"I'd better see to my mother," Regina said, and she left them before they reached their table.

Louise slid into the seat Sadie had saved and looked at the full plate of food before her. She'd met the other grownups at the table before, but couldn't remember their names. They were complaining about how expensive Spain had become since the war. Sadie was asking them questions about climate and food. Everyone in the Park except her mother and sister, and Jimmy, were always just finishing with a trip or just beginning one, Louise thought. Sadie never seemed to mind. "How nice for them," she'd say if Louise told her that her classmates were going to the Riviera or to ski in the Alps. Louise always understood that to be poor in a rich person's place meant you were stuck and they weren't. Her fingers itched for tickets and a suitcase. She imagined herself looking across a big, empty room at her father and the dark woman.

She looked past the lawn and the crowd of people she half-recognized over to the woods. Louise wondered why she was here and not elsewhere. She might be floating above the guardian woods. She looked at her hands, which might be someone else's, and then the feeling passed.

"Why is it," Jimmy asked, "that Mary insists on giving these mass gorges and doesn't ever have sufficient food?"

"Gorgeous?" Sadie asked. She was cautious with him, though he seemed friendlier.

"As in, to gorge. I mean, you know the chicken is counted out to the piece."

"The potatoes were boiled too long," Marilyn said, "but the dressing's all right."

"Who cares?" Louise said. "She always serves the same thing and we eat it. Who cares?"

"I do," Jimmy said. "Someone has to keep up standards."

"You can have my chicken," Louise said.

"Louise," Sadie said sharply, "eat something."

"Eat, eat," Louise said.

"The chicken's good," Marilyn said. "The way you like it."

One side of Louise's drumstick was coated with potato salad. On the other, the wrinkled skin had pulled away from the flesh. It reminded her of Sadie when she was naked, her thighs mapped with varicose veins, pocked flesh hanging loose in back. She swallowed hard and returned the meat to her plate.

Jimmy pushed away his untouched plate and picked up his glass. He said, "This is my swan song. No more Justice birthdays."

The high-layered cake, heavy with burning candles, was carried from the house and set before Mary. All around them, people stood, raising their glasses and calling out "Happy Birthday!" and "Another one, Mary," then whispering to whoever stood next to them. There was clapping and singing, and cries for a speech that Mary ignored.

Louise stood and walked away from the table. Sadie called after her, "Louise! Sit down. You can't leave before the cake," but Louise shook her head and ran.

SHE RAN ALONG THE COOL DARK ROADS, FEELING AS IF everyone else in the empty Park was behind her at the party, or the bomb had dropped and she was the only person alive in the Park. She was inside the shell, safe at last, the final disaster over. She need never leave now and go into the world to find her father. All of the Park was hers alone.

When she got home, Louise realized that she hadn't eaten enough. She was trying to train herself out of hunger, but it wasn't working yet. She stood outside her room, head tilted, finger on her chin, staring at the ceiling, just as her mother did on her gloomy mornings. Louise hated it when her mother broke out of her stupor and said, "Oh, sweetie, you know everything—what was it I was supposed to be doing?"

Down in the kitchen, she opened the refrigerator and stared at the dishes and containers, covered with wax paper and rubber bands or by odd plates. There were pork chops from the night before lying uncovered and she picked one up and carried it to the sink. She scraped off the congealed fat with her fingers, then ate the tough morsel, chewing until it was pap, and throwing it in the garbage. She looked around for something to wipe her hands on and reached for Sadie's apron. As she pulled the layer of grease from her fingers, she heard the crackle of paper from the pocket, and she remembered Sadie at the front door, the odd look on her face.

APRON AND LETTER CLUTCHED IN HER HAND, LOUISE went to her room and shut the door. She could still smell pork on her fingers.

The letter, foreign stamp, lightweight paper, was addressed to Sadie. Louise recognized the handwriting. She studied the curves and straight lines, staring at her mother's name and *Tuxedo Park*. His handwriting was still cramped, secretive, and precise, but slightly shaky, as if he'd written the envelope while moving. When Louise held the envelope and closed her eyes, she could feel him standing as still as a boulder. There was no return address on the letter, only the identifying postmark, *Venezia*, and on the stamp a man in armor on horseback.

The letter began *Sadie*, no salutation as Louise had been taught to start a letter, but a bold dash after *Sadie*—. *It has occurred to me that you consider that it would be a failure if you granted me a divorce. I ask you*

*to admit our mistake. Be as kind as I remember you
wanted me to be. If you dream that I will some day come
back—and I believe that you are capable of such childishness—disabuse yourself of the notion.* It went on and
ended without a mention of Louise or Marilyn.

Louise opened her bedroom door and crossed the hallway to her mother's room. Sadie had left her gardening
clothes in a heap near her bathroom door. Her underwear
was on top, the bra stretched out, its elastic turning color
with age.

Louise opened Sadie's desk drawers and closed them
again. She looked around the familiar room, noticing a
place where the wallpaper was coming loose, a chip on
the door, smudges on the carpet. Sadie's bedside cabinet
was piled with books, half read, unopened, and a small
brass key was in the lock. Louise opened the cabinet.
Beneath old articles on gardening, a cosmetics sample,
packets of photos Sadie meant to put in albums, she
found airmail letters tied together with a Christmas rib-
bon. Louise took them out and locked the cabinet door.

SHE FELT SO TIRED HALFWAY UP THE CASTLE HILL THAT
she thought of turning back. The air was full of lightning
bugs and the sounds of crickets. But when she was inside, she was happy that she'd come, and walked slowly
up the stairs by the dwindling light. Cars stopped and
started on the road below. But inside the castle the only
sounds were those she made.

She spread out the letters on her table, pushing aside
Willard's portfolio, and Louise read the letters from her
father to her mother. *You may wonder that I communi-
cate at all, or that I persist and stay away. You may think
you will wear me down, but this is a miscalculation. I am
in exile and will stay so until I am freed.*

Louise looked at the dates, thinking, I was ten, I was
eleven, I waited for him. She had expected him to come
back at Helen's Christmas party, then during the summer, when everything looked so green that she was sure

the return would happen then. She had worried if he was sick or in need, feared that he might be dead. But here he was, writing letters to Sadie. And Sadie, whom Louise had despised for being fluttery and silly, for being abandoned, she was just as bad. Louise hated herself for hoping for so long and for being wrong.

She went to the window and looked down at her house, wishing someone would come out onto the terrace, look up and see her, come up and get her.

She picked up *Anna Karenina* where she had left it earlier and, just able to make out the page, flipped through the book, passing by chunks of philosophy, Levin's boring peasants, trying not to think until she came to the train station, and Vronsky with his toothache and his vision of Anna. Would he marry? she wondered. Now that Anna had freed him?

Louise emptied her pockets onto the table, and spilled out her tins of pills beside the new ones. Green and red, white and yellow, she separated them into neat piles.

He could have come home, she thought, taken a boat and a train, a bus to Tuxedo, walked through the door anytime. She breathed deep gulps and stopped herself from crying. She was meant for this, she thought. If she wasn't, one of the castle rats would have opened her tins and eaten the pills.

She kept water at the castle in a magnum bottle from one of Jimmy's flush times, and she filled a chipped crystal goblet she'd taken from the house. The yellow ones first, a gulp of water, a handful. She changed to the red capsules, smoother and lighter, easier to swallow. The light in the room was fading, but she didn't care to light her candles. There would be a full moon tonight, Louise thought, waxing or waning, she couldn't remember. She started on the little triangles, she could feel their shape in the dark. She looked around for a piece of paper to write something on, a letter to her father or her mother, they were one now. On the wall, she saw metal ferns that were not her home roses. She pressed damp hands against her eyes and squinted out the window at the moon as it rose

over the lake. She wondered if she could swallow more
pills and when she would start to feel them. Where were
the letters? The other side of the table was too far away.
She would write a letter of her own: Good-by Sadie,
Good-by Willard, Good-by Marilyn—but the last made
her want to cry. The water bottle was so heavy and full,
she hadn't made a dent in it, as if she could dent such
heavy glass. She tried to stand but her ears felt funny,
and she thought how tired she was. She heard a ringing
in her ears, as if she were inside a seashell listening to
the ocean. She would have liked to be in her armchair
but it was too far away. There was something she should
be doing, she thought, something she had forgotten. She
closed her eyes and saw the familiar darkness of her
dreams. She moved forward into the darkness. All
around her something was alive, a wall or a person,
something streaming in the darkness, water or air. This
was what happened when the shell cracked, the darkness
came inside. Her chin hit her chest and she woke as if
she'd been struck by lightning. The moon made a pool on
her table, and she thought how pretty it would be outside.
She held up her hand to the moon and saw the light
through her bones and flesh. What a relief, she thought.
This was what I forgot. She wanted badly now to leave
because she wanted to be in the woods, that's what she'd
forgotten, and so she tried to stand, making the effort of
a giant, not a girl. Eyes closed, ears open, she made her
way out of the room, feeling along the castle hall until
she knew she was at the stairway, opening her eyes and
smiling because she was right. She could see in the dark
at last. Down the stairs, eyes closed again, out the door,
clutching the doorjamb when the cool night air struck
her, waiting until her heart was quieter before she went
on. The road was below, silver in the moonlight, and
beyond it the golden lake. She would swim down there
through the rocky black bushes, then roll along, eyes
open this time, pushing forward into the steep darkness
that was not like air, path, or woods, more like water into
which she might dive and swim, straight as an arrow.

JIMMY'S CAR WAS IN THE GARAGE, SO SADIE OFFERED him a ride home. Once they were at the car, he insisted on driving.

"But, Jimmy," Sadie said, "I don't think it's such a good idea. You're so—"

"I'm a better driver when I've had a bit to drink, you see, because I watch so carefully. I'm more single-minded. Less distracted. But if you'd rather not, I'm sure someone at this party would let me drive home. I really am the best driver in the Park. Don't you think, Marilyn?"

"Oh, leave Marilyn out of it," Sadie said. "I'll drive us home and then you can take my car and drive it into the lake for all I care."

"Was I that bad?" Jimmy asked sadly.

"You were and you know it," Sadie said, forgiving him.

"Another birthday for Mary polished off. I can't say that I enjoyed myself. I feel quite ill in fact, and yet I'm sorry it's over. Nostalgia," Jimmy said. "Habit. Feel the same?"

"Maybe," Sadie said. Leaving with Jimmy was often her favorite part of dinners and parties. This time she felt as though she were rescuing him. He was acting as though one of his binges were starting. She had never seen one in full swing, never seen him in a fight, only one time when he showed up at her house, sick and covered with bruises. She thought he had never shown her his violent side to spare her. Now she realized it was pure chance.

Sadie sailed the heavy silver car along the tree-lined road, so familiar and mysterious in the moonlight. The blind curves and the unexpected cars, the half-lit houses and the glimpses of moonlit rose gardens—how lucky she was, after all.

Marilyn sat in the rumble seat, the wind in her face. She didn't listen to what they were saying, only the rhythm of their voices, and she thought how much she loved both of them and how happy she was to be there in that car at that very moment, flying through the summer moonlight in a silver car. She wanted the journey to go on forever.

When they were almost at the bottom of the castle driveway, Sadie slowed in preparation for the turn up the Weavers' hill.

"By the way," Jimmy said, "I believe I lined up a new job for—"

A deer, Sadie thought. A raccoon. Oh, no, Marilyn thought, as suddenly a shadow appeared from the underbrush at the castle drive and rolled toward them. The car slammed into the shadow, and it fell away from them, crying out, into the bushes. Sadie turned the Packard into a spin that ended when they slammed against the boulders at the edge of the lake.

"Oh, God," said Sadie, "what was it?" but Marilyn was already out of the car, climbing over the rocks and bushes. The castle, she thought, the castle is up there. She found her sister thrown on her back, eyes closed, her party dress torn and dirty. "It's Louise," Marilyn called out. "Go get someone quickly. Oh, Louise." She started to shake her sister to wake her, but Sadie ran up, breathing heavily, saying, "Don't touch her, don't move her."

"Wait there," Jimmy called from the road. "I'll get someone. Wait there."

"Oh, God," Sadie said, "how did this happen? Look at her, Marilyn, is she all right, is anything broken? There's no blood—maybe a little on her arm—how did this happen, did she jump in front of the car or fall, but why would she jump, Marilyn? Go get someone, Jimmy, go fast."

They listened to Jimmy struggling to start the Packard. Finally the engine caught, and he pulled the car from the boulders, metal tearing. When he drove away there was no sound but the wind through the trees, and rustling in the underbrush. Sadie began to cry.

"Wait," Marilyn said.

In the cold moonlight, Sadie and Marilyn watched Louise breathe and move her lips. Oh, God, Sadie prayed, if she's all right, I'll do whatever I should. This is why I'm here, for her. This is all there is.

The girl moaned and turned her head. Sadie saw her eyes move beneath her pale lids. When Louise was first born, Sadie watched her like this. The woods smelled like something sweet and something rotting, sharp pine becoming soil. Louise opened her eyes. "Don't move," Sadie said. "Don't move, dolly."

Louise looked up: two mothers, two sisters. Two moons, many trees. "Oh, no." She wanted to sleep again.

"Don't talk," Sadie said. "Don't worry. Just wait. Help's coming."

Not moving, not talking, just waiting, they rested on the forest floor in the cool summer moonlight, half dreaming as the moonlight traveled from one rock to another, covering the trees with silver. Then came the red lights and the men—waited for, hoped for—frightening them. Sadie and Louise wept together in the ambulance.

Four

Sadie drove home slowly at dawn, parked the Straight Eight, and stood in the oil-smelling garage, wanting to be outside while the light created the garden. She ran her hand over the damaged silver fender and wondered if she'd ever care to get it fixed.

Under the light of the kitchen lamp, Marilyn and Jimmy were playing gin rummy. The kitchen smelled of hot chocolate. Marilyn had a cup next to her, and Jimmy a glass of water. Marilyn looked rumpled and sleepy in her nightgown and old plaid robe. She was holding her cards droopily. Jimmy could see what she had.

They turned and looked up at her. Her eyes were red —from crying, Marilyn wondered.

"Sweeties," Sadie said. "I'm back."

"How was it?" Jimmy asked. "How's Louise?"

Marilyn put down her cards and came to her mother, hugging her, saying, "I think there's some chocolate left. Do you want me to make breakfast?"

"For once, I'm not hungry," Sadie said. "I'm fine. It's okay." She kissed the top of Marilyn's head and pushed her away. She couldn't bear the weight of her daughter's nearness. "I just want to sit down for a minute."

Jimmy threw down his cards. "How's Louise?" he repeated.

"Asleep," Sadie said. "They wanted to put her in a locked room, you know, but I convinced them that she wasn't going to do anything else. She wouldn't. I know her. They pumped her stomach and found all kinds of pills. Not very digested, so she was just kind of woozy, they said."

"Woozy," Jimmy said. "Marilyn, you must know where she got the pills."

"I don't. I really don't."

"Hush," Sadie said. "I believe you. A little intoxicated and sleepy. She's just a child, I told them, not used to taking anything like that—tranquilizers, sleeping pills. She told me before I left. She took them from Mary Justice. Some other people too."

"When can she come home?" Marilyn asked.

"She has some bruises too," Sadie said. "Where the Packard bumped her, so for a few days, they're watching her. They took some x-rays but she's fine. Just fine. They said, Youth."

"So all's well that ends well?" Jimmy asked.

"I don't know what that means in this case," Sadie said. "She's alive."

Jimmy said, "It's so late, it's early." He stood and gathered his hand and Marilyn's and shuffled them neatly into the deck. Jimmy's hair was slicked back and wet. His face looked pale and caved-in.

"You took a shower?"

"Marilyn thought it would make me feel better."

So her daughter had ideas on what would make a drunk feel better. For once she wished Jimmy were gone, though in their years of friendship, each time he left felt like a minor defeat.

"Do you need a ride home?" she asked.

"No, no. I'll walk," he said. "I think I'd like the air. Don't fuss, Sadie. Don't worry."

How lean he looked, how wrinkled in the unfair kitchen light. He was older than she, Sadie remembered, and he didn't like other people's troubles.

"If you like, I'll be back later," Jimmy said. "Most

probably. I don't know when. I have to go up to Tower Hill for the afternoon, but—"

"You've done a lot already," Sadie said, "playing cards with Marilyn. Don't worry about us," but she thought, Good, he'll be back, wanting to believe that he would.

ONCE HE LEFT, MARILYN WENT UP TO BED AND SADIE cleaned the kitchen. She put the deck of cards back into the drawer with balls of string and broken can openers. She went around the house turning out lights. Marilyn was asleep with her bedside light on. Sparky was curled at the foot of the bed, a gray smudge against the flowered quilt. Dandelion slept on the rug, snoring heavily. Sadie turned out the light and tiptoed to her own room.

She was still wearing her blue dress, with dirt and pine needles at the knees where she'd knelt at Louise's side, and blood from Louise's arm. Sadie lifted the skirt and smelled the sweet antiseptic hospital odor. She hoped that Louise was asleep. She looked around her room, at the piles of mending, and at the open door of her bedside cabinet. Staring, she struggled to unzip the back of her dress, then dropped her arms. She went to her dressing table and ran her brush roughly through her hair until her forehead was red where the brush hit it. She crossed the hallway to Marilyn's room and turned on the light. Marilyn lay on her back, her arms flung open, her mouth a little slack. Sadie touched her daughter's shoulder. "Marilyn," she said. "Marilyn."

Marilyn moaned and tried to turn away. The cat turned, looked at Sadie through slit eyes, and settled back down.

"Where did Louise come from?" Sadie asked. "Where did she come from?"

"What is it?" Marilyn said.

"I want you to answer me. Where did your sister come from when she fell down? What was she doing in the woods?"

Half asleep, Marilyn snuggled down beneath the bed-clothes. "At the castle," she said.

"The castle? You mean the place up the hill? Oh, Marilyn, wake up, for Christ's sake."

Marilyn opened her eyes wide and looked at her mother, her hair brushed back sharply, her face distorted in a frowning grimace. "The castle," she said. "Stop it. You're scaring me."

Once Marilyn and Louise were playing and knocked over a glass of milk, soaking the newspaper that lay on the kitchen table, their sandwiches, Sadie's glasses. Sadie came into the kitchen in time to see the river of milk flowing from the table, and she rushed over to the girls and grabbed Marilyn and hit her across the face. Marilyn ran up to her room and locked her door. Sadie followed her upstairs, crying, saying, "Forgive me, I thought you'd spilled the milk, but Louise said she did it." Marilyn thought now that Sadie might hit her again and be just as sorry.

Dandelion, woken by their voices, stood and stretched, then went to the bedroom door, her tail wagging, ready to go with them.

"Get out of bed," Sadie said. "Show me. Show me the castle right now. Stay, Dandelion. You stay here."

BAREFOOT, HER NIGHTGOWN SNAGGING ON SHRUBS AND weeds, Marilyn led Sadie up the stone steps. Ground fog rose from the chilly garden beds. When they were past Sadie's tended territory and in the woods, there was just enough light for Marilyn to see her way and to avoid stepping on things she didn't want to. When she looked back, she saw her mother behind her, silhouetted against the thick trees, strange in her party dress.

They reached the front of the castle, and Sadie asked, "Do you have a key? How do you get in?"

"It's unlocked now. But Louise has the key," Marilyn said.

"Where did Louise get a key? This isn't her *house*,"
Sadie said.

Marilyn shrugged, and Sadie walked a few paces away,
returning quickly to ask, "But when does she come here,
what does she do here? What's inside?" Marilyn
shrugged again and looked away. Sadie said, "You have
to tell me, Marilyn. I know you think you're betraying
your sister's secret but there can't be any secrets anymore. Do you hear me?"

"She fixed up a room here," Marilyn said. She had
wished for a long time that Sadie knew about the castle,
but now it seemed too late for any good to come of it. All
she could think was how much Louise would hate her.

"But she has a room at *home*," Sadie said. "She has
two rooms, twenty rooms."

She went up the steps, and leaned on the front door,
pounded on it, then turned the knob and opened it.

The half-oval foyer smelled musty, and the doorjamb
where she rested her hand was damp to the touch. She
could barely see past the furniture shrouded in cloth, to
the windows where the draperies were long closed. Sadie
was reminded of her own house as she first saw it with
Willard, unlived in, waiting for the next life.

Marilyn said, "Okay, Sadie. If you really want to see,"
and walked past her mother to the stairs.

Sadie followed Marilyn up two flights of stairs and
down the long broad hallway. The barefoot girl in her
white nightgown disappeared around a corner. Sadie
walked faster.

Marilyn stood outside Louise's tower room and ges-
tured for her mother to go in. Sadie went to the window
and looked out, saying, "You can see our terrace from
here," then turned and looked around the room.

A book lay open on the arm of an overstuffed armchair,
and there were indentations in the hassock where Louise
put her feet. Sadie found a candle in a broken crystal
candlestick, and lit it with matches that lay on the small
desk. In the new light, she saw two oval tins, lids off,
overturned, and scattered pills. She saw a glass and a

magnum bottle. Where had that come from, she wondered, what celebration? There was no suicide note waiting there addressed to her, so, she thought, maybe it was a kind of accident after all. If Louise had really wanted to die, she could have done so in this room and not been discovered until it was too late.

Sadie picked up the candlestick and set it on a table across the room. There were old western photos, fanned out and displayed on an open black portfolio that Sadie recognized, her heart sinking: Willard's scarf, Willard's photographs, and his books on Japanese prints. From the cover of one of the books a black-haired Japanese maiden in a kimono laughed at Sadie, her mouth pursed into a perfect red bow. Cast down in a loose bunch next to the books were Willard's letters and their envelopes. Hands shaking, Sadie gathered them together and held them against her. Marilyn still stood at the door. Sadie looked at her second daughter's beautiful face. Marilyn didn't know what the letters were or what a liar her mother was.

"How long has she been in this horrible place?" Sadie asked. "You'd better tell me, chickie."

"Forever," Marilyn said. "For always. She likes the castle. She likes being here alone. I told her she'd get caught. It doesn't have anything to do with you. Don't feel bad."

"I feel—I've been a terrible mother."

"You're one of the best mothers in the Park," Marilyn said. "Everyone says so. It doesn't have anything to do with you."

THE SUN WAS UP, AND THEY WALKED HOME THROUGH the woods. They thought they heard a rustling in the underbrush, but when they turned, there was nothing there. For almost a decade, Sadie thought, she'd been waking up in Tuxedo, waiting for Willard, and she had risen prepared and expectant. Now, coming down the hill through her garden, she felt dread instead of expectation, and she knew it was what she should have been feeling all along.

She sent Marilyn to sleep, hugging the girl first and saying that she shouldn't worry, things always worked out in the end. Holding her, Sadie thought how easy her second child had always been, so much like herself only thoroughly good. When Marilyn hugged her back, Sadie shuddered, wanting again to pull away from the trusting embrace.

She made her round through the house, checking doors and windows, straightening piles of magazines in the library, picking up a jacket carelessly thrown over a chair, a half-drunk glass of milk forming cheese on the porch. For all these years the shabby house had been her fortress, and a good one. It was hers, by a right greater than legal ownership, and she wouldn't give it up. And yet—she moved a finger along the broad back of the piano—she had brought her daughter harm and she had done it in this house.

Upstairs, Sadie put the letters back into her cabinet, took off her dress at last, and ran a hot bath. She would sleep, she planned, have breakfast, go back to the hospital. She lay down in her dressing gown, listening for the water to reach the right level.

Their first autumn in Tuxedo, when she hadn't known a thing about house, country, or winter, she had woken each morning with her heart pounding and gone to sleep each night thankful for some time off. She bought the beef from the slaughterhouse, but it took them forever to get through it. Jimmy helped her cut wood for the fireplaces, and showed her how to install the few storm windows they found in the garage. Each time Sadie was ready to give up, Helen appeared to invite them for dinner to celebrate a heavy snowstorm or to take the girls off for the day, and Sadie revived. She learned to rush her visitors through the living room and music room to the library, the one comfortable room. She set out the family photos, of Willard, Reed, of Willard's mother, of her parents, of her and Reuben. She learned to wake in winter and to listen for the sound that would tell her what had broken or crumbled overnight, what she had to do for the girls.

She wanted to make the girls a wonderful place, a safe place with a gate and a fence, the lake and the road, so that it would never seem to them that they had been abandoned in Tuxedo Park, left behind as if Willard had forgotten who they were and what their claims were to him.

Now she thought, We could have moved back into the city. Things would have been easier for me. I could have done something—a job, school, it didn't matter. I should have moved back there to be with people just like me. For the first time it occurred to Sadie that something else might have happened to her, something unpredictable and unforeseen, if she'd left Tuxedo Park. Staying had seemed the only way to stay alive, and she was wrong about that.

Sadie got up, turned off the bath water, and went downstairs. She looked at the living room. "Well, what could I do?" she asked. "I was all alone here, just me to do it all."

She stood at the center of her room, listening to the house.

She went outside to her garden, whistling for Dandelion, clapping her hands softly in the still early morning. The flowers that bloomed all over the hill were at their best now, near the peak; delphinium, and roses with dew on their half-opened petals, cleome and cosmos shimmering in the breeze. She looked toward the vegetable garden and saw a doe standing still as a tree, staring at Sadie fixedly. Sadie turned her gaze to the garden. A spotted fawn grazed inside the fenced-in lettuce bed, finishing the stubs of lettuce heads left the day before. The doe stirred, and Sadie thought, She's dying to run away but she can't leave the baby. "Take it," she said, and she turned and went into the house.

Five

THE HOSPITAL WAS ONCE THE MAIN HOUSE OF A LARGE estate north of Tuxedo Park. The gloomy redstone building was at the crest of a tree-covered hill, and Sadie had heard stories of babies born during snowstorms halfway up the drive. In beds where she guessed there were once more demanding plants, there were woody shrubs, trimmed crisply, and across the drive from the main entrance tennis courts original to the place. Though it had once been a home it had the institutional look of a prison or a school.

On Louise's bedside table were flowers, one bouquet sent by Helen from a florist, the other more abundant and undisciplined. Jimmy had cut some of his best roses and arranged them in an art pottery vase for Louise.

"What beautiful roses," Sadie said, "I hope—" Louise looked small in the bed, and beaten.

"As soon as I bust out of here, I'll write him a thank-you note. Okay?"

"And Helen too," Sadie said.

She wanted to be serene. Along the hospital's broad, empty corridors she'd looked into other patients' rooms —she couldn't help herself—and saw that Louise was one of the few young people there, which made it all seem worse. She wanted to be serene and calm for Louise, who was refusing to look at her. Sadie set down her pocket-book and a bag containing an orange, a magazine, and a box of Kleenex, and sat in the plastic chair beside Louise's bed.

Louise's room faced the woods, not the broad lawn, which Sadie thought would have been a far better view for her daughter, one that implied perspective. She wished Louise would realize that they were in danger, and that she had to act well. What if the doctors decided that Louise had a mental affliction and had to be taken away from Sadie? Sadie set the Kleenex on Louise's table by the hospital box of tissues, and took out the magazine.

"Reuben's coming to see you. Tomorrow. He had to go to court today. But he sends his love," Sadie said.

"When do I get out of here?"

"Tomorrow. Or the day after. Unless you still feel sick."

"I'm fine," Louise said. "I just feel . . ."

She lay back on a nest of white pillows, aware of the wan picture she made. She rubbed her stomach, which still hurt, and closed her eyes, listening to Sadie turn the pages of a magazine—*Yes! Embroidery Is Worth the Effort!* She tried to feel empty and hard as she imagined she should after so much vomiting and cleansing. At moments, she felt almost happy when she recalled flying through the dark. She touched the bruises on her legs, her badges of courage. Her mother was parked there acting as if nothing had happened, boring her, which surprised Louise. Everything should be different now, she thought. Nothing should be the same ever again.

The night before when Sadie had left, Louise had felt panic engulf her, like one of the fits of vomiting. The nurse came to give her a last shot and turned out her light, and Louise realized that she had done something that couldn't be ignored. She had been half asleep, startled to see a stranger, she'd been counting the number of nights she'd spent away from Marilyn and Sadie. She cried when the nurse left, and vowed she would tell no one she cried. She slept off and on, waking with a jerk. In the blackness, she saw creatures who were half alive and half dead.

Her hearing might be slightly impaired, the doctor had said that morning before Sadie arrived, and Louise wondered what that would be like. The doctor asked her about her parents, if she had brothers and sisters, where she lived, how she felt—questions that left Louise feeling exposed, and she felt that way still. She was altered but didn't know in what way. She wondered if this would be the one great act of her life and the rest would be memory, like a movie that flashes ahead to the heroine as she becomes older and smaller, until no one could believe that she'd ever done a thing out of the ordinary. Her story would be added to the Park annals, but no one would understand.

"Be nice to him," Sadie said. "For me."

"Who?" she asked.

"Your uncle."

"Oh, I wish he'd stay away. I don't want to see him," Louise said, feeling tired suddenly.

"Please," Sadie said. "Please see him."

"I want to see Marilyn."

"Well, you can't. You'll see her when you come home. She's too young to visit."

"That's dumb," Louise said.

"Probably," Sadie agreed. She put down the magazine and came to Louise's bedside, touching her scraped hand. "Is there anything you want to tell me, duckie? Or ask?"

"No," Louise whispered, avoiding her mother's eyes, hating the feel of her mother's calloused hand.

"I know I've done a lot of things wrong, Louise."

"No," Louise said, unwilling to listen to Sadie take the drama for herself. "He's the only one who can do anything. It's him."

"Him?"

"My *father*."

"What about him?"

"He wanted to stay away," Louise said. "He could have come back but he didn't want to."

She turned her head from her mother and closed her eyes. Sadie watched her, wanting to say, It was all my fault, I should have called him back long before, but she couldn't. Who would have thought that the child would find the letters?

"All right, look at me, Louise." When Louise didn't move, Sadie said, "Do you remember once, right after Willard left, you asked me if I was going too and I said, Never. I meant it, Louise, I still mean it. I'll always be here for you. I know it's made you unhappy that your father's left, but—"

"You," Louise said, stiffening in the bed. "You're just as bad as he is. You've been lying to me all these years. Oh, poor Sadie, Willard left her. You could have gotten him back here anytime."

"But not to break up the family. You don't understand, Louise. The only condition was divorce and think of what that would do."

"Think of what it did, Sadie. Look at me, look at me, this is all your fault." She sat up in bed and held out her pale arms, displaying the red and blue scrapes and bruises. Along her forehead, a cloudy bruise was deepening. "You did this to me, you did it."

"I didn't tell you to jump in front of the Packard."

"Oh, who cares about the Packard? I'll never forgive you, never. If you'd gotten a divorce, we would have seen him."

"You would have seen him if he'd come home as he should have all along," Sadie said.

"You knew," Louise said, sinking back against the bank of hard white pillows. "You knew all along where he was. I was so stupid. I thought he'd told me a secret. I was going to go after him. But you knew."

"Not *really*," Sadie said, but Louise interrupted and said, "Really, really, you knew, you knew."

Sadie looked at Louise, and thought, Look how young she is. She'll be healed in no time, good as new. Nothing will show. She has everything before her. Sadie looked down at her hands, the garden dirt that stayed in the cracks season to season, the nails cut to the quick, the stubby fingers. She wasn't even forty and she was old. Nothing would ever happen to her again. Sadie stood. Her hands were shaking and she had to cough before she could speak.

"You don't know what you're talking about," she said. "You don't know what this has cost me. None of it. Don't be so quick to judge. You think you'll never forgive me? You think you're so miserable? The day will come when you have to forgive yourself, and I don't envy you a minute of it."

"Oh, God," Louise said, "just stop talking, just leave me alone. Leave me alone. I just want to die."

"No, you don't, Louise. You could have died last night but you didn't. And I'm warning you—don't announce to anyone around here that you want to die. I'm going back to the house now. I'll tell the nurse you're alone."

Louise waited until the sound of her mother's footsteps faded, then she opened her eyes. A time would come when she wouldn't be able to remember what the truth was and what the letters said. But this is what would remain, this version of the story: he could have come home anytime. This made her father smaller to her, and changed everything else, reducing the world to nothing she wanted, and making all the moments and people Louise had ever cared for unimportant.

Six

THE FLOWERS LOOKED TOO FULL AND BLOWSY AS SADIE drove home through the Park. She should be deadheading, she thought, picking bugs off the vegetables, cultivating around plants, but she was weary and uninterested in the garden, and for once she was in no hurry to be home. Sadie saw herself and the dog in the house together, and the girls gone. That would be her old age, which might start at any time. Sadie drove past her driveway. She wanted nothing more than to be with Helen or with Jimmy. They had saved her from so much and would do so again. It was their friendship that had enabled her to survive in Tuxedo Park.

Sadie knocked on Helen's front door and, receiving no answer, opened it. She called Helen's name, then went upstairs.

"There you are," she said at the doorway of Helen's dressing room. "I let myself in."

Clothing was spread over every surface—piles of lingerie, suits and dresses on hangers. Helen stood in the large closet, staring at the garments still hanging there.

"Oh," Helen said. "Hello. Any news?"

"Not much," Sadie said, clearing a space on a chair and sitting down. She wished Helen would offer her tea or coffee. "Louise is shaken up, as you'd imagine. But she'll be all right. Reuben's coming tomorrow. Anyway, I was driving by, on the way from the hospital, and I decided to visit.''

"How's the patient?'' Helen called from inside the closet.

"I told you, a little banged up. Very upset. Spring cleaning?''

"It's a little late for that, isn't it? I'm packing.''

"I see,'' Sadie said. Don't go, she wanted to say, don't leave me now. "What a pretty blouse.''

"I'm tired of it. Do you want it? It's not really your color. And it would be much too big.''

"No. I guess not,'' Sadie said. "Thanks anyway.''

"You must want to know where I'm going.''

"Is that wrong?''

"God, no, everyone else around here knows everything within minutes, why shouldn't you?''

"I don't gossip about—''

"Okay, Sadie,'' she said, emerging from the closet. "Calm down. I'm taking a cottage in the Cotswolds. For the summer. The fall too. Longer, if it suits me.''

"I didn't know you liked the Cotswolds.''

"I don't know a thing about the Cotswolds, but Suzanne Fletcher's cousin has a place with a cottage on the grounds. Which I'm renting. I hope the cousin either minds his own business or isn't half as dull as poor Suzanne. It's not a bad ride from London.''

Helen was so matter-of-fact that Sadie felt numb in response. Absently, she straightened a pile of lingerie on the chair next to her.

"What about Packy?'' she asked. And what about me, she wanted to say.

"He's selling their place. As you probably know. Everyone else does. Or rather Terrell is. After all these years, she's decided that she wants her husband to herself. I suppose she's had her fun. He has too. There's been another woman. Another another. Some young girl in Texas. So I guess Terrell decided to rein him in. Oh, don't look so shocked, Sadie. What do you expect people to do—live the way you do, mending your socks and being good? Anyway," she said, "I'm not going to sit around here and be mooned over by the Park hags and harpies."

"I don't blame you. I mean, it'll probably be better," Sadie said cautiously. "The whole fall?"

"Who knows how long? The good thing about being rejected is that you get your freedom back."

"I guess I never wanted my freedom," Sadie said. "What a shame. I always thought he loved you so."

"Oh, Sadie, sometimes you're more of a child than your children. I can't imagine even Marilyn saying a dopey thing like that. You talk about love as if it were a block of cement. Loving someone has very little to do with it."

"Maybe that's true. But it's been the whole shebang with you and Packy," Sadie protested.

"So I thought. Apparently I was as stupid as could be. The one good thing . . ." Her voice trailed off as she looked back in the closet. "I feel like throwing away everything I own. I feel like such a fool." She stood stonily, holding a striped dress by one sleeve like a ragdoll.

"I guess everything will change now," Sadie said.

"Oh, I hope so," Helen said. "Look, Sadie, kids do all kinds of crazy things—"

"Louise found the letters," Sadie said. "That's why she did it."

"What letters?"

"I never wanted to tell you. Willard's been writing to me for years, nagging at me to give him a divorce. But I couldn't, Helen, you can see why. It would be the end of everything. Would have been. And I thought, all along, you know this better than anyone, I thought he was coming back. I hoped he was coming back."

"Wait," Helen said. She sat down on the couch opposite Sadie. For the first time that afternoon, she stopped looking furious. Her old look of amusement and interest returned. "You mean all these years that everyone's thought he just dropped you like a hot potato, you two have been corresponding?''

"No," Sadie said. "I never wrote back."

"But, Sadie, you knew where he *was?*" She began to laugh uncontrollably. "Oh, God, it's priceless. Does Jimmy know? He'd love it."

"No," Sadie said, "no."

Helen wiped at the corners of her eyes. "Oh, the martyr of the Park, the saint of the Park, it's too much. It's too good. Oh, bless you for telling me. I haven't laughed in a week. So she found the letters?''

"Yes," Sadie said. "That's what I've been trying to tell you." She was sorry now that she'd told Helen anything. "She blames him. That's new. But she blames me too. As she should."

"Well," Helen said, standing and returning to her closet, "I never thought you could keep a secret. If I'd known you were such a deep well, I'd have told you things years ago . . .''

"Helen!" Sadie shouted. "This isn't so funny to me. What do I do now?''

"Oh, Sadie, darling. You just get a divorce, collect alimony, buy a new wardrobe, move to Florida, I don't know. Do you think I know what you should do? By the way," she said, and she passed her hand across her forehead in a gesture that meant she was nervous, "by the way, Jimmy's coming to England with me. He's in terrible shape. He'd be in a funny farm if he could afford it.''

"He was drunk last night, but it didn't seem any different . . .''

"If he isn't crazy now, he will be soon. Crazy, drunk, whatever it is. And this is one way to get him out of this place. He's been drunk for a month. More or less," Helen said. "And you know the kind of thing that's happened before at the end of a spree. He's getting a little old for this.''

She spoke as if Sadie had been Jimmy's caretaker and had failed.

"What will he do there? What will you?''

"Set up house. He's awfully handy, as you know. Gardener, valet. I won't be lonely this way, you see, and he'll be taken care of, which is what I think Jimmy wants. What he's always wanted, really. He's very dependent. We'll see how it works out."

Sadie stood and said, "When do you go?"

"A few days."

"I guess you won't have any time to come over . . ." She hated the humility in her voice.

"I'll come by," Helen said. "Of course I'll come by. Look, Sadie." She emerged from the closet and leaned against the doorjamb, her arms folded. "I might as well level with you. Not that it makes so much difference, but you might as well know. Packy saw Willard in London recently. And he was with a woman. All Packy said was dark hair. Did you know about her too?"

"The lawyer said—"

"I don't know what that means, a woman. Maybe it was just someone he met, but you might as well be prepared for that. Sadie, dear—stop being so dreamy about Willard."

"But you're the one who's always said love was worth it. Your husband—"

"Yes, and look where it's landed me. A word to the wise, Sadie." She put a heavy tweed suit to one side and said, "By the way, you might consider apologizing to Mary Justice."

"What for? Did she tell you to tell me that?"

"Really, Sadie. Louise did steal from her."

"How did Mary find out about that? Did Jimmy tell her?"

Helen shrugged. "Do as you like. But it might make future years more peaceful around here."

"Where's Jimmy now?" Sadie asked.

"He's dividing his time between here and the Round House. We just decided this morning. He came by at dawn and passed out on the couch. I don't know where he is now. I don't keep track of him. I'll send him over if I see him."

"He asked you to tell me?"

"He wants you to hire someone to keep the business going."

"Oh, I'll be all right," Sadie said. "The gardens are winding down soon. It's a good season for him to go."

"I'll let him know you said that," Helen said. "I'm sure he'll be happy to hear it. Look, Sadie, I hope there's no hard feelings. I'd hate to go off feeling depressed about you too. It's probably much better this way. For you. Oh, Sadie, stop looking like that. People live as they can and they do what they have to. Haven't you learned that yet?"

Just as she reached home, Sadie remembered that once Helen told her about her mother's closest and longest friendship. One day, for a small provocation—a book or a piece of costume jewelry loaned and not returned, forgotten on one side and not on the other—the friends quarreled and drifted apart. For the rest of her life, Helen's mother wondered how her friend was and bristled at news of her as she might have at news of a former lover. She even began to have lunch with her, toward the end of her life, but it was never the same. Sadie had thought, What could ever make me feel that way, what could ever end our friendship.

Seven

REUBEN ARRIVED AT THE HOSPITAL THE NEXT AFTER-
noon, bringing treats from the city: *Seventeen* magazine,
caramel-covered marshmallow squares wrapped in wax
paper from a shop on Broadway, French soap in pink
paper. He settled in the visitor's chair and watched
Louise push the gifts from one side of her bed to the
other.

"You don't have to talk to me," she said. "You can
read your paper. Sadie read that magazine on the floor all
morning."

"I read the paper on the train. Twice."

"Nobody reads the *Times* twice. Not even you."

"Test me," he said. "Try me on the financial page."

She turned her head away.

"So your mother was here." He put an unlit cigar in
his mouth and inhaled its wet odor.

"You don't have to stay," Louise said.

"I like it here," he said. "It's restful. The last hospital
I visited it was a very sad occasion. An old friend. If you
were being unkind, you'd call him a party hack. Came to
America with nothing. Died a pauper. Spent his life
working for what he believed in. So this—a visit with my
favorite niece."

"I'm not your favorite," she said. "How come Marilyn won't come to see me?"

"She can't, Louise. Visitors must be sixteen years of age. Rules is rules."

"She thinks I'm creepy, doesn't she? So do you."

"I haven't seen Marilyn to ask if she thinks you're creepy," he answered in a lawyer's voice.

"You know what I mean," Louise said. She breathed in deeply to stop from crying. "What's going to happen to me? Am I going to be locked up? Or arrested?"

"If you're hospitalized, it'll be from choice."

The pale color washed from her face, leaving the accident's marks vivid, and he said, "It's a possibility. You run these risks, you know. There are consequences for actions most places on the planet. I suppose your mother's acting as if you're on a vacation or something. All right, don't answer that. But you and I, Louise, we can't just act as if nothing's happened here, you know. We're different kind of people from your mother, aren't we?"

She could barely keep her eyes on him. She wanted to look out the window to the green forest, up to the white cracked ceiling.

"Well, what did you think, you stupid kid? You thought you'd get a medal? This is your life. Your *life*."

Reuben stood, his suit wrinkled from the train, looking for a place to put his cigar. Exasperated, he jammed it in his pocket.

"Maybe my father will come back," she said.

"You think he'd bring a lot to this party? I promise you he won't."

"You don't *know* that," she said.

"No. You're right. But I'm willing to make an educated guess. Look, Louise, let's make a deal, you and me. Once you start jumping in front of cars—"

"I didn't *jump*," she said. "I *rolled* down the hill. I *fell* in front of the car. On the road."

"Congratulations," he said. "Whatever you did, I got the impression you weren't happy. So . . . I think it's time you got out of this hothouse. If you'll agree to go to boarding school, I'll pay for everything. Fees. Clothes. Trips home for vacations.''

"Have you talked to Sadie?" Louise asked suspiciously.

"I said I wanted to make a deal, not start World War Three.''

"Why should I go to boarding school? I don't know what it's like. I wouldn't know where I was.''

"Well, you know what this is like.''

"This is my *home*, Uncle Reuben.''

She had always felt this about her uncle, that what he seemed to be giving, he was really taking, and now he wanted to take the Park, her mother, her sister.

"Nice home," he said, "taking pills at your age. Rolling in front of cars.''

"If I didn't like it at school," she asked, "could I come back?''

He hesitated to answer, guessing that once she left Tuxedo, it would be almost impossible for Louise to return. And he couldn't believe that any boarding school would be a good thing. But after what Sadie had done to Louise, bringing her up here, what difference would a few more years make? The school would at least remove her from Sadie. He said, "Of course you can come back. And everything would still be here. Your mother hasn't changed anything in years, right? But you'll give it a shot, right, Louise? You'll be fair about it?''

"I guess.''

He looked around the room as if he might get help from the window or the door. He gathered his paper and asked, "You need anything? No? Think it over. I once asked your mother—For whom shall you live? So—who knows in your case. You might like it out in the world.''

"Maybe," she said doubtfully. "And what about Marilyn?''

"She stays," Reuben said. "Unless—''

"No, she would stay if there was an earthquake," Louise said. "Anyway, Sadie wants her.''

"Sadie wants everything. Chin up," Reuben said.

"This is probably the best offer you'll get for a while. But remember, however misguided—your mother has your interests at heart. Right?" He made a gesture, thumbs up, and she shrugged her shoulders, then succumbed suddenly to her tears.

"No one cares about me," she said. "You just want to get rid of me. Willard could have come back anytime. Anytime. Did you know that too? Did you know where he was?"

"Okay, okay," he said. Her shoulders shook and he reached over and patted her gingerly, as if she were an unpredictable animal. "That's not so. We all care, but—"

"You don't understand," she said.

"Louise," he said. "Grow up. I understand. It's tough, but—it's what is. You know? Your father and mother are just who they are. Nobody chose it to be this way," which he didn't think was strictly true either but it seemed to make Louise feel better. She dried her tears and looked straight at him for the first time.

"I'll think it over," she said and he guessed that she would agree to his proposition. He imagined Louise at a school in the mountains, somewhere north of Tuxedo Park, one of a group of girls. There were autumn leaves, the girls wore plaid pleated skirts. They kicked the leaves, their arms full of books. They were teaching each other how to behave out in the world, and, he supposed, worse things could happen to Louise. He smiled, and Louise gave him a quick thumbs-up, using her hand to cover her face as soon as his back was turned.

EXPANSIVE, COMFORTABLE, REUBEN LIT A FRESH CIGAR, and blue smoke clouded the air around him. He leaned back and spread his arms over the back of the couch on the glass porch.

"You look as though you just sold the Brooklyn Bridge," Sadie said. "Pleased with yourself."

"Just relieved," he said. "Reflecting on the remarkable properties of youth—the ability to recover. Louise looks like hell, but in a week she'll be right as rain."

Sadie, on the other hand, looked awful. Her face was puffed with worry and crying, and she held her arms crossed over her chest or around her waist, her shoulders hunched over.

"Come on," he said. "Relax. What's so awful? It's over. Don't shut the barn door now to keep your chicken at home."

"Nothing's ever over," she said. Her eyes reddened and she looked like an old woman. "I thought yesterday, for the first time, I thought—"

She was looking out the window, and Reuben came up and stood beside her, looking out also, trying to see what Sadie saw. The Park lay before them, the dainty, mid-summer sky reflected in the placid lake, the tops of the large dignified houses rising above the groups of enormous hardwoods, the pines pressing jaggedly upward, covering the rocky hills. He wrinkled his nose at the lake, at Sadie's bouquetlike flower beds lining her terrace, at the Park.

"Helen thinks I should apologize to Mary Justice."

He made a snorting noise and said, "An interesting idea. And here I was contemplating the whole train ride the merits of a negligence suit against that woman. So careless with her deadly drugs. What nonsense these people have for brains."

"Helen said it would save grief in the future around here."

"Ah, Sadie," her brother said, "you've saddled yourself with morons and fools, and you've settled in for life."

"But you're fond of Helen," she protested.

"Helen, Helen's all right," and he dismissed her with a shrug. "Look, Sadie, Louise and I had a talk just now."

"She doesn't talk to me much," Sadie said. "Yesterday we had what I thought was a good talk. I didn't like what was said, but we talked. Today—it was like we were at the dentist. Waiting. Sitting there together."

"She said you read a magazine."

"Maybe I did."

"Sadie," he said, "try to listen to me and not to talk. Have you ever thought that Louise jumped in front of the car because she wanted out of Tuxedo Park?"

"A ride?"

"Sadie. Listen to me," he said, "try not to make jokes or worm out of this."

"Helen's leaving," she said. "She's going to England and she's renting a cottage. Things have gone wrong with Packy, you see, so I can understand . . . She says Jimmy's going with her, but I don't know. He hasn't come around."

"Nothing stands still," he said impatiently. "So they're taking a trip. They'll be back."

"But why leave now?" Her eyes were filled with tears and her mouth was twisted. "Now when I need my friends, when I have no one else. I wouldn't do it to them."

"Don't be naïve, Sadie. People don't live for other people's convenience. You, for instance. Your crisis with Willard, when he left. It was a very bad time for me—"

"You never said."

"It was a bad time, if I said so or not. And who's to say if you would have listened. Did you listen to me then, or before then, about anything?"

"No," Sadie said. She was so glad now that she hadn't told him a thing about Louise's castle or what she had discovered there. If she told Reuben now that she saw that she might have made a mistake in staying here, it would incriminate her. "Well, if it was a bad time for you, Reuben, it was a worse time for me."

"So it's a bad time for Helen," he said. "Do you deny it?"

She left the window and sat heavily on an armchair, pushing around pillows in back of her to try to get comfortable.

"My theory is that she jumped because she wanted out. A simple idea. So I made a proposal to my niece.

Louise and I talked,'' he said. He might have waited and chosen a better time for his announcement, but he was tired of watching out for the right moment. "She's agreed that she'll go to boarding school."

"Agreed with whom? You?"

"It's the best thing. She'll get some perspective on the Park. This atmosphere. You can't keep her wrapped up here forever. She has to see something of the world."

"No boarding school," Sadie said. "This family stays together. My God, what do you think my whole life has been about, for me to send her to boarding school?"

"I'm sending her," he said. "Not you. She has a mind of her own and I'll pay for the whole thing. Remove her from a place where there are pharmaceuticals at every turn."

"And you call *me* naïve? You think on West End Avenue there aren't pills? People don't have the same troubles they have here?"

"They may have the same troubles," he said, "but they go about solving them differently. She's picked up some bad habits."

"And taking her away from me will cure them?"

"Not you," he said. "The Park. This place."

"Me," she said, "me. This is pure spite. Because I won't move back into the city with you. I wouldn't live in that apartment again if I had to live on the street. You think this place is so bad? It's a garden, Reuben, a garden. My garden."

She was crying now and wished she could stop, for her tears weakened her words.

"And you've done all right in it, for a person with two black thumbs. Look, Sadie," he said, lowering his voice. "I found a nice place, smaller than Mama and Pop's, of course, just for me. It's on the river, closer to—you know, I've mentioned her, the woman I see. I have a life of my own, Sadie. I don't need that apartment, the furniture. Everything. I've lived my whole life stepping around china urns. And we thought—it's a start for me.

Nothing like marriage. Not even living together. Just a river view. I've always wanted a river view."

"I see."

"So. If you decide you want the apartment. If you want anything," he said, relieved that his announcement was over, "just let me know. Anything of theirs. I know you like some pieces, though God knows you don't need furniture. Maybe the silver for the girls."

"This house is Willard's," she said. The idea of the apartment gone was unimaginable. "So it's theirs eventually, I suppose. All the furniture and everything in the house. They won't need anything. He may want it someday, of course. Willard may have other ideas."

"Sadie, for Christ's sake."

"I'll help you pack up the apartment," she said. "I'll help you because you've always helped me, but I don't need anything."

"My last bit of advice," he said. "Forget Willard. Call his lawyer. Get a divorce by mail. Train will handle it for you. You're crazy by now, Sadie, waiting so long."

"It's not so much me anymore," she said, though this wasn't the whole truth. "It's Louise. She thinks all her unhappiness comes from him being gone. She wants him home again. And I see—" It hurt her to say this to Reuben, but she felt she deserved it. "I've been selfish. She said it and she's right. I've kept her from her father. I thought I was doing the right thing, I thought I was living for them. That I was doing what I did for them. Willard thought it was safer here for children than in the city, and look, it hasn't been all bad. I thought it was the right thing, the thing I was meant to do."

He interrupted because he couldn't bear to hear her say again that she was right to stay in the Park. What is, he repeated, what is.

"So what will you do?" he asked.

"I don't know. Nothing too quickly. I'll make up my mind."

"Has it occurred to you," he asked, "that Willard might not want to come back?"

He put out his cigar and patted his chest, making sure his cigar case and matches were in it. He knew his sister. She had mixed everything up in her wishing.

"Helen told me something," she said. "She told me Packy saw Willard in the British Museum. With a woman. So maybe he has someone else. Maybe that's why he left. Wouldn't that be corny? I always thought he'd come back. Maybe he will even now, one way or another."

She had done it fast, Reuben thought, absorbed into her dream Cherry or whoever she imagined at Willard's side, absorbed the other woman and brushed her aside, keeping her focus fixed on Willard. At least Sadie would never learn that he'd known about Cherry from the start. He thought of the years he had protected Sadie from finding out about Cherry. He had waited for the right moment and now it was too late.

"I never liked him," Reuben said, surprised at the anger in his voice. "I never wanted you to marry him. You ruined your life and your children's lives—Sadie, what have you done?"

"I don't know," she said, "I don't know." She felt emptied out, as far away from feeling as if she were dead and watching Reuben from inside a tomb.

"I won't stay for dinner after all," he said. "I have to get back to town."

"All right," she said. "I'll drive you to the station. Let me find my keys."

She left the porch, roaming the house like a spirit, shutting windows in case it rained, locking doors as if she were leaving for good. She presented herself to him again, her hair combed, car keys in her hand, and she meant to thank him for coming, but when she spoke, Sadie said, almost shouting, "Reuben. How dare you never tell me there was a woman? What kind of monster have you made me into? If you have a girlfriend, a lover, a woman you love, how could you not tell me? How could you not bring her here to meet us? You offend me, Reuben. You treat me like an idiot, a fool. I swear, Reu-

ben, you haven't said a word. You treat me like a child
and you hate me because I'm not grown-up. What do you
expect me to do?"

"I'm sorry," he said, sure he had mentioned her. "I
thought I had. At some point. It's not a marriage. It's just
—we're fond of each other. She has a boy, she works—
"

"Reuben," she said quietly, "you've done everything
for me and I'm grateful. Ever since the accident you've
watched over me. But I'm grown-up now, Reuben. I have
two daughters who are almost grown-up. You have to
leave me alone now, Reuben."

"That's what I was afraid of, you thinking that because
I'm moving it means—"

"It does," she said, "and don't you see, it's a good
thing. You think I need you to be an old bachelor?" She
was crying now and trying to smile. "You have to let go
of me, Reuben. You can't have it both ways, telling me
I'm wrong, not telling me ever, ever what to do except
come home. That's all you've ever really said, do you
know that? Don't think I'm not grateful, not appreciative.
But you have to let go now, Reuben, you know that,
don't you? It's what you want. You did your duty.
You've done the right thing, but now it's over."

From his new apartment by the river, Reuben would
look over the yacht basin and the Spry sign and, if he
leaned his head out, a corner of the George Washington
Bridge. He would eat breakfast alone, as he preferred,
his tie flung back to avoid the sour cream. He saw himself
at breakfast, the sunlight falling on the river, and he was
not worrying about anyone else. He was watching the
river, his newspaper and binoculars by his side.

"If it's what you want, Sadie," he said. "I've never
done anything but want to help you. Nothing for myself."

"I know. It's just the way it's turned out. Look, if you
want to go, there's a train in ten minutes," she said.
"Come on. I'll drive you. Or stay the night. Though I'm
tired, really tired now."

Halfway to the station, rolling between tall elms, he said, "This car—"

"Let's not go backward. Pretend I'm an eccentric Tuxedo Park lady with an old car and my old dog. What difference does it make? Or you could think everything is my fault, start to finish, car, house, Park, everything. Just be quiet so I can drive without killing us."

At the station, before Reuben stepped on the train, she ran from the car and joined him at the track. Sadie said, "I won't shut the barn door if you won't, Reuben."

"What do you mean?" he asked, distracted now, looking up for the train.

"Never mind," she said. "Call me."

"I always do," he said.

ON THE TRAIN BACK TO MANHATTAN, REUBEN thought of the time and money he'd wasted keeping track of Willard and Cherry. They had rambled over Europe, Paris for a month at least, London for half the year, Berlin for the archaeological museum, Rome, Venice. There was a place in Kent they went to sometimes at the end of winter, or after Venice. Cherry had spent a few months in a Swiss clinic five years before. A breakdown, Reuben guessed, a drinking problem, female trouble. Whatever, they went on to Venice that spring as usual. He imagined them slowly replacing their American possessions with European ones, shedding their clothing and baggage as a snake does its skin.

He had told Sadie about his lover, he was sure he had, and if she hadn't heard, it was because she didn't want to. Sadie was in for more surprises, he thought, if she was on her own. Louise had always been pig-headed, and once an idea was presented that was frightening and would cause difficulty for her mother, she would go through with it, he was sure.

As for Willard, Reuben thought that Sadie's greater difficulties would start if he came home. How would she rid herself of him a second time?

In the city, he thought, he'd catch a movie or call Train and see if he was in the mood to meet for a drink. Reuben felt light-headed and in need of a way to acknowledge the occasion.

The moment Reuben learned his parents were dead, without hesitation he put a marker in the book on torts he was studying, closed the book, and took his suitcase from the closet. One by one he pulled from the wall the thumbtacks that held his Soviet workers poster above his narrow bed. What had it looked like? A woodcut in three colors, a stylized phalanx of workers holding a flag, words he could not read. He worked steadily for the short time it took to return the little room to what it had been before he claimed it as his own. He went six steps to the window and looked out at the courtyard and the corner of Riverside Park that showed between the high buildings, then left without another look, knowing he would never return. Reuben carried his suitcase of clothes, a leather satchel of books and papers, and, crushed under his arm, the poster, which he'd rolled up clumsily. He could feel the weight of the luggage even now cutting into his hands.

Reuben wondered if it was wishful thinking to believe that at last she would manage without him. What is, he thought, what is. Everything changes except people. The link to his sister was too strong to break. Something else would happen and she would need him. The story of the girls was just beginning after all. Reuben turned uncomfortably in his seat and wished that he was already back in the city.

Eight

AFTER AN EARLY DINNER, THE RESTLESS HOSPITAL night began. Louise lay against hard pillows in the high bed, and thought that she might as well be a million miles from Tuxedo Park already.

When she looked back on the night of Mary Justice's party, her act seemed no more serious than if she'd lost her temper at her mother. She had to make an effort—press on her sore belly, swallow hard on her poor throat, to summon up a sense of emergency. She chanted to herself—*He could have sent for you, He could have come anytime*—but the words were losing their power.

When it was dark and Louise could no longer see the woods through her window, the nurses turned on dim night lights in the hall. A small shadowy figure appeared at the door. Louise wondered if the figure was real, it was so still and dark. Then it moved and Louise said, "How did you get in here? You aren't allowed."

"I walked in and no one noticed me. What do you think they'll do if they find me?"

"Get over here. You can hide behind the bed if anyone comes."

Marilyn came up beside Louise. "Are you okay?"

"I figured Sadie was lying when she said you couldn't visit."

"No, it's true. There's a big sign downstairs."

Louise lifted her head to get a better view of her sister. "Where's Sadie? Is she coming too?"

"She took Reuben to the train. And she said she was going to the store or something. She doesn't know I'm here. I told her I was going to Regina's. Jimmy's going away, she told me. Did she tell you?"

"She reads a magazine when she's here," Louise said. "We don't talk much."

A nurse came to the door, and Marilyn crouched down, half hoping she would be caught and sent away. She listened to the swish of the nurse's nylons as she walked, a little grunt as she picked up Louise's tray.

"You didn't knock yourself out eating," the nurse said.

"I ate some," Louise said. "I ate as much as I could."

"All the chocolate cake," the nurse said with a sniff, and she left the room.

Marilyn straightened up and said, "Maybe I should close the door."

"They have to have it open," Louise said, "in case I try something."

"Would you?" Marilyn asked. "Would you try again?"

Louise stared at Marilyn and said, "I don't know."

She was unable to explain that she hadn't really wanted to do anything in particular. Everyone gave her more credit than she deserved. What she had done unplanned had unhinged so many things that it would sound like lying to deny its purposefulness.

"How *could* you, Louise? How could you do this to me and Sadie? Were you that unhappy? I mean, really unhappy?"

Louise thought of telling Marilyn about what she'd overheard and the letters she'd found. She said, "It wasn't so much like unhappiness. I didn't have any choice, it was like there was nothing else to do. Like something that had to be done."

"But why? Everything was fine. Why did something have to be done?"

"If you don't know, you just don't know," Louise said. "Why are you bothering me like this?" She wished the nurse would come and take Marilyn out.

"Suppose it had worked and you'd died," Marilyn said. "Where would I be?"

"Right where you are," Louise said. "I guess you want me to say I'm sorry for being in the hospital and for Reuben having to come out in the middle of the week. But I'm not."

"Well," Marilyn said, shifting from one foot to the other. "I guess I'll just be mad at you for a while," though mad wasn't exactly what she meant. She couldn't conceive of life without Louise. Even looking at Louise's bruises and scrapes made her feel weak. "But I'm glad you're coming home. Sadie's coming in the morning. Or after lunch. I forget."

"Goody," Louise said.

"You won't do it again, will you?" Marilyn asked.

"I can't *say,*" Louise hissed, wishing she could yell at Marilyn, who pressed for a pledge that couldn't be given. Marilyn didn't understand that adults could do anything they wanted with her. Louise didn't have a choice: something might happen again, something unimaginable, and then she would want to do something, maybe something worse. Marilyn stood by the bed, frowning and chewing her rosy lip. If she knew the truth, Louise thought, she would hate us all.

"You have to promise me," Marilyn said, "that you'll never try it again."

"Otherwise?"

"Everything's ruined. Don't you see that?"

"Well, it's too late anyway. Reuben's going to send me to boarding school," Louise said.

"Sadie will never let him," Marilyn said. "You'd never go. You won't."

"Don't be so sure," Louise said.

"So you won't promise me. You won't even do that for me."

"I can't talk to you about this stuff. Don't you remember, Marilyn? Do you really not remember? When Willard used to come home at the mews house and we'd be waiting for him?"

"I remember things, early things, but what difference does it make? We're here now. It's where we've always been, pretty much. Look, Louise—I have to tell you something bad. You'll probably hate me. I took Sadie to the castle. I had to. I had to show her. Don't you see? Do you forgive me? Will you forgive me ever?"

She thought she'd feel better once she told Louise but she didn't. Instead she remembered leaving Louise at school after throat inspection, walking away from her sister down the long hallway, up the dark stairs, happy to have Sadie to herself and ashamed of her happiness.

Louise looked shocked, then relaxed and lay back, looking as relieved as Marilyn had expected to feel when she confessed. Louise's resignation frightened Marilyn, as if her sister were a balloon with the air going out, changing shape as Marilyn watched.

"You don't know anything," Louise said, "I can't explain. And I can't promise. Promises don't do any good, don't you know that yet?"

When Marilyn left, Louise got out of bed and went to the window. Her knees were wobbly. The big window was open to the fragrant night air. Past the window was a screen, and past the screen, she saw for the first time, a barrier of linked wire.

Nine

SADIE CHECKED THE STOVE, WALKED THROUGH THE glass porch and the library, inspected the ashtrays for embers from Reuben's cigar, checked the kitchen again. She climbed to the third floor, which burned like an oven, holding the day's heat. On the second floor, in Louise's room, which she'd cleaned that day, she smoothed the bedspread, straightened a book that lay on the bedside table. Dandelion followed her on night rounds, her long nails clicking, but stopped in Louise's room and lay across the doorway in the breeze from the open window. The dog had a sense of the right gesture to make, Sadie thought.

In Marilyn's room there were piles of clothing and books covering every surface, food-crusted plates and glasses with milk and juice rings stacked at the door.

"I hope you marry a rich man," Sadie said. "You need room service in your life."

"I'm not going to marry a rich man," Marilyn said. She was lying in bed, *Little Women* face down beside her.

"Are you like Louise, you're not going to marry anyone?"

"Oh, I'll get married. But I'm just not going to marry a rich man. I'm going to marry someone, I don't know who, but someone, and I'll still live with you. There'll be lots of room even when I have children."

Sadie considered her daughter's grave face and said, "You don't have to stay here and take care of me. Now you think you know everything, darling, and you think you can see into the future. But you don't know what could happen to you in a life. Things happen that you could never guess at, or they happen just as you want them to and then it turns out to be a disaster."

Marilyn listened to her mother, polite and disbelieving.

"What's the use?" Sadie asked, smiling a little. "People do just as they like. Do you want to come in the morning to pick up Louise?"

Sadie meant the offer to sound like a favor to Marilyn, but her voice betrayed her.

"Don't worry. I'll come," Marilyn said.

"You don't have to." Sadie settled on the edge of Marilyn's bed.

"That's okay," Marilyn said. "I don't mind."

"I hope I didn't make you tell your sister's secret. I wouldn't want to do that. I always believed people should have privacy. Normally. Of course now it's different." She was talking too much, she thought, wishing for Helen. Did she believe in privacy really? Privacy for her children?

"It's okay," Marilyn said. "Don't keep talking about it. You would have found out sooner or later, I guess."

"Later. You've been a big help."

Marilyn's hand strayed to the book.

Marilyn was turning into a beauty, Sadie thought, her eyes the color of the first violets, her fuzzy hair that clung like fog around her delicate face. She had always worried that Marilyn would grow up to look like Reuben. She didn't know what to say. The things she wanted to say about Louise and her usual domestic warnings seemed inadequate.

"Reuben told me he's going to send Louise to boarding school," Sadie said. "What do you think?"

Marilyn said, "That's just what he says. Maybe she won't go."

"School starts in a little over a month," Sadie said, "so maybe it's too late for this year."

"Maybe," Marilyn said.

"Do you want to go too?" Sadie asked.

"No," Marilyn said. "I told you, I'm staying in the Park with you forever." It wasn't up to her, Marilyn thought. If she ever left, it would be because something came from outside herself and forced the change.

"Forever?" Sadie asked.

"Yes. I just told you that, Sadie. I'll never leave. We'll live here forever and ever," Marilyn said, her eyes clouding over. "I never wanted to leave and why should I now? Don't worry, we'll be fine here."

"Well, only if it's what you want. I wouldn't want to . . ." Sadie stood and went to the door. She wanted to insist that Marilyn would leave too, but she tried to imagine her life without the girl. Marilyn looked placid and solid, her decision made, and Sadie thought, Who am I to know what's best? She knew she was indulging herself but couldn't stop. Later, she thought, when I feel better I'll make Marilyn see that she's wrong. And in the meantime, if it makes her feel good, I'll leave it alone.

SADIE COULDN'T SLEEP. SHE LAY IN BED AND PLANNED out the next morning—breakfast (dry cereal, fruit, coffee for her, milk for Marilyn), drive (around the lake, the road, through the gate, to the hospital and up the steep drive) and pick up Louise (should they do grocery shopping before or after?), come home. She'd always thought Louise liked being outside, walking, but now that she thought of it, how long would a person really walk? All that time, Louise was in the castle, and Sadie never knew.

She gave up, and, wrapped in her old blue robe, Sadie wandered through the house, looking into rooms that hadn't been used for months, trying to open windows that had been stuck for years. If Willard saw the house now and the gardens at the height of their summer bloom, if he saw the girls now, grown into lovely girls, even Louise, what would he think. She looked around the darkened rooms, the night covering the wear and tear, and she thought that she had done nothing but make his house into a home, no crime, even a work of art. In that moment, she believed that when he returned, he would be able to see her whole, see her love for him, see the girls, see even the Park, their home, all for him, and that he would be grateful to her, that he would love her at last as she wished to be loved. At last Willard would be happy with them, happy with her, and though she felt far from her afternoons in the white kimono, he would bring her love in a new form, suitable for people married as long as they had been, and cruelly separated for so long.

And yet—she sat stiffly on the living-room couch that looked out toward the glass porch and the lake—when he left, he took little with him, not even his Whistler. How cool he must have been, she thought, how little attached to leave empty-handed. Always before she had thought that of course he could leave that way because he knew she would take care of everything for him, preserve his clothes, his papers for him. Now she thought, He didn't care what happened to his things. He didn't count on her looking after them at all. He wouldn't care if she'd done a good job.

In the library she found a new Rex Stout that Reuben had given her, and she brought it down to the kitchen.

Sadie took out a saucepan and poured milk in it, put it on the stove and lit the burner, put the honeypot and a cup on the table. She looked around for her gardening notebook. She was sure she'd left it in the kitchen, but looked over into the servants' dining room to be sure. She looked and looked again, thinking she saw a figure in the room, and for a moment her breath stopped, and her heart beat hard in her throat. It might be Willard, returning as oddly as he'd left. For years, she had been mistaking him around corners and in crowds, though she had never seen him so distinctly before.

"Who's there?" she called, walking toward the familiar shape.

"It's me, Jimmy."

"For heaven's sake. How did you get in?"

"The door from the garage was open."

"God. I missed it. I never think about that door. What are you doing wandering around this time of night?" she asked.

"I escaped my keeper," he said. "I came to make amends. For going away and leaving you with the business, if it can be called a business. How do I apologize in advance?"

"I don't know," she said. She was so glad to see Jimmy that it seemed ridiculous to have believed he would go off without saying good-by to her. "Have you consulted Emily Post?"

"Maybe they'll have a copy of *Etiquette* in the cottage. You know that I'm going with Helen? A sort of private asylum cum broken-hearts recovery room cum English cottage garden? Did you know? It must be all over the Park by now."

"Helen told me. Don't worry about anything. I can get a boy from the village to help me with mowing and weeding, I think. And it's almost the end of summer. So many people leave in August."

"The thing is, Sadie, I don't know quite what will happen to me."

She had often thought that Jimmy might show up one night, just like this, to tell her that he'd changed, that they should be together in some relation she couldn't imagine in detail. The person she'd worked side by side with was not the same person in her nighttime thoughts, and always the next day she was startled to see Jimmy as he was.

"Who can know what will happen to them?" she asked. "Maybe Willard will come back, you know, and want the girls and the house. Everything but me."

"He can't just saunter in and have them," Jimmy said.

She stepped back into the kitchen a few feet, thinking that they might sit down and have a good talk, but Jimmy stayed where he was, giving no indication that he wanted to stay.

"Look, Jimmy, what would you do if you were me? Would you try to track him down? Bring him back? Divorce? Try for reconciliation? I think of every single possibility, but none of it fits."

She moved closer again. Jimmy stood stiffly, waiting for her to stop talking.

He said, "I don't know, Sadie. I'm not very good at these things."

"It's all right," she said, "it's all right. I'm stupid to have asked."

"Helen's been talking to me, and convincing me that this kind of isolated life . . . Maybe I'll scare up something in London. Or New York. I don't mean to upset you," he said. "But I thought you'd want to know. I may not come back."

"I know," she said. She could feel how much he wanted to turn and leave, yet she willed him to want to stay.

"I'll probably be back in a few weeks. This is just an idea, anyway."

"I understand," she said. "I understand."

She heard a noise in the kitchen and turned to see the milk foaming over the stove, and she smelled the sweet candy odor of burned milk.

"Oh, no," she said, and rushed into the kitchen, turning off the fire, starting to scrub the black enamel before the milk welded to it. She looked back at him, saying, "Well, it never rains . . ."

Jimmy was gone. It was the way Jimmy was, she had known it all along. It was one thing for him to be that way, she thought, but why had she expected something different for so long.

BACK IN BED, SADIE THOUGHT OF THE PARK AS A CIRCLE drawn in the dirt, enclosing her girls, Helen and Jimmy, herself. Reuben came in and out of the circle; Willard, though he wasn't visible, was almost the circle himself, for he was the reason and origin of everything in the Park. Now a wind had come along and blown the circle away. She imagined Jimmy and Helen scattered, flying off, Louise going off to school, Reuben somewhere in the city, only she and Marilyn remaining. There was no unity now. Nothing held them together.

It had seemed so natural to stay where fate had brought her, to insist on no divorce. Yet the thought returned to her, as chilling as it was in the castle—she might have left, and something she could neither imagine nor predict might have happened. Staying in the Park, she stayed within the circle.

Now Sadie felt something new, shame that she had done so, shame at her secret pride at her beautiful daughters, her house, her Park, her survival, and her loneliness.

There was something worse than fate, there was her own character. The bad things weren't only what happened to you but what you did. It was not fate, she thought, it was her character that had kept them there. Her childishness, her fears, her stubbornness. How childish she had been to think she had found rock bottom for once and for all when she lost her parents, when Willard left. Sadie wept for shame at herself and for sorrow for her daughters, and because she knew that at the origin of her love for Willard was this stubborn waiting for a miracle, waiting for the dead to rise, and now she would have to give up. It was too late for her. She would never leave, she didn't even wish to leave. Whatever was in store for her could happen here as well as anywhere else,

and she guessed that this was true of Marilyn as well. But
it was different with Louise. Louise thought she could
leave the Park by walking through the gates, but Sadie
guessed that she would come back home and leave again,
and that no matter how far away she seemed to get,
Louise would always be on her way back home.

For Louise's sake, she had to bring Willard back. She
had to stop waiting, she decided. Immediately she worried that she was giving up too soon. She wondered if she
would still love him if he stood before her in the Tuxedo
house, and Sadie thought of the woman in London. Of all
the women in the world, what was she like? Sadie remembered the blonde outside their art history class. She
thought of a painting by Ingres and a Whistler portrait of
a woman in black. It didn't matter, she thought, feeling
defeated at last. If there was a woman, nothing mattered
but that she would not hate Sadie's girls, and it was up to
Sadie to find a way to ensure that.

Sadie lay on her back, tears rolling down her cheeks,
sobbing—like a girl, she thought, I'm still like a stupid
girl—but by the time she fell asleep, she felt as if events
had already moved forward.

Toward morning, Sadie dreamed that she was with her
mother and father, walking along a tree-lined street. The
dream was yellow and white, like a very hot day. They
reached their building and went upstairs to the apartment
where everything was in its place. Sadie's mother
frowned and bent over the table of family photographs,
squinting at the elaborate frames, blowing on a silver
edge, checking for dust. Her father settled in his armchair, her mother took her place on the sofa next to
Sadie. They were back from Florida. Sadie said that she
had to go soon, that she was expected elsewhere, but
they didn't hear her. She said it again. They didn't ask
where she was going or who waited for her.

Her father leaned back heavily into his plump armchair. Her mother sighed, and talked about making tea,
having a cookie, inspecting the house, unpacking the luggage. But she didn't move. Sadie knew—as they did not

—that they were dead and that when the dream ended she would return alone to life without them. Perched at the edge of the sofa, her legs bent like a runner's, Sadie waited for her chance.

Ten

SADIE WOKE LATE THE NEXT MORNING, WHEN THE SUN was above the edge of the trees and the bedroom began to feel hot. She dressed quickly and left her room, glancing at Marilyn's sleeping form. Dandelion raised her head as Sadie passed Louise's room and lay back again. Sadie went downstairs and settled at the chair and table in the entranceway by the phone.

Mr. Stratton had retired, but the firm had appointed Mr. Horn to Willard's affairs.

"I understand perfectly," he said. "No need to explain, Mrs. Weaver. I've read the memo of your conversation with Mr. Stratton."

"You sound prepared," she said. She stood at the phone in the entryway, looking at her garden. Overnight, rose petals had blown over the hillside. "Can you find my husband?"

"Easily," he said.

"Then tell him two things for me, please," she said. "First, that his daughter Louise has been in an accident. She's fine, but he should come see her. And second, what he wants, he can have it."

"What he wants? Do you mean the divorce?"

"Yes," she said. "He can have it. But only if he comes

to Tuxedo Park. And you'll tell him that exactly, won't you?''

"I'll write him—"

"Cable," she said, "telephone."

"Your daughter is in urgent need?"

"Oh," Sadie said, "what's urgent? Tell him, Mr. Horn, Louise has been in an accident but she's fine, and that she needs to see him. I won't argue about need. Find him, Mr. Horn, speak to him in whatever way you like. But let me know."

She hung up and bent her head over the phone. When she looked up, she saw Marilyn on the stairs.

"You heard?" she asked.

"Is Willard coming back?"

"I've started it," Sadie said. "We'll see what happens. Maybe he won't want to come."

"Oh, he will," Marilyn said. Marilyn came slowly down the stairs and stood by her mother. They looked at each other, acknowledging the lengths they would go to for Louise. She had always needed them both so badly and she never understood that to the smallest degree.

"He could have before," Sadie said. "Maybe—but this is for Louise."

"I'm scared to see him, Sadie," Marilyn said. "Everything will be different." She hugged Sadie and hid herself in Sadie's embrace.

"Not everything, chickie," Sadie said, holding Marilyn tightly. "Let's wait until it happens and see."

Eleven

MARILYN WAITED OUTSIDE THE FRONT DOOR FOR Sadie, who was bringing the Packard up from the garage. The high-skied summer morning made Marilyn sleepy, and she settled on a stone step, her eyes closed, her face lifted to the sun. She heard rustling in the bushes at the edge of the driveway, and looked around quickly. She saw Dandelion's red head peeking around the stone fence, and she called, "Dandy! Dandy!" but the dog wagged her tail and ran up into the woods.

When Sadie pulled up with the big silver car, Marilyn got in and looked over at her mother. "You're squinting, Sadie," she said. "Don't feel so bad."

"I don't feel bad," Sadie said, starting down the drive. "I feel . . . I feel stupid."

The peak-of-summer day pulled at Marilyn, and every time she began to feel the way her mother looked—squinting forward at the road, shoulders hunched—the sun and the loaded, fragrant air pulled her back, as if from the edge of a crack in the ice. The Park never changed, and each evidence of its sameness reassured Marilyn that she was still herself, even if she had now what Louise had always had, a crack in her life. From now on, she thought, everything will be measured by the one event, before Louise's accident and after. Only to herself did she say, When Louise died.

Just before Sadie crossed the highway and turned up the steep hospital drive, Marilyn asked, "Do you remember when we lived in the city? When we used to take Louise to school?"

"Of course I remember," Sadie said. "It was a Scottish Presbyterian nursery school. Everyone said it had a very good reputation. Also it was the closest school I could find. I'm surprised you remember."

Marilyn watched the lake go by and the club, then caught sight of the church by the gates. She remembered when they came to Tuxedo for her grandfather's funeral, the first time she and Louise saw the castle. She remembered what was important, she thought.

"I used to hate leaving Louise at school," she said.

"What was there to like?" Sadie asked. "I didn't understand why she had to go to school. Reuben and Willard said she needed other children, but she had you. I suppose you have to go to school to learn to read. Things like that. But I never felt easy until she was home."

DRESSED IN FRESH CLOTHES SADIE HAD BROUGHT THE day before, Louise sat on the edge of her bed, waiting to leave the hospital. She'd eaten the rubbery hospital egg, burned her tongue on the hospital tea, dawdling over the meal, her last, she thought. She longed for home and dreaded going. It had been only days since the accident, but she felt like a traveler who'd been gone too long and seen too much to be fit for home. She wanted nothing more than to lie down again and stay forever.

A nurse, one Louise hadn't seen before, appeared at the door with a wheelchair.

"I can walk," Louise said.

"Sure you can," the nurse said. "Hospital rules. Something to do with insurance."

So Louise gathered her paper bag of magazines and her hairbrush, and the flowers from Jimmy and Helen, and

climbed into the chair. It seemed shameful to be wheeled
so smoothly and quickly along the linoleum floor, and she
kept her eyes on the floor, not wanting to see other patients who might really need the wheelchair. She was
relieved that they were alone in the elevator.

When the elevator came to the ground floor, the nurse
pushed the chair away from the elevator doors, and told
Louise she would be gone only a minute. Then she disappeared down the hall. Louise looked after her and then
the other way, in the direction that she thought led to the
lobby. She wanted to get up and run, maybe go to the
road and find a ride, disappear somehow. But she felt
obligated to stay in the wheelchair. Minutes passed, filled
with the clanging of the elevator as it left Louise and went
up, back into the hospital. She listened for the nurse to
return and looked around, then Louise despaired. Sadie
had forgotten her. She had gotten a job and now when
she should have been at the hospital, she was picking
around in someone else's garden. It would be like this
forever, Louise thought, and it always had been, waiting
and not knowing whether to hope that the person would
really come.

Then she heard voices and saw Sadie and Marilyn at
the end of the long hall, coming to get her. And Louise
felt the opposite of what she'd felt a second before, not
left but retrieved, not forgotten but remembered, not
abandoned but beloved. She could almost forget where
she had been and why, Louise could almost believe that
she would never be away from them again.

"WHAT'S THE MATTER?"
When she saw the Packard, Louise stopped for a moment, then walked straight to it and got in, ignoring the
fender.

Sadie drove down the hospital drive, and Louise
twisted around and looked back.

"What's wrong?" Sadie asked. "Did you forget something?"

"Nothing. I never saw it from the front," Louise said. "It's so gloomy."

"Anyone hungry? We can go up the road for a hamburger and a shake," Sadie said.

"They serve real goo in the hospital," Louise said.

"Does that mean yes?"

"No. I want to go home."

"Okay," Sadie said. "I have to pick up a few things at the IGA." She pulled into the store parking lot and said, "You girls wait in the car."

"You're ashamed of me," Louise said. "You think the Park snoots are going to stare at me. 'That Weaver girl who . . .'"

"No," Sadie said quietly. "You should be ashamed, Louise, if anyone. Everyone's trying very hard."

When Sadie was out of earshot, Louise asked, "Are you trying very hard?" and Marilyn answered, "No, but Sadie is. And you're not trying at all."

"You don't know a thing about it," Louise said. "I feel like . . . something happened. Something big. But I'll go home and it'll be as if nothing happened. It won't count for anything."

"It's counting, all right. Willard's coming," Marilyn said.

Louise looked at her sharply. "How do you know?"

"Sadie told me. She called someone and sent a message that he should come."

"Did she talk to him?" She stuck her hand out of the car and opened and shut her fingers into a fist.

"No. I told you. She called someone. So you got what you wanted."

"Not exactly," Louise said. "When?"

"I don't know. And she didn't want me to know. Just take it easy. She'll tell you when she's ready."

SHE HAD INTENDED TO PICK UP A CAN OF TUNA FISH and some bananas, but Sadie took a shopping cart and

began walking up and down the narrow aisles medita-
tively, as if she didn't have two girls waiting for her in
the car. She paused at canned soups though she always
made her own, and squeezed the white bread absently,
though she drove once a week to buy bread at a bakery
in a town where Italians lived. She had decided not to
mention Willard to Louise until she knew when he was
coming, if he was coming. Sadie bought Hostess cup-
cakes and a carton of ice cream, a chicken and carrots,
then rushed toward the cash register as if she were about
to miss a train.

When she emerged from the store, the bags of groceries in her arms, both girls were in the rumble seat, Louise
looking down the road, Marilyn in the opposite direction.
Nothing mattered, Sadie thought, as long as the three of
them could be together. It wouldn't be for very long now,
she knew, but for a moment her heart lifted and she no
longer dreaded anything. Thank God there was no justice, thank God there was no perfect accounting in this
world.

Instead of driving straight home, Sadie took the long
way around the lake, meandering up little-used drive-
ways and onto roads she hadn't traveled in years. There
were no houses in sight. The wooded land rose steeply to
one side, and on the other side was the lake. Across the
lake somewhere was Helen's house—Sadie couldn't find
it on the shore—and their own, invisible, up on the hill.
She drove slowly around the lake, past English and
French castles, past hills of day lilies. There was nothing
tentative about the day or the time, and Sadie felt
strengthened by the confidence around her. The trick of
summer in Tuxedo, Jimmy told her years before, is that
everything in the Park—houses, gardens, lawns, woods,
lake, gates, people—everything looks just as it should. It
didn't last. Before you knew it, the air in the morning
was so cool you wanted a sweater, and you began to
think of wood for the winter. While it lasted, Sadie
thought, it blessed them all.

WHEN THEY GOT HOME, LOUISE SAID SHE WAS FINE, BUT Sadie made her put on a nightgown and get into bed. Louise was surprised (she hadn't felt sleepy) but she slept until evening. When she woke up, she remembered that her father was coming. She went to her window and looked out at Sadie's garden and the woods. She looked up, trying to see a corner of the castle. She would never go there again, she decided.

Below, Sadie was in the kitchen, and the smell of cooking reached Louise. She touched the bruises on her face and arm. They didn't hurt as much as they had in the hospital. And when she leaned her head against the window screen, the pressure hurt only a little. She watched the fading light over the garden, saw something move, and heard a sound. It was Marilyn, coming down from the woods, calling for Dandelion. Louise's heart told her —This is all yours, every bit of it is yours, and Louise wished she would never get better and be forced to leave the place to which she might never return.

Twelve

IN THE *PENSIONE* DINING ROOM, EACH TABLE WAS LAID with a heavy white cloth. The napkins were folded to sharp, starched points, and around each wine bottle hung a silver ring imprinted with the room number of the table's occupant. Cherry and Willard had come to Venice in the spring to stay for as long as they liked, and they had settled, perhaps temporarily, at a *pensione* they knew on the Zattere.

Martin Bowles, who spent each September in Venice, suggested that they rent an apartment for the year in the palace of an acquaintance of his. "I can recommend both the company and the surroundings." But Cherry and Willard had learned that one danger of their life without property or family was that they tended to welcome and then resent restrictions.

They made rules: Never to discuss returning to a place before they left, never to purchase anything that couldn't be carried easily (except for Willard's collection), never to fuss about where they would stay, and never to stay in a place that demanded a long lease. The rules worked best for times of transition, moving from Venice to London, or when they were trying to decide on their next place.

Cherry had watched people buying and wanting to buy,

burdening themselves, trying to take home a piece of a foreign place. She watched them struggle with luggage, willing to stagger through airports and train stations, aboard ships, because they had a home to sink down in eventually, exhausted. It was for home that they made their time so miserable. Cherry felt superior to the burdened, though sometimes she envied them, for there was no place into which she and Willard could sink.

This year they had determined to make up their minds right on the spot about such problems as apartments and hotels, meals and museums. "It's honest guilt that makes us worry so much about the next meal," Cherry said after one restaurant argument. "If we had something big to worry about, like a light bill, the petty stuff wouldn't matter." They stayed on at the *pensione* through the crowded Venetian summer, but they might have done better, she thought. Their rooms were all right—ceilings of ecclesiastical height, marble floors, an ornate glass chandelier hanging over their too-soft beds. She was sure that in the luxury hotels that catered to foreigners they would be given one bed rather than two pushed together. But Willard was never anxious to spend more than he had to.

At the largest table was a German family, brown-haired and undistinguished-looking, very happy to be in Venice. They ate all their meals in the *pensione,* which was far more expensive than eating out, but Cherry guessed that they had worked something out with the signora. Two English spinsters—one fragile and blue-eyed with a wispy bun, the other with a helmet of gray hair—ate at the table closest to Willard and Cherry. They spoke of nothing but the price of things, but was it because they had limited money or because it seemed the right way to take on Venice? Willard and Cherry didn't speak much at their table. She had years before discovered that silence between couples in public—something she had always pitied and dreaded—might mean comfort.

A Swedish couple, possibly unmarried, had been given the table near the door, where the waiters—Nevio was thin, red-haired, and generous, Mario nervous and over-weight—brushed by them as they moved from kitchen to dining room.

"It was good enough for Ruskin," Willard said when she complained one morning about the shared toilet.

"He never stayed here," she said. "He stayed around the corner. And what did he know about toilets or anything else?"

On the morning before their departure day Cherry wished that she had a better memory and could bring this distinctive, ordinary European place back with her.

"Of course," she said, "there's no reason to ask the signora to keep rooms for us. Or to pay for them while we're gone, unless—"

"I've told you," he said, "there's simply no way of knowing when we'll be back."

"But we will?"

"If we choose," he said firmly. "We're not going to die, we're simply going back to New York, and there we'll settle my business. We've been in Venice long enough." First, he had decided, they would travel to London and settle their business there, matters to do with the lease on the warehouse, which would soon be up. A raise in rent was being threatened. In a week, two at the most, they would fly to New York. He insisted on order, for he could not bear to go back immediately. When he thought of the girls, they were six and four, almost babies, as if time had not passed since his leaving. He could not imagine them grown. "We'd be off to Kent soon anyway. It's a chance for you to see your mother."

"You know better than that," Cherry said, wishing that she could control herself better. He was nervous, she could see that for herself, and in no position to reassure her. "Explain it to me again."

"I don't know any more than you."

"But you spoke to the lawyer. I didn't."

"He said that Louise was in an accident, and that Sadie asked him to tell me that and to tell me I should come home. There's no hurry, Cherry. That was abundantly clear. Not urgent, he said. If I came home, I would get the divorce. Now you know as much as I do. I won't say it again."

"It isn't a trick? To get you back?"

"Oh, Cherry, after all these years? No, it means that she'll grant the divorce. She might have spared me the worry and told me what kind of accident."

Or he might call and find out, she thought. She tried to break a piece off the roll Mario had presented with ceremony, but it was too hard.

"You could stay here or in Rome. You could go to London or stay in Kent without me," he offered. "I would be back in a few weeks, a month at the most if I knew you were waiting for me."

"No," she said. "I'd feel like you pawned me. I'll come."

"That will make it easier for me," he said. "Possible."

She looked out across the watery alleyway to window boxes of brilliant red geraniums.

"I can't help it," she said. "It all feels so definite and final. We've had so little time—"

"Years," he said. "We'll have more years. Unless the plane crashes."

"I suppose I want to see my mother," she said.

"That's the spirit. Who knows when we'll be near New Jersey again."

She feared the injured child. He had left his daughters once but could he again? Already, Willard was calling them by name to her. If her own father, now probably dead, had come back one last time, he might have stayed, Cherry thought, but probably not.

In the afternoon, Willard napped, and Cherry went out into the moist Venetian air.

She liked Venice when the shutters were closed and she was one of the few abroad, moving through the heat like a cloud of hot air. Sometimes she stopped at a café and watched the *vaporetti* and the strollers go by, but now she took a boat herself in the direction of the Piazza San Marco. Cherry took a seat next to a young woman

who was enormously pregnant. She tried to keep her eyes
from the woman's swollen breasts and stomach that were
covered by a flowered dress, stretched to its limits, its
cabbage roses rising and falling as the woman breathed.
The woman turned to Cherry and smiled, patting her
stomach as if she and Cherry shared a happy secret.

Cherry walked across the Piazza San Marco, past the
church and palace. There, along the canal, were the ven-
dors she remembered. She walked up and down, inspecting their goods, ignoring their greetings and calls for
attention. When she couldn't look anymore, she bought
a pair of glass earrings for her mother, crude pineapples
hanging from wires. Martha would never wear them; they
would join the mosaic guitar pin from Florence, the cor-
onation cup and saucer that Cherry had sent home.

On another stand, she found two necklaces. One was
purple and green, clusters of grapes, fashioned delicately.
The other was green, dull, flat leaves hanging from rings,
a laurel necklace for the one who managed to be in an
accident, Cherry thought. The victorious one, the older
one, the one who looks like Willard.

On her way back to the *pensione*, Cherry stopped in a
paper shop and bought a small box for her mother. Martha had refused their invitations to come to Europe, and
she had never come on her own, though she had retired
years before. Something always came up and now it was
probably too late. Cherry asked how long it would take
to make up portfolios and notebooks in this pink design,
that deep blue. Though she had admired the paper shop
for years, Cherry had never ordered such cumbersome
articles before, but all at once Cherry was bone tired of
traveling, and she guessed that they would not see Venice
again soon. She wanted to buy more in Venice, feeling
the visitor's panic that this was her last chance.

If they had to stay there near the children and if they
could stay together, it might be the best thing, but Cherry
feared their return to New York as she feared the dull
gray in Willard's blond hair. It was one thing to live as
they did, but how would they live together in just one

place? Martha had written her that the prettiest farm around Long Valley was up for sale. Maybe Willard would buy the Black Angus farm, and they would live the life she'd glimpsed down the long tree-lined drive. They would have a living room and armchairs of their own. They would have to sell the cows. She could not imagine the cows. They might live in the city, of course, surrounded by Willard's collection. If he could stand it, if he could stand any of it. The thought of settling made her shudder and she grabbed the edge of the counter to steady herself.

"Five days," the saleswoman said, "and we never mail. You must come for it yourself." She looked bored and clicked her teeth while Cherry looked quickly again at the patterned paper. Cherry said, "It's no good. We're leaving Venice tomorrow. *Grazie*." She gathered her small packages as if she were in a terrible hurry, and left the shop.

Thirteen

SADIE KNEW THE VALUE OF THE DAYS BEFORE WILLARD
came. They were precious jewels that they could not
save. She saw the line dividing the time before Louise's
accident and the time after. It was always the same, she
thought; when her parents died, when Willard left. The
first days of mourning had an edge of excitement to them,
as if it were still possible to choose to return to life as it
was, a life seen as sweeter now than it ever seemed before.

For days there was a rainstorm that broke off weak
branches and trampled flowerbeds, part of a hurricane
that threatened from the south, a sure sign of an early
autumn. Sadie wished she could make the rain stop,
warm the cool air, and start summer again.

LOUISE WENT ALONE TO THE CASTLE, BUT THE PLACE
that used to make her feel safe spooked her. She smelled
the dampness of the walls, felt the rain coming in a mist
through cracked windowpanes. She couldn't bear to look
at her desk or the magnum bottle. She was embarrassed
that others had seen her place. Quickly, she gathered up
the western photographs and her books and left.

After, Marilyn took the castle key from Louise's top

dresser drawer and went up the hill to the castle, where she removed everything of her sister's and brought it home, to an unoccupied room on the third floor. It took several trips to the house and back, and some time to remember and to restore the castle furniture as it had been before Louise moved in, but Marilyn managed.

On the way down the hill, Marilyn detoured at the spring. She took the rusty cover from the spring, and looked down into the black water that reached into the middle of the earth, and she saw the cloudy reflection of the sky. She looked again and saw her face, chiseled as an image on a coin. Marilyn dropped the key to the castle in the spring, and waited to hear it drop.

Sadie had said there must be no more secrets, but that couldn't be. There were secrets all around now, in the sky and the woods, in the animals that waited quietly for her to go and in the leaves that would turn color and fall, and in the spring that never changed. Marilyn trusted that she would learn a few of them in time, and that there would always be more that she would never know.

NONE OF THEM WANTED TO LEAVE THE HOUSE IN THE rain, nor did they want to leave each other. Louise stayed either in the library or in her room. Sadie and Marilyn cleaned out their bedroom closets.

"We have to be very strict," Sadie said, and she forced Marilyn to part with clothing that no longer fit but that Marilyn loved, like the pink cardigan with seed pearls that Helen gave her one Christmas. "It's too tight," Sadie said. "We'll go to the city and get some new clothing. Before school starts. We have to have some rules."

It was harder with Sadie's clothing because all of it fit, more or less. Her closet looked like a sandwich, Louise said, standing by the door, watching them.

"Too much stuff," Louise said. Every day she checked in the mirror and saw that her bruises were fading. Without thinking, she walked almost upright, not hunched over to protect her ribs.

It was hard for Sadie to give any of it up, especially clothing that she'd never worn or worn only once. It made her breath catch in her throat to think of giving the clothes away, and she had to force her arm to pick up a garment and take it from the closet for the last time.

"When we go into the city," Marilyn said, "we'll get you a suit. And a dress. A nice one."

But Marilyn didn't really believe in parting. At night, when her mother and sister were asleep, Marilyn went downstairs to the kitchen, where Sadie kept the bags of clothing they would give to the Salvation Army, and she retrieved her pink sweater and a white silk bathrobe that Sadie had stuffed in the bag.

It was no good parting with things that you liked, Marilyn thought, because then you were doomed to roam the planet trying to find them again.

LOUISE LAY ON THE COUCH IN THE PINE LIBRARY, listening to the sound of the rain and the wind through the trees. It was almost cool enough for a fire. This fall when Sadie decided to gather pine cones to burn in winter fires, she'd be gone. She'd be in a place now unknown, and the cones would be gathered without her, and the fires burned.

On the table in front of her were folders from the schools she'd applied to, and some she hadn't. She had to write an essay for the applications. It began: *I believe that so far my education has been limited by where it took place.*

She wondered if Mr. Kaiser, her Latin teacher, would ever see the essay, if there was a central school bureau somewhere that would alert him to her treachery. There's nothing wrong with my education so far, she wished she'd written, there's something wrong with me.

Now that her application forms were mailed out, there was nothing to do but wait, and look over the folders again.

She liked the folders with pictures of students walking

around the schools. All the schools she chose to apply to were all-girls schools. She held the folders close to her face so that she could inspect each detail: the stone walls of the buildings on one campus, the clapboard of another; and the way the girls dressed. Louise tried to match up each item she could make out in the blurry photos—pleated skirt, cardigan, oxfords—with what she had and what she didn't. Sadie had relented, saying that if Louise wanted to go, she was welcome to try it. Sadie said they'd go to the city and buy clothes for school, but Louise didn't believe that it would happen. At the last minute, Sadie would decide that they didn't have the money, and Louise would go to school with what she had, all of it wrong.

When Louise looked in the mirror now she wondered how she'd look to the girls she didn't know at a school she hadn't seen. She held up her hair behind her and turned her head to one side, then the other, then dropped the hair again. There was a closet on the third floor filled with Reed's leather bags, Willard's canvas and leather duffels. Excellent quality, Sadie would say, but Louise longed for the matched luggage sets she saw advertised in magazines.

She could still refuse to go, she thought, still change her mind at the last minute.

WHEN SADIE THOUGHT OF WILLARD AND THE OTHER woman, it was like trying to turn a wheel stuck in mud. She couldn't believe that Willard would return, yet she had a vision of what it would be like once he got back. She would be alone. The house would be cold, her daughters gone. Her dog would go for walks and be given up for dead, though Sadie would listen for her at night and look for her in the snowy woods.

A letter from Helen came, sent during their first week at the cottage near Cirencester. Helen wrote that the cottage was darling, but not enough room to swing a cat. She adored elevenses and tea, and found the English country-

side divine. Packy had proposed at the last minute that
he join her for a week, and she was thinking it over.
They'd probably be back in plenty of time for Christmas.
"What would Christmas be without my party?" Helen
wrote, "Did you get my package yet?" Jimmy scribbled
at the bottom of the page: "You haven't seen gardens
until you've been here. Sell something, Sadie, and join
us runaway boys and girls."

No one wanted change, Sadie thought, even those who
sought it. All she could think of now was, Get him in and
out. Willard must come for Louise's sake. He must leave
for Sadie's. And she must stay. Like it or not, any of
them, it was her girls' childhood home, and that was
enough reason to keep it. She had continued the garden
that Willard's mother started, and that gave her a right of
property greater than Willard's legal claim. Childless she
might soon be, but the garden would remain hers.

Sadie tested herself, bringing up her most precious
memories of Willard, the ones she allowed only before
sleep. They were frozen, like ice statues. They were no
longer memories of living people, but memories of memories. Was it possible to love someone for so long and
then to stop loving him? And if she didn't love him,
would she be able to let him go? Because that was all that
was important now, to move him in and out again. Not
like Packy at the end of a fine golden thread, but really
out.

The other woman would have lots of dogs, better bred
than Dandelion. She would have roaring fires in every
room. And sometimes she would have Sadie's daughters.
But how to make sure she didn't have everything all the
time?

Fourteen

CHERRY FELL ASLEEP AS SOON AS THE PLANE LEFT LONdon, her neck twisted against an airplane pillow, covering herself with a blanket and her traveling-suit jacket. Willard held a book open on his lap, but he was unable to focus on the letters, make the letters into words, the words into sense. He looked over at Cherry and adjusted her blanket.

His time with Sadie seemed as long ago as his childhood years. He had been with her and his daughters for less time than he'd been away, but his life since leaving Tuxedo had gone by so fast. In memory it was all of a piece. He did not say that he loved Cherry because the word was for people like Sadie—"Do you love me? Am I pretty?" For him and Cherry there was the superiority of not naming, of this companionship. Cherry looked older and more worn out when she slept, more like a Frenchwoman than an American.

Willard gave in and shut his book, turned off the overhead light, and closed his eyes.

He had known that his escape couldn't last forever. He'd urged Sadie to divorce him because it seemed a way for them both to become free of a mistake. Now he guessed that he would be engaging in a more official and binding relationship with her. He was leaving behind in

Europe a precious anonymity. He thought of Louise who had looked at him the same way from the time she was newborn: full of love, staring and consuming. The lawyer had been vague on the telephone about the nature of Louise's accident, and Willard hadn't pressed. If she were in real danger the lawyer would have given him details, Willard thought, and urged him to hurry. They were reeling him in, as they might have long before. But he would never stay, he thought, not if he could help it.

The last time he came back to New York was just before America entered the war. Paris was lost, London under siege. It was the end of the best time Willard ever had. Despite his fear there was a new purpose to his life —to stay alive. He returned, assuming that despite his age some branch of the American military would use him. He might work with refugees, use his languages somehow. He didn't foresee that he wouldn't be accepted or that the years of war would be years of exclusion and lethargy, leading to Sadie. If he had, would he have chosen to stay in Paris and risk the Occupation?

When the liner he had taken across the hazardous ocean docked at last, Willard stayed in his stateroom. His luggage was removed, but he delayed his own disembarkation, lying on his bunk while the other passengers rushed away. He listened to the sounds and feel of the ship settling into New York harbor, to the people pushing through the corridors and onto the deck, ready to be done with the ocean. Many of the people on board were refugees, and surely for them the landing should be more frightening than for him. The ocean liner took on the air of a theater, backstage after a performance when everyone's gone home. The purser opened the cabin door and was surprised to see Willard there. "Here we are, sir," he said, "New York. End of the line."

IN THE MIDDLE OF THE NIGHT THEY ARRIVED AT IDLE-wild, and it was two before they passed through customs and stepped out into the stale night air. Willard flagged down a cab, and when he looked around for Cherry he saw her standing a few yards away, her head tilted up at the sky. When he called her name, she hurried toward him as if she were afraid he'd leave her there.

They'd made no reservation and there was a delay when the night bell at the Algonquin failed to rouse the doorman. They waited on the pavement, their suitcases around them. They stared at the height of the midtown buildings.

"We're inside a big machine," Cherry said. "Who'd have thought Manhattan would ever seem so strange?" She felt excited too. They were here. Willard pressed the bell again and cursed.

Finally, they were admitted, checked in, and they settled in a small room on an upper floor with a view of an airshaft and barely enough space for their luggage and themselves. Willard tipped the night man who'd brought them up, opened the window as far as it would go, and the curtains were pulled out into the night.

They took baths, then stretched out naked on the bed in the dark, listening to the traffic. Willard reached over and rubbed Cherry's back, tracing the smooth curves of her torso. She turned over and as he was leaning over to kiss her mouth, she said, "I'll just wait here for you."

"When?"

"Tomorrow. When you go to Tuxedo. To see your family."

He sank back onto the bed and covered himself. He said, "You won't come?"

"I can wait," she said. "I'd just like you to know in advance. That that's what I'll be doing."

"No," he said. "You'll come out there with me."

It was what she had hoped for, but she said, "Are you sure?"

"I want you there," he said.

He crossed his arms over his face, and she waited for him to make love to her, or to say that he couldn't face them without her and that he would never leave her. She waited until she recognized his rhythmic breathing as sleep, then she stood by the open window trying to see across the river, in one direction to Long Valley and home, in the other to Tuxedo. When she was tired, she closed the windows halfway, and pulled the curtains together against the city where they'd met.

Fifteen

MARILYN BROUGHT HELEN'S PACKAGE TO SADIE IN THE garden. The box was from a fancy nursery in Connecticut, and there was a message: "A commission from me —plant these for Jimmy to make his spring. Love, H." Inside were four hundred red Rembrandt tulip bulbs.

"Oh, dear," Sadie said. The note was so cheerful and trusting that Sadie realized that Helen was counting on her to be in Tuxedo when she came back, and it made Sadie feel proud and important. That's all right, Sadie thought, but I mustn't count on her again.

"I haven't even mown his lawn. Get Louise, Marilyn. We'd better all be in on this."

MARILYN STOOD AT THE DOOR OF THE PINE LIBRARY, shivering in T-shirt and shorts.

"What are you trying to prove?" Louise asked.

She lay on her back, tracing the paneling from wall to ceiling and down the opposite wall. Someone had worked hard to line up all the grooves.

"The sun's supposed to come out later," Marilyn said. "Come on. Sadie needs us to come with her. We're planting tulips at Jimmy's."

"I don't feel like walking all over for everyone to see."

415

"No one will see you," Marilyn said. "Anyway, we'll
be in the car."

"Oh, great. No one will recognize the Packard."

"Come on," Marilyn said. "Sadie wants you."

Louise sat up and looked around. "Okay," she said.
"I'm coming."

THEY CLIMBED INTO THE RUMBLE SEAT, AND SADIE
started the car. She shouted back to them, "Let's take
the long way."

First they drove past Helen's house. The lake was calm
and gray, resting after the storm. Though the house
wasn't shuttered it had the sleepy quality that it always
did when Helen was gone.

The next place was unfamiliar to the girls. It was the
timbered cottage Sadie drove up to by accident when
they first came to Tuxedo. She told them about the man
threatening her and how scared she'd been. The hedge of
roses had gone crazy, she saw, and weeds were growing
up through the stone drive.

Next she paused before the unhappy house. Regina
had taken her mother to Maine for the month, and the
people who'd borrowed the house left the cushioned lawn
furniture out during the storm. The place looked more
forlorn than ever. "They've been in the house longer
than anyone," Marilyn said. "But it's still the unhappy
house."

Sadie pulled up at the Round House. She had fallen
down on the job, she thought. She meant to get someone
up here to do Jimmy's lawn, and she'd promised herself
to weed the rose beds that lined the marble parapets.

"This is a mess," Louise said.

They piled out of the car and walked around, looking
into the windows of the abandoned house. It didn't feel
to Sadie like a place that anyone was going to return to,
and she felt freer because of that. Even if Helen and
Jimmy had let her down, she wanted them back. But not
too soon.

"Okay," she said, calling the girls back to her. The tulip bed was full of weeds and fallen leaves, in no shape to be planted yet. "Okay," she said. "We'll clean it up and work on the lawn. Then when it's drier and cooler, we'll come back and plant the bulbs."

They worked until they were hungry for lunch, but decided to keep on working. Sadie got out the mower and they took turns on Jimmy's lawn, weeding in the rose beds, and cleaning the tulip bed. It was even quieter at Jimmy's than at their house, with no sound but the wind. Every once in a while, Louise stopped working and looked up to locate her sister and mother. Once she saw where they were, she ducked her head and went back to work.

When they were ready to leave, Sadie said, "We'll have to come back and prune the roses."

"I'll do it," Louise said. "Jimmy showed me how once. I can come on my bike."

"Good," Sadie said, and tried not to say any more.

They drove out the gate to the Carvel stand a few miles down the road and ordered the largest cones. Marilyn and Louise got theirs covered in chocolate, and they had a slow-eating contest, catching drips from under the firm coating. "Be careful of the upholstery," Sadie warned, listening to their giggling and teasing as if it were music.

Slowly, long after the cones were gone, she pulled up to their driveway. Louise should lie down, she thought, and Marilyn and I should start lunch. Louise, seeing her mother's lips move soundlessly, was afraid.

WHEN SADIE, LOUISE, AND MARILYN STEPPED FROM the Packard, the front door of their house was opened from inside. A man stood in the doorway.

He was thin, his posture slightly stooped. His hair was a faded silver-gray, the color of cornstalks after a winter in the field. His skin, too, looked silvered, dried and fragile. His clothes were bulky, as if once they belonged to a larger man. He held a lit cigarette in his hand, and the smoke smelled strong and foreign to them. He stood in the doorway as if he should be comfortable there but was too shy or afraid to move.

He looks like someone I once knew, Sadie thought in the instant before she recognized Willard. She stared at him, understanding that that was what he was, someone she once knew. He looked uncared for. He looked like a tramp, like someone used to sleeping where he could.

Sadie smiled involuntarily, her heart glad to see him. "It's you," she said, too softly to be heard. She would have stepped forward if Louise hadn't made a clicking noise in her throat.

In back of Willard stood a woman who looked his age, maybe older. She was a small woman, her hair a fading mixture of black and gray, like an afternoon storm. Her clothes were simple and worn. She wore noiseless, sensible shoes. The woman's suit would be a little heavy for the late summer afternoon in Tuxedo. They were not tramps, Sadie decided, they were travelers, and their clothes were like a soldier's uniform, practical and durable.

They were blocking her doorway.

Marilyn remembered him perfectly now, as if he and she hadn't changed at all. She remembered how Willard's hand felt to hold, enormous, gentle, and she remembered that he left without a word for her.

Marilyn moved so that her mother was flanked by her and Louise.

Louise stared at her father, frowning, wondering how she would account for herself to him. Years later, when Louise still didn't understand why she had done what she had, nor how she had left Tuxedo Park for school and love, for jobs and other places to live, Louise thought of her father at the door. She wished herself back there. She wanted more than anything to have been the first one to speak. But no matter how many times she thought of Willard standing at the door with Cherry behind him, Louise could never imagine what she might have said.

Sadie looked closely at the woman's face. She must have been awfully pretty once, she thought, prettier than I ever was. She saw lines around the woman's eyes, a tightness to her lips. She is as afraid as I am, Sadie thought. The woman was a match for Willard. They were a pair. Something we never were, Sadie thought.

They stood frozen in place. A cloud passed across the sky, releasing northern light, exposing their faces, and their motionlessness.

Then there was something up in the woods. Sadie turned to see Dandelion at the top of the hill, her long tongue hanging out, her ears alert behind her. Her coat was matted with burs. The dog began running, and she became a red blur hobbling down the stone steps, past the flowerbeds and fenced vegetable patch, barking at Louise, Marilyn, Sadie, and the new people. So simple to be happy.

There was nothing else, no other way to move Willard and the woman in and out of her house, in and out of her children's lives, but to welcome them. Quickly, before anyone could speak, before the dog reached the bottom of the garden, Sadie put her arms behind her daughters' shoulders, and moved them toward their house.

"Willard," she said, "I didn't know when you were coming. Won't you introduce your friend? Louise, Marilyn . . ." Sadie forced her arms to release her girls, and she stepped back.

At the sound of her words, Willard and Cherry looked at each other, and Cherry withdrew into the house. The girls filed slowly past Willard, looking up at him as they passed. Dandelion licked Sadie's hands, then pushed straight through the door.

"Well, Sadie," Willard said, "aren't you coming in?"

She came up beside him in the doorway. She looked up at Willard and let the years roll from her, and it was Sadie and Willard again at the door to their house, and she was filled with her old happiness. Then it was over. Here is my miracle, she thought, back from the dead.

"How are you?" Willard asked. "How have you been?"

"You can see," Sadie said, "look around."

Sadie made a gesture to include children, dog, house, and the garden that covered the hill, even the hill itself. "Leave the door open," she said as she went in. "It's one of the last beautiful days of summer."

ABOUT THE AUTHOR

LAURA FURMAN was born in New York City and now lives in central Texas. She is the author of THE GLASS HOUSE, THE SHADOW LINE, and WATCH TIME FLY, and her short stories appear in *The New Yorker*.

SUPERIOR FICTION *from the* FINEST CONTEMPORARY AUTHORS